PRAISE FOR GAV THORPE

"Thorpe writes strong, uncluttered ~~~~~~~~
and his characters ~~~~~
people."

Tom Holt, SFX

"I tore through *The Crown of the Blood* in one long sitting, after which I felt ready to conquer an empire or punch a dinosaur of my own. *The Crown of the Blood* is a collection of violent conquests and vicious battles, from the fields of war to the equally-bloody arena of politics. Not *I, Claudius*, but definitely *Rome*, this book is hairy, gory, sweaty, shameless… and perhaps even a little bit thoughtful."

Pornokitsch

"The battle scenes are truly epic and Thorpe doesn't give anything away until the final sword stroke has fallen."

Graeme's Fantasy Book Review

"I immersed myself in the book and devoured it in four sessions; it reads extremely well, the story unfolding at a measured pace, gently (but repeatedly) coaxing you into reading 'just to the end of this chapter'."

My Favourite Books

GAV THORPE

The Crown of the Blood

**ANGRY
ROBOT**

ANGRY ROBOT
A member of the Osprey Group

Lace Market House,
54-56 High Pavement,
Nottingham
NG1 1HW, UK

www.angryrobotbooks.com
Your enemies closer

Originally published in the UK by Angry Robot 2010
First American paperback printing 2010

ISBN 978-0-85766-058-9

Printed in the United States of America

9 8 7 6 5 4 3 2 1

To Phillip, Alexander and Julius,
who were the inspiration for this series

THE CROWN OF
THE BLOOD

TEMPLE

The stones echoed to the sound of a gong. Lakhyri opened gold-veined eyes that reflected the glow of a guttering candle. The high priest's face was the texture of ancient parchment, etched and tattooed with swirling designs. As he rose up from the low slab that served as his bed, the dim light revealed his naked body; a tracery of scars covered him from scalp to foot, shoulder to fingertip, faded and barely visible against his dark skin. Astrological symbols decorated his body, from a zodiac first recorded thousands of years before his birth. Alchemical sigils for elements not yet identified by man ornamented his weathered flesh. All were linked together by intersecting lines scarred into his half-rotted meat, enveloping Lakhyri in a life-sustaining web.

He walked to the slit of a window, through which crept a sickly yellow light. All about the great temple was dead. An expanse of rock and dust stretched to the horizon, pale and lifeless. Cracks had been ripped into the fabric of the desolation in ages past, like welts upon the surface of a petrified corpse. Gasses issued from these crevasses, heavy with the taint of rotted flesh and sulphur. Even the skies felt the temple's taint; no insect buzzed and no bird flew. No breeze stirred the air and fumes choked the plain.

Though nothing lived, there was movement. Flickers of fire danced across the ground; glimmers of purple and blue and green that swayed and veered of their own accord. The witching lights merged to create hues not found in rainbows but in diseased bowels and plague-ridden cysts. They twirled about each other and evaporated into the skies, adding to the haze.

The temple rose up on seven colonnaded levels, built from white stone hewn from quarries long since eradicated by the wear of millennia. Black smoke drifted in oily wisps from chimneys at the temple's heart, staining the stones with streaks of soot.

The temple had no name; none that was remembered save by those ghastly creatures that dwelt within, clasped to the world through magic though long devoid of physical form or rational thought. Spectres of limbo, they hid in the dark and whispered to each other of the day when they would again rise to rule all other creatures.

Within the temple's dreary confines, murmur of prayers echoed about labyrinthine halls and passages as naked worshippers shuffled in single file towards the central shrine. Lakhyri left his room and took his place at the head of the line. For an age he had ruled, eking out his withered life with the most ancient sorceries he could glean from the mad utterances of his masters; a wraith-like figure whose body was nothing more than a skeleton wrapped tight with desiccating skin. Lakhryri nonetheless strode with head high, eyes alert in their shrunken sockets.

The chief worshipper was perturbed. The sorceries that perpetuated his half-existence and his masters were failing. The temple no longer drew in the life force needed for the eulanui and their followers. All creation within range had been sucked dry of its essence; the parasitic-yet-sustaining miasma was thinning.

Lakhyri had called together the faithful to consult with the ancient masters on this vital issue. About the shrine they gathered, in concentric circles of twelve hundred worshippers, each cut to a greater or lesser extent with prehistoric runes. The newest acolytes stood at the back, only one or two sigils carved upon their young bodies. Each ring corresponded to another step in enlightenment, the worshippers within each successive circle ever more decrepit and scarred. They prayed and chanted in a tongue they could barely pronounce, much less understand. By rote they hissed the praises and names of the almighty eulanui.

Lakhyri stood at their centre, before an altar stone fused from black volcanic rock and primordial bones.

Kneeling before the shrine, Lakhyri laid his hands upon its ridged surface, his fingertips tracing the lines of ribs and femurs, joints and vertebrae. He did not feel the shiver of exultation that usually electrified him at the altar's touch, for none of its magic passed to him.

"Magnificent, immortal masters, I beseech thee to speak with us." The high priest's voice was a whisper as dry and cracked as his skin, barely audible above the wheezing of the worshippers around him.

A stench of decay filled the shrine room and the air moved with formless energy. A tenebrous presence coalesced upon the altar stone, indistinct yet indescribably powerful. The stone melted, slewing away from the skeleton melded into the block. Bones reorganised themselves, sliding into place with each other while black rock slicked over them, forming pitch-like flesh.

Many-limbed, crooked and gangling, the Last Corpse took form, infused by the spirit of one of the eulanui. From many centuries of experience, Lakhyri recognised immediately the particular stance and disposition of the creature and knew it to be the *huoyakuitaka*, second most powerful of the masters. That such a senior figure had addressed his call demonstrated that the eulanui were well aware of the growing problem with the temple's sorceries.

11

SPEAK.

The voice came not as sound but as thought, entering Lakhyri's mind not with language but as pure concept. No creature apart from another of the masters could communicate in a physical fashion with an eulanui, though sometimes their words could be heard on the edges of sleep; a bass throbbing that shivered through Lakhyri's bones and resounded within his shrivelled guts.

"The temple strains to maintain your presence," the high priest said.

KNOWN. QUESTION.

"How can we increase the power of the shrine?"

DISTANT. SACRIFICE. SEEK.

"Seek whom? Seek what?"

KING. CHILD. RESTORE.

"How might we find this king? Which land does he rule?"

STRONGEST. TERRIBLE. COMING. SEEK. FAST.

The body of the *huoyakuitaka* dissolved, flowing back into the shape of the bone-clad altar stone. It had been a short exchange; shorter than any Lakhyri could remember, and his memory stretched back far indeed. The masters were struggling to maintain their grip upon this world, and had little power to spare to animate a body with which to converse with an underling.

"Acolytes stay, all others leave," declared Lakhyri, turning away from the altar.

Within a short time the eldest followers had hobbled away, leaving only the youngest of the order, eighteen in all. They were naked and shaven-headed, their skin fresh and their muscles tight and fit. Lakhyri looked at them with disgust, offended by their youth.

"You," said the high priest, pointing a skeletal finger at one of the boys. "Go now to the chamber of souls, I have a task for you."

The acolyte nodded solemnly, his eyes fresh and eager. Lakhyri sneered at his enthusiasm. He did not yet understand the true meaning of service. A hundred more years tending to the masters and these acolytes would better know the fate that had been decreed for them.

The one he had sent away would not have time to learn the lesson.

MEKHA DESERT
Early Summer, 208th Year of Askh

I

The behemodon bore down on Ullsaard as he lay on the hot sand, the enormous reptile's blue-scaled flanks slicked with the gore of the commander's warriors. Ropes of saliva drooled onto the dune from its dagger-long fangs and the stricken general could see his bearded face reflected in plate-sized black eyes. The lizard's panting was interspersed with bass growls, punctuated by cracking bones and wet splashes as it pulped the dead and wounded beneath its clawed feet.

Atop its back red-skinned Mekhani tribesmen leered and shouted from their howdah, jabbing the air with their stone-tipped spears. Among them was one with an elaborate headdress of green and black feathers: a Mekhani chieftain. The tribal leader snarled and spat at Ullsaard from his vantage point, waving a club edged with sharpened flints, furious at the Askhan general's offer of peace.

"I'll take that as a 'no', shall I?" Ullsaard said, the niceties of the pre-battle parley having been ended by the attack on his bodyguard. He had expected the Mekhani to refuse his conditions of surrender, but the barbarians had not withdrawn as was usually the custom. Ullsaard had been surprised by their sudden attack. He was angry with

14

himself for trusting the Mekhani to conduct the parley with any kind of honour or dignity; a misjudgement that had cost him losing twenty good soldiers.

Looking up at the towering behemodon, he hoped he would not pay the same price for his mistake.

The general pushed himself to his feet, fuelled by indignation. The morning sun glinted from his bronze greaves, vambraces and breastplate, his armour carved with designs reminiscent of spiralling clouds and crashing waves. Ullsaard brushed sand from his black leather kilt and adjusted his high-crested helm so that he could see properly. Snatching up the scored remnants of his shield and tightening his grip on his golden spear, he took up a guard position.

With a coughing bark, the behemodon snapped its head forwards. Ullsaard slammed his shield upwards, smashing its rim into the creature's lower jaw. The impact sent Ullsaard sprawling to his back again, the shield splintering in his grasp, its bronze rim catching him in the mouth as he fell. The behemodon reared back for a moment, cracked shards of fangs spilling from its bloodied mouth. Ullsaard tasted blood, but considered a cut lip a fair exchange for the behemodon's mouthful of broken teeth.

"I gave you the chance to surrender," the Askhan leader muttered as he regained his footing. "Let's get this over with."

The shrieking Mekhani fell quiet at the general's defiance. Even the behemodon paused for a moment. Something in the puny human's slate grey eyes was beginning to register in its tiny brain. Prey was supposed to flee and be hunted down, not stand and fight.

Adjusting to a throwing grip Ullsaard took one pace, his eyes fixed on the behemodon, and cast his spear with an arcing arm. The gilded shaft punched into the beast's left eye and erupted from the top of its skull in a carmine fountain. With snorts of pain the creature thrashed its head in an attempt to dislodge the weapon as dark blood poured from the grievous wound.

Half-blind and in agony, the behemodon lashed out wildly, driving its head towards Ullsaard with mangled jaw gaping wide. Ullsaard bounded to his right, pulling his sword from its sheath. He spun on his heel and drove the point of the blade backhanded into the roof of the creature's mouth. The behemodon staggered as blood and spittle foamed, wrenching Ullsaard's sword from his sweat-slicked grip. With a rattling hiss the monster collapsed, sand billowing into a cloud beneath its gargantuan death throes. The dying behemodon's heaving spasms snapped the ropes tying the cane howdah to its back and the structure slid sideways, spilling tribesmen to the dusty ground.

The Mekhani pulled themselves to their feet and edged uncertainly towards the unarmed warrior confronting them. They grunted at each other in their guttural tongue, urging each other to make the first move, the chieftain growling commands from behind his warriors.

Ullsaard cast the remains of his shield aside. He cracked his knuckles and smiled at the Mekhani. It was a wolf's grin and Ullsaard fervently hoped they would not see through his bravado. His guts writhed but he kept the fear inside and stared at his foes with the expression of a man confident of victory.

As one the chief and his guards fled, their bare feet kicking up clods of sand in their haste to get away.

Ullsaard strode to the twitching corpse of the behemodon and ripped free his weapons, hands trembling at the shock of what had just happened. Taking a deep breath to steady himself, Ullsaard sheathed his sword and rested the spear jauntily over his shoulder. He turned to face his army.

Seven legions of Askhor, nearly fifty thousand men, cheered their gore-spattered general as he raised his spear in triumph. Ullsaard spat blood to one side and flicked glutinous strands of reptilian filth from his hand. He gestured over his shoulder with a thumb, indicating the seventy thousand tribesmen advancing down the ridge beyond the behemodon's twitching body.

"What am I paying you for?" he called out.

II

There was no sight or sound that stirred Ullsaard more than an army on the march, and today was no exception. Drums thundered as the regiments of Askhor moved into action. Beneath circular gold icons depicting the face of mighty Askhos, the warriors raised their red-hafted spears and black lacquered shields and advanced. The sun glinted from red-crested helms and serrated spear tips while the desert sands shifted under the tramp of sandaled feet.

From the flanks of the army skirmishing kolubrid riders peeled off and dashed forwards. The reptilian mounts hissed as they ploughed through the sand drifts, black and red scales dirty with dust and grit. The riders aimed their bellows-bows towards the Mekhani who were descending the opposite slope. As the Mekhani closed, the riders pumped inflatable bladders to prime their weapons and let loose a volley of barb-tipped bolts. Arrows arced across the dunes in a crimson-shafted cloud before plummeting like bronze rain into the tribal warriors. The Mekhani's hide shields and animal skin cloaks offered little protection against the heavy projectiles and scores fell to the first volley, their blood quickly soaking into the sands.

Watching this impassively, Ullsaard was joined by Cosuas, his co-commander. It was frequently joked that the aging officer was the oldest man in Greater Askhor, but his taut muscles and springing step betrayed no infirmity. His clean-shaven, lined face was awash with rivulets of sweat as he stomped through the sand, a mace in his left hand and a long oval shield in his right.

"Are you trying to make me die of worry?" Cosuas snapped, glaring up at Ullsaard who was a head taller. "You could have been killed, or worse."

Ullsaard answered with a shrug. He had called the parley with good intent and although he wondered if it had been rash now was not the time to second-guess events beyond his control; what was done, was done. Hindsight might be good for others, but to Ullsaard it only encouraged doubt and regret and he had no time for such indulgences.

"It's your wives that scare me," Cosuas continued, casting his eyes up to the sky in exaggerated despair. "Do you think my life would be worth living if I let you die? I'd be nagged to death, if not actually ripped apart. I'd rather have my cock gnawed off by a wintermouse with one blunt tooth. "

Ullsaard laughed and shrugged again.

"You have to start a battle somehow," he said. "None of us want to be out in this sun longer than we have to be. I just got the Mekhani warmed up for the boys."

"We can't stand here passing the time of day, pleasant as it is," Cosuas said, clearly not amused by Ullsaard's indifference. "We've got a battle to win."

Ullsaard nodded and signalled to Prince Erlaan. The youth rode up on his ailur, leading Ullsaard's mount by its reins. Bred from the grey-furred mountain lions that had once plagued the tribes before the coming of Askhos, ailurs were regarded as a badge of office amongst Askhans and a leader's merit was often judged by the quality of his steed. In this regard, Ullsaard was very fortunate, for his was a prime specimen of the breed: Blackfang, a vicious she-ailur that was almost as old as Ullsaard and as tall at the shoulder as her master, her mane thick and black, plaited and bound with golden thread.

She was placid enough at the moment, her head encased in a spiked metal mask that covered her eyes with plates, held on by riveted straps that left her jaw free.

Though blinkered, Blackfang's hearing and sense of smell meant she was still more than capable of fighting. Ullsaard patted her shoulder and pulled himself up into the high-backed saddle, swinging his bloodstained spear into a strap behind him.

"I don't understand why you walk everywhere," Erlaan said to Cosuas. "An old man like you surely needs whatever rest he can."

"The day I need one of those piss-stinking, flea-ridden, hot-breathed rugs with claws to get me around is the day you can light my pyre," said Cosuas. His well-known disdain for ailurs was his only deviation from Askhan orthodoxy and a source of respectful amusement amongst the officers that had served him over the years. Ullsaard thought it an odd view, but unremarkable in comparison to some of the affectations and habits of other commanders he had fought alongside.

Blackfang padded forwards, flanked by Cosuas on foot and Erlaan on his ailur, Render. Behind them slithered a coterie of messengers riding more kolubrids, ready to take Ullsaard's orders to his subordinates. In the desert valley the battle was quickly unfolding and Ullsaard was pleased to see the legions following the precise orders he had given them the previous night. Not that he had harboured any doubts: an Askhan legionary was highly trained and well-rewarded in return for his obedience and bravery.

The Mekhani were herded into the centre of a sandy depression by the harrying of the kolubrid riders. Ullsaard wanted them forced together so that their numbers would be a hindrance more than an advantage. Their foes thus hampered, the Askhan spear regiments formed into tight phalanxes and closed for the kill from both flanks. With their attackers coming at them from two directions, the tribesmen huddled about their behemodons, sheltering under the bows and slings of the giant reptiles' crews. Against the bronze-bound shields and helms of the Askhan legionnaires, these missiles had little effect; here and there an Askhan bled on the sands but the phalanxes marched implacably onwards.

Ullsaard knew the Mekhani's faith in their war beasts was misplaced. As the disciplined columns of the Askhans stopped a short distance from their unruly foes, six-man teams carrying lava-throwers emerged from between the advancing companies. Dragging wheeled barrels of combustible ammunition through the deep sand, the fire teams laboured to set up their engines, directing their iron muzzles towards the behemodons. Pumping furiously at the pressure-bellows, the teams readied their weapons.

At a shout from their commanders, they unleashed the burning fury of their machines. Jets of black-red flame leapt out like incinerating tongues, lapping at the behemodons and setting fire to the howdahs on their backs. The panicked grunts of the beasts sounded over the roar of flames. The monsters ran amok, throwing off their crews and crushing tribesmen in their angry stampede. Ullsaard spared a thought of thanks for the Brotherhood, keepers of the lava-fire's secret since the time of Askhos.

One of the behemodons loped into a charge towards the nearest lava-thrower. The men turned their machine clumsily towards it, a gout of burning fuel searing an arc through the air. Seeing that the enraged beast would not be stopped, they abandoned their engine and ran for the cover of the nearest spearmen. Behind them the behemodon, patches of fire still smoking on its hide, smashed into the lava-thrower and seized the machine in its jaws. As the gargantuan reptile lifted the lava-thrower into the air the fuel tank exploded, splitting apart the creature's head and neck in a blossom of dark fire. Charred flesh rained down onto Askhans and Mekhani alike.

With their beasts slain, the desert warriors raised their crude spears and charged, churning up a huge plume of sand in their wake. Unintelligible battle cries hooting from their lips, the Mekhani hurled themselves towards the Askhan phalanxes.

Ullsaard exchanged a knowing look with Cosuas. The Mekhani had just made the fatal mistake the generals had been expecting.

Orders shouted along the line of companies, the drilled spearmen set themselves to receive the charge, forming a wall of shields and spears. Unheeding of the jagged barrier, the Mekhani leapt to the attack. Their stone spear tips crashed against shields while their bodies were spitted on the pikes of the Askhans.

Ullsaard watched the butchery without emotion. It was bloody and it was one-sided, which was the best way to fight a war. He turned in his saddle and gestured to one of his subordinates, a youth with sunburnt skin and a shock of red hair.

"Karuu, tell the cavalry to encircle the enemy," Ullsaard said to the herald. "I don't want any escaping to poison the wells or inflict other sabotage."

"What do you want to do with the survivors?" Karuu asked.

"Why don't we ask the young general-to-be?" said Cosuas.

"What do you think, prince?" Ullsaard looked at Erlaan. "Let's pretend this is your army."

Erlaan was deep in thought for some time; long enough for Ullsaard to think that he wasn't going to answer.

"There is no market for slaves these days," Erlaan said eventually. "With the expense of sending them back to civilised lands, it would cost us heavily. We cannot have them roaming around the camp, they will just cause trouble."

"So we just let them get away?" said Cosuas.

"No," replied Erlaan. "These savages will not learn. They will only come back again. We have to kill them all."

Ullsaard nodded in agreement, pleased that the young man had come to the right decision.

"There will be no survivors," Ullsaard told his messenger, keeping his eyes fixed on the slaughter.

As Karuu goaded his mount and slid away down the ridge, Ullsaard looked back to the battle. The phalanxes were driving into the heart of the Mekhani, their spears ruthlessly cutting down hundreds of tribesmen, their flanks protected from encirclement by lava-throwers and kolubrid riders. The Askhans advanced over a carpet of the dead, leaving piles of mangled bodies in their wake.

Ullsaard felt Erlaan's stare upon him as the battle unfolded with bloody predictability. He looked at the prince and saw a hint of distaste in his eyes.

"Horrible, isn't it?" said Ullsaard.

"It's a massacre, not a battle," said Erlaan.

"Good," grunted Cosuas.

"You're enjoying this?" Erlaan said, and shook his head. "What can be good about this?"

Cosuas did not reply immediately. He walked behind Blackfang to stand next to the young man's ailur. Erlaan stared down at the ancient general with faint disgust.

"Don't look at me, look at them," Cosuas snapped, raising an arm to point at the ongoing fighting. Erlaan once more directed his attention to the bloody work before them. "Would you rather it was Askhans that were dying? Perhaps you would prefer it if those poor Askhos-cursed Mekhani bastards were left maimed and wounded, to die bleeding in the desert sun, or to perish from thirst or diseased wounds?"

"They lost the moment they decided to fight," said Ullsaard. "The offer of peace was made and the Mekhani leaders refused it. We bear no responsibility for what follows. It is a mercy that we despatch them with the minimum of grief. We allow their families to collect the dead and perform whatever rites they wish to practice."

"I understand the principles." Erlaan puffed out his chest

and tried to appear unconcerned but his eyes kept straying back to the fighting.

"You understand the principles, but here you will witness the practise," said Ullsaard.

"Those families will tell stories of what happened here," Cosuas said, grinding home the Askhan logic of war. The screams of dying men and crash of weapons illustrated that logic. "News will spread that Askhor has no mercy for those that oppose us and benevolence for those that do not raise arms against us. Some will not listen and they will also die. A generation from now, nobody will remember why so many were killed in this pointless place, if they even remember at all. They will remember only that Askhor is merciless and from that fear, peace prevails.

"News will spread that Askhor has no mercy for those that oppose us and benevolence for those that do not raise arms against us," the grim officer continued. "Some will not listen and they in turn will be killed. Over time, others will heed the warning and lives will be saved. A generation from now, nobody will remember why so many were killed in this desolate, pointless place, if they even remember this battle at all. They will remember only that Askhor is merciless to our enemies, and from that fear peace and harmony will prevail."

"As Askhos decreed," said Erlaan. "I am one of the Blood; there is no need to teach me about Askhos' legacy."

Erlaan's eyes were fixed on the fighting, unable to drag his eyes away from the gory scene, his expression perturbed.

"What of glory?" he asked.

"Overrated," grunted Cosuas.

Ullsaard laughed and Blackfang padded left and right for a moment, sensing her master's mood.

"This is glory," Ullsaard said, his humour gone as quickly as it had come. "Do you think that poets will write of Askhor legions butchering defenceless tribesmen? The noble houses of Askh will resound to verses about the brave soldiers of Askhor winning against hordes of red-skinned savages. Maniacal and bloodthirsty, in numbers without counting, the Mekhani terrors poured across the deserts intent upon rape and pillage until the bronze spears of our warriors held them at bay."

"That is why I pay little attention to poets," Erlaan said.

"Which would you prefer your husband, or brother, or father, or son to be? Called a hero or a murderer?" Cosuas said. "People don't care about the truth, they only care if their lands and children are safe, and they have a few Askharins to spend at the market. It isn't our place to give them other concerns."

The clash of weapons and hoarse cries of soldiers were diminishing as the Askhans crushed the tribal warriors. Those Mekhani that tried to flee from the relentless press of spears were cut down by the fangs of the kolubrids or the bellows-bows of their riders.

It was barely mid-morning and the battle was almost over. Ullsaard wiped the sweat from his face with the sleeve of his tunic. He needed a drink.

III

The walking wounded marched back to the Askhan camp while the honoured dead were set upon biers carried by their comrades. Those who had lost limbs or suffered other grievous wounds but still lived were gathered in three lines along the floor of the shallow valley, one hundred and thirty-eight in all. Some sat in groaning agony; others had slipped into fitful sleep. A few were lucid and sat muttering quiet thanks to Askhos while the rest endured the blazing sun in stony silence.

Behind each injured man stood a soldier with his dagger drawn.

Ullsaard stood with his hands on hips looking at the wounded, Cosuas beside him. Behind the pair, Erlaan sat upon Render holding Blackfang's reins. The ailurs bobbed their heads, flicked their thick tails and pawed the ground at the scent of so much blood. Ullsaard gave Cosuas a nod and the aging general took a step.

"Soldiers of Askhor, we salute you," he said. "As a son will lay down his life to protect his mother, so you have given all for the defence of the realm that raised you. You are heroes, one and all, and the memories of your deeds will be respected and cherished alongside the other favoured fallen in the Hall of Askhos. The king mourns for your sacrifice, as do we all."

At a signal from Cosuas the line of soldiers raised their blades and slit the throats of the wounded. None struggled, for they had been resigned to this fate since joining the legions. They knew that their families would be fed and sheltered by the king for three generations and each was thankful that he would not suffer a future as a crippled parasite suckling at Askhor's bosom. As blood dried in the sun, more biers carried away the newly slain.

Though he kept his expression stern, Ullsaard felt a little pity for those who had to die in this manner. In the press of melee it was not bravery or skill that decided who lived and who died, but luck. Those who had just given their lives for Askhor had been no less devoted, no less worthy of life than those who had survived.

Ullsaard was reminded that he might one day share the fate of those being taken back to the camp in honour, for the oaths of service he had taken were the same as those of every soldier. Some men might be swayed to cowardice by that vow, to avoid the danger of injury, but such men did not become Askhan officers. They became clerks or engineers, or priests of the Brotherhood, and suffered no dishonour because of it. From the teachings of Askhos, the king and people of Askhan recognised that some served with courage and some with other qualities. Like many military men, Ullsaard had his reservations about those that risked less than their lives for their empire, but it was impolite to mention such thoughts openly.

No Askhan legionnaire marched to war expecting to return, and such fatalism bred a stubborn courage that won battles other warriors would lose. If a legionnaire was fortunate enough to fight for ten years he earned himself a generous pension from the king and had a chance to live out his life in peace with his family. That more than half refused retirement at so young an age was testament to the appeal of life in the legions. Ullsaard knew well that the common man cared only for three things: his family to be safe, food in his belly and a little money to spend freely on whatever pleasures he saw fit when he could get them. For many, a life in the legions was preferable to labouring in the fields, or digging canals or building bridges.

"How many dead and injured?" Ullsaard asked as Cosuas joined him.

"Including those?" the general replied. "Seven hundred and forty-three dead, one thousand and six wounded but still capable of fighting."

Ullsaard nodded solemnly. It was not a bad toll, in truth. He had expected the price of victory to be higher but the Mekhani's spirit had broken early and they had been cut down in their rout. He grunted and waved for Erlaan to bring Blackfang. Ullsaard looked at the youth.

"Nothing to say?" Ullsaard said.

The young man shook his head.

"Good," said Ullsaard. "We'll return to camp and tomorrow morning escort the engineers and masons back to the bridge."

Ullsaard decided to walk with Cosuas, and sent Erlaan ahead with Blackfang. The tramp of thousands of feet had packed the sand into a rough road, cutting across the desert towards the Askhan camp.

"Why are we both here?" Ullsaard said after a while.

"To push forward the borders of Greater Askhor," Cosuas replied with a frown. "What else would we be doing?"

"No, I mean why send two generals to command a single army?"

"Scared of having the old man looking over your shoulder?" laughed Cosuas and Ullsaard chuckled at the thought of the much smaller man looking over anything, much less his shoulder. "I can still teach you a thing or two."

"I'm sure you can," said Ullsaard. "That's not my point. Either one of us can command this army, the other is a waste. Surely there are other campaigns that you or I could lead. Legions stand idle on the borders of Salphoria while you and I – and Prince Kalmud! – grub around in the sands. There is nothing here to fight over. The real prizes are to duskwards."

"You'd war with Salphoria?" said Cosuas, his mood suddenly serious. "Salphoria is divided, no threat to Askhor. Why start a costly fight when we can simply help the tribes fall out with each other?"

"Is that really what has become of us?" said Ullsaard with a sorrowful shake of the head. "Agitators? When did Askhor need any reason to go to war other than to expand the empire? Salphoria is rich with grain, ore and wood. Think of the great works we could undertake if we controlled those resources rather than paying the exorbitant prices of the Salphors? Askhos himself declared it our destiny to rule all of the lands between the seas. Yet what gains have we made in these last twenty years? Truly?"

"The king is consolidating our power," Cosuas argued. "You can't simply lurch from one war into the next. You take ground, control it, build towns and roads and only then move on. You know this, Ullsaard."

Ullsaard pointed ahead to the many pillars of smoke rising from the horizon.

"The king wishes a new settlement to be built here," the general rasped. "What for? There's no real farmland for a dozen days' marching. The river isn't even that plentiful. It's a trinket dangled in front to keep us busy, nothing more. Give me a hundred thousand men and I could take Salphoria in a year. Raise more legions and give me two hundred and fifty thousand and I'd do it for the king in a summer."

"The legions are the king's soldiers," said Cosuas. "You would have every soldier of the empire at your call? What of the princes and governors? Are they allowed any legions? We command only in the king's name. We do not choose where and when we fight, that choice lies only with the Blood. As Askhos promised, the empire has grown and prospered under the rule of his heirs. I would not doubt his teaching just because you're sore of the sun and have sand in your boots."

Ullsaard said nothing, knowing the truth of what Cosuas said, but finding it hard to reconcile with his own desire to push on for the glory of Askhor. He liked to think of the empire as an ailur, a beast with hunger and passion that needed to be constantly fed and directed, its energies focussed on strength and growth.

Talk of consolidation irritated him. It sounded like the language of politicians, not generals. His respect for Cosuas and his achievements prevented Ullsaard from voicing these thoughts. That, and for all Cosuas and Ullsaard shared a history, the older general would no doubt report back to Askh with any comment by Ullsaard that might be considered improper. Cosuas had lived to his ripe age by following orders well, not by showing too much initiative.

"You are right," Ullsaard said eventually.

"When aren't I?" replied Cosuas with no hint of humour.

They followed the column of soldiers heading duskwards across the dunes. It would be two more hours before they reached the camp.

"Camp" described the Askhan settlement as well as "cat" described an ailur. It was a whole town of canvas, wood and leather dedicated to war. In firmer ground coldwards of the desert, it stretched across several miles, atop a hill that had been flattened by legions. The land here was just about fertile and patches of tall grass broke through the dry earth and stands of short trees clustered around invisible underground pools, fed by the Nakuus River that ran lazily through the scrub at the base of the hill.

The camp was surrounded by a wooden palisade twice the height of a man with twenty roofed towers, built on an embankment of packed earth. Each log had been carried hotwards from the forests of the empire, the stunted trees of Mekha unsuitable for timber. A ditch as deep as the wall was high girded the palisade, an obstacle impassable save at the eight wooden bridges at the gates. The bridges were down at the moment, but at the call of Duskwatch, they would be drawn back behind the walls.

Smoke from hundreds of fires drifted over the tents of the legionnaires and the colourful pavilions of the officers. Each legion, six to eight thousand strong, was garrisoned in its own area, complete with kitchens, armourers and a forge. From a mile away the workers of the camp could be heard; hammers on metal, axes on wood and chisels on stone drifted across the dunes.

This was not just a place for soldiers to rest; it was a statement of intent. The gilded faces of Askhor stared down from the gates at the surrounding land. The blare of a horn marked the passing of the watch. This was the empire incarnate, a construct of ambition and conquest.

Here was to be the next town of Greater Askhor. Before any construction work could begin on the settlement, engineers and masons had to get a bridge across the river to allow more supplies to come from the Askhor territories far to coldwards. At the moment the hundreds-strong supply caravans had to travel down the Greenwater River before forging upstream along the Nakuus for many days to reach the camp.

A bridge would be the first part of a road stretching directly to coldwards, cutting at least ten days from the journey. When the bridge and road were finished, settlers would come – and some of the legionnaires would stay with their families – planting farms to feed a fresh move further into Mekha.

The harassment by the Mekhani tribes had put the force five days behind schedule and Cosuas was not happy at being forced to spend more time than was necessary in the blistering heat. His skin, much tanned from many campaigns, was peeling nonetheless and his stomach was knotted from eating starchy march rations.

The company of guards at the gate of the wooden palisade surrounding the Askhan fort raised their spears in salute as Cosuas approached, just ahead of Ullsaard and Erlaan. Cosuas returned the respect with a nod and walked between the two squat wooden towers flanking the entrance. Young boys scurried past him to take the reins of the two ailurs and Ullsaard and Erlaan swung down to the parched ground.

"I want to see Haraa, Entiu and Dor in my tent at High watch," Ullsaard said. Erlaan nodded and walked off across the camp to find the master masons.

"Do you need me for anything?" asked Cosuas.

"No," replied Ullsaard.

"I'll be taking a bath then," said the aging general, pulling off his helmet and striding away along a walkway of wooden planks sunk into the dirt.

There were waves and calls of greeting as the general strode through the encampment, heading towards the bath tent. Cosuas returned the welcomes with nods, keeping his feelings hidden behind the blank mask of his face. As he looked at the many hundreds of soldiers, he knew that at least one in ten of them would never see Askhor again; or whatever province they had once called home. In the time of Cosuas' ancestors the Askhor legions had all been from Askhor itself. Now Greater Askhor stretched thousands of miles beyond the old borders and the army was filled with foreigners like himself.

He had always thought of himself as an Askhan, never an Ersuan. Cosuas had been less than a year old when King Tunaard II, father to Askhor's current ruler, had conquered Ersua. Just like the thousands of other Ersuans now under his command, Cosuas had faced the decision of staying at home to labour in the fields or build the towns, or joining the army and campaigning to bring the rule of Askh to other lands. He saw no irony in a conquered nation aiding their conquerors to bring the same fate to others. It was simply the way things were; the strong got stronger and the weak did well to recognise their fate in time to survive.

And there were plenty of benefits to being an Askhan, Cosuas reminded himself as the horn sounded the quarter-watch. The large, steam-filled tent ahead was one such boon. He pushed through the flap into the antechamber and stripped naked, handing his armour and weapons to a Maasrite orderly. The young man passed the general a wooden scraper and opened the next flap into the main portion of the huge marquee.

The four large wood-sided baths had been dug into the sands and they were filled with soldiers washing and laughing, gossiping and dozing. Cosuas stood upon the preparation mats while more servants doused him with cold water. He used the scraper to get rid of the worst of the dirt from his skin and climbed into the nearest bath. The water was cool and pleasant after the heat of the desert and Cosuas sunk into the water up to his chin, eyes closed. He ignored the chatter of the other soldiers around him and instead tried to clear his mind of everything.

After a few minutes' contemplation, Cosuas opened his eyes and ducked his head into the water. He washed away the grime of the battle, using a stiff brush to clean the dried blood from his fingers. With a renewed spring in his step, he pulled himself out of the preparation bath and plunged into the rinsing tub. The cold caught his breath in his chest and he gasped, much to the delight of his underlings. Cosuas shared their laughter, splashing a few with a sweep of his hands.

"Some of us actually worked up a sweat today, you layabouts," the general joked.

The whole group left the rinsing pool and headed towards one of the two main baths. Several dozen warriors were already in the bath, swimming back and forth, others lounging around the edge, dangling their feet in the water or resting against the sides. Steam filled the air, the water kept hot by lava tanks buried beneath the packed earth.

Cosuas lowered himself gingerly into the water, letting his feet get used to the heat, then his legs, then his body and finally he submerged himself for a moment, the heat draining the last vestiges of stress from his body.

Yes, there certainly were advantages to being an Askhan.

V

Ullsaard's gaze followed Cosuas for a while until he turned between two tents and disappeared from view. The old man displayed as much energy and stamina as ever, an irrepressible vigour Ullsaard had known since he was young, but Ullsaard knew his mentor would not live forever. Cosuas had never taken any wives and had no children; the last of the line of Ersuan kings. With his death the royalty of Ersua would come to an end, his realm forevermore a dependant of Greater Askhor. More than that, when Cosuas died, Ullsaard would be the last general in Askhor not of the Blood. It seemed that men capable of leading armies were a dying breed; another sign that the King's ambitions were not as grand as his predecessors'.

Ullsaard's musings were interrupted by the approach of Karuu.

"General, a messenger from Askh awaits your attendance," the officer reported. "He bears missives from Prince Aalun."

Ullsaard nodded and shooed Karuu away with a wave of the hand. Tidings from the capital would be important; the prince would not send a messenger this far hotwards without good reason. Ullsaard mused on what it might be as he walked through the camp towards his pavilion at the centre. Kalmud, the king's eldest son, was campaigning to dawnwards along the Greenwater River. Perhaps the news concerned that.

Ullsaard caught scattered snatches of conversation as he walked through the camp. Morale seemed to be high, though he overheard many complaints about the heat and sand. Soldiers always moan, he told himself. Though the conditions were less than tolerable, today's battle had been the first serious fighting since passing into the desert. Most of the warriors seemed to think that the Mekhani had been dealt such a harsh blow they would be returning to their families soon. Ullsaard would not dissuade them of the notion for the time being, though he knew the Mekha war was just beginning; better that his men enjoy what peace they could; by the best guesses of the empire's scholars as many as three times the number of tribesmen slain today awaited the army's bloody attentions, spread across the vast desert. The summer would be long this year for many of his soldiers, and brutally short for others.

A bright red pavilion rose high above the orderly rows of white tents that surrounded it, Ullsaard's personal standard gleaming in gold from its central pole. Hunting scenes had been embroidered in black on the red cloth; visions of Askhor's lush forests and cold mountains that reminded all of what they fought for, not least Ullsaard himself. The quartet of guards stood at the doorway bowed their heads in greeting as Ullsaard approached.

"Send word for the prince's herald to attend me," Ullsaard said as he strode into the huge tent.

The floor was covered with rugs woven from Askhan wool dyed a dark red, deep and soft beneath his booted feet. Here and there sandy footprints trailed across the carpets, from the bare feet of servants and the sandals of soldiers. Linen partitions decorated with spiralling patterns divided the pavilion's large space into smaller compartments. Lamps hung from the roof beams, unlit for the moment for there was plenty of light provided by window flaps opened in the high roof.

The central area was lined with wooden screens painted with scenes from the plazas and avenues of Askh; the approach to the royal palaces, the racing circuit at Maarmes, the fruit markets of the lake quarter. Other officers decorated their tents with portraits of themselves and their families, but Ullsaard felt no need for such affectation. His family were kept in his heart and there they would stay. The scenes reminded him instead of his duties as a general of the legions, dedicated to the protection and future of Askhor before all other concerns.

Flanked by stools carved from black wood, Ullsaard's campaign throne was set upon a marble plinth that had been quarried from the hills far to coldwards in the general's native province of Enair. The stone was black and veined with red, like blood trickling down a bare slate. The throne itself was wrought from bronze and gilded with white gold, padded with cushions of blue velvet stuffed with the hair of ailur cubs, the back lined with white meimur fur. There was no doubt in Ullsaard's mind that it was indeed a magnificent chair, but just a chair nonetheless. His less intelligent subordinates were impressed by their general giving his orders from such a magnificent perch, and that alone was worth the effort of bringing it on the long march.

Upon seeing their master enter, two tan-skinned Maasrite servants came with clay ewers of wine and water, and another with a bronze tray set with a single golden goblet. Ullsaard nodded to the water bearer, who poured him a draught from his jug before the trio retired wordlessly to their positions at the side of the chamber. After taking a gulp of the refreshing drink, Ullsaard placed the goblet on the arm of the throne, sat down on the marble plinth and began to pull off his boots.

With a grunt the right boot came free and Ullsaard wriggled his toes, enjoying the cool breeze wafting through the open door. Sand was caked between his toes and on his instep and he waved to one of the servants.

"Fetch me a bowl of water, soap and a towel," said Ullsaard. The mute Maasrite bowed and departed.

By the time the servant had returned with the cleaning provisions, Ullsaard had wrenched off the other boot and sat with his feet in the deep pile of the rug, clasping and releasing the thick wool between his toes. The servant knelt down with the bowl and picked up the soap, but Ullsaard took it from him and waved him away.

"I'll not have any man clean another man's feet, no matter what they do in Maasra," Ullsaard declared.

"A sensible if unfashionable choice, General," said a voice from the doorway.

The short, slim man standing there was garbed in the red sash, kilt and cloak of a king's herald, his crestless helm under one arm. He was a little younger than Ullsaard, with long blonde hair that showed no signs of the grey that had assailed Ullsaard in the last few years. His face was softer though not chubby, and stubble betrayed that he was normally clean shaven but had not had opportunity to attend to his cheeks and chin in the last few days. A longsword hung at his belt, its hilt and pommel wrought from gold.

To Ullsaard's eye it was a ceremonial duelling weapon, unsuited for real fighting.

"Noran!" exclaimed Ullsaard. Grinning, Ullsaard pushed himself to his feet and paced across the rugs with his arms open for an embrace. The messenger met him halfway and they hugged, clapping each other on the back and kissing each other's left cheek. "They just said a messenger had come, they never mentioned it was you."

"I asked them not to," said Noran, stepping back and smiling. "Why spoil the surprise?"

"Indeed, indeed," said Ullsaard. He waved his lifelong friend towards the stools and clapped his hands twice. "Wine and food for my guest!"

"Wait," Noran said as he raised a hand to stay Ullsaard's servants. "As much as I would dearly love to indulge in some reminiscing and wine, I have important matters to discuss with you first. We can eat and drink later."

"Leave us," Ullsaard snapped at the approaching servants. He turned to Noran, apprehension written on his face.

"Prince Aalun has demanded your attendance at the court," said Noran as the servants melted from view. "His older brother has fallen ill."

Ullsaard, slumped into his throne. "What is it? How long has the prince been afflicted? More to the point, why do I have to travel all the way back to Askh because of it?"

"Word came to the court only the day before I left," explained Noran, seating himself as Ullsaard slouched in the throne and took up his goblet. "It is an affliction of the lungs. The prince's life is in no immediate danger, but if his condition deteriorates, it jeopardises his campaign. I believe Prince Aalun wishes to discuss this, along with other matters to which I have not been made privy. I'm sure the prince is aware of the burden of travel and would not summon you for an inconsequential matter."

"We've only just fought a battle," Ullsaard said, rubbing his chin in thought. The notion that Aalun perhaps wanted him to take over Kalmud's campaign encouraged him, but he was loathe to leave his army to Cosuas without knowing when he, or if, he would return. "There are preparations to be made for the cremations and honour to be given to the dead. If I leave suddenly, rumour will quickly engulf the army. And there's the matter of this unfinished bridge."

"Cosuas can deal with all of that," said Noran with a dismissive wave. "Probably better, he's been doing this sort of thing even longer than you have. The prince was insistent that you attend him at as soon as it was practical. In fact, he was adamant."

Ullsaard frowned and stood.

"Then I have no choice," he said, suppressing a rebellious sigh. "Though I would rather continue the campaign here, one of the Blood has spoken and I must obey. It will take some time to get ready for a return to Askh. If this concerns Kalmud, I should take Erlaan back to the capital as well, to see his family. He'll have to get everything packed away for the journey. It will be too late to leave tonight; first thing in the morning will be soon enough."

"That would be good," said Noran. "I will inform him of what I know while you get yourself ready to depart. I have a galley waiting at Atanir to take us up the Greenwater."

Noran stood and stepped towards Ullsaard.

"I wish that we had met again in better circumstances," said the messenger. "All the same, it is good to see you, Ullsaard."

Ullsaard smiled and laid a hand on Noran's shoulder.

"It is good to see you as well, my friend," Ullsaard said. "On the road you will have to tell me what you have been doing with yourself these past two years."

"Well, maybe," Noran said with a wink. "There's a few tales I'm not sure that I trust you with!"

Noran gave a nod of reassurance and turned towards the doorway. At the edge of the rugs he turned back to look at Ullsaard.

"And get your feet washed, I could smell them as soon as I came in," he said with a grin.

Ullsaard nodded and smiled, and watched his friend leave the pavilion. He suppressed another sigh. A trip back to the capital was no small diversion, even if there was the promise of a more profitable command at the end of it. His servants would have to pack up everything needed, gather supplies from the storehouses; there were wagons and abada to requisition, handlers needed for the ailurs.

There was also the question of whether or not to take a bodyguard. There was little physical danger travelling to coldwards; the Greenwater was patrolled by the galleys and soldiers of Askhor and prosperity had swept away most of the brigandage that had plagued the empire in earlier generations. On the other side, it was expected that a general of Askhor travelled with a certain amount of style and gravitas. Tradition and appearance were considered by many to be as important as practicality.

On balance, it would be less of a pain to leave the soldiers and travel with servants alone. The presence of legionnaires escalated matters; they needed officers, their own supplies and other considerations that would turn what was already a considerable journey into a major expedition.

"Attend me!" yelled Ullsaard and moments later a dozen servants came scurrying from amongst the wooden screens.

VI

Hills rose up on either side of the rude turnpike, crowned by stunted trees and thorny bushes. The bell-laden harnesses of the abada jingled pleasantly as the beasts of burden plodded along the stony track that led dawnwards towards the Greenwater. Six abada carts rumbled and pitched over the uneven roadway, each pulled by a team of four beasts. Red and white awnings were hooked onto poles over the wagons and amongst the chests and sacks Ullsaard's servants dozed while the drivers flicked long switches across the backs of the abada to keep them plodding on.

Ullsaard, Erlaan and Noran rode ahead of the wagons, their ailurs panting in the heat. The sky above was cloudless and the sun beat down relentlessly as it had done since they had left the camp earlier that morning. Noran noted that Erlaan was quiet, no doubt wrapped up in thoughts concerning his father. Ullsaard was his usual taciturn self, so Noran was talkative enough for the three of them and had entertained Ullsaard with tales for two solid watches.

"So I was on Neerita's balcony, with nought but my scabbard to shield my dignity, when her father returned," Noran was saying. "I saw his chariot come through the gates and hid behind the parapet, all the while listening to the shrieking of Neerita's mother from through the open doors."

"Isn't her father Neerat Aluuns?" said Ullsaard. "He's Prince Aalun's treasurer!"

"Well, Aalun will need to find someone else to keep his accounts, I'm afraid," said Noran. "Neerita confessed all, and my involvement in the affair, and old Neerat called me out on it. The prince tried to persuade him otherwise but he was insistent. I killed him on the bloodfields at dusk the next day."

"So you've finally settled down," said Ullsaard. "Good for you. Did any sisters come with your new bride?"

"An older one, and a sour-mouthed, ill-eyed, poison-tongued bitch at that," snarled Noran. He shuddered as he remembered his first encounter with the icy Anriit. "Suffice to say, she shares my roof but not my bed! Still, Neerita is game enough for the bedroom athletics, and may be

39

bearing me a child. We'll know for sure once she has visited the loremother."

Ullsaard shook his head in disbelief.

"I leave you to your own devices for two years and you end up a husband and probably a father," said Ullsaard, leaning across to slap Noran on the arm. "You'd avoided it for so long I thought you were going to join the Brotherhood."

At this Noran broke into a deep laugh, almost falling from the saddle.

"My father would have loved that, I'm sure," said Noran. "The Astaan lands around the city would have made a fine addition to someone else's inheritance. Suffice to say, the Astaan legacy is now safely mine once more. I'll not be ceding my lands to the throne and running off to a Brotherhood precinct, I'm afraid. You'll just have to conquer some more of Mekha if you want new farms."

"I can't say I ever saw you as fit for the Brotherhood," said Ullsaard. "Well, for a start, you'd have all that reading to do first. I'd bet half a third-born's dowry that you haven't picked up a copy of the Book of Askhos since you left your father's house."

"I didn't even read it before then, I must admit," said Noran with a guilty smile. "What's the point of the Brotherhood dedicating their lives to understanding its meanings if we all go out and make it up for ourselves?"

"To find personal enlightenment, perhaps?" said Ullsaard, suddenly serious. "I never figured you for a heathen."

"Heathen?" said Noran with a choking cough. "Have you actually read that book? It's so tiresome."

"They are sacred words," warned Ullsaard, directing a glare at the herald. "They guide us, and give us meaning. The great Askhos laid down some pretty specific instructions for his descendants. You'd know that if you bothered to read the book."

Noran held up his hands in surrender.

"I did not intend to offend," he said. "As you say, I am a man of means and responsibilities now, so perhaps I will pay more attention to the mighty ancestor's teachings."

The two rode in stiff silence for a while longer. The light was beginning to fade and their shadows lengthened on the dusty cobbles. Eventually, Noran turned back to Ull-saard with a twinkle in his eye.

"I don't suppose you could direct me to the pages where old Askhos had any advice on what to do with axe-faced second wives, could you?"

Their laughter drifted across the hills to join the background chorus of buzzing insects and birdsong.

VII

That night, they made camp under open skies. Not since a hunting expedition n Ersua more than a year before had Ullsaard been away from the company of several thousand other men for more than a watch. He took delight in the peace, and wandered away from the camp as his servants prepared the evening meal.

His stroll took him coldwards and dawnwards from the road, towards Askhor, his adopted home. Cresting a hill a few hundred paces from the wagons, Ullsaard stopped and gazed around him, savouring the cooler night air and basking in the chirrup and chitter of small wildlife. Bats flitted above him, and darted towards the circle of light surrounding the camp to feast upon the many flies and other insects brought out of hiding by the fires.

There must be caves not far away, he considered as he watched the bats. He did not know for sure and the bats could have flown some distance searching for food. The thought brought more depressing one: how much of these lands did he really know? His holdings in Askhor had been mapped by the best cartographers many decades ago, but this new realm hotward of the border was as unknown to him as the Straits of Lerbrieth or the source of the Green-water.

There were no people here yet, that was the problem. He needed to build the town so that settlers could come and tame his newly acquired dominions. For that to happen, he needed to build that damn bridge and move on with the army; something that was not going to happen while he was away pandering to Aalun's whims.

Angry with himself for bringing up to troubling thoughts, Ullsaard moved down from the hilltop into the dark shallow beyond. His boots slid on the sandy slope and he stumbled over roots and tussocks of thick-bladed grass. Picking his way through these obstacles by the light of the stars, he couldn't help but wonder how much more of the world there was to see? How much further did the lands spread before they reached other seas? Would he live to see them all?

Askhos had proclaimed it the destiny of his line to rule over all the lands between the seas, and for two hundred and eight years the First King and his successors had laboured towards that goal. Who would be the first wearer of the Crown of the Blood to lay eyes upon all of the domains under the sun?

As was his wont, Ullsaard's musings turned from reflection to action. Things didn't happen just because one wondered about them; things happened because great leaders made them happen. The empire had taken two hundred years to grow as large as it was, and it would take many more years before Askhos's goal was accomplished, but Ullsaard chafed at the thought that his generation would not be the ones to succeed. Cosuas had a few more years left at most, and while Ullsaard could happily look forward to another twenty years at least, there was no guarantee that would be long enough.

In that darkened hollow on the edge of the Mekha desert, Ullsaard vowed to live to see all that the world had for him, life willing. Greater Askhor certainly had the resources and the means. All it required was the will, and he had that aplenty even if others did not appear to share his ambition. In this king's reign or the next, Ullsaard would lead Askhor to the greatest heights of power and create a legacy for his children and grandchildren that no other could match.

Erlaan's voice drifted on the breeze, calling Ullsaard's name. Ullsaard ignored it for the moment, determined to mark this place in some way so that he could return here when he had accomplished his dream, and say to his descendants, "Here I stood when I decided we would rule the world."

He searched around in the twilight until his fingers came upon a smooth, flat rock slightly wider than his outstretched hand. Picking it up, he ran his hands over it – it was hard but not so unyielding that he could not etch a mark onto its surface. Drawing his knife, Ullsaard began to scratch the rune of the Crown upon the stone, working by touch rather than sight. After some considerable work, he drew his fingers over the roughly carved sigil, confident that the engraving was deep enough to withstand the depredations of wind and sand for many years.

With a deep breath, Ullsaard looked up to the stars once more and closed his eyes. He felt the stone heavy in his grasp, knowing that upon it he had sworn an oath to himself and to Askhos. Opening his eyes, he crouched and placed the stone at his feet, reverently pushing it into the thin soil. He stood and turned back towards the camp, strengthened by his private ritual.

The flickering of the campfire entranced Erlaan. He sat alone, the remnant of a half-eaten meal scattered about the clay plate on his lap. The young prince was troubled by the news of his father's illness, a mixture of concern for his family and for himself. If his father died, Erlaan would become heir to the Crown of the Blood. His grandfather, Lutaar, was old, and within a few years Erlaan might become king. The thought repelled him, though he had known since childhood that it was his destiny. He didn't feel ready at all. The campaign with Ullsaard was meant to be a stepping stone towards learning the craft of the ruler but it had so far left him wanting nothing to do with war.

All he had learnt was that Greater Askhor was a huge wilderness, devoid of the comforts he had been raised to enjoy. His handful of servants could barely provide a decent meal and he had already been away from noble company for more than a hundred days. Back in Askh, fashions were changing, friends were drifting away, girls were casting their eyes elsewhere. He was left to grub around in the dust and sand like a dog scavenging for scraps, and it seemed most unfitting for one of the Blood.

There was also the question of the veteran generals. Cosuas seemed deferent enough, in his own crude way. Ullsaard treated him like an inferior sometimes, barking orders and giving Erlaan menial duties. He might be only a Second Captain by rank, but he was a prince by the Blood. It occurred to Erlaan that Ullsaard was punishing him in some way, simply for the benefit of his birth. Just because the general's meagre heritage – a bastard no less if gossip was to be believed – had forced Ullsaard to claw his way to the top from being a lowly legionnaire, there was no reason Erlaan had to suffer similar indignities.

"Care to share your thoughts?" asked Ullsaard, appearing on the opposite side of the fire. The general was stripped to the waist, his muscles carved in shadow from the fire. Erlaan glanced guiltily at Ullsaard and saw a warrior-born, utterly unlike himself. The prince was short and thin, utterly at contrast with the tall, athletic officer.

"Not really," Erlaan replied. He picked up a stick and tossed it into the flames.

"You are worried about your father," said Ullsaard, sitting on the ground a little way to Erlaan's right, looking at the fire rather than the prince.

"Of course," said Erlaan.

"I had no father," said Ullsaard. "Well, no father to raise me, though obviously a man exists who gave his seed to my mother."

The rumours had been true. Erlaan looked across at the general and saw that Ullsaard's gaze was fierce, directed at the flames as if they were somehow responsible for his hard life. The prince said nothing and simply waited for Ullsaard to continue.

"I became a legionnaire and it was Cosuas who raised me up to be an officer, and your uncle who supported my rise, all the way to the position of general."

"I know this," said Erlaan.

"Yes, but you are missing my point," said Ullsaard. "Had you asked me twenty years ago what man I would become, I could not have said. My horizon was the next battle, the next march. Now? Now I have three wives who have each borne me a strong son and I lead the greatest army in the world. Circumstance shapes us every day, Prince. You must learn to recognise when events are changing you and when you are changing events."

"And right now events are changing me?"

"No, they are not, and that is what should concern you," said the general. He grabbed a brand from the fire. Stoking the flames, he turned his gaze upon Erlaan, the fire glittering in his eyes. "You do not wish your grandfather and father to die. That is understandable. Yet, all men must die and even those of the Blood are no different. You have the certainty of fate on your side. Your lineage stretches back to Askhos himself and in your veins runs his strength."

"But what if it doesn't?" blurted Erlaan.

Ullsaard laughed, but his humour was not born from mockery.

"You can no more be weak than I could be a red-skinned Mekhani," said the general. "You are what you are, and it is in you to embrace that destiny. You owe it not only to yourself, but to the people you will rule and your forefathers. You are young, like metal soft in the flames of the smith. The skill of the smith can fashion a great sword, but only so far as the quality of the metal will allow. Life will beat upon you and fashion you into something else, but the quality of the bronze, your heritage, is without question. You are of the Blood, I cannot put it more plainly than that."

Erlaan considered this, nodding gently. His father and all the fathers before him had ruled Askhor since its founding. Each must have had their doubts at times. Ullsaard was right; it was a measure of him as a man how he reacted to his troubles.

"Thank you," said the prince with a smile, his confidence already a little restored by Ullsaard's words. "You are a thinker as well as a warrior, I see."

Ullsaard laughed again and stood up.

"A warrior who does not think is a corpse," said the general, tossing the brand onto the fire. "Get some sleep, we break camp at dawn."

There it was again; a casual dismissal that betrayed the insincerity of the man. Erlaan hid his thoughts as he watched Ullsaard leave. The prince stood, sparing a last glance at the fire. "The Blood holds its own destiny," he remembered his grandfather once telling him. Erlaan walked to his tent, wondering what that destiny would be.

THE GREENWATER
Summer, 208th Year of Askh

I

Noran stood at the starboard rail of the galley's aft deck, enjoying the shelter of the sail while Ullsaard reclined on the deck, his hands behind his head. Clad only in tunic and kilt, the general was less imposing than normal, but even unarmoured and lying down his massive frame and muscular body dominated the afterdeck. Noran idly wondered what it would be like to have such a remarkable body, to have eyes turn to you whenever you entered a room.

The slosh of the water, the creak of ropes and the warm evening air dulled the senses. Bare feet padded on board as the sailors turned out to trim the square sail, urged on by the quiet orders of their captain. The sailors cast glances at the reclining general as they tiptoed around him, whispering to each other.

"A welcome sight after so much desert," suggested Noran, pointing to the vine-crowded terraces of Okhar rising up the banks of the river.

Ullsaard sat up and looked at the fertile slopes.

"Not as welcome as the streets of Askh, but it's a start," replied Ullsaard with a languid stretch. "Twenty-five days we've been travelling, and we're barely halfway."

"It'll be quick enough, you'll see." Not for the first time, Noran compared Ullsaard to an ailur; seemingly quiet and passive, but masking a capability for immense violence and destruction. His rank, his affected civilisation, were the blinkers that kept him from going wild. Some of the stories of the general's exploits moving up the ranks had made Noran glad he was a friend; he had resolved to keep that friendship for as long as possible. The tales of Ullsaard's enemies generally ended badly on the bloodfields.

"We'll pick up a few barrels of wine to celebrate your homecoming. It's been a good summer, by all accounts."

"Stopped by to check on your estate while you were coming to see me, by any chance?" Ullsaard said, giving his companion a dubious look.

"I had to resupply somewhere before that interminable trek into the sands! The quays at Geria just happen to belong to my father. That's not my fault."

"Yes… and I'm sure your visit didn't delay your duties as herald any longer than necessary."

"I may have sampled an amphora or three while I waited for fresh provisions to be brought aboard. What's a day here or there when you're travelling such a long way, anyway? You're just sour because you could have left all the dust and heat a couple of days earlier."

Ullsaard grunted and lay down, closing his eyes.

"It's not natural to have no rain for so long," he said. "Ever been to Enair in the winter?"

"Thankfully, no."

"Pisses down every day. I don't mean the little squalls and showers you get in Askhor; I mean solid downpours day and night from harvest to spring. And the wind! Howls down from coldwards, bringing the sea with it."

"It sounds truly dreadful. I'll be sure to avoid it if I can. No wonder all you Enairians are such a miserable lot." Noran leaned back against the rail and looked down at

Ullsaard, becoming serious. "You haven't really told me much about what it was like growing up in Enair."

"No, I haven't."

Noran waited but nothing else was forthcoming.

"Oh, come on! Throw me a bone here. You must have friends there still; perhaps there was a lass or two you tumbled in the rain? What about family? I know your mother still lives there, but haven't you got any cousins, uncles, alluringly mature and experienced aunts?"

Ullsaard sighed deeply and remained silent.

"Fine," pouted Noran. "It's not like this journey isn't long enough, without you playing dumb for the whole voyage."

"If you want to gossip, talk to the crew," mumbled Ullsaard. "I'm sure they'll be happy to tell you about the harlots they've humped in every town along the river, if that's what you're after."

"You can be such an arsehole, Ullsaard. I try to take an interest in your life and you throw it back at me."

"Don't be such a woman. We could talk about hunting, or the races, or fighting, but you just want to pry into my sex life. You're as much as a gossip as Meliu!"

"Tell me about it! I swear she and Neerita are more like old women than any of their sisters once they start jawing. Did you know that Princess Meerina has gilded rose petals scattered on her bed every night in an attempt to entice Aalun to sleep with her? Imagine that, bribing your own husband to fuck you?"

"I can't imagine that, and I'm pretty sure I don't want to try."

"Me neither, but it's the sort of prattle I have to put up with once Neerita and Meliu start talking. I swear I'd have Neerita's tongue cut out if it wasn't for all the other things she can do with it. I tell you, she does this thing where she can curl her tongue into a tube, and when she sticks–"

"If you finish that sentence I'm going to chop off your balls," growled Ullsaard. "I don't care what you and Neerita put where, just don't tell me about it."

Noran fell into a sullen silence and watched the sailors returning to the thin strip of shadow beside the duskward gunwale, the sail having been trimmed to the captain's satisfaction. Maybe Ullsaard was right; he would be better off talking to someone else. He looked at the sailors again; most appeared to be catching what sleep they could. It was probably better not to disturb them.

Noran turned back to the river, scanning the surface for flying fish or other delights to distract him. Here and there a small dhow bobbed on the water, nets trailing behind it while the three or four fishermen aboard lounged in the setting sun. Evening was coming on and clouds of midges were rising from the rushes along the bank, gathering over the water. Birds gathered for the feast, diving and sweeping just above the river, snatching mouthfuls of the swarming flies.

It was pleasant enough, but intensely boring. Back in Askh, someone would be holding a feast, or there would be games held at Maarmes; something to stimulate the senses and the intellect, or at least rouse the flesh. Noran made one more attempt to animate his lethargic friend.

"These Okharans are a bunch of lazy bastards, aren't they?"

"Most of them," replied Ullsaard. "Had a couple of Okharan porters a few years back. They were always wanting to take rest breaks. Still, the ones I've got in my legions don't give me any problems. Not officer quality, mind you, but diligent enough when they've been trained, and damned obedient."

"You'd be obedient too if you have Nemtun for your governor. He scares the shit out of me, and I'm a family friend."

Ullsaard dismissed his friend's concern.

"He's the king's younger brother, that's what scares the shit out of you; because you're scared of the king. Nemtun's all talk, a bully. King Lutaar gave him Okhar so that he doesn't come back to Askh too often. Too many willing girls and hot days for him to want to leave."

"He trained Aalun and Kalmud; he can't be just full of farts."

Ullsaard yawned again and stared out towards the sunset, shielding his eyes. His tone was distracted.

"True enough, he was a tough bastard in his prime, from what Cosuas says. Pretty much conquered Anrair singlehanded if some of the stories are to be believed. But after that, he couldn't be arsed anymore; he had that one great campaign and has lived off it ever since. He hung around the palace knocking up maids until Lutaar sent Murian to take over Anrair and gave Okhar to him."

"You see, that's the sort of gossip I'd like to hear from Neerita. Useful stuff to know."

The pair fell quiet for a while, contemplating the vagaries of the sexes. Noran took a knife from his belt and began cleaning his nails, flicking dirt into the swirling waters. Ullsaard broke the silent reverie, sitting up.

"Ever felt like going for a governorship?"

"What?" said Noran, whose thoughts had strayed back to Neerita's bedroom talents.

"A governorship – ever been interested?"

There was an intent look in the general's eyes; the question wasn't out of idle interest.

"Why? Have you heard something?"

"No, no!" Ullsaard warded away Noran's intrigued look with a wave of his hands. "I mean, I don't see any of the current governors shifting any time soon. What I meant was, if we settle northern Mekha, for instance, or somewhere else, would you want the king to bear you in mind?"

Noran considered this for a while, lips pursed.

"Not really. Well, maybe. Well, of course I would, but it'd have to be somewhere nicer than Mekha. Though, I suppose if I was to station myself in that new town you'll be building, with some proper irrigation in and everything, it wouldn't be too bad. I think my father was once offered Maasra, but didn't like the idea of living on the Nemurians' doorstep. And that he said being a governor wasn't as great as it seems – more a case of getting the blame if things go wrong and none of the credit if things trickle along nicely. It's like having an ailur – impressive until someone has to clean up all the shit."

"What about a piece of Salphoria?"

Noran's eyes widened with surprise and then narrowed.

"Is that likely? I mean, that would be a bit of a jewel, wouldn't it? Yes, Magilnada would make a fine seat." A look of consternation clouded Noran's face. "Magilnada would either be fantastic or terrible, no middle ground. What with all our damned gold and ore going to the city, it's pretty rich already, but it's hanging its arse out in the wind, right on the edge of the wilds. You'd be dealing with bandits, rebels and who knows what other vagabonds and idiots, not to mention probably a whole army of pissed-off Salphors plotting to get their lands back. They're not like Okharans, or Maasrites, or Ersuans. They wouldn't piss on their king if he was on fire, so how do you conquer that lot? The more I think about it, the more it seems like it'd be more trouble than it's worth. Anyway, that's not going to happen any time soon, is it? *Is it?*"

Ullsaard shrugged.

"Who knows? I think I could persuade the king that Salphoria is achievable, if we decide to really go for it. It's definitely worth it. Gold and silver. Gems. Copper, timber and coal. As much grain as Okhar and Nalanor put together. More of everything than Askhor has already, just over the mountains, being wasted on a bunch of long-haired barbarians. More than that, it's the route duskwards. Nobody knows what lies past Salphoria, not even the Salphors!"

Noran was doubtful and his look expressed as much.

"Even if we assume that the king was to go for it, it's a tricky proposition to become governor. I mean, there's Prince Aalun to consider first, surely he'd want a piece of the action. Younger son, no governship yet, he'd be the first in line without a doubt. Even if he wasn't interested, which is unlikely, I'm not sure my family has enough clout to make any realistic stake. There's better-placed families than ours that have been sticking their tongues right up the king's arse for generations for just such an appointment, while my father's been blinkered by his trade interests. We've got plenty of lands, plenty of produce and even some ore, but how's that any use? The king gets a damned good share in levy anyway, it's not like you can bribe him."

"Maybe you're right," sighed Ullsaard.

"It's not like you to give up on something so easily," said Noran. "What is it? Come on, something's been gnawing your cock for a while now, why don't you tell me?"

Ullsaard glanced at the crewman at the tiller, who appeared to be dozing fitfully. The general stood up and joined Noran at the rail, keeping his voice low.

"I really want to have a go at Salphoria. Right now. It's like we're a legionnaire standing at the door of the whorehouse tugging himself rather than going in…"Ullsaard sighed and frowned. "Cosuas and the princes won't argue against the king, the governors are more concerned with keeping their posts than expanding, even that old warrior Nemtun, so the king sits on his hands. I figured…"

He shrugged, helpless. "I thought that maybe I could use a bit of greed to fire the ambitions of a few of the big families. You know, start them jostling for the spoils, putting some pressure on the king."

He sighed again heavily and spat over the rail. Noran said nothing. It was the most talkative Ullsaard had been in years and he didn't want to interrupt.

"Problem is," Ullsaard continued, "I'm just no good at the politics. All I've done in my life is kill people, either with a sword or a spear or an army. I'm bloody good at it too, but it seems that after all these years, what has it got me? Askhos knows, I love the legions, I really do, and I've got a damned big house, three wives, three sons and plenty of askharins to show for it. But nobody listens to me. I'm just a general, I just do what the king wants me to do, kill the people the king wants me to kill.

"Ah shit, I don't know what I want."

Ullsaard started to turn away, disgusted with himself, but Noran grabbed him by the elbow and pulled him back.

"While I'm no politician, I've picked up a thing or two from my father over the years," Noran said. "If you're going to dabble in politics you have to take two views: the short and the long. In the short view, you have to be ready to exploit any opportunity that might arise and then deal with the consequences later. For the long view, you have to manipulate the situation for the present so that opportunities you are looking for come about in the future."

Ullsaard's nod was uncertain and his frown deep.

"But how do you do that?" he asked.

Noran chewed his lip, formulating an answer that would make it clearer for the straight-thinking Ullsaard.

"Right," said Noran with a smile. "Think of a battle. You go into it with a plan, right? In your mind you have everything set, the way things should turn out. That's the long view."

"Yes, I see that. And when things go wrong, or really well, you react and adapt the plan. If the enemy makes a mistake, you exploit it, if they do something unexpected, you move to counter it. That's the short view."

"That's right! But if you spend too much time reacting,

you end up going nowhere, and the same is true with politics. At some point even the most equivocating politician has to make his opinion known, even if he later changes it. The good thing about a battle is that you know what you want to do and who your enemies and allies are. That's not true of politics. Sometimes you're not sure what it is you want to achieve, but you know what it is that you *don't* want; usually something somebody else wants to happen. People change sides according to self-interest, and often the battlefield itself changes."

"Sounds complicated."

"To one of the family heads or a governor, mustering an army, marching it for fifty days to a battle, organising your troops and then laying out a battle plan is complicated. It's just a matter of how you think about things."

"Maybe I shouldn't get involved, maybe Cosuas is right."

Noran slapped a hand to Ullsaard's shoulder and grinned.

"You would make a lousy politician, friend. For a start, you actually have some loyalty to those around you. You're generally honest, which is a definite drawback in politics. The biggest problem I see, and some would say this is a good thing, is that you actually care more about the empire than you do your own circumstances. No matter what they say in public, those nobles are only thinking about one thing: how does this benefit *me*?"

"Surely the king and the princes aren't like that. After all, the empire's interests and the fortunes of the Blood are the same. Aren't they?"

"At the basic level, of course their fortunes are the same. But when you think about it, what does the king want for? He's the king! Everything in Greater Askhor is his, one way or another. You are, I am, my house, your soldiers, it's all his. The king allows us certain freedoms to make sure we continue to do the things he wants us to do. On the other hand he is nothing without us. If everybody in the empire decided tomorrow that we didn't like Lutaar, what could he really do about it? He can't physically take everything from us."

"He could send a legion to kick you off your estate and put you to the spear," laughed Ullsaard.

"Only if the general and the soldiers agree to do so."

"Why wouldn't they?"

"I don't know. Perhaps because they've met me and realise what a wonderful person I am and they think Lutaar is being mean to take my estates from me. It doesn't matter. The reason you obey the king is out of loyalty to his position, and the threat of reprisal. If you turn against the king, whoever he is, then you are inviting anarchy. If you ignore the king, your captains can ignore you, and their legionnaires can ignore them. The whole thing breaks down. Suddenly you find out that you're not living in Greater Askhor, you've become a Salphor!"

"I see where this is going. For the empire to work, it needs everything in agreement. The armies have to fight, the farmers have to provide the armies with food, buildings have to be kept, roads maintained, all of that. The king has to keep everyone happy so that they do their bit."

"No..."

"What? If the farmers stop farming, we'd all be starving. Surely he has to keep them happy, and those that own the estates?"

"Only if he wants to be nice. This is where we come back to you, the general, and the threat of reprisal. If the farmer decides not to grow food, he gets his door kicked down by your booted foot and told to grow food at spearpoint. Well, that's the implicit punishment for disobeying the king; he doesn't actually have to do it to everyone. By the same measure, *you* have to go and kick down the farmer's door unless you want Cosuas or Nemtun or some other swordswinging bastard paying you a visit."

Ullsaard shook his head and scowled.

"But if legions start fighting other legions, the whole thing becomes a mess. The king doesn't achieve anything by letting that happen."

"Which is why it's the *threat* of force that is his most powerful weapon, and your loyalty to the empire your greatest weakness. You can't act out of place, because the long-term consequences could be disastrous for the empire and your future prosperity. Enlightened self-interest keeps everybody and everything working, with the occasional reminder from the king to make sure nobody starts getting ideas that would cause trouble.

"The only real threat to the empire is a person who doesn't care about the empire because they don't care about their future prosperity and well-being. Nobody sane would want to destroy the thing that guarantees their future, so we all go along with the whole enterprise. It doesn't matter what we really think about the empire, as long as it's there, because it's better to have it than not."

"That's… terrible. You're saying that people are only loyal to the empire because they're scared of not having it?"

Noran shrugged. He pointed to a fishing boat passing a spear's cast away from the galley, two men hauling at their net.

"Do you think they care about any of what I've just said?"

"Probably not."

"They want to know that they'll get a good price for their fish and nobody is going to turn up and burn down their home in the night. Before the Askhans came, that could never be guaranteed, and now it is. That's what the empire means to them. They don't have to see the huge interacting interests that drive Greater Askhor to appreciate what it's brought them. Before Askhos, we would have been rivals, sending our little warbands to raid each other's villages for a few abada and maybe a comely wench.

"Askhos did away with all of that, showing that if we took a step back and looked at the wider world, we could do so much more. I may not have read his book, and I don't have much time for the Brotherhood, but Askhos was a very clever man. He didn't have to conquer the whole world to get what he wanted; he just had to show people that it was possible. Their ambitions did the rest; whether that ambition was to rule over Enair or just to have a stretch of river that could be fished without risking an arrow in the eye."

Ullsaard absorbed this in silence, fingers tapping the rail. He nodded to himself, but then his brow furrowed again.

"I think I understand what you've been telling me. But what does any of it actually *mean*?"

Noran leaned back against the rail and gave an expansive shrug.

"Probably nothing at all. Greater Askhor is what it is. You're frustrated at the moment, but you can't fight the whole empire. People are happy with the way things are, from the farmer to the king. Unless you can prove to them that you're offering something better, why would they want to change?"

"You're right," Ullsaard said with a grimace. "Cosuas said the same thing, but in a different way. I'm putting my desire for war above the needs of the empire. If Greater Askhor doesn't need a new war now, who am I to demand one? That's just being selfish."

The general patted Noran on the arm and smiled. "Thanks."

"That's not really what I meant..." Noran muttered to himself as Ullsaard set off across the deck towards the ship's captain. "Ah, bollocks to it."

The king's herald headed in the opposite direction, seeking the comfort of the Okharan wine stashed amongst his belongings.

OKHAR

Midsummer, 208th Year of Askh

I

Ullsaard ducked under the deck beams and moved to the front of the hold where the ailurs were being kept. Bred from cave-dwelling cats, reared by the Brotherhood beneath their precinct buildings, the war beasts didn't mind the dark. The three of them – Blackfang, Render and Noran's ailur, Thunderbolt – stirred restlessly at Ullsaard's approach, rolling to their bellies. Blackfang raised her blinkered head, catching the scent of her master. He reached through the wooden bars and patted her shoulder.

"Perhaps I need one of those hoods," Ullsaard whispered to her. "Stop me looking at things I shouldn't look at."

He stroked her mane, checking the fastenings on the armoured hood as he did so. He did the same for the other two. Assured that all three cats were secure, he reached into the bucket of bloody meat beside the door and proffered a chunk through the bars. Blackfang took it gently, lifting it from his fingers with her teeth with the delicate touch of a mother lifting a newborn. A few chews and a long gulp and it was gone. Ullsaard allowed her to lick the blood from his fingers, her thick tongue rasping at the flesh.

"Your turn," he said, grabbing another hunk and offering it to Thunderbolt. She was a bit snappier, snatching the meat from his grasp and retreating to the far corner of the cage. Ullsaard tossed a third hunk of meat to Render.

The meat was laced with special drugs made by the Brotherhood and Ullsaard waited for the cats to show the signs of their effects. Ullsaard felt mean every time he had to drug an ailur, it didn't seem fair or honest. On the other hand, it was a wise precaution. Though they were mature and trained, it was best not to take chances. He had never seen an unmasked ailur, but apparently it was not good for anyone that had.

The ailurs settled down, heads swaying. Ullsaard waited a while longer before opening the door. He took a chain hanging from the bars and attached it to Blackfang's collar, gently tugging at the rein so that she rose groggily to her feet. He whispered encouragement as he led her out of the cage, closing the gate with his heel.

The ailur's paws thudded heavily on the boards as Ullsaard led her to the ramp placed at the hatch. She followed passively up onto the deck, stupefied by the Brotherhood's concoction. With gentle coaxing, Ullsaard took her to the gangplank while Noran headed below to fetch Thunderbolt.

The sailors shrank back from the plodding beast as Ullsaard took her down to the quayside. They had their dumb superstitions about women on board ship and seemed to think that a female ailur was just as bad. Ullsaard ignored them. All trained ailurs were female, so there wasn't any way to avoid having them on board ship. As far as he knew, the males were kept in the Brotherhood's Grand Precincts as studs.

The docks at Geria were well-established, stretching along both sides of the Greenwater for some distance. The river had been widened and deepened here in the reign of the previous king, to provide a better anchorage for ships moving up and down the empire's greatest river. Most of the ships were single-deck galleys; trading vessels that kept the lifeblood of Greater Askhor moving along the arteries of its waterways. A couple of warships stood out in the centre of the river, patrolling back and forth with sweeps of their oars. An impressive trireme stood proud at the next dock, whitened hull gleaming, obviously newly commissioned. The banks of oars were stowed and her twin sails furled, but the rows of torsion-armed spear throwers on her upper deck leant her an air of ready menace.

Beyond the grey stone wharfs rose the low warehouses of Geria, made of thick wood planks, roofed with tiles of naked fired clay. Cloth banners hung over the doors, displaying the colourful emblems of their owners – more ship captains were illiterate than could read so it was a simple system of identification to make sure goods ended up where they were supposed to. Wood was in much evidence elsewhere, in the chests and barrels, crates and pallets stacked along the dockside.

Further coldwards were the dockyards, where the skeletal beams of two new galleys were being laid down, towered over by complex cranes of wood and rope. Ullsaard watched the construction as he sat down at the quayside, pulling Blackfang down next to him while he waited for her to recover enough to continue.

Shouts echoed from the shipyard as teams of tanned, loincloth-clad dockworkers pulled at ropes, swinging a long deck timber down onto the struts holding the ship carcass beneath it. The workers made fast their cables and returned to lounging along the riverbank while carpenters milled over the ship with mallets and wooden wedges. There seemed to be little sense of urgency or discipline.

A shadow crossed Ullsaard and he glanced over his shoulder to see Noran leading Thunderbolt. The pair sat down next to him.

"Told you they were lazy bastards," said Noran, picking an errant tuft of hemp from Thunderbolt's fur.

"Right enough," replied Ullsaard. "Look at them! While the carpenters are fixing the decking, those others could be getting the next beam ready."

"Maybe they're worried about dropping it onto their friends," suggested Noran.

"Meh, only if they don't organise themselves properly." Ullsaard shook his head and looked at Noran. "This is what I mean. There's no urgency any more. Everyone's happy just to dawdle along; everything's fine, like we've already got what we're after. It's comfortable contentment, people happy with what they've already got. Where's the hunger for more? What happened to Askhos's pledge to rule over all the land between the seas?"

"Why stop there? Why not rule the seas as well?"

"Why not?" exclaimed Ullsaard with a laugh. "It's only water, no reason it should get away with running around doing its own thing."

Blackfang purred and flicked her ears.

"They'll be back with us soon, we might as well start walking to the villa," said Noran, standing up. Ullsaard fell in beside him and the pair made their way up the cobbled road, heading for the centre of the town.

The large warehouses gave way to smaller wooden buildings, long terraces of one-storey houses for the hundreds of dockworkers. Children ran about in the street and stopped to stare at the ailurs as they passed; mothers shouted out of narrow windows and fell silent when they saw the pair, eying the general and his noble companion with more than just passing interest, expressions coloured by lust and awe.

The road led straight to the central plaza, at the foot of the hill upon which stood the palace of Nemtun, governor of Okhar. The grey building loomed over the town, its shadow cast across the roofs of the town's centre. From this direction the palace presented a narrow front, its columned portico painted white. The hall itself stretched directly away from the square and could not be seen.

"Going to pay him a visit?" asked Noran.

"Not if I can avoid it. I'd rather he didn't know I was even here."

"Me too. He might start asking awkward questions, like why you've been called back to Askh and he hasn't, when it's his nephew that is ailing."

"Were messages sent to any of the governors?"

"Not that I know of, none had been sent when I left," said Noran with a shake of the head. "It was Prince Aalun that sent for you, not the king. I don't think King Lutaar wants anyone to know about Kalmud's condition just yet. He is the heir after all."

"I hadn't thought of that," admitted Ullsaard.

"Best keep it to yourself for now," suggested Noran, casting a meaningful glance at the troop of legionnaires standing guard by the large gilded gate that barred the road up to the palace.

The activity in the plaza was winding down for the evening; market stalls being wheeled away; wares being loaded back onto abada carts; customers drifting down the side streets. A few desperate merchants continued to hawk their perishable wares, offering fruits and vegetables at prices so ridiculous it couldn't be true, if their patter was to be believed.

The ailurs were lively enough to mount by the time the pair had crossed the plaza. There were more stone buildings further from the river; homes of the wealthiest merchants and offices of the governor's small army of sychophants and money-lenders. Only the ground storeys were of stone, the upper levels made of the same pale wood as the warehouses. The buildings had high, narrow windows covered with colourful awnings, and stepped porches up to their slender doors. Here and there a servant or maid swept dust onto the cobbled streets, while workmen laboured on tiled roofs or repainted the stones with thick coats of white. Of the owners, there was no sign.

Slightly apart from them was the three-tiered precinct of the Brotherhood. Atop the precinct a huge golden disc depicting Askhos's face glared down at passers-by, flanked by two limply hanging flags. None of the bureaucrat-priests could be seen, though Ullsaard had no doubt that his arrival and progress would be noted from within the narrow windows.

The cobbled road gave way to a packed dirt track a short way from the plaza, and the houses were again made solely of wood, roofed with grasses and leaves. They had no windows and smoke drifted lazily from chimney-holes. Children ran through the narrow alleys between the commoners' huts, chasing goats and chickens, shrieking and giggling. Knots of women sat in scattered groups grinding flour, kneading dough, scraping roots and sorting through baskets of vegetables and fruit bought at the market or foraged from the hills around the harbour town.

They seemed happy enough to Ullsaard, chattering away in their odd, guttural Okharan dialect. Just like the fishermen, he thought, content with what they have. No dreams, no grand desires. Perhaps is it better to have low expectations fulfilled than loftier goals thwarted.

Now and then one of the women would see the pair riding past and look up with broad, broken-toothed smiles. A few waved. Ullsaard hesitantly waved back, while Noran ignored them.

"What are you doing?" Noran asked.

"Saying hello," replied Ullsaard.

"Why?"

The question caused Ullsaard to pause. He glanced at the women and looked at Noran.

"Why not?"

"You shouldn't encourage them. They'll become over-familiar. First it's a wave and a smile. Next time, you stop and ask how they are, what they're doing, if the harvest has been good or if their man has come back from his voyage upriver. The next thing you know, there's a bunch of them at your villa asking you to represent their complaints to the governor..."

"Speaking from experience?"

Noran nodded sourly.

"Not here, but up in Parmia. I spent a summer on my farms around there and thought it would be good to get to know a few of the locals living on my land. They wouldn't go away until I'd promised to speak to Adral about drainage ditches being blocked on Crown land, drowning their crops."

"What did Adral have to say about that? Did you get the problem sorted out?"

"Never mentioned it to him. Would have been a bit churlish, considering I was trying to negotiate for that land at the time."

"You said you promised your tenants..."

"It's not a real promise though, is it? Not like I'd promised you something, or my father, or a prince."

Ullsaard grunted with disappointment and shook his head.

"And what do your tenants think of you now?"

"No different, I guess. They don't know I didn't say anything to Adral. For all they care, he heard their case and then told me to piss off; which is what he probably would have done if I had spoken to him. Anyway, all got sorted. I bought the land from him and those whingers ended up clearing it themselves. Problem solved. For all I know, they're eternally grateful to me for buying the land and resolving the situation."

"So you haven't been back since?"

"Yes, a couple of times. But, like I say, I don't talk to underlings any more, it just causes trouble."

The path forked ahead, the right-hand trail leading up towards the hills that heaped upon each other until they stopped abruptly at the coast of the Nemurian Strait. The other fork continued ahead, with rutted branches leading off to the farm buildings dotted about the fields and pastures. Goats were everywhere, freely wandering the heathery slopes, the young boys responsible for them following their charges aimlessly dragging their long switches along the ground.

"There it is!" declared Noran. He pointed to the right, at a low white building on a hotward-facing slope half-hidden amongst the vine terraces. The pair split from the main road onto a narrower path that wound up the hill through half a dozen switchbacks, until they came to a walled courtyard. The wooden gates were open, a handful of Noran's servants waiting for them just inside.

"You can see down to the bottom from the kitchens," explained Noran, nodding towards a long, narrow wing of the villa that ran along the outer wall to the right. "Gives them plenty of warning when someone is coming."

Ullsaard looked around and nodded appreciatively.

"Pretty defensible position. Not bad." Ullsaard swung off Blackfang and a young stableman trotted across the courtyard, head bowed, and took the chain from him. Noran laughed as he dismounted and handed Thunderbolt's reins to a waiting attendant.

"Doesn't count for much these days, nobody's wanted to attack the Astaans for at least three generations. But yes, you're right. This place started out as a marching fort when my great-grandfather Asoniu was a general subjugating the Okharans. He didn't bother pulling it down when they capitulated and instead it grew into this lovely place."

The whole front of the villa was open, a semicircle of ten pillars holding up the front of a domed stone roof in the shade of which lay storerooms and stabling on one side and reception chambers on the other. Noran led Ullsaard between them into a grassed garden, also circular, in the middle of which there was a square pool. Colourful waterfowl floated casually on the pond, bobbing their heads to feed on fronds of weed just below the surface. Wooden benches surrounded the pool and white gravel paths cut across the lawn to the three main parts of the villa.

"Dining and entertaining over there," said Noran, pointing to the right-hand stretch of the arcing building. "Next to the kitchens, obviously. On the left are the bedrooms and lounges. I suggest we head to the baths, get rid of this travel-dust."

"I live in the king's palaces and I don't have my own baths!" complained Ullsaard. "How do you get your own all the way out here?"

"I told you, this used to be a marching fort... My great-grandfather was a clever fellow, built the whole villa around the baths the legionnaires dug! Actually, they aren't as good as the real thing, wood-heated you see; the Brotherhood refuses to sell us lava."

"It's a pain in the arse to transport, anyway," said Ullsaard. "Well, not just a pain in the arse; it's dangerous stuff. You'd be better off having one of the Brotherhood on hand to keep an eye on it, and I'm sure you would love that."

Noran's lip wrinkled in distaste at the suggestion. Servants waited to take their clothes as they entered the steam-filled bathrooms. There were only two baths, in fact; one cold, one warm. Despite Noran's modesty it was a rare civility to find in a private house outside Askh. Ullsaard lowered himself into the water with a groan of pleasure. He splashed around for a while before he noticed Noran had not joined him.

"Better than washing in river water, eh?" he said.

There was no reply and he turned to see that Noran had left. A blank-faced functionary stood by the door, holding a fresh robe for Ullsaard.

"Where did he go?" Ullsaard demanded. The servant looked towards the doorway pointedly and returned his gaze to impassively staring ahead. Ullsaard pulled himself from the bath with a snarl at the mute orderly. "Fucking Maasrites."

As Ullsaard was pulling on the robe, Noran reappeared, a concerned look on his face.

"Shit!" he said. "It seems that you can't ride a couple of ailurs through the centre of a town without someone running off to tell the governor. Probably someone from the Brotherhood. Nemtun's invited us to his palace for a feast tonight."

"Tell him we're very sorry but we're in a hurry and are setting off at first light. It's not really a lie, after all."

"It's Nemtun, he won't take no for an answer, and if we don't go to him he's bound to come to us, with all of the fucking about that will entail. Shit, I really could do without this."

Ullsaard tied the belt of the robe tight and smirked.

"I'm not sure why it's such a problem. We'll go to the palace, have a few drinks, eat some of his food and then be back here before midnight."

"It's Nemtun! How many times do I have to say it? Aalun was very explicit that he didn't want any of the governors, least of all the king's brother, coming to Askh at the moment. I've no idea why, but he only wanted you."

"Then why in Askhos's name did you have us stop off here? We could have sailed on to Paalun in another two days and Nemtun would have been none the wiser."

"Because I'm a fucking idiot, sometimes." Noran strode back and forth across the bathroom cursing inaudibly. He rounded on Ullsaard with a gleam in his eye. "I've got it! You can go and see Nemtun and I'll stay here. That way Aalun can't blame me if Nemtun finds out about Kalmud's illness."

"Not a chance," growled Ullsaard, crossing his arms. "If you think I'm going to be the one to tell Nemtun his nephew might be dying, you can think again."

"No, think about it. You can just tell Nemtun you've been summoned to Askh, and don't know why. Nemtun doesn't have to find out anything."

"I'm not lying to Nemtun just because you wanted to show off your fancy villa. He may be an arsehole, but he was a commander of the legions and is still a Prince of the Blood. That deserves some respect."

Noran paced some more while Ullsaard watched with wry amusement. The general quickly grew bored and threw off the robe, slipping back into the relaxing bath. A thought occurred to him.

"Wait a moment," he said. Noran fixed a hopeful stare on Ullsaard. "Don't get excited, it's just something that doesn't fit. Kalmud would have come back along the Greenwater from where he was campaigning. How is it that Nemtun doesn't know already that the prince is ill?"

"Well, clearly..." began Noran. He scratched his chin as he sought an answer. "You're right. Word gets around, no matter how clever you are. The ship carrying him back to Askh would have to put in somewhere along the Greenwater, and it's only a sailor's tongue away from becoming common knowledge."

"That still doesn't help you out of the shit you're in."

"Maybe it does, maybe it does," Noran said slowly, wagging a finger at Ullsaard. His gaze drifted away as he fell into thought. "Yes, that might work."

"What might?"

Noran looked down at Ullsaard lounging in the bath, startled from his contemplation.

"Oh, nothing. Just let me do the talking when we first see Nemtun."

"Is this going to be political?" asked Ullsaard with a wary sigh.

"Oh yes. The heir to the empire doesn't fall dangerously ill without a whole shitheap of politics falling on the rest of us..."

II

A troop of forty legionnaires stood in ranks either side of the palace portico. They had white crests on their helmets, denoting that they were the governor's guard. Ullsaard didn't like that; he never had, even though he had started as guard to Allon of Enair. To his mind there were just legionnaires of Greater Askhor. Giving them different coloured hats didn't change that. What it did was make some governors think they were military commanders, when most of them – Nemtun excepted – had never come closer to a battle than hearing about it from a herald.

Something else irritated Ullsaard as he and Noran walked towards the shallow steps leading to the palace entrance. He stormed towards the guard captain, who recoiled as the general stopped just short. He couldn't have been more than twenty-five years old, his eyes bulging with sudden apprehension.

"Stand up straight!" rasped Ullsaard and the captain went rigid, his gaze hovering over Ullsaard's right shoulder. Ullsaard leaned closer, his voice a hiss. "When a general of the legions and a herald of the king arrive, I would expect a fucking salute!"

"Present spears!" screamed the captain, his voice almost breaking. The guard lofted their weapons in salute with shuffling feet. The lines of spearheads bobbed uncertainly.

"Pathetic," said Ullsaard. "Practice that until we come out. I expect a smarter farewell than the welcome we got. Do you understand?"

"Yes, General," the captain replied.

Ullsaard stalked away and rejoined Noran as he reached the steps.

"Fucking soft-arsed captain, I bet his spear's never seen a drop of blood," muttered Ullsaard as the two of them mounted the steps. The heavy wooden doors swung inwards to reveal a pillared hallway down the centre of the palace, archways along each side leading to other chambers.

"Temper your mood before we see Nemtun," cautioned Noran.

"I'll try."

A bowing factotum appeared in front of them, dressed in a blue linen kilt and sleeveless white vest. His head was shaved and he had a golden ring piercing the side of his nose.

"General, herald, please follow me," he said with another bow.

"Fuck me, a talking Maasrite," chuckled Ullsaard. The factotum directed a weary smile towards the general.

"Not everyone from Maasra takes the Vow of Service, General," the man explained, speaking softly. "It is only those committed to the life of domestic service that do so."

"I knew that," Ullsaard lied quickly. "Just never met one of you lot who wasn't a servant."

The functionary nodded in understanding and led them to the end of the hall and turned right, passing through an archway into a broad, square chamber. Rugs were scattered on the stone floor and the walls were covered with patterned hangings. Young, half-naked maids walked with trays amongst the clusters of Nemtun's guests, offering wine, water and fruits. Ullsaard ignored them though Noran quickly lifted a clay cup from the tray of the closest and filled it with undiluted wine. Ullsaard directed a questioning look at his friend.

"I need something strong before I see Nemtun," Noran explained before taking a long draught of the drink. He smacked his lips appreciatively.

Ullsaard walked through the throng of merchants and ship captains. He suddenly stopped, spying a middle-aged, handsome woman standing at the centre of a knot of aging admirers.

"Is that...?" he asked, turning to Noran.

"Lerissa? Yes, that's her."

Ullsaard gazed at Nemtun's wife, admiring her smooth, tanned skin and firm limbs through the slits in her dress.

"I didn't realise it had been so long since I last saw her," Ullsaard remarked quietly. "She's certainly matured well. I hope Nemtun looks after her properly."

"This is where listening to the gossiping Meliu and Neerita comes in useful," replied Noran with a wink. "Apparently Nemtun is besotted with Lerissa, but has never once laid a finger on her. They don't even share a bed."

"Why would any sane man pass up the chance of bedding such a woman?"

"Are you interested? Apparently Nemtun isn't too fussy about who his wife chooses as her lovers, that's why all those wrinkled vultures are circling so intently."

"I hope she doesn't settle for these old goats," Ullsaard said with a disconsolate shake of the head. "I can't imagine any of them having the necessary endurance."

Lerissa looked across the room and caught Ullsaard's gaze. Her warm smile melted another piece of his heart. He nodded in acknowledgment and turned away, cursing his faithless thoughts. This was no time to get distracted. He had to keep an eye on Noran to make sure he didn't get himself, or Ullsaard, into more trouble.

The Maasrite functionary coughed politely to catch their attention. He looked pointedly towards an archway barred by a heavy curtain of black and red beads.

"Governor Nemtun would like to speak with you in private before he joins the festivities."

"In there?" Noran asked with a gesture towards the curtain. The factotum nodded. Ullsaard heard Noran taking in a deep breath as he plunged towards the archway. "Best not to keep him waiting."

III

The small room beyond the curtain was filled with brightly

patterned divans, and low wooden tables brimming with fruits and various dishes made from the fish of the Greenwater. Nemtun reclined in the dim light from the room's one narrow window, his gross form filling the couch on which he sprawled. He looked up at the clatter of beads and smiled, droplets of sweat dripping from his heavily lined brow and bald scalp.

"Ah, my special guests!" Nemtun declared in his bass voice, jowly cheeks wobbling. He raised a beringed hand in greeting but made no effort to sit up.

"Governor," replied Noran with a nod. He glanced towards a divan and Nemtun motioned the pair to seat themselves. "Thank you for the invitation, but I must start with an apology."

"Eh? How so?" Nemtun's crumpled forehead deepened into a frown. "You've only just arrived; you can't have got into that much trouble already, Noran!"

"Not at all, Governor," Noran said with a light laugh. His face grew sincere. "We must apologise for not being able to enjoy your hospitality for long."

"Got an early start," added Ullsaard with what he hoped was a look of disappointment. Noran shot him an exasperated look, piqued by Ullsaard's interruption.

"As the general says, we must be away by dawn tomorrow to make all speed to Askh, and I've never had much of a stomach for boats at the best of times."

"Shame."

Noran blinked in surprise at the governor's flat retort. He rallied quickly. "We are also eager to learn if you have heard any further news of Prince Kalmud's condition."

Now it was Ullsaard's turn to be surprised. Wasn't Noran supposed to keep the prince's illness secret from Nemtun?

"I had hoped to ask you the same," Nemtun replied heavily. "You're the first man from the court I've seen since poor Kalmud went upriver."

"He was as well as could be hoped when I departed, and

I have no reason to believe he will not make a full recovery."

Nemtun shifted his bulk, causing the wooden frame of the divan to creak alarmingly. Once upright, the governor leant forwards, wiped a hand over his sweaty pate and fixed Ullsaard with bright blue eyes.

"And what about you, General?"

Ullsaard managed to avoid glancing towards Noran for guidance.

"I am well, Governor. The campaign in Mekha is slow but progressing."

"Those sand-eaters giving you much trouble?" Nemtun plucked a bowl of roe from a nearby table and scooped a handful of the black eggs into his mouth.

"Not so far," Ullsaard replied, ignoring the cluster of small spheres now stuck to the governor's chin. "The lava-throwers are a match for the behemodons, and they've got nothing else to offer in the way of threat."

"Reckon you should be done by winter."

"I don't know. The Mekhani keep moving around, it's hard to bring them to battle in one place. They split up and disappear into the desert where we can't follow."

"Why not?"

Ullsaard was taken aback by the question; a general of Nemtun's experience should have realised the difficulties of maintaining an army in such conditions. He kept his tone even.

"Not enough to drink, Governor. There're lots of scattered water holes, but each can only sustain two or three thousand men, and many are up to a march apart. The Mekhani would love us to spread all over the place, letting them gather their numbers and come at us while we're divided."

Nemtun grunted in understanding.

"What are you going to do about that?"

Ullsaard considered the question, grabbing an orange to fill the gap before his answer.

"When the bridge is built, we can stockpile better, and then we can launch a proper offensive. I'm just hoping they're stupid enough to have a few more goes at us over the summer."

"Seems like you're making slow work of it."

"When has war ever been speedy?"

"When I brought Anrair into the empire," replied Nemtun. "Two summers, that's all it took to get those barbarians to concede defeat."

"It was a masterful campaign," Ullsaard admitted. "Though Anrair is very different from Mekha."

"The same excuses," Nemtun said, waving away Ullsaard's answer with a flick of his wrist. "Just bloody well get it done. I've got labourers fucking and drinking and doing nothing else while they wait to go hotwards to build your town. I don't know why they were sent here first; dull Enairians and horny Ersuans filling up the streets and barracks, eating my food and chasing the local women."

Ullsaard killed an angry retort and finally looked to Noran for help. The herald was peeling an orange with his knife and looked up at the sudden silence.

"It might not be Ullsaard's problem for much longer," Noran said hurriedly, glancing between the general and the governor. "Depending on Kalmud's state of health, I think Ullsaard might be taking over the Greenwater campaign."

Ullsaard wanted to throttle Noran at that moment. Why had he brought up the Greenwater campaign with Nemtun? The governor grunted again; Ullsaard detected a note of disapproval.

"I am sure Kalmud will be healthy enough to rejoin his legions soon," said Ullsaard, thinking that Nemtun was perhaps annoyed by Noran's assumption that Kalmud would be unwell for some time. "Maybe before the winter, with any luck."

"I don't know why Lutaar doesn't just ask me to do it," grumbled Nemtun. "I mean, who is better placed than me? I'm right on the river already, got plenty of experience."

"I'm su–" began Noran but Nemtun cut him off.

"It's all well and good making sure his sons get in on the action, but I've had my eye on going hotwards along the Greenwater ever since I came to Geria."

"I would have thought being a governor was far more rewarding and comfortable than the campaign road," suggested Noran. "All that bad food and… long marches."

Ullsaard suppressed a smirk, imagining Nemtun waddling along at the head of a legion column, gut bulging between breastplate and kilt.

"You think I'm too old and fat?" rasped Nemtun, heaving himself to his feet to totter towards Ullsaard. "Pah! It's sitting around here every day that got me this way. My heart and lungs are still strong; the fat would melt off me after a few days. Then I'd show you idiot youngsters how to lead a legion!"

Ullsaard could ignore the overstatement of Nemtun's victories but it was more than his mood could bear for his accomplishments to be dismissed so easily. He surged to his feet with a growl and confronted Nemtun, whose eyes were on a level with Ullsaard's chin.

"The Anrair tribes were ready to surrender after one summer, but you decided to take another year so you could add half-a-dozen pointless battles to your name; battles fought against half-hearted, broken warriors who just wished their chiefs would be allowed to hand over their weapons. If you were such a great leader, why didn't you press on into Salphoria?"

"Be warned, I am not a man to be mocked!" Nemtun's cheeks and chins trembled with indignation, his face growing ever redder. "I ought to summon you to the bloodfield to teach your generation a few manners."

Ullsaard couldn't stop the short laugh that erupted from his lips.

"I would not meet you there, even if you called my mother a whore," the general said. "You're right; you are too old and too fat to fight, either as a general or a warrior. I'd take no pleasure and no honour from gutting you on the bloodfield, so why would I bother?"

Noran was horrified and grabbed Ullsaard's arm, fearing perhaps that he would strike the governor. Instead, Ullsaard took a step back, picked up a bowl and raised it to Nemtun. "Okharan spiced fish head, Governor?"

Nemtun's eyes flickered between the beady eyes of the dead fish and Ullsaard's hard stare. A smile crept across his thin lips, creating deep dimples. The governor plucked a fish head from the bowl and met Ullsaard's gaze.

"Go fuck your mother, Ullsaard," Nemtun said amiably. "You're not of the Blood; you're not even Askhan. Aalun's already promoted you beyond your ability. I've no idea what he sees in you. Hurry up; scurry off to Askh to wipe his arse for him. While Kalmud is incapacitated, you'll need to keep on Aalun's good side. Your shortcomings will become obvious soon enough. I'd start being very nice to the few friends you actually have; you never know when you might need them."

The governor slumped back into the couch and continued, tossing the fish head at Ullsaard's feet.

"If you do get the Greenwater campaign, don't think of stopping off here on your way back from Askh, because there'll be no welcome for you. You know, sometimes stores get spoiled, or ships spring leaks."

"Perhaps we should be getting away," said Noran, stepping between the two of them. "Early start and all of that."

"We'll leave the governor to his party," agreed Ullsaard, pulling his arm from Noran's tightening grip. "I'm sure he needs to save his strength for that."

The general turned sharply through the curtain, as Nemtun snarled a last retort.

"Enairian cockeater!"

Ullsaard's face was a mask of polite respect as he emerged into the main chamber. He cast around the room for Lerissa but the governor's wife was not to be seen. The old goats that had been crowding her were still present, with the glum looks of men who were sure they had missed a certain chance.

"I think that settles business for the evening," he said to Noran, who had become quite pale and agitated. After another quick look for Lerissa, Ullsaard headed for the door. "There's nothing else to keep us here."

IV

Noran silently fumed during the ride back to the villa and Ullsaard said nothing. The herald kept his tongue while the ailurs were taken away and he led Ullsaard to one of the reception chambers. Servants in plain white tunics entered quickly, bringing wine and water. Ullsaard slouched on a rug and pulled one of the ewers next to him, pulling out the stopper with his teeth. Noran snatched the jug away, spilling red liquid onto the ochre tiled floor.

"You stinking heap of abada shit!" Noran snarled. Ullsaard smiled without shame. Noran wanted to punch or kick the idiot, but thought better of it and contented himself with hurling the jug against the wall. "You selfish, childish, moronic, cock-gnawing..." He floundered around for the right words before giving up. "Arsehole!"

Ullsaard's smile faded and Noran thought for a moment that he had gone too far.

"Nemtun only got what he deserved; the fat, useless toad," grumbled Ullsaard.

"That's not the point!" shrieked Noran. He turned as a servant entered and started picking up pieces of the shattered jug. "Get out! Get out!" The servant quickly retreated.

Noran began pacing again, stopping only to fill a cup to the brim with wine, downing half the contents in two long gulps.

"I really didn't need Nemtun as an enemy, you fucking idiot," Noran rasped before finishing off the cup of wine. The sharp liquid took the edge off his anger a little. "Why did you do it? Why in all the world did you pick a fight with him?"

"If he's got a problem with anybody, it'll be me," Ullsaard said placidly. "You've got nothing to worry about."

"Oh, I do, I really do. I was in the room with you, for Askhos's sake. I thought I'd got away with being here against Aalun's wishes, but you've made sure he'll find out. Nemtun will be sending a message to Askh right now; telling the king and his sons about how you've insulted one of the Blood, one of the king's appointed governors. They really don't like that sort of thing."

"Psh! Lutaar despises his brother for his behaviour of these last years, and surely if Aalun held him in any regard he wouldn't have told you to avoid him. Believe me; Nemtun has fewer friends in court than I do."

"It's not about Nemtun, it's about the dignity of the Blood." Noran slammed the cup down on the low table and glared at Ullsaard. "They can't let people go around insulting members of the Blood and getting away with it. They'll have to punish you to maintain respect."

"What can they do?" Ullsaard said with a shrug. "I'm already campaigning in the arse end of nowhere; it isn't like they can send me anywhere worse. And if they want me to take my chances on the bloodfield, I'm more than happy."

"It's a matter of the Blood, and that means the Brotherhood will get involved," Noran said. He shook his head in exasperation. "They don't send you on shitty garrison duties or make you prove your mettle on the bloodfield. They've got much nastier ways of punishing folks. They could name you as an enemy of the empire, take your family away, cut off your balls and then have you strangled."

"I think you're overreacting…"

"Yes? Tell me that again when you're a ball-less, family-less man being strangled to death."

Ullsaard laughed so hard that Noran couldn't stop himself from smiling.

"What? What's so funny?" said the herald.

"You are. All of your concern isn't for me, it's for you. You've got far more to lose than I have. It's you without bollocks that worries you."

"That's not true! We've been good friends for most of our lives, I wouldn't want to see you ruined because of a stupid outburst."

"It's done now, so we'll just have to see what happens," said Ullsaard, gesturing to the stoppered jugs of wine. Noran sullenly tossed one over to him.

"You could apologise," suggested the herald.

"Not a chance!" Ullsaard pulled free the stopper and drank directly from the jug, a trickle of wine staining his tunic. "If Nemtun senses weakness, he'll go in for the kill. At the moment, he's wondering whether I'm going to call him out. He's probably just as distressed as you about the matter. He knows I'm on good terms with Aalun and Co-suas, and is probably worried about what *I* might say about *him*."

Noran crossed the room and took the jug from Ullsaard, swigging a mouthful of wine as he sat down next to his friend.

"You know, if I'm going to get fucked on this, I'm not going to let you forget it."

Ullsaard retrieved the wine and slurped a mouthful.

"It'll be a sad day for Greater Askhor if two fine upstanding citizens like us get fucked for speaking our minds."

Noran shook his head at Ullsaard's naïveté but said nothing. They shared the wine for some time, leaving three empty jugs on the floor, and Noran began to feel sleepy. He was about to excuse himself and send for a servant to take Ullsaard to his chambers when the general turned a bleary but accusing gaze on Noran.

"You brought up Kalmud first!" Ullsaard exclaimed.

"What do you mean?"

"With Nemtun. You didn't want him finding out about Kalmud's illness, but you were the first one to mention it. Why'd you do that?"

Noran smiled smugly and winked.

"I figured that Nemtun just *had* to know something already. Kalmud came through Geria and, by fair or foul means, Nemtun would have found out. Or found out something, even if it wasn't the whole truth. You know, I'm sure someone would have lied to him about it, put him off track. By being open about it, I pretended there was no secret about Kalmud, so there was no reason for Nemtun to suspect anything he had already heard. That way, I could work out what lie, if any, he'd already been told. Simple."

Ullsaard scratched his bearded chin and his eyes glazed over for a moment before he focussed again.

"What lie?"

"Did he seem all that concerned to you?"

"No. He was very calm about the whole thing; more interested in trying to relive his glory days."

"Exactly. Nemtun clearly knows that Kalmud is ill, but it looks like he doesn't know quite how ill he is. He's happy to stay out of the matter because he thinks Kalmud will be back on his feet soon enough. Why make him think anything else?"

Ullsaard nodded sagely, eyelids drooping. He squinted at the almost-empty jug.

"That's strong stuff; we should probably have watered it."

Noran suppressed a heavy yawn and silently agreed. He stood up uncertainly and patted Ullsaard on the shoulder.

"Someone will show you to your rooms when you're ready. I'll see you bright and early."

While Ullsaard and Noran slept the heavy sleep of the drunken, Erlaan stared into a camp fire, not far from the duskward bank of the Greenwater. He was alone – except for two Maasrites – and was depressed. He grabbed pinches of dirt from between his legs and flicked them at the flames.

"I'm glad Noran suggested I not stay in Geria," the prince said. The tongueless servants looked across to him from where they were preparing his bedding, their bald heads reflecting the glow of the flames. "The last thing my father or grandfather need at the moment is Nemtun raging around the palace making trouble."

The two Maasrites – Keaila and Aminea – nodded sympathetically and returned to their chore. Erlaan didn't notice and continued talking softly.

"He trained my father and uncle in generalship, you know? I think that's why they both agreed I should learn from Cosuas and Ullsaard; didn't want me to suffer whatever it was they had to go through."

The servants exchanged a knowing look and glanced with mock pity at the Prince of the Blood. Erlaan was still looking at the dancing red and orange of the fire.

"I'm still not sure why I need to learn to be a general," he muttered, grabbing a fistful of dry earth. He let it trickle through his fingers. "When I'm king, I'll have generals to lead legions for me."

Concealed from Erlaan's view, Aminea's fingers flickered in secret sign language, "King one day?" Keaila gave a slight shrug and softly shook his head in disappointment. They shared a smirk while they plumped up the prince's feather-filled pillows.

"It isn't as if a king since Askhos has actually led a legion. A king's far too valuable to risk on a battlefield." The prince considered this realisation for a while. "When you think about it, surely an heir is as valuable as a king? I'm a king-to-be. If anything happens to me before I have an heir... I really should do something about that. Find some wives. The sooner the better, in fact."

Erlaan sat deep in thought, drawing circles in the dirt with his booted toe.

"I'll speak to my father when we reach Askh. I'm sure he and my mothers have already lined up some likely candidates for me to think about, that's the sort of thing parents do. Askhan, obviously. Pure families. Dark-haired and dark-eyed beauties, with any luck. Three would be nice; one my age and a couple a little older. They say experienced women make the best wives. Full breasts too, and hips you can grab onto without worrying about breaking them. Good for breeding and good for bedding. Hmm, I think that was one of Nemtun's sayings. Perhaps I should go for small tits and thin hips to spite him."

Erlaan sighed long and deep. Thinking about women was giving him an erection. He absentmindedly rubbed his crotch through his tunic.

"I haven't been with a woman since the winter," complained Erlaan. Out of the prince's sight, the Maasrites exchanged alarmed glances and pointed at each other insistently. "It's a shame Ullsaard doesn't have any maidservants. Hopefully my balls won't burst before I get back to Askh."

The Maasrites breathed quiet sighs of relief and ducked out from under the awning that would serve as the prince's shelter for the night. Erlaan looked up at their approach.

"We need to be ready to leave by dawn," he said. The Maasrites nodded in understanding. General Ullsaard had been quite specific with his instructions. "Wake me up at the start of Dawnwatch."

The Maasrites patiently nodded again and followed the prince to his mattress, quickly helping him undress. When he was under the blanket, head sunk into the pillow, they turned away and shared a conspiratorial smile. As they tidied the camp, Erlaan began to grunt quietly with pleasure. They kept their gazes away from his tent.

"Wanker," signed Aminea. The other Maasrite bit his knuckle to suppress a laugh and they headed to their rough pallets, sneaking a jug of fiery Enairian spirit from their packs. They took a swig each and giggled quietly as panting began to sound from Erlaan's bed.

"Not a lot," Keaila signed. "Early start."

Aminea nodded, took one more mouthful and stashed the liquor. The frenetic sounds of self-pleasure from Erlaan died down. The two mute servants looked past the guttering fire and saw the prince burying himself deeper into the bedding.

"You wash sheet in morning," Keaila signed to his friend.

"Fuck you," Aminea signed back with a grin.

VI

The galley's boat picked up Erlaan and the two servants not long after the next day. Noran and Ullsaard were both aboard already, nursing sore heads. The prince was happy to keep to himself, while Ullsaard and Noran were in no fit state for conversation and winced every time the sailors' bare feet padded on the boards or the sail cracked in the wind. Ullsaard was relieved that a steady duskwards wind carried them against the sluggish current without need for the sweeps. The thump of the drum and creak of the oars would just about have broken him.

The ship was brimming with fresh supplies from Geria. Barrels of pickled fish and salted goat meat filled the hold and were roped onto the deck. Bales of white Okharan linen had been stowed as well, for dyeing in the towns of Nalanor before being shipped to markets across the empire. The captain had also used the opportunity to acquire some slabs of Okharan marble – jade-veined stone highly prized in Askh – which he had distributed throughout the ship as expensive ballast. Up in the bow two bulky abada munched at their feed, thick ropes through their nose horns tying them to rings in the deck. No patch of deck was wasted, everything bound tight and close-packed.

There was little cloud and the captain made use of the pleasant weather to set his crew to cleaning and maintaining everything from bow to stern. Bronze fixings were polished, planks scoured, the mast lacquered with thick resin from Maasra, knots were tightened, ropes spliced and a hundred other things besides that kept a ship afloat and orderly. All was done with a quiet bustle that carefully avoided the guests when possible, as if they were a necessary inconvenience rather than the purpose of the journey.

Ullsaard lay on the deck, a coil of rope for a pillow, eyes closed, sleeping in short snatches. He found his troubled stomach could handle the rising and falling of the ship better than when upright. In the periods of wakefulness, he thought about his confrontation with Nemtun. Should he have held his tongue? He dismissed the regret. Both he and Nemtun wanted to take over the Greenwater campaign in Kalmud's absence. They were going to become rivals anyway, so Ullsaard's little outburst didn't matter. If anything, it might discourage Nemtun from getting too carried away, knowing that a fully active, experienced general was offering to continue the advance along the river.

Thoughts of the Greenwater campaign banished any chance of catching up on lost sleep. Ullsaard's mind filled with the possibilities. So much more could be done than in Mekha. An easy, constant supply line meant he would be able to push hotwards as far as the river would take him. Who could say what was waiting down there? The sea, at some point, and that probably meant a harbour. The Greenwater was the main artery of Ersua, Nalanor and Okhar, and doubtless in the uncharted reaches of the river there were undiscovered tribes and towns that depended on the river. For all that Ullsaard knew, it was a prize worth even more than Salphoria. He would sooner risk the wrath of Nemtun than let the bloated fart get his greasy paws on the Greenwater without a fight.

"Here," said Erlaan. Ullsaard opened his eyes to find the prince standing over him with a jug of water and a cup. He sat up and took them with a nod of thanks.

"Now I remember why Askhos forbade hard drink in the legions," Ullsaard said with a grimace. He downed two cups of water swiftly and emptied the remaining contents of the jug over his head with a gasp.

"Thank Noran, it was his idea," said Erlaan, sitting down next to Ullsaard. "He was throwing up over the stern when I last saw him and was begging for some water. I thought you might appreciate some as well."

"You don't approve of drinking?"

"Nothing wrong with indulging now and then," Erlaan said with a shrug and a grin. "I know I've not had much experience of life, but I've had a few wine-filled evenings. I've learnt that they're best reserved for when one has nothing to do for several days after."

"True, too true," said Ullsaard. He studied the prince and scratched a bearded cheek. "I got into something of an argument with your great-uncle."

"You were drunk?"

"No such excuse. No, he just annoyed me."

"I wouldn't worry too much about that, he annoys everybody. I'm pretty sure he and my grandfather used to have fights all of the time. I don't think he's ever got over the sad fact of his birth."

Ullsaard raised himself to one elbow.

"What do you mean?"

"Second-born of the Blood," explained Erlaan. "As soon as my father was born he was next in line, meaning Nemtun was not going to become king. I think that's why he couldn't stand to stay in Askh and decided to lead the legions duskwards."

"I hadn't considered that," said Ullsaard. "Must be hard knowing that you're never going to be at the top no matter what you do."

"You seem to handle it without any problem."

"What? I'm not of the Blood."

"Which means that you'll never be king, either. It's not a problem for you, why should it be a problem for Nemtun? And Uncle Aalun is very supportive of my father. He doesn't seem to be jealous."

"Maybe you're right. Maybe it is just jealousy." Ullsaard saw small wooden houses crowding the banks of the river, fishing boats bobbing up and down on their moorings outside. The Greenwater was even wider here and barely a sound could be heard from the banks. His head throbbed again, the previous night's drinking not quite ready to free him of its effects.

"Believe me, it is jealousy," said Erlaan. "Askhos was always careful never to give his followers any reason to doubt the right of the Blood to rule. My father has always told me that although being of the Blood gives us the right to rule, the reputation of the Blood depends upon all of us to rule with dignity and fairness. It is not only a privilege, but also an honour that needs to be lived up to."

"One that I am sure you will," said Ullsaard, guessing that Erlaan was worrying again about his inheritance. It would be better to change the subject than listen to more of the prince's self-indulgent woes. Unfortunately, Ullsaard couldn't think of anything Erlaan wouldn't complain about.

"I should leave you to recover in peace," said Erlaan, mistaking Ullsaard's silence. The general affected a grateful smile and lay back with his eyes closed. Erlaan's footsteps receded across the deck and Ullsaard drifted again into sleep.

VII

They sailed past the slate-roofed buildings of Paalun and continued upriver, the mountains of Nalanor and Askhor growing larger every day. The vine terraces and grassy meadows of Okhar gave way to Nalanor's crop-rich fields, swathes of gold and green as far as the eye could see. Here the Greenwater narrowed, the current growing stronger. The wind kept strong across the flat plains of Nalanor, but every dusk and dawn it stilled and the sailors brought out the oars for a watch to keep the ship at its steady pace.

The tedium of the voyage gnawed at Ullsaard and he became irritable. Without the needs of command to distract him with its everyday inconveniences, the general realised just how repetitive life could become. There were no disciplinary matters to oversee, no provisioning requests, no scouting parties to send or officers to instruct. Every few days, Ullsaard ordered the captain to put into the bank to allow the ailurs some exercise. Ullsaard, Noran and Erlaan would ride along the bank, easily keeping time with the ship, and board again in the evening. The general enjoyed these short excursions, and listened patiently to Noran's exploits in Askh or Erlaan's hopes for quickly finding some suitable wives. He let their babble wash over him, paying just enough attention to answer the occasional question or respond with suitable comment when it was required.

The Greenwater curved dawnwards towards the Askhor Mountains and the banks grew steeper, reed beds giving way to chalky cliffs cut with zigzagging paths. River traffic grew with each day they came closer to Nalanor's capital, Parmia. The grey city dominated the hills to coldward of the river, across five mounts that dropped steeply to the shores of Lake Parmia. The Greenwater disappeared into the inland sea and the wind died, broken up by the surrounding ring of hills. The crew bent their backs to the sweeps for five watches out of eight, as the steersman guided the galley around other ships and the low, tree-filled islands that broke the lake's surface.

The ship stopped in Parmia for two days while the captain exchanged some of his cargo for Nalanorian goods. Ullsaard and Noran had no desire to repeat the fiasco of Geria and stayed on board lest Governor Adral became aware of their presence. They left the city without incident and carried on dawnwards along the Greenwater, every day bringing them closer to the docks at Narun and the border of Askhor.

NARUN
Summer, 208th Year of Askh

I

Though it lacked the general splendour of Askh and could not compete with the sheer size of the Askhor Wall, Narun was perhaps the greatest achievement of the Askhan Empire, at least in Ullsaard's mind. Just hotwards of the sprawling docks the Greenwater ceased to be a river; for three miles the river broke into a dozen channels created by a series of lock gates and dams. Each channel was divided and divided again into a criss-cross of canals and aqueducts, creating a huge gridded area of waterways, wharfs and dry docks.

Teams of abada trudged in circles around capstans to open lock gates or pump water along the aqueducts. Thick-beamed cranes – more than ten times as many as were found in Geria – loomed over the still waters, more beasts of burden chained and roped to the sprawling network of pulleys and levers. Swarms of dockhands busied themselves on the ships' decks and wooden quays, loading and unloading, a constant stream of wagons and handcarts arriving and leaving with the goods of the empire. A stepped hill had been built to duskward, rising in twenty levels reached by winding ramps, each tier filled with cavernous warehouses.

Along the waterside overseers cajoled and bullied their teams with cudgels and curses, warning off rivals with hoarse shouts. They haggled unloading fees with ships' masters as they passed and called out to Ullsaard's ship to make dock at their quay. Pilots sat in boats on the water, offering their services to captains unfamiliar with the maze-like harbour.

"Where are we going to berth?" Ullsaard asked the ship-master, Eoruan, who thrust a hand into a leather pouch at his belt and pulled out a gilded crown-shaped token.

"King's Wharfs," Eoruan said with a grin. "Your friend, the herald, knows all the right people."

With slow sweeps of the oars, the galley slid serenely between the ships, coracles and boats filling the waterway, the smaller vessels hurrying out of its path as it headed implacably coldwards along the main canal. The water opened into a large artificial lake, broken by anchored rafts on which were piles of wood for fires. The clean-hewn banks of the reservoir jutted steeply at the water's edge, and there stood high beacon towers.

"You should see this place at night," the captain said. "It's not called the Harbour of a Thousand Fires for no reason. The firelight glittering on the water, the shadows and silhouettes of a hundred ships. Makes my old heart stir, it surely does."

Ullsaard nodded but said nothing. He had seen plenty of firestorms by night; when Lehmia had burned; when his legions had put the torch to Mekhani settlements hotwards of Khar; when lava-throwers had torched enemy encampments. He chose not to share the memories with the ship's master.

"About time," muttered Eoruan.

"What's that?"

"The harbour authorities have talked about a halfway bridge for the past three years. Good for unloading light, perishable goods without having to dock fully. You know, using just boats. Looks like they're finally doing something."

The captain pointed to a long pontoon bridge stretching about a third of the way across the lake from the coldward bank. Dozens of men laboured on the extended bridge, naked save for black scarves that covered their heads and shoulders; slaves taken by the legions and criminals labouring to atone for their acts against the empire, under the watchful gaze of robed members of the Brotherhood. Soldiers with black crests stood at regular intervals along the line of labourers, carrying long clubs rather than spears. More coloured hats, thought Ullsaard. Black hats to match the black robes of the Brotherhood. More nonsense.

The King's Wharfs were built of stone blocks, unlike the wooden quays and jetties that made up the rest of Narun. On solid piles sunk into the bottom of the lake, three wide piers speared into the water, each large enough to berth four ships, two to each side. Only one was in use at the moment, the middle quay providing mooring for a bireme and a small yacht. A blue banner embroidered with the gold symbol of the crown fluttered at the masthead of the smaller vessel.

"Prince Kalmud's ship," said Eoruan. "Was here when we left. I guess the prince has been spending some time in Askh."

"Very likely," grunted Ullsaard.

"I thought he was hotwards along the Greenwater," Eoruan continued.

"He was," said Ullsaard. "Now he isn't."

The captain caught Ullsaard's stare and quelled whatever he was going to say next. He coughed self-consciously.

"We'll be in berth soon enough. Time to start getting the stores ready to unload."

"Right," said Ullsaard. "Do that."

With another glance at Ullsaard, Eoruan headed along the deck, bellowing for the crew to muster. The pounding of feet on the deck roused Noran, who sauntered from be-lowdecks. Erlaan was behind him.

"Not long now, eh?" Noran said to the prince as they joined Ullsaard. "Soon we'll be back in Askh, chasing the women and drinking the finest wines."

"I am more concerned with my father's health," replied the youth.

"Of course, of course," said Noran. "I didn't mean to be dismissive. It's just… I'm sure there's no cause for serious concern."

Erlaan's eyes were fixed on the dawnward shoreline.

"I hope not," he said. The prince turned and his gaze moved between Ullsaard and Noran. "I know you think me inexperienced, and you're probably right. But I know enough to wonder what's happening when my uncle sends a herald so far hotward to bring back his favourite general."

"Probably the Greenwater campaign," said Ullsaard, meeting Erlaan's look. He smiled in the most encouraging fashion he could. "It doesn't mean anything, really. I'll probably just be sent to keep an eye on his troops while your father recovers. We'll be back kicking sand at the Mekhani next year."

Erlaan shook his head.

"Why bring you to Askh just to send you all the way back down the Greenwater again? Seems like an awful waste of your time."

Ullsaard looked to Noran to provide an answer. The herald shrugged, earning himself a frown.

"I just know what I am told," said Noran. "Prince Aalun gave me no instructions other than to bring you back to Askh; and no information other than Prince Kalmud had been taken with an illness."

"You don't think it's something worse, do you?" asked Erlaan, grabbing Noran's arm. "About my father, I mean."

"Not at all, young prince," said Noran, patting Erlaan's hand. "Your father was not well, but far from death when

I left. His condition did not seem to be worsening, and with the attentions of the Brotherhood there is no reason to think things are so bleak."

Erlaan was about to say something but the captain intervened. There was a gaggle of sailors behind him, with ropes and lading hooks.

"Please excuse us," he said.

The group moved out of the way and stood to one side of the tillerman. The sailor kept his gaze solidly ahead, affecting the blank expression of a man who is deaf to all things, as the galley slid towards the nearest quay of King's Wharf.

"Look at this way," said Noran, keeping his voice quiet. "If there really was some problem with your father, it would have been the king who sent me, and many other messengers beside. Your family are keeping this quiet because there is no cause for alarm, but rumour could be very disruptive."

"I suppose you are right." Erlaan folded his arms and bit his lip.

With a rough scraping and a couple of thuds, the galley was brought in alongside the wharf. Thick cables were thrown over to the landsmen who had swarmed out of the buildings along the length of the pier. A short, heavyset, sweaty man in a thick blue robe puffed and wheezed as he pulled himself over the side of the ship on a rope ladder.

"Token," he said, reaching out an open palm towards Eoruan.

"Here it is," said the captain, holding the golden crown between thumb and forefinger, forcing the jettymaster to take it from him with a frown. The functionary pulled a small wax tablet from his belt. Line after line of perfectly formed script almost filled the tablet.

"Make your mark," he said, thrusting the tablet to Eoruan. The captain turned towards Noran.

"It's your mark that's needed, not mine," Eoruan said.

Noran gave a huff of annoyance and crossed the deck. He took up the official's stylus and wrote his name into the wax. The jettymaster brought forth two thin sheets, almost transparent, and a block of charcoal. He made a rubbing of the impression in the wax on each piece and handed one to Noran. The other he carefully folded and placed in a bag at his belt. He smeared Noran's mark out of the wax and returned the tablet and stylus to his belt.

"Token," prompted Noran, beckoning with a finger. Absent-mindedly, the jettymaster handed back the royal seal.

He dragged himself back over the ship's side without another word and disappeared into the crowd of labourers waiting for instructions from the ship.

"We'll get the ailurs off first, and be out of your hair," said Ullsaard, slapping a hand to the captain's shoulder. "My people will unload the rest of our baggage."

"It's been no burden for me," Eoruan said with wink and a nod to the cargo being made ready for unloading. "Crown business never is."

As always, Ullsaard was conscientious and deliberate during the disembarkation of the ailurs, while the crew heaved and pushed the abada down the gangplanks to the dockside and the servants loaded the wagon with their master's baggage. It was almost nightfall by the time they were ready to leave the quayside, and Ullsaard decided that they would spend the night in Narun.

They found lodging in the house of Araan Nario, a fleet owner who had regular dealings with Noran's family. The wiry, elderly merchant was more than happy to put up such esteemed guests when Noran sent one of the servants with word of their presence in the harbour town. They spent the evening in the company of Nario and his mercantile friends, fending off questions regarding their business in Askh. Glad of no repeat of the incident in Geria, they left Narun mid-morning the next day and headed dawnwards towards the Askhor border.

There was much traffic on the road as traders moved their wares between Askh and Narun. Abada pulled carts from the capital laden with stone and metals from the mountains, or carried finely spun linens in bushels on their backs. Towards the city the merchants ferried grain for the most part, the interior of Askhor being unsuitable for widespread farming. Though plentiful in game and fish, the highland pastures were good for goats and a few hardy cattle and little else. Fish came from the Sea of the Sun to dawnwards, but animal fodder was always in high demand, as were the more exotic gems and spices of hotwards, and the wool and textiles from coldwards in the lands of Ersua and Enair.

The prince, herald and general were the subject of much attention, their ailurs advertising their status more than anything else, but other travellers on the road did not involve themselves other than to exchange pleasantries and occasionally break bread.

They made steady progress and three days of riding brought them to the edge of the Askhor Mountains, which reared up steeply from the flatlands of Nalanor. Snow-capped all year round, the impressive peaks formed a wall that stretched from coldwards to hotwards as far as could be seen. Low clouds shrouded the peaks, but in the foothills the summer air was clear and hot.

Almost directly to dawnwards lay the Askhor Gap, where the mountains were parted by a steep valley. The road cut straight and true through the steep hills leading up to the gap, and by mid-afternoon of the third day Ullsaard and the others laid eyes on the Askhor Wall.

The Wall stretched the entire width of the gap, nearly twenty Askhan miles almost directly from hotwards to coldwards. The lowering sun shone bright from the grey and black granite and glinted from bronze speartips and helmets. It took the four patrols, each a thousand-strong, two whole watches to march from one end to the other, each patrol being roughly thirty thousand paces long. Some five thousand more soldiers were stationed in twenty fortified towers along its length. The Wall ran across the narrowest point of the valley, its rampart as level as a race track so that where the hills were highest it stood no more than three times the height of a man, and where the ground was lowest it seemed as much as ten times as high. As well as two hundred and fifty men, each garrison tower housed three bellows-launchers capable of hurling a spear-sized projectile a considerable distance, and a small lava-powered forge similar to those taken on campaign by the legions. Each tower held enough stores to feed its men for fifty days.

There were six gates, but only the main gate was ever in regular use, wide enough for four carts abreast and guarded by two massive bastions twice as tall as the Wall itself. Lava throwers jutted from the towers in the lowest levels while murder holes and bow slits punctured the upper storeys. The gates themselves, now wide open, were low and broad, made of bronze-clad wood as thick as Ullsaard's outstretched arms. They were opened and closed by means of counterweights and a water wheel fed by an aqueduct that redirected one of the mountain streams, and ran the length of the Wall to provide the garrison with fresh water.

For nearly two hundred years the Wall had stood; a testament to the power and ingenuity of the Askhans.

In all of that time, it had never been attacked.

"Just a day's more travel before we're home!" announced Noran with a clap of his hands. "I can almost smell the city already."

"It is a most welcome sight," said Erlaan. "Though I have seen the Wall several times from this direction, this is the first time I have laid eyes upon it after being so long away."

Ullsaard merely grunted.

"Not happy to be back?" asked Erlaan.

"I will be when we reach the palace," Ullsaard replied. "This is just a wall."

"It's more than just a wall," said Erlaan as they rode between two high embankments where the road cut straight through a hill, heading directly towards the main gate. "It's the Askhan border. Here Greater Askhor ends and true Askhor begins. Surely that means something."

"It's a big wall, that needs several thousand good legionnaires and countless artisans to maintain," replied Ullsaard. "It is a magnificent wall. I am sure that the Nalanorian hordes who capitulated to Askhos shortly after it was completed were very impressed by its size. Since then, it has had no useful purpose other than to drain resources from the legions."

"You are in a surly mood," said Noran. "It's the Wall! It's on the king's coins, and celebrated by a dozen murals and a hundred poems. Everything that is Askhor and Askhan: ingenious, dependable, unbreakable."

"And pointlessly expensive," added Ullsaard. "Just who is it defending, and against what? The Salphors? They'd have to cross all of Greater Askhor to even get here. The Nemurians? The Mekhani?"

"And what would it say to the people of Greater Askhor if it was just allowed to fall into ruins?" snapped Erlaan. "Would you have us abandon our heritage and let the great monuments from our past tumble to nothing?"

"Spoken like a poet and not a soldier," Ullsaard replied calmly. "I think the people of Greater Askhor would far rather have the stone and the men used to build bridges and homes and man forts elsewhere in the empire. On the Salphorian border, perhaps. It may be a symbol of Askhor's past, but surely the empire is about the future and where we are going as much as it is about where we come from?"

"You have a dull spirit at times, Ullsaard," said Noran. "I would say it is because you are a soldier and soldiers have practical minds, but it is more than that. Surely you see some merit in maintaining such a glorious structure as a testament to Greater Askhor's strength?"

"Askhor's strength," Ullsaard said quietly.

"What's that?" asked Erlaan.

"Askhor's strength," Ullsaard said, louder than before. They passed through the defile and the Wall could be seen again, dominating the valley. "The Wall was built by Askhor, not Greater Askhor. It is not a symbol of the empire, it is a symbol of Askhor itself."

"Ah, I see!" said Noran. "As someone born outside the Wall, perhaps you resent what it represents?"

"It is a division between Askhor and Greater Askhor, for sure," Ullsaard admitted. "I have done well and made something of my life, but for some the fact that I was born on this side will mean I can never be a proper Askhan, though I have achieved more for the empire than most who happened to be spawned behind its stones."

"I did not realise you were so ashamed of your lower birthright," said Erlaan. "I think it is marvellous that you have attained the station you have despite your humble beginnings."

Ullsaard reined in Blackfang and swung towards the prince with a glower.

"Ashamed? I'm bloody proud of what I've done. From legionnaire to general in twenty-seven years, through all the blood and piss on the way. But I would have done it in ten if I'd been born in Askh."

"And perhaps not at all if not for the patronage of my uncle," Erlaan said, stopping next to the general, his voice and gaze steady. "I think you overlook the favour of the Blood."

Ullsaard ground his teeth for a moment and saw nothing but incomprehension in the eyes of Erlaan and Noran. It really was that simple for them; they were born Askhans, nobility even, and had never had to face the obstacles

Ullsaard had overcome in his career. He realised he was treading on uncertain ground, and his reaction to seeing the Wall confused him. He had ridden past it a dozen times or more and had never felt this way before. Perhaps it was the irritating presence of the prince that was really the cause. The general frequently forgot that Erlaan was one of the Blood and not just another junior officer.

"It's just a bloody wall, eh?" Ullsaard said with a forced smile. "I hate the last days of the journey, so close to where you're going but not there yet. Forgive my gruff manner."

"Of course, Ullsaard," said Erlaan with a magnanimous look. "You have your wives waiting for you so close at hand and here's us chattering away about symbols of Askhan glory."

They rode on for a little while longer as the shadows lengthened and the air grew cooler.

"He built Magilnada as well, you know," said Noran.

"Who?" asked Ullsaard.

"Beruun, the man who constructed the Wall for Askhos."

"Never heard of him."

"Why should you have?" said Noran. "He turned out to be a traitor and a thief. Fled to Salphoria with half the workforce and built that damned city for their king."

"How do you know this?"

"While you were learning how to gut Mekhani and avoid the boy-fondlers in camp, I had my nose shoved into Artus's *Chronicles and Conjectures* by my father. He thought it important that every noble son of Askh should learn his history, to understand where we come from."

"And yet you have an utter ignorance of the most important book from history. The Book of Askhos."

Noran shrugged.

"I've never claimed to be even-handed. I didn't enjoy the learning, but some of it sticks in the mind despite numerous attempts to wash it away with fine liquor and rampant sex." Noran turned to Erlaan with a wink. "Those taught me far more important lessons about life than any number of dusty old scholars."

"I'll be sure to broaden my education when I have the chance," replied the prince.

Ullsaard ignored them as they continued to talk about their tutors and upbringing, maintaining a grumpy silence until they reached the Wall. The sun was almost set and the traffic on the road was all but gone.

"You two should enjoy the hospitality of the garrison," said Noran.

"And you?" asked Erlaan.

"I need to ride on, to bring news of your impending arrival to the palace. I'm sure they wish to organise a suitable welcome."

Ullsaard shook Noran's hand and clapped him on the shoulder.

"Ride safe, friend," said the general. "It's been good to see you again. Your wives should make arrangements with mine so that our families might spend some time together."

"I wouldn't be surprised if the whole thing hasn't been planned already," laughed Noran. "I'm certain they've already got festivals and celebrations in mind. Askhos knows how much it's going to cost us!"

The herald gave a nod to Erlaan.

"It is a pleasure to have met you, Prince."

"Likewise, Noran. I am sure I will see you around the palace in the days to come."

"Your father will be heartened to hear that you will be joining him very shortly. With any luck, he'll be back on his feet and ready to go, and this whole journey will have been a waste of time."

"With luck," Erlaan said quietly.

Noran looked at the two of them and then through the great gate to the darkening hills beyond.

"Right," he said, quietly as if to himself. "I'll be going then."

Ullsaard watched his friend ride through the gate and signalled the captain of the watch who had come out of the gatehouse to greet the general.

"Beer, bread and bed, Captain," said Ullsaard. The young officer nodded in understanding and headed back to the gate, snapping orders.

Ullsaard looked at his companion, hiding his annoyance that Noran had abandoned him with the prince. At least he only had to tolerate his company alone for one day. He waved Erlaan ahead.

"Welcome back to Askhor."

SALPHORIA
Summer, 208th Year of Askh

I

The clanking of chains from the debtors' cranks filled the sweaty confines of the landship's hull. The planks vibrated and rumbled with the grinding of the wheels beneath. Stripped to the waist, shackled men bent their backs to the turn shafts with metronomic regularity, stooping and heaving to the steady banging of the drivemaster's drum. Skins of many hues glistened in the yellow light from the three lanterns swaying upon the hull beams. All eighty of the labouring men had close-cropped hair to prevent the spread of mites and other parasites, and their chests, cheeks and chins were clean shaven for the same reason.

Grimaces of pain were writ upon the faces of the new-comers; the old hands stared stolidly at the backs of the debtor in front with expressions of detached determina-tion. They worked with hands bound with leather thongs, gripping wooden shafts smoothed to a polish by a genera-tion of internees, on benches eroded into dipping shallows by countless buttocks.

Anglhan Periusis walked along the narrow aisle between the two rows of his workers, checking hands and feet for blisters, examining joints for inflammation. Behind him his second-in-command, Furlthia Miadnas, ladled water to the perspiring prisoners. Even with the hatches open it was sweltering in the bowels of the landship and Anglhan regularly dabbed at his forehead and fatty jowls with a sweat-soaked rag.

"Only four more days, Gelthius," Anglhan said, patting a grizzled debtor on the shoulder. "I bet you thought the day would never come."

"Never did, right enough," the man replied, puffing between the words as he continued to push and pull at the turncrank. "Fourteen years, right enough."

"I'll be dropping you off in Magilnada," the ship master said, hooking his fingers into the belt holding up his baggy trousers. "It's a day earlier than I should, by rights, but we're heading all the way to Carantathi after that and I wouldn't abandon you at least a day's walk from civilisation."

"Magilnada?" wheezed Gelthius. "Free Country, that is. Take me forever to work my way back to Landensi."

"You're welcome to join the deck crew at full pay, until we head back towards the central plains," Anglhan offered. "An experienced hand like yourself, that doesn't go unrewarded."

"I might do that," said Gelthius.

"Just let me know in the next day or two and I'll make the arrangements one way or the other," Anglhan said with a warm smile.

"Right enough," said Gelthius.

Anglhan continued the inspection of his detainees, marking off another day's service in his ledger for each of the debtors. He noticed that three of them would be finished paying their way before they reached Carantathi. He would have to transfer them to another debt guardian in Magilnada, or come up with some other form of arrangement so that they did not labour longer than was allowed.

"Everything seems in order," he said to Furlthia, who nodded in agreement.

"This new lot are as fit as a rat catcher's dogs," Furlthia said. "That was a good deal; don't usually get so many last this long."

"Aye, Byrantas earnt his commission this time," said Anglhan as he stepped onto the bottom rung of the ladder leading up to the main deck.

The fresh breeze that swept over Anglhan as his head popped through the hatch caused him to stop and savour the air for a moment. A not-so-subtle cough from Furlthia goaded him into action once more and he heaved his portly frame the remaining few rungs onto the upper deck. The wind was freshening, tugging at his scarlet tunic, tousling his mop of blond and grey hair.

With a quick eye, Anglhan checked that all was brisk and ready; crew stood by the spear throwers along each side of the hull; the lines of the single square sail were taut and the canvas full. Atop the mast four men stood upon the crow's-nest, eyes shielded against the low sun. Casting his gaze further afield, the captain could see the dust from his outrunners spread out around the landship. Should danger approach they would light warning flares and sound their curhorns.

From the foredeck a large shape ambled towards Anglhan. It was Pak'ka, one of the Nemurians. He stood half as tall again as Anglhan, and almost as broad. He was covered with thick grey scales, darkening to black around his flat face and surprisingly delicate, long-fingered hands. His back and shoulders were patterned with pale orange stripes that faded away halfway down his knobbly spine. His loins were concealed behind a heavy skirt of studded leather, split at the back to allow his tail to move freely; the appendage was adorned with silver bands and ended in a knobbly club-like growth that thumped. The Nemurian's green eyes caught the sun with a flash as he bent down in front of Anglhan. Pak'ka's slit-like nostrils flared as he took in a deep breath.

"Nothing to report." Like all of his kind, Pak'ka spoke in with a slight lisp. His voice was quiet and measured.

"Let's hope it stays that way," said Anglhan. Pak'ka's cracked lips wrinkled back to reveal two rows of small, flat teeth in an attempt at a smile.

"We hope, but the rocks are unhappy," said Pak'ka. With this baffling proclamation, the Nemurian turned heavily and rejoined his warriors basking in the sun by the starboard rail.

The lookouts and guards were a necessary precaution these days, with the number of brigands and escaped slaves hiding out in the Altes Hills growing every year. Anglhan had heard tales from fellow debt guardians, of outlaws growing bolder and more organised with each passing season. Three landships had been lost since the turn of the growing season and Anglhan was not prepared to take any chances; he had brought on the Nemurian mercenaries and doubled his outunners for this long voyage to the coast.

"Dusk or dawn," said Furlthia.

"What's that?" said Anglhan, turning his attention back to the first mate.

"Raiders usually strike at dusk or dawn, out of the sun," said Furlthia.

"The king should send an army into the hills and clear them out," said Anglhan with a shake of the head. "I pay tithes for safe roads and freedom to trade."

"It's a brave king who sends an army into the Altes," countered Furlthia. "The expense and risk doesn't match up to the complaints of a few caravan masters and landship captains."

"The Askhans would do it," Anglhan said as he turned towards the quarterdeck, running his experienced gaze across the ropes and beams of the landship's workings. The road was rutted and the whole vessel sagged and swayed as it rumbled along the uneven stones. Despite the movement the mast and braces were sound, the wood and ropes creaking softly.

"You'd want the Askhans here, wouldn't you?" said Furlthia. "You wouldn't keep Aegenuis on the throne for a moment, given the choice."

"It's nothing against the man personally, it's a matter of trade, is all," explained Anglhan as he mounted the steps up to the quarterdeck. "In fact, if we became a protectorate there's no reason he couldn't stay on in some capacity. I've travelled a bit in Ersua and never seen trouble. Good prices too; their economy is far more stable. They don't have a king who fritters away half a year's taxes on statues, for a start."

"The tribal chiefs would never stand for it," said Furlthia. "You want to be ruled from Askh, foreigners making decisions? Not me and not them. If the Askhans do come here next, I'll be leaving you and joining the army."

"Then you'll be dead," snapped Anglhan as he took up his position in the shade of the broad sail. "Nobody fights Askhor and wins."

The captain's expression softened.

"Anyway, I'd miss you," he said. "Good mates are hard to come by and I would not see a friend march off on a hopeless cause."

"You think the Askhans would allow you to keep your trade?" Furlthia persisted. "They don't have slavery, you know. Not of their own people."

"Neither do I," said Anglhan. "I've told you before. Don't get squeamish about it. These men work off their debts. They earn money. Okay, so it all goes to me, but that's not the same as the field serfs or the slaves in the Labroghia mines, is it? They knew the risks when they got into debt."

"Do you think the Askhans will see it that way?"

"Like I said, I've never had any problems when I've been there, debtors and all," said Anglhan. "Of Askhor and Salphoria, which has rebels hiding out in the hills attacking people, eh? I tell you, it won't be more than a season or two before some clever bastard gets them organised and attacks Magilnada, and I don't see the garrison holding out until the king decides to do something about it. Say this about the Askhans, they're brutal but they get the job done.

"It's the Crown of the Blood, you see, and that book of theirs. They know what they want to do and just do it. King Aegenuis, on the other hand, has overturned half the things his father brought in, and no doubt that halfwit son of his, Medorian, will do the same again when he finally knifes his father in the back and takes over. Stability, Furlthia, stability."

The mate said nothing and turned away to look over the starboard side of the landship. The purple hills of the Altes rose higher and higher to duskwards, the sun settling down behind them. Night would come quickly.

"We best rotate the watch," Furlthia said.

"Aye, do that for me," said his captain, casting another wary glance across the hills. "I'll be in my cabin."

ASKH

Midsummer, 208th Year of Askh

I

Blackfang padded back and forth, mirroring her master's growing impatience. The city walls were but a stone's throw away and the general sat atop his ailur, glaring venomously at the blue-garbed official standing in front of him. Erlaan whistled quietly beside them, occasionally patting the mane of his mount.

"What's the delay?" snapped Ullsaard. The official shook his head solemnly.

"I do not know, General." He turned back to the gatehouse where the signal was to be flown. He gave a deep sigh of relief when a black and red flag fluttered from the tower. "They are ready!"

"About time," growled Ullsaard, flicking the reins. Erlaan took his place beside the general.

A roll of drums echoed from the walls and a solitary horn sounded, alerting the city to the return of their prince. Ullsaard's heart quickened as the noise of the crowd reverberated through the open gate. The pair rode into the shadow of the gatehouse as the noise swelled. A company of a hundred legionnaires broke into a march, keeping twenty paces ahead of the returning heroes.

Coming through the gatehouse, Ullsaard and Erlaan were bathed by the setting sun. It glinted from their armour and helms, from the masks of the ailurs and the tips of their spears. To either side the crowd erupted into a roar. Ullsaard saw a sea of faces; men and women, old and young, merchant and soldier, all with eyes bright and mouths open. Young girls naked but for red cloaks skipped ahead of the parade, scattering offerings of salt and grain onto the road. Garlands were cast from the crowd, showering Ullsaard and the prince with leaves and petals.

The general held up his spear in a salute and the noise became deafening. Lines of legionnaires shouted warnings and pushed back the mob as the people of Askh surged forwards to see their betters. A buxom woman broke from the mass, ducking beneath the cudgel of a soldier to grasp at Erlaan's leg. She reached up and stroked a loving hand inside his thigh. Her words were lost in the din and a moment later she was dragged away and pushed back into the throng.

The prince leaned towards Ullsaard, his voice raised to a shout to be heard.

"Shame we don't have a few Mekhani to show off. That would drive them wild."

The crowd had made their own substitutes. Amongst the waving bouquets and hastily-daubed signs he saw rag dolls of red-dyed wool being vigorously waved. Here and there red-painted straw effigies burned atop poles, hung with tin coins on slender chains.

In the crowd were many off-duty legionnaires and a fair number of veterans. Their close-cropped hair and scars marked them out amongst the mass, and Ullsaard took care to smile and wave at each of those he saw.

The parade continued past the market forum, which had been emptied of its stalls save for a few licensed traders selling food, beer and wine. Here the street opened out into a vast cobbled square, packed with humanity. The windows of the upper storeys of the surrounding buildings were packed with the shopkeepers and their families; children excitedly waved bunting made from dyed twine and papyrus, their shrill cries cutting through the throatier roars of their elders. Buoyed up by the crowd's appreciation, Ullsaard beamed back at them, shaking his spear triumphantly.

From the forum, the Royal Way continued upwards, straight into the heart of Askh, past the three-storey homes of the noble families, with their semi-circular facades and steepling roofs. Here the tumult was lessened, though servants packed the doorsteps of the street, while their masters and mistresses crowded balconies and roof terraces to wave appreciatively; more at Erlaan than Ullsaard, the general noticed.

Ahead rose the Royal Hill, the highest point of the city, where centuries before Askhos had been born and founded his empire. The palaces sat like a crown atop the mount, surrounded by a white wall. A maze of flat roofs, towers and domes could be seen above the wall, flags of red and black hanging limply from dozens of poles. Wooden scaffolding obscured the dawnward wing of the main palace and several other buildings; Ullsaard had lived in the city for thirteen years and never known a time when there was not some construction work being undertaken.

To coldward and duskward of the palaces, on top of a secondary crest just below the palaces, stood the Grand Precincts of the Brotherhood. The grey edifice was built on five levels, a ziggurat of drab stone surrounded by a flat plaza reached by winding steps that traced back and forth along the duskward side of the Royal Hill. The precinct was older than the city, the ancient centre of the Askhan tribes' culture, the hub around which their civilisation had revolved. Smaller versions of the temple could be found in all of the other cities of Greater Askhor, physical extensions of the power of the Brotherhood. It was from here, not the palaces, that the true power of Askh was wielded. The Grand Precincts had created the first laws of Askh, formed the first courts, kept the Archive of Ages; all of the foundations of the empire that Askhos had taken across the lands behind the spears of his legions.

Half a mile more brought them to the central area of Askh, where a wide road encircled the landscaped palace grounds and gardens. The group turned dawnwards, to come around the palace past the bloodfields and racing track. More companies of soldiers stood to attention along the roadside, icons freshly polished, commanders calling them to attention. Their shields were etched with the device of a crown; the famous First Legion, bodyguard to the Blood. In a long ripple, spearpoints were dipped in salute and raised again when the pair passed by. The procession continued around the circuitous avenue, heralded by a clarion of horns when they came to the fields of Maarmes, where duels were fought and athletes contested in feats of speed and skill.

Here the crowds ended. Instead there stood long lines of the Brotherhood, heads bowed in solemn silence; row upon row of shaven scalps and black robes. The higher Brothers stood at the end of each line, eyes ahead, faces hidden behind blank silver masks. After the earlier furore the quiet was profound; not even the birds stirred in the trees that lined the Maarmes circuit.

Finally they came to the palace steps and dismounted. Dozens of functionaries flocked around the arrivals, to take the ailurs, offer wines and meats on gilded trays, and escort the pair up the long flight of stairs to the coldward gates of the palace. Ullsaard took a cup of light beer from one of the trays and downed the draught in one long gulp. With the note of a solitary gong, the gates opened into the palace's interior.

Erlaan was the first to pass the threshold, as was his right by tradition and his rank. Ullsaard was happy to hang back as more flunkeys bustled around. The hall within was lit by a few oil lamps placed in front of curved mirrors, while the last of the sunshine trickled through narrow windows in the ceiling paned with thick triangles of glass that broke the light into dim rainbows.

A clapping of hands sent the horde of servants scurrying to the sides of the hall, revealing a tall, slender man who looked a little older than Ullsaard. His hair was greying but still thick, cut straight at his shoulders. He was swathed in a long robe of vermillion, a sash of white embroidered with golden spirals across his chest. He sported long sideburns plaited with red and green beads, though his lip and chin were clean-shaven.

"Erlaan!" The man welcomed the prince with a hug. He turned to Ullsaard. "My good friend! It is a pleasure to see you."

"You also, Uncle," said Erlaan.

Ullsaard and Prince Aalun gripped wrists in a warrior's greeting. The general said nothing, but nodded his head and smiled.

"My father?" asked Erlaan, his voice breaking suddenly. Ullsaard realised that for all his own impatience, the young man must have been even more frustrated by the delays in organising the procession.

"He is in the king's throne room, with your grandfather. Run along and see them now; we'll have important business shortly."

The youth smiled his thanks and headed quickly up the hall, a swarm of servants descending upon him as he reached the arch at the far end.

"You should have some time to see your family," said Aalun, turning his attention back to Ullsaard. "Come to the throne room in the last call before Howling."

"Thank you, Prince," replied Ullsaard. He waited for Aalun to turn away and head after his nephew before

113

crossing the hall to his right and pushing through a curtained doorway into the corridors that led to the apartment wing. He walked quickly, exchanging nods and smiles with a few familiar faces until he reached the wooden doors of his chambers.

He hesitated, taking a deep breath.

II

"He'll be here soon and Luia hasn't even dressed!" Meliu slapped her hands on her thighs in frustration.

"Sit down for a moment," soothed Allenya, guiding her youngest sister to the low couch by the window. "If Luia wants to play her silly games, let her."

"But it reflects badly on us as well," Meliu said, tears forming in her eyes.

"Stop that," said Allenya, snatching up the hem of her long yellow dress to dab at Meliu's cheeks. "You being all puffy-eyed is not going to help."

Meliu huffed indignantly.

"Luia always wants to spoil everything."

"Yes, and now you're acting spoilt. The last thing our husband wants to come back to is one of your tantrums."

"I suppose you're right." Meliu beckoned to one of the maids, who approached with a bowl of white powder and a fine brush. She dusted Meliu's cheeks heavily. "It's not fair, is it? Luia has skin like snow and here's me stuck with the ruddy cheeks of a farm girl. It's wasted on her!"

"Believe me, Ullsaard will be just as happy if you were as red as a beet. Just smile and let those sweet dimples do the rest."

Meliu couldn't help but comply, her smile hesitant.

"Why is he keeping us waiting?" snapped Luia from the next room. She stalked through the door, her dark blue robe still unbelted, open at the front, servants trailing behind forlornly. "Noran said he'd be here by noon. It's just

114

typical. The food will spoil and he can strut off to see the king, leaving us with mouldy scraps."

"The procession was delayed, sister," Allenya said calmly. "I am sure he is as anxious as we are."

"Anxious to see you, sister, perhaps." Luia turned her scornful glare on Meliu. "Askhos's cock, you look like a garden slut; or worse, a poet."

Meliu pouted and was about to say something when Eriun, the head maid, slipped in behind Luia.

"The master has reached the palace, mistresses," she announced quietly.

With a wordless hiss, Luia darted from the room, scattering her attendants.

"Let me have a last look at you," said Allenya, beckoning for Meliu to stand. She smoothed a few stray locks of her sister's golden curls, adjusted the hang of her low-cut dress to display her fine cleavage and smoothed out a crease in her broad white belt. "Nothing to worry about, sister, you look lovely. How am I doing?"

Meliu laughed. Allenya was the tallest of the three sisters, with wide hips and long legs. Her hair was a deep brown, falling in oiled curls about her shoulders, with no sign yet of greying. Her face was narrow, her chin and cheekbones prominent, with only the slightest wrinkles to testify her middle age. He eyes were a startling sapphire blue. Allenya wore a plain white dress, gathered tight about the waist with a broad belt of blue fabric embroidered with silver threads, bronze and gold chains about her wrists and neck.

"You could wear a sack and shave your head and Ullsaard would still give you that look."

"What look?"

"Don't come all coy. You know, that longing look he gets whenever he says goodbye to you, the one he only gives you. I try, Askhos knows I try, but that look is only for you."

"He loves us each in a different way."

Meliu looked doubtful.

"Even Luia?"

Allenya let out a short laugh.

"Well, perhaps not Luia. Still, she hasn't ruined it for the pair of us yet, so let's not let her start now."

There was a whisper of warning from the next room and the two women linked arms and walked through to the main chamber of the apartment. Meliu could feel Allenya trembling as a foot scraped on the far side of the doors. It seemed like an eternity before the door swung open, revealing Ullsaard, skin dusted with dirt, streaked with sweat.

As ever, his eyes went first to Allenya, and he crossed from the door in a few long strides to embrace her. He kissed her on each cheek, delicately stroking her back. As they parted, Ullsaard turned to Meliu, his eyes roving up and down her petite form, lingering on the curve of her half-exposed breasts. He clasped a hand to her neck and planted a long kiss on her lips, his body swallowing her up with its hard bulk. She returned the kiss, feeling his other hand roughly caressing her buttocks.

"Where's the other one?" Ullsaard asked, pulling away from Meliu, dragging a gasp from her parted lips.

"The 'other one' is here," announced Luia, standing at the door to the dining hall, one hand languidly raised to the frame, the other held behind her arched back. Her dress hung beautifully from her curved body, her hair tied simply but neatly into a braided coil atop her head, a golden pendant hanging from her alabaster neck, its point angled towards the cleft between her breasts. Meliu wanted to spit. She had spent all morning getting ready, and Luia had upstaged her in a few moments.

Ullsaard nodded, his eyes straying past Luia to the table beyond, upon which foods of all kind had been heaped.

"We have a watch and a half before I must attend the Blood," Ullsaard declared. "Let me get cleaned up and then we'll eat."

"As you wish, husband," said Luia.

"It is wonderful to see you again," said Allenya, laying a hand briefly on her husband's arm. "Be swift, we want to hear all about your adventures."

"You have been away such a *long* time," whispered Meliu, trying to make her voice husky. She let the back of her hand stroke the front of Ullsaard's leather kilt. "Why don't I show you a proper welcome?"

Ullsaard grinned and snatched her around the waist. As he led her towards the door of the main bedchamber, Meliu directed a sly wink towards Luia. Her sister turned away sharply, hips swinging, and disappeared into the dining hall.

Pulling her through the beaded curtain of the bedroom, Ullsaard rounded on Meliu, clasping her close, his lips and tongue seeking hers, his chest crushing against her breasts. He grunted and pushed her towards the bed, where Meliu allowed herself to fall on her back, her slit dress parting to show her legs.

"On your knees." Ullsaard's words were little more than grunts between clenched teeth.

Meliu did as she was told, rolling over to expose herself to her husband. There was a slap of leather hitting the wooden floor and a moment later Ullsaard's muscled arm encircled her waist. His other hand engulfed her breast roughly. His breaths came in short pants, as did hers. Ullsaard's murmuring was joined by a groan from Meliu as he pushed himself inside, forcing himself as deep as possible. She winced at the momentary pain and clenched her teeth as he grabbed her hair, pulling back her head.

Three stretching thrusts later Meliu felt his seed flooding into her. Ullsaard let loose a fierce growl, fist twisting her hair painfully. She felt him shuddering for a few more heartbeats, pressed up against her, his grip like iron on her head and breast.

With another grunt, he pushed her off, leaving a wetness leaking onto her thighs.

Ullsaard leaned against the bedpost, breathing heavily, eyes closed. Meliu slithered to her back, parting her dress to reveal her breasts fully. She stroked her nipples, eyes fixed on her husband.

"Why don't we take a bit of time to enjoy this next one?" she purred.

Ullsaard's eyes snapped open and fixed her with a steely glare.

"You have a complaint?" he rasped.

"No! I only thought that perhaps you might allow me to lavish greater attention and pleasures upon you."

"Maybe after I've seen the king." Ullsaard crossed the room to the bowl of hot water that had been left on a stand beside the bed. He splashed his face and pulled off his tunic, revealing a muscled chest and back criss-crossed with scars.

Meliu rolled off the bed to her feet and stood behind him, dipping her hands into the water. She rubbed her hands over the taut muscles of his back, massaging the liquid into his tanned skin. Ducking beneath his arm, she took a bottle of scented oil from the table and poured a little into her palms. Rubbing them together, she warmed the oil a little and reached up to apply it to his broad shoulders. He nodded and knelt down, allowing her to better knead his knotted muscles. She moved closer, so that her arms encircled him, caressing his pectorals, and ran her fingers down the ridged muscles of his stomach towards the thick mat of curled hair at their bottom.

"I said perhaps later." He gently grabbed her wrists and pulled them away. "Send Donaal in with more soap and my ceremonial armour."

"Of course, husband," said Meliu, holding her tears behind a smile. "Whatever you want."

III

Garbed in a thin skirt of white linen and a black tunic, Ullsaard joined his wives in the feast room; he would put on his gilded breastplate and don his helm when it was time to leave.

"What have my sons been up to?" he asked as a servant poured wine and water for him.

"Ullnaar has been accepted into the colleges of Meemis," Meliu announced with a proud smile. "Luckily he has your mind and not mine."

"And your looks and not mine," said Ullsaard with a grin. "I had forgotten he came of age in the spring. It doesn't seem possible that it has been sixteen years since you brought him into this world."

"Urikh has bought himself a stake in the copper mines at Saartia," said Luia.

"What has Ullnaar decided to study?" said Ullsaard, ignoring Luia's interruption.

"Law," replied Meliu.

Ullsaard absorbed this as he filled his plate with slices of roasted fowl and dark bread.

"He's not joining the Brotherhood," the general declared heavily.

"Not at all," said Meliu, passing her husband a platter of hard-baked grain cakes. "He is going to study city law, not criminal. Like Ahsaam and Heriot, he said."

"Never heard of either of them."

"Me too," laughed Meliu. "I think they were advisors to the last king. He is so clever."

Ullsaard turned his gaze on Luia.

"Urikh is expanding his mercantile influence quickly," he said. "Kolubrid breeding, part ownership of a ship, and now copper. I suppose he'll want me to put in a word for him with the legion provisioners again."

"It wouldn't hurt," replied Luia. "Though he says he already has a contract with a consortium of Ersuan kettlemakers."

"Kettlemakers? Not interested in making armour and weapons?"

"He thinks that the legions are well-equipped as it is; he sees little profit in military supply at the moment. But every farmwife and kitchen master needs a good copper kettle."

"And where is he at the moment?"

"In Caprion, talking to his Ersuan customers. He could be back quite soon, perhaps before you leave. You might see him. That would be nice, wouldn't it?"

"You are staying for a while, aren't you?" asked Meliu.

"I've no idea," Ullsaard said with a shrug. "For all I know, I'll be packed off down the Greenwater come tomorrow. We'll have to wait to see what Aalun and the king have to say this evening."

"Please at least try to stay for a few days," Allenya said quietly. "Enjoy the comforts at home."

Ullsaard smiled and sank his teeth into a peach, the juice running into his beard. His eyes stayed on Allenya. He took another bite and sighed.

"If I stay too long, I'll get used to all this again, and then it'll be harder to leave."

"Let's not talk about leaving then," said Allenya. "You have only just come back to us."

"Good idea. So, I know about my eldest and my youngest, tell me about Jutaar."

"He remains in service to Governor Allon. He is still third captain."

"Not yet made second?" Ullsaard could not hide his disappointment.

"He doesn't have the fire of his father," said Luia. "He has neither Urikh's ambition nor Ullnaar's wit. You really should find something more suitable for him than the legions."

"Perhaps a foreman somewhere," suggested Meliu. "He is very practically minded."

"He loves being a soldier," said Allenya, directing a frown towards her sisters. She turned her gaze upon Ullsaard with a slight smile. "Allon writes to me frequently, praising Jutaar's dedication to duty and steadfastness. Our son is content, happy even, which is more than can be said for many who aim above their means."

"It is just as well that Urikh has a mind to grow the family's fortunes in the years to come," said Luia. "If Jutaar were your heir, his happiness and contentment would see our grandchildren labouring in the fields or mines."

"That won't happen," said Ullsaard. "Despite your extravagances, there is still enough put by to give our grandchildren a good start in life."

"A good start?" There was a sneer in Luia's tone, though her face did not betray her scorn. "I want my granddaughter to have more than a 'good start'. Luissa will be the envy of noblewomen across Askh, perhaps even marry a prince."

"She is only four, I think we should stop gossiping about Luissa as if she were come of age," said Meliu.

Ullsaard laughed, but there was no humour in him. He leaned an elbow on the table and pointed at Luia.

"Not a chance! You may have lofty goals and ancestors of name, but there is not a drop of the Blood in this family's veins. You think your granddaughter will marry into noble lineage? No Prince of the Blood will look at her twice. You might have your fine Askhan heritage, but her name is wrong, her grandfather of Enairian stock. Perhaps you should set about finding her a wealthy merchant or perhaps a respectable officer."

"Something else to thank my wise sister for," Luia said, darting a venomous stare at Allenya.

"Enough!" growled Ullsaard, slapping his hand down, sending a wine jug spinning, its scarlet contents splashing across the lacquered wood of the table. He fixed Luia with a stare. "I am not ashamed of who I am. I have given you healthy sons, provided food for your table and brought you to the palace of the king. Do not think you have somehow missed out in life because of your marriage to me! Lands in my name rival those of the oldest Askhan families. Lands, I might add, that I took by my own hand, unlike most of those entitled bastards that are our neighbours."

"You have done well by us all, husband," said Allenya.

"I would choose no other," added Meliu. "You know that, don't you?"

Ullsaard kept his gaze on Luia, who returned it with an expression of apathy. Ullsaard mentally dared her to show some sign of defiance. Instead, she smiled thinly and stood up.

"You are one of the greatest generals of the empire and any woman would be proud to call such her husband," Luia said. "Please excuse me, husband, I am quite worn out by the excitement of today."

Ullsaard nodded, eyes still fixed on his middle wife. When Luia had gone, he turned to Meliu. Her lip quivered and she gripped the edge of the table fiercely.

"Ignore your sister's barbs. She is just jealous that you are younger and far prettier than she is."

"Yes, she is," replied Meliu with a half-smile. She glanced between Ullsaard and Allenya and the flicker of a smile disappeared. "Please excuse me also; I wish to write a letter to Ullnaar."

"Of course," said Ullsaard. He took two steps towards Meliu with an outstretched hand, but she turned away hurriedly and left.

"You confuse her," Allenya said quietly.

"I do not mean to," Ullsaard said, pulling Allenya to her feet. He stooped to embrace her, burying his face in her thick hair. He whispered in her ear. "She is a lovely woman, full of joy and devotion, and brings out a lust in me that I cannot control. But she is not you, my love."

Allenya stroked the back of his head and kissed him on the cheek.

"I know," she sighed. "Do not trouble yourself over it. I will talk to her. And Luia."

"If Luia is the price I pay for you, I gladly accept it." Ullsaard tightened his arms around the wife he loved and wondered why he had ever agreed to the stupid Askhan custom of marrying her sisters.

"Luia is the price you pay for Aalun's favour," said Allenya, guessing his thoughts. "You know I would have married a captain and lived happily in Enair."

"I know," replied Ullsaard as he straightened. He looked at the thick hangings on the wall, the plates of food on the table, the marble underfoot. "But then we would have none of this, and you deserve all of it."

A gong sounded from outside, echoing through the palace. It was followed quickly by two chimes of a bell. Ullsaard pulled himself away, as reluctantly as if he peeled off his own skin.

"Second hour of Dusk," he sighed. "I best get ready and go to the king. Hopefully I will not be gone long."

Allenya took his hand and followed Ullsaard as he made his way back to the hallway, where servants stood waiting with his armour. He gave her hand a squeeze and let go, gesturing to the servants to approach.

"I will wait up for you," Allenya promised. Ullsaard nodded and his eyes followed her as she walked through the archway to her rooms, his gaze lingering there for a moment after she had disappeared from view.

IV

Ullsaard entered the king's hall with little ceremony; a captain in dress armour opened the high door and announced the general's arrival. Stepping through, Ullsaard saw four men. All looked down the narrow hall towards the door. King Lutaar sat upon a throne of black marble, slight and severe, his skin heavily folded, his hair close-cropped to his balding head. Beside him, Prince Aalun sat on a high-backed chair, his golden sash dangling over its back. On the other side, Prince Kalmud lay on a low bier, head and torso propped up by a hill of cushions. There was a waxy, sallow sheen to his skin and his eyes were sunk in the sockets, dull and listless. The fourth man stood at the king's right shoulder, clad in a black robe with its hood thrown back, face concealed by a silver mask blank save for a mouth-slit, and two oblong holes behind which dark eyes regarded Ullsaard carefully: Udaan, head of the Brotherhood.

"Welcome back, Ullsaard." The king's voice was strong and deep, carrying down the hall easily as Ullsaard approached the throne. "I trust that your endeavours in Mekha progress well."

"It has been a hard summer, Majesty, but as the weather cools I hope that progress will be quicker," replied Ullsaard, stopping before the throne with a short bow. "The men have been in good spirits and the Mekhani have suffered their first defeat."

"If you are in need of anything – soldiers, masons, supplies – be sure to let Aalun know before you leave."

Ullsaard did not voice his disappointment at this statement, but he could not stop a slight frown.

"Is there something you wish to tell us?" asked Udaan. His voice was a hoarse whisper, given a metallic ring by his mask.

Ullsaard looked to Aalun, seeking help. The prince nodded slightly in response.

"I believe that Ullsaard wishes to discuss the Greenwater campaign," said the prince. He glanced at his brother and continued. "Kalmud is not fit to lead his legions for the moment, and I thought it would be wise to discuss the ongoing prosecution of our exploration hotwards."

Udaan turned to the prince, inscrutable behind his mask, but it was the king that spoke first.

"No decision need be made until the spring. The legions are well-camped and under no immediate threat. If Kalmud is still unwell, Cosuas deserves the honour. In all likelihood he is on his final campaign."

"A campaign that needs vigour and strength, Father," Aalun said while Ullsaard fought to quell his anger at having been brought to Askh on a fool's errand. "As you say, Cosuas is nearing the end of his days. It would be foolish to have to change commanders again soon."

"Are you saying the king is a fool?" Udaan's whisper left the accusation hanging.

Aalun ignored the Brother and looked directly at his father.

"It is time to let Ullsaard show us his full capabilities," the prince said evenly. "The Greenwater campaign is an opportunity for all of us, and it is too important to chance on the vagaries of Kalmud's recovery and the continued health of Cosuas."

Lutaar pursed his lips and nodded.

"I will consider your petition," the king said. His eyes fixed on Ullsaard like a hawk spying its prey. "Is this what you desire? I cannot say when you would be returning, for it would be your task to follow the Greenwater until it reaches the seas. Are you willing to do that?"

"Without hesitation, Majesty," replied Ullsaard. "I live to serve Greater Askhor and push back the boundaries of the empire. I would consider it an honour, not a chore."

"I believe you would," said the king. He glanced at Aalun and at Udaan. "I will consider the matter."

"That is all I ask, Majesty," Ullsaard said, bowing again.

"I sense you have concerns beyond the Greenwater campaign," said Udaan. "You have avoided asking them as yet, but you have other questions arising from your brother's condition."

Ullsaard was amazed that the others spoke as if Kalmud were not a few paces from them. Perhaps, he wondered, the prince's sickness had rendered Kalmud deaf.

"I did not think to raise my questions until Erlaan had returned, since they concern him also," said Aalun.

"Just say it," rasped Lutaar. "What is on your mind?"

"The succession. Kalmud is unfit to become king and you should name me as heir."

Ullsaard drew in his breath. He studied Aalun's face, but saw no apprehension there.

"No," the king replied. "While Kalmud still lives, the succession does not change."

"The eldest surviving son is heir," said Udaan. "The Book of Askhos is clear on this. There are no exceptions."

"It is too much of a burden for one made so frail," said Aalun, looking with pity at Kalmud. His face hardened as he returned his gaze to his father. "While it is the wish of all your subjects that you live forever, such is not possible. You are almost as old as Cosuas, and though strong of will and thought, your body grows weaker. If you should die while Kalmud is still heir, it could be disastrous for the empire."

"When I die, Kalmud will become king if he outlives me. If not, Erlaan will inherit. This is how it has always been and always will be."

"Erlaan is barely an adult, no more fit to wear the Crown than his father currently is."

Lutaar was about to say something when Kalmud stirred. He coughed harshly for a few moments, gauze held to his mouth. As he brought it away there were flecks of blood on the material.

"You have something to say on the matter, my son?"

"I feel no better and no worse than when I was brought here." Kalmud's voice was quiet, wavering, but his eyes had regained some of the strength Ullsaard had seen in them during previous encounters. "With the Brotherhood

126

to aid me through my times of weakness, I can still rule Askhor."

"That settles the matter," said Udaan. "Your brother himself claims fit to rule."

"It matters not," snapped the king. He lifted his hand to quell Aalun's protest and continued in a calmer voice. "The succession stays as laid down in the Book of Askhos. To break from that now would invite disaster in generations to come. The Book of Askhos does not give us advice, does not give us guidelines. Its rules are absolute and must be followed as such."

Lutaar stood and stroked Kalmud's forehead. He paced in front of the throne, stooped and weary, and laid a hand on Aalun's shoulder.

"I know that you do not say this out of malice for me or your brother, and I do not deny you out of malice either. There can be no contention over the succession. If we were to equivocate, then we open the door for further exception. It matters not who wears the Crown, other than that he be the legal heir of the Blood. That is the rule. It matters not his merit or standing, his physical condition or his personality. There can be no other claim to the Crown other than that laid down by Askhos, for it means that there is no ambition from others to claim it for themselves. It matters not what you think, for the Crown will accept no other than the rightful heir."

"What do you mean?" asked Aalun. "The Crown is a symbol, it does not have a say in this."

Lutaar hesitated, again glancing toward Udaan.

"It is more than a symbol, it is the embodiment of Askhos. It carries his wisdom and his strength. What does the Book tell us? 'He who wears it will be without weakness.' Trust in the Blood, trust in the Crown. For two hundred years we have prevailed over our foes, and that will not change when your brother becomes king."

127

"I understand," said Aalun, though his eyes confessed a different opinion. The prince stood, kissed his father's hand and turned away. He gestured for Ullsaard to follow.

"By your leave, Majesty," said the general. Lutaar smiled and nodded.

"Spend some time with your family," said the king. "Whether it be to Mekha or the Greenwater, I will not send you on your way too soon."

"Thank you. You are considerate as well as wise; a true inheritor of Askhos' legacy."

The king smiled, eyes alive with humour.

"I am."

V

The inner gardens were dark, lit only by the scattered light from courtyard windows. Erlaan stared at the distorted shadows through the thick glass, trying to see past his reflection, his eyes constantly returning to his slender face and light brown eyes. Weak eyes, he thought, with neither the depth of his grandfather's not the brightness of his father's. Average eyes providing a window onto an average intellect and character.

He turned away, sickened at himself. His father needed him to be strong now, stronger than before. But how could he be, when everything he had drawn strength from was now so weak?

He paced back and forth across the carpet of the apartment's main chamber, alongside the low table crammed with stuffed birds, roasted swine cuts and bowls of nuts; to the fireplace, empty for the summer, and back to the tapestry hanging by the door. He stopped to look at it again; Askhos in all his fiery glory, purging the hills of the Demeetris. Even in blue and white and black thread, the First King's eyes held more life than Erlaan's.

He turned about and ambled towards the fireplace again, eyes fixed to the watch-candle burning on the shelf above. It seemed to shrink so slowly; surely more time had passed since the gong had signalled the Watch of Howling.

He started as the main doors thudded open. Suddenly self-conscious, Erlaan threw himself down onto a couch, and affected an interest in the hidden view beyond the window.

Four burly servants entered; Enairians by their wide build and thick beards. Between them they carried a bier of polished wood, Erlaan's father lying on the thick mattress amongst red-and-gold pillows. It was the first Erlaan had seen of him since arriving in Askh and his heart fell at the sight. Forgetting any pretence of decorum, he hurried across the room as his father was set down beside the table.

Kalmud's eyes were closed and there was a thick sweat upon his face. Dried blood crusted his nostrils and the corners of his lips. His thick hair was unkempt, plastered over his scalp. His chin was thick with bristles, some dark, others grey. The servants lifted him from the bier and carried him to a couch, where they lay the prince carefully, leaning him against its curved back. Two maids entered as the porters left, carrying dishes and wet sponges. Erlaan was fixed on his father's face as the two elderly women dabbed at his skin, washing away the sweat.

"Fetch someone to shave him and clean his hair," the prince snarled. "It's a disgrace that you allow him to look like this."

One of the maids bowed and left. Erlaan sat on the floor beside his father and gently laid a hand on the sheet wrapping his body.

"Give that to me," Erlaan said, taking the cloth from the remaining maid. "You'll wake him up with your heavy pawing."

The maid placed the bowl next to Erlaan and pattered out of the room on bare feet, casting a glance over her shoulder before she was out of the door.

"Is there anything else, Prince?"

Erlaan ignored her and placed the back of his hand on his father's brow. The skin was flushed, hot to the touch. Erlaan wrung out the sweaty cloth onto the floor and dipped it into the water bowl. He carefully laid it on above his father's eyes.

There was tightness in his chest as memories came back to him; of sitting watching the maids do the same for his mothers and brother when the flux had swept the palaces ten years ago. None of them had survived; his cousin and aunts also had been taken. Though Uncle Aalun had married again, Erlaan's father had refused to take a new wife and had instead thrown himself into his command of the legions. The thought that Kalmud might die was too much for Erlaan to contemplate. His father was so strong, it was impossible that anything could end him; not the flux, and certainly not this foreign disease.

Kalmud's eyelids opened hesitantly, Erlaan's heart fluttering with them.

"My son…" Kalmud smiled and tried to lift a hand, but struggled to pull it from the confines of the binding sheet. Erlaan put an arm beneath his father's back and lifted him up, loosening his coverings. Supported by his son, Kalmud ruffled Erlaan's hair slowly. "You look well."

"Have no concern for me," replied Erlaan, fist clenched unseen behind his father as he fought to control his emotions. "Save your strength for your recovery."

"I see Ullsaard brought you back. Is he treating you well? Is he teaching you how to be a leader?"

"He has been dutiful in his attention, though he does not spare me the more odious chores of his officers."

"Good, I would not have you learn only the privileges of command."

"I wish that you could teach me yourself."

"Family complicates things." Kalmud motioned for Erlaan to allow him to lie back. He wheezed as he settled. "Just ask your uncle what it was like to serve with Nemtun."

"But you are not him, and would be a far better teacher."

There was a delicate cough from the doorway. A short man with olive skin stood there holding a small towel and barber's tools.

"What do you want? Wait outside! Can't you see we're busy?" Erlaan turned back to his father, not sparing the servant a second glance. "Sorry about the disturbance. Do you need some rest?"

Kalmud shook his head slightly and swallowed hard.

"Why does he have no water?" bellowed Erlaan. "Would you have an ill man suffer from thirst?"

The maid who had left scurried in with jug and cup, spilling water onto the carpet in her haste. She dithered, caught between pouring the water and cleaning up the spillage.

"Just give me that," snapped Erlaan, snatching the ewer from her. She held the cup out in a trembling hand as Erlaan poured. He set the jug on the table behind him and took the brimming cup from the maid, dismissing her with a glare. Erlaan lifted his father's head to allow him to drink, as much water dribbling down his chin as passed his cracked lips. Erlaan dabbed away the excess with the edge of the sheet and put the cup aside.

"You'll make a fine soldier," his father said as he settled back against the couch.

Erlaan sighed and his father looked at him sharply, his eyes regaining some of their former life for a moment.

"You think otherwise?" said Kalmud.

"The killing… I have little stomach for it. Ullsaard and Cosuas, they take it all in their stride. But when I saw all of those bodies being carried back to the camp, it choked me."

Kalmud nodded and weakly stroked at Erlaan's arm.

"I'm not a coward, you understand?" Erlaan continued. "I'd happily match a foe with spear or sword, in battle or on the bloodfield."

"Of course you would," said Kalmud. "You're of the Blood; there is no fear in you."

"But war, that's something else. Thousands of men putting their lives in my hands? I don't know if I could take that. And to think that one day I'll be king, and the fate of millions will rest on my shoulders... I am not ready for that."

"No boy should be." Kalmud closed his eyes but his hand squeezed Erlaan's arm reassuringly. "You think I was ready at your age? I was interested in drinking as much wine as possible and putting my cock in any girl that didn't move fast enough. You're better than that already."

Erlaan laughed uncomfortably, horribly aware how much he thought about sex.

"I do my fair share of hole-chasing."

"Of course you do." Kalmud's voice was growing weaker and for a moment Erlaan thought his father had fallen asleep. A cough brought him around and his gaze settled uncertainly on Erlaan. "What was I saying?"

"It doesn't matter. Get some rest."

Kalmud's eyes roved across the room for a while, perhaps seeking inspiration. He settled on some anonymous point of the tiled ceiling and when he spoke his mood was distant.

"To rule people is to change, son. Your grandfather taught me that. You have only known him since he was king. Before he took up the Crown he was a gentle man like you, full of compassion. When he became king it changed him. The Crown weighs heavily on those that wear it. It made him stronger, for sure. Stronger, but colder and harder, like hot ore that becomes deadly bronze. It changed him. It'll change me, I'm sure, and you too. Askhor has never had a weak king, and you won't be the first."

These last words were barely a whisper as Kalmud faded away. Erlaan was gripped with panic, certain that his father had died. He laid his head upon Kalmud's chest and gave a sigh of relief when he heard a faint beat and felt a gentle pulse.

Erlaan stood, eyes lingering on his father.

"Don't leave me on my own," he whispered.

VI

Aalun's apartments filled half of the coldward wing of the palace, a sprawling collection of reception rooms, halls, feasting chambers and bedrooms. Woollen rugs patterned with designs from all across the empire covered the floors. The main halls were painted with murals depicting the most famous sights of Greater Askhor: the cataracts above Narun; the four-towered bridge at Karnassu; the white peaks of the Ersuan highlands; the Maasrite aqueduct from Lehmin to Osteris; the ziggurat of the Brotherhood in Oraandia; and many others with which Ullsaard was not familiar. Walking from room to room was like taking a tour of the Askhans' conquests and achievements.

A small army of half-seen servants kept the apartments in order, filling water bowls, replacing dying blooms and wreaths with fresh flowers, washing the marble floors and brushing the hangings.

Aalun led Ullsaard to a circular chamber containing cushioned benches along three-quarters of the wall, the row of windows above showing the city beyond to hot-wards and duskwards. The general took his helmet from under his arm and placed it carefully on the bench, gaze drawn to the view outside. The last rays of the sun trickled over the slate roofs as torches sprang into life along the criss-crossing streets and windows glowed from within. The Askhor Mountains stood like jagged teeth against the red and purple, the sliver of the dying sun perfectly centred on the Askhor Gap where the Wall stood.

"A remarkable piece of planning," said Aalun as Ullsaard stared at the view. "My ancestors showed good foresight to choose such a place for their capital."

Ullsaard said nothing. He was still surprised by Aalun's argument with his father and his dismissive attitude to his brother's health. The prince stood beside him and looked out of the window.

"Greater Askhor did not happen by chance," Aalun said quietly. "It was conceived by the intelligence of Askhos, forged by his strength and that of his descendants. The empire cannot be ruled by any man of lesser character or ability if it is to continue to grow."

Ullsaard looked at the prince.

"You think your brother a lesser man?"

"Not in heart or spirit," Aalun said with a doleful shake of the head. "But this sickness, it has weakened his body and clouds his thoughts. Three things keep the empire intact and allow it to expand. Firstly, common cause, self-interest if you will; the benefits of being an Askhan citizen far outweigh the burdens. Secondly, fear of Askhor's legions; men like you who are willing to be ruthless against the few to protect and expand the interests of the many. Thirdly, a strong king who will wield that power in defence of our ideals. A strong king who will temper the greed and ambitions of other men so that those who serve are not reduced to slaves and those that govern do not become corrupt."

"You think that Kalmud would fall prey to these other men should he become king?"

Aalun sat down on the bench and nodded for Ullsaard to sit next to him. The prince leant towards Ullsaard, hands clenched in his lap.

"We both know that to lead takes stamina, of the body as well as the mind. When we are tired we make poor decisions, when we are hungry we are hasty in our judgements. I have no doubt that Kalmud would rule to the best of his ability, and would never willingly surrender the interests of the empire. But should one of the governors, Nemtun perhaps, or Asuhas, wish to gain some advantage or other they need only wage a gentle war of attrition to get their way."

"But what about your father's argument? To suggest that circumstance might change the succession seeds doubt for the future. If you wish to help your brother and the empire, why not allow him to succeed his father and stay close to him? Between you and Udaan, I am sure you could protect him."

Aalun drew back, folding his arms across his chest.

"Protect him? What sort of leader needs protection? It is unfair to the people of the empire to be ruled by a man in name only. It is also unfair to Kalmud to put him in such a position. Such stress could labour his health further. I would be the last man to wish to hurry him to his pyre."

"I have seen good officers humbled by minor injuries and infections," said Ullsaard. "Still, many kings have ruled well into old age and not suffered. That includes your father."

"Old age and clinging to life are not quite the same things," replied Aalun. He sighed lightly and stood. "I may be worrying about nothing. My father may live several more years yet and my brother may recover. You are a good citizen, Ullsaard; loyal, determined and dedicated. I recognised these virtues in you long ago, which is why I have always supported you. There were those that said a coldlander could never aspire to greatness, but I saw your potential, nurtured your ability, provided you with the means to aspire. In your judgement, have I ever acted out of selfish reasons or against the good of the empire?"

Ullsaard shook his head.

"And do you trust me?" asked Aalun.

"Of course," said Ullsaard. "You have shown great trust in me and you deserve no less in return."

"I am glad to hear that, friend. It is these bonds, between the legions and the Blood, which make our people strong. I will exert what influence I have over my father to grant you the Greenwater campaign. Cosuas has had his opportunities, I think you deserve one now."

Aalun waved a hand towards the door. Ullsaard stood.

"I should not keep you from your family any longer. Thank you for coming."

Ullsaard was taken aback by the abrupt end to the conversation.

"I am happy to be of whatever help I can," he said uncertainly, picking up his helm. He fidgeted with the crest for a moment. "Thank you for explaining the situation. If you need me for anything else, just ask."

"I am certain I will," Aalun said with a smile.

Ullsaard left the prince's apartments with his thoughts dragged in different directions. Foremost in his mind was the notion of commanding the Greenwater campaign. The prospect filled him with excitement. His mood deflated as he remembered the warning of the king; that he would be away from Askh for a very long time. As he strode along the still stone corridors of the palace, his thoughts began to stretch further into the future. Ullsaard considered the alternatives Aalun had presented. He suspected that Kalmud, and later Erlaan if Kalmud was not to survive long, would be a conservative king. There was little chance that either would endorse an invasion of Salphoria; even less that either would not promote one of their Askhan First Captains to the rank of general to lead such a conquest. Aalun, though, had always acted in Ullsaard's best interests. With his sponsor as king, Ullsaard felt he would be in a position to drive forward Askhor's fortunes.

Bells sounded the third hour of Howling just as he arrived back at his apartments. The main room was empty, save for his chief of servants, Ariid. The aging retainer stood up as Ullsaard entered.

"Your wives have each requested the pleasure of your company for this night," Ariid said as he helped Ullsaard take off his breastplate. The general tossed his helmet onto the main table and stretched, feeling more tired than after a day of battle.

"I shall sleep with Allenya. Bring us both breakfast in her chambers, no earlier than Low Watch."

The servant nodded his acquiescence and withdrew, leaving Ullsaard alone in the quiet. He stood in the hall for a moment and closed his eyes, savouring the stillness. No growl of ailur, no snort of abada or kolubrid hiss could be heard. No clink of armour, scratch of whetstone or pad of sandaled foot. No crackle of campfires, flap of tent door or creak of pole. Everything was still. He smelt roses and hill daisies, burning wax of the watch candles, fresh lacquer on the table.

He listened to the slow beat of his heart, counting each long breath as he drew it in. Peace. No clamour, no attention, no pressure. Memories of the fight with the behemodon flashed at the edge of his thoughts and he opened his eyes, unwilling to face the reality of how close he had come to never being here again.

He cut across the apartments to Allenya's bedroom and quietly pushed his way through the heavy curtains across the door. A red-panelled lantern bathed the room with a soft glow. His wife lay on her side in the bed, sheets and blankets covering her up to the waist, her hair spilling across her arm and covering her breasts. Ullsaard watched the gentle rising and falling of the covers, the wisps of her hair fluttering with each exhalation. He pulled off his tunic and let it drop to the carpeted floor, loosened his belt and stepped out of the embroidered skirt. He kicked off his sandals and walked slowly to the empty side of the bed, eyes still on Allenya, her face ruddily lit against pillows bordered with golden thread.

He slipped as gently as he could beneath the covers, but Allenya stirred with a murmur. She rolled to her back, eyes still closed.

"Husband," she whispered, half-asleep.

"Wife," he whispered in return, stroking a calloused hand across her hair, pushing it from her face with a thick finger.

She smiled and a hand flopped languidly towards him, absently stroking his hairless chest. He encircled her with his arms and buried his face in the brown curls, kissing her lightly on the side of the neck. His desire stirred as his eyes travelled from her eyes, down her cheek, passed her slightly parted lips, finishing on her breasts. The sight of her naked skin caused his heart to beat faster, while his lust began to swell him. He reached out a hand but stopped before he touched her, his fingers hovering just above her flesh. He looked back at her face, the embodiment of the peace he had felt earlier, and pulled back his hand.

Allenya rolled back onto her side, away from him. He settled further into the bedclothes, sinking into the soft mattress and pillows. He felt her warmth against his stomach, the curve of her backside and legs beside him but not touching. She was not Meliu, to be turned this way and that as his lusts dictated. This was Allenya, his wife and love. He kissed her again, on the back of the shoulder, and closed his eyes. She reached back and their fingers entwined.

Ullsaard's hot ardour cooled to a warm wave of contentment, and he fell swiftly into sleep.

FREE COUNTRY
*Near Magilnada, Midsummer New Year,
209th Year of Askh*

I

The pealing of a warning horn ripped Anglhan from his sleep. He surged out of his bunk, head crashing against the roof beams of his cabin. Rubbing his head, he stumbled to the door, dressed only in his long shirt.

Outside, the landship reverberated with footsteps as the crew boiled up from their quarters below decks. Three large lanterns hung from the bow, mast and stern, their yellow glare spilling across the deck. Anglhan blinked in the light, still dazed by the blow to his head. Furlthia hurried past and Anglhan grabbed him by the arm.

"Where?" the captain demanded.

Furlthia pointed towards the hills ahead, where a lone flare burned with a stuttering white flame.

"Prepare to defend the ship," said Anglhan. His second-in-command replied with a pointed look as the crew busied themselves around the spear throwers and handed out axes and swords from the chests beside each hatchway. "Right. Sorry."

Anglhan ducked back into his cabin and hastily pulled on his trousers, pulling the belt tightly into his soft gut. His head still throbbed and he snatched up the half-empty jar of beer on the table and took a long swig. Smacking his lips, he pulled on his boots and grabbed the curved sword that hung above his cot before hurrying back outside.

"Where's Pak'ka?" he demanded.

The first mate nodded towards the bow of the landship. The Nemurians were putting on their armour; huge vests of grey metal scales that hung to their knees. They donned coifs of the same, reinforced along the top with a thick studded band. Anglhan wondered again at so much iron, calculating its worth; Pak'ka's armour alone would be enough to buy land and livestock for a small farm. Any thought of acquiring that wealth vanished as the huge creature straightened, his right hand hefting a spear twice as tall as the ship master, the other holding a long, triangular shield. There was many a corpse that had tried to steal from a Nemurian.

The landship's axles creaked and the vessel listed to the side as the Nemurians approached along the starboard rail.

"The wind carries the news," Pak'ka said quietly. "Four dozens of men. Where shall we fight?"

"Four dozen?" said Furlthia. "That does not seem so many."

Anglhan doubted the accuracy of the Nemurian's assertion but decided against remarking on it. He considered his options; his crew were paid whether they fought or not, while the Nemurians were promised extra for actual fighting. There was no need to use them unless he had to.

"Stay aboard for the while, and we'll wait to see what happens," Anglhan told the mercenaries. "I'm sure the outrunners and spear throwers will see them off."

They waited, the still night air disturbed by the mutterings of the crew and the creak of the landship's timbers. Clouds covered the sky, hiding the stars, the light of the moon a fuzzy glow to aft. The flare had guttered and died and the only light was the haze surrounding the landship.

They waited some more. Anglhan was about to return to his cabin, thinking that the raising of the alarm had scared off the brigands. A hushed call stopped him and he looked to the masthead to see the lookouts pointing over the starboard bow. Three figures came dashing into the lantern light: outrunners.

Anglhan and Furlthia hurried to the rail and called down to the men.

"Rosion and Dabbis are dead," announced the closest, a young man named Rigan. "The bastards snuck up on them and took them by surprise. Colthiun sounded the alarm, but we haven't seen him since."

"Where?" growled Furlthia. Rigan pointed coldwards, towards the hills. "There's a narrow stream cuts down towards the valley. I think they must have crept along the defile and got behind our line."

"Any idea how many of them?" asked Anglhan, still wondering whether he would have to employ the Nemurians' services.

Rigan shook his head and looked to his two comrades. Both shrugged.

"You can count, can't you?" rasped Anglhan.

"Yes, but we're not owls!" argued Murlthin, another youth Anglhan had recently brought on board.

"Or perhaps you didn't stick around long enough to see them," said Anglhan, his grip tightening on the rail. "Get back out there and do your job!"

The three exchanged nervous glances and headed back into the night.

"And split up!" Furlthia called after them. "You can cover more ground."

Anglhan crossed to the larboard side, seeking some sign from the rest of the outrunners. There was no sound or movement in the darkness. As he peered into the gloom, something hissed through the air, missing his ear by a finger's breadth. He hurled himself to the deck.

"Slingers!" he bawled, instinctively covering his head with his hands and pulling his knees up to his chest.

The crewmen at the spear throwers began to shout to one another, demanding to know where the enemy were. A few paces from Anglhan, one fell to the deck with a cry, blood pouring from his nose, a gash between his eyes. Another span to his knees clutching at his elbow as more stones whirred out of the darkness.

"More light!" bellowed Furlthia as the crew ducked and took cover behind the bulwark and mast. The mate growled a wordless curse as the crew continued to take shelter. He jumped down into the bowels of the landship and emerged a moment later carrying one of the beam lanterns from below. With a grunt, he spun on his heel and hurled it out into the night.

Flaming oil spilled across the rocky ground as the lantern burst. The puddle of flames showed little, but now the crew had seen what to do, they organised themselves quickly, passing up more lamps from below to throw around the landship. By the flickering light, men could be seen skirting from rock to bush, slings in their hands. One stood up, swinging the sling about his head. The spear thrower crew at the bow reacted quickly, pulling the lever of their machine. With a slap of twisted ropes hitting wood, the thrower hurled its bolt towards the slinger, punching into his shoulder. The impact nearly severed his arm and flung him backwards out of the light. The crack of other shots sounded around Anglhan as he pushed himself to his knees and peered over the rail.

The captain glanced around the deck to see who else was hurt, but his attention was drawn by an unexpected space; a space that should have been filled by five Nemurians.

"Where'd they go?" he demanded, surging to his feet. "Where's my fucking muscle gone?"

The crew exchanged dumbfounded glances, until one of the lads at the tiller called out.

"They slipped over the side when the first slingstones were coming in."

142

"Shit-eating, dog-fucking mercenaries." Anglhan continued to curse as he prowled up and down the deck, oblivious to the sling bullets whirring past him.

"Captain! Look!" Anglhan turned at Furlthia's shout to see his second-in-command pointing over the rail towards the brigands' position. Larger shapes moved in the gloom and a moment later he heard a hoarse shriek. Something sailed out of the darkness and slapped heavily against the steep side of the landship. Anglhan ran to the rail and looked down. He saw the mangled remnants of an arm in the dancing firelight.

More cries of dismay sounded from the rebels, along with the wet crunch of weapons cutting flesh and breaking bone. By the dimming light of the burning oil, Anglhan saw one of the bandits crawling along the ground, blood pouring from his gut. A massive shadow loomed up behind him. The Nemurian – a green-crested beast even larger than Pak'ka – slammed a punch-dagger into the back of the man with an audible crack of vertebrae. The slinger fell to the dust, arms and legs twitching. The inhuman warrior brought its broad foot down onto the man's head, pulping it with a single stamp.

"Take some alive if you can!" Furlthia called out. Pak'ka lumbered out of the night and raised his axe in acknowledgement. He hissed something in his own tongue and disappeared from view. More panicked shouts and sounds of grievous wounds quickly followed.

"Get down there and help them," shouted Anglhan, grabbing the nearest crewman to shove him towards the side of the ship. Those men not crewing the spear throwers clambered over the side and down the rope ladders. As the first pair advanced cautiously towards the guttering patches of oil, Pak'ka and his warriors emerged. Each of the five carried a man; three hung limply, two struggled weakly against the powerful grips of their captors. Pak'ka shook his prisoner to quell his moving, thrashing him from side to side for a moment like a child having a tantrum at a doll. The brigand fell limp, clutched his head and moaned loudly.

Ropes were passed down and the crewmen on the ground quickly bound the captives hand and foot, and tied them to one another around their waists. While the brigands were being secured, Anglhan heaved himself through the gap in the rail and carefully lowered himself down the rope ladder. Puffing from the short exertion, he strutted up to the prisoners, who were pushed to their knees, surrounded by sword-poking crewmen and the silent bulk of the Nemurians.

He kicked the closest in the ribs. The prisoner fell to the side, the rope around his waist pulling at the man to his right.

"Attack me?" yelled Anglhan. He grabbed the man by the hair and pulled him upright. "You piss-drinking sons of boar farts! Who do you think you are fucking with?"

The brigand turned his head to the side and spat dust from his mouth. He looked up at Anglhan, mirroring the captain's contempt.

"We are soldiers in the army of Aroisius the Free. These are his lands."

"Really?" Anglhan's laugh was short and filled with scorn. "Here's me thinking this was the Free Country, not land of any man. And you are soldiers? Pathetic, that's what you are. Fifty men are not an army. Which one of you is this Aroisius bastard?"

The prisoners laughed and shook their heads as Anglhan glared at them.

"We are just the vanguard of Aroisius the Free. He has many thousands of followers, and soon he will be lord of Magilnada!" one of the men announced. "If you do not wish to join him, you would be wise to leave his lands in the morning."

"Ah, so you're rebels, eh? Not just petty bandits?"

"Aye, that is right. We fight to free Magilnada from the corrupt rule of that overfed swine, Aegenuis."

There were jeers and laughs from the crew but Anglhan said nothing. He walked back to the ship and laboriously hauled himself back up to the deck. Furlthia was waiting for him at the top.

"Should we just slit their throats and have done with it?" the mate asked.

"No," said Anglhan. He looked back at the prisoners and ran a hand through his hair, deep in thought. "No need to make more enemies than necessary."

"They're rebels, Anglhan. They'd kill us as soon as look at us. Most of them are escaped slaves, and they don't take kindly to our trade."

"Always debtors, Furlthia, not slaves." Anglhan headed towards his cabin, motioning for Furlthia to follow him. When they were both inside, the captain closed the door and spoke quietly.

"What if they're telling the truth?" He found the remnants of his beer and finished it off. "What if this Aroisius is ready to make a claim for Magilnada?"

"A fool's hope if ever I heard one. I don't care if he's got ten thousand men, no inbred mountain boy can take the city. The sooner we get there and out of here, the better."

Anglhan flopped down onto his cot with a frown.

"Maybe you're right."

"But?"

"But where there's war, there's profit. If nothing else, it wouldn't hurt to find out more." He came to a decision and nodded to himself. "Yes, bring the prisoners on board. Don't rough them up. Give them something to eat and drink. We'll get to the bottom of this in the morning."

Furlthia's expression plainly showed that he did not agree with this course of action.

"If they prove to be useless, we'll hand them over to the king's men in Magilnada, no harm done," said Anglhan.

"It's only a few more mouths to feed for another day or two. There might even be a reward."

A sly, hesitant smile spread across Furlthia's face.

"And if there's a reward for this lot, there could be a much bigger one for Aroisius, right?"

Anglhan beamed and clapped his hands.

"Now you're thinking like a man of trade, Furlthia! I might yet make something out of you."

II

The debtors sat patiently on their benches with bowls in hand as two crewmen moved along the below-deck with buckets of hot porridge. Another followed behind, giving each man a small dollop of honey from a clay jar. It was better fare than could be expected, Gelthius admitted, but it was not given out of Anglhan's generosity. The cost of food came out of the debtors' "payment," and thus little touches like the honey just added more to the time it took them to pay off Anglhan. Gelthius didn't begrudge the landship captain this subterfuge; if not for Anglhan, Gelthius would have spent these last years in a mine or quarry, and most likely would have died in debt, condemning his oldest son to the same fate. Of all the woes that could beset a man whose business had failed, working as a turnsman under Anglhan was relatively kind.

"D'ya hear what went on last night?" said Henglhid, the benchmate who sat on Gelthius' right, closest to the hull. The haggard little man put his bowl in his lap and rubbed his hands gleefully. "Rebels it was. I heard the crew up top talking about it. A lot of 'em."

"You think they'll free us?" asked Methrian from behind. His excitement was understandable; the former tax collector had been serving Anglhan even longer than Gelthius, in exchange for his embezzlement being paid off by the captain. It was probable that he would never pay off his debt before he died.

"I'd rather rot on the bench than be a rebel," growled Cormarindis. "Traitors and cowards, the lot of them."

"Most of 'em was slaves like us," said Henglhid. "S'only right to give back as you get, and there's a fair few treated us poor, the king and his lackeys among 'em."

"I'd join them, right enough," muttered Gelthius. "I'd love to march up to that fat pig what stole my seed with a few friends at my back. I'd show him what 'rights of the land' really means. I got nothing against the king himself, it's them what does his dirty work should know better. Stealing from honest men like us, that oughtn't be allowed."

Murmurs of agreement rumbled along the benches but soon quietened as feet thudded on the aft steps. As he ducked beneath the deck beams, Furlthia's eyes narrowed at the silence.

"Less muttering, more eating. Captain wants you up and out, so finish off your breakfasts quickly."

"Ain't freeday till tomorrow," said Gelthius. "What's going on?"

"I'll be buggered for a whore if I know," Furlthia replied with a shrug. "The captain has something he wants to tell you and the crew together."

Muttered speculation and scraping spoons filled the below-deck as more crew came down with heavy keys for the debtors' ankle chains. Trio by trio they were freed from the deck rings, still shackled together. The men shuffled up to the ladder and carefully climbed onto the deck. Gelthius arched his back and took in a deep breath as he was jostled into position by the mast, Henglhid to one side, Lepiris to the other. When all were present, Anglhan emerged from his cabin and clambered onto a box on the aft deck. All eyes turned towards him. The prisoners from the attack stood in a line behind him, now unbound, their appearance causing a swell of hushed gossiping.

"As you all know, I am not a malicious man," the debt guardian said, his voice raised to carry the length of the landship, silencing the hubbub. "I think no less of any of you for the circumstances you find yourselves in. It is my hope that I have treated you fairly, more than some of your previous masters have done, and that my demands of you have been tough but not cruel. For all of you, crew and debtors alike, I have justly rewarded your service to me and allowed you to share in my profits."

"He's worried," whispered Lepiris. "The rebels have got him rattled."

Gelthius grunted in agreement. It seemed like Anglhan was trying to make some kind of case to his audience.

"No man likes to see another fall on hard times, and I have been there to provide useful employment for all of you. For some I even put food on the tables of your families when you could not, and for most I spared you the horror of being turned from your homes without a thread on your backs or a barley grain in your pocket. I do not claim that I did this wholly out of kindness, but I believe that a man should be allowed to rectify his mistakes if he can."

"What's 'rectify' mean?" asked Gelthius.

"Payback," chuckled Lepiris.

"It is with these thoughts in mind that I want you all to consider an offer; a choice each of you must make."

Anglhan paused and all across the ship was still, the air silent with anticipation.

"Today, all agreements are considered fulfilled."

There were a few shocked gasps, mainly from the crew, followed by a buzz of confusion.

"As of now, you are all free men, your debts to me paid in full," announced Anglhan, throwing his arms wide.

Some took the proclamation in stunned silence; others gave cautious cheers or laughed. Gelthius heard a sob and a thud, and looked over his shoulder to see Methrian had fallen to his knees. He looked back aft and saw an agitated Furlthia whispering angrily into Anglhan's ear. Clearly the first mate, who had a small share of the landship, had been telling the truth when he had said he had no idea of the captain's intent.

Gelthius turned to the nearest keyman.

"You!" he called out. He looked down at his shackles. "You heard your captain. I don't need these no more."

The keyman took a few uncertain steps and looked back at Anglhan, fumbling with the square-headed key at his belt. He stopped when the captain's voice boomed out again.

"As free men, I now present you with the choice I spoke of. That way," he pointed towards the low hills over the larboard bow, "is Magilnada, no more than two days of solid walking. As free men, you can head there and follow whatever path life presents to you."

He turned around and pointed towards the higher mounts to starboard.

"Before you all dash off, I must warn you that a man called Aroisius the Free leads an army not so far away. As you might guess from the name, he was once a debtor, but now he would see the tyranny of the king and his servile nobles ended. Magilnada is perhaps not such a safe place as you might think. You all know me well enough to know that I do not like being on the losing side of any deal. So trust me when I say it is in our interests to join with Aroisius the Free, so that we might all have an equal stake in the future of a new Salphoria."

Anglhan plopped down from the box and strode amongst the crew and debtors, clapping some on the arm, smiling and nodding to others.

"It is my intent to deliver this ship into the hands of those who would fight for our freedom. It needs a crew, and you are all welcome to join me. Those who wish to leave can do so, with food for three days and my best wishes. Those who wish to stay will be signed in as full members of the crew, with no obligation beyond our meeting with Aroisius. Our new allies will announce our coming," Anglhan waved a hand towards the captured bandits, "to avoid any unpleasant surprises. From then on, you can continue to serve with me, join the army of Aroisius or go your own way without recrimination."

"What's 'recrimination'?" Gelthius quietly asked Lepiris.

"That's payback too."

Anglhan had a key in his hand. With a flourish, face reddening, he bent down and unlocked the shackles on the closest debtors. He handed the key to one of them and waved towards their companions.

"As you enjoy that first taste of freedom, hear the turn of that key, I want you all to think about what you will do. I trust you all to make the right decision."

As their chains clanked to the deck, the debtors milled around aimlessly, unsure what to do. The key made the rounds, passed from each set of three men until it arrived at Gelthius and his benchmates. As it was handed to him, Gelthius grabbed the key like a hungry man offered bread and unshackled himself first, handing the key to Lepiris. Gelthius crouched and rubbed his chafed ankles. As he straightened, he found himself being stared at by Anglhan. The captain surged through the crowd and flung an arm around Gelthius's shoulders. The former debtor tried to shrink away, but the captain's grip was as solid as the ankle-chains had been.

"Here is Gelthius, a steadfast man we would all agree!" declared Anglhan. Gelthius cringed as the captain turned a broad smile upon him. "Tell us, Gelthius, what are you going to do?"

He felt the stares of everybody aboard, from the captain to the other debtors. Some were expectant, others encouraging.

"I figure," Gelthius began, but fell silent, unsure what he did figure. He took a deep breath and started again. "I figure that I got a better chance of having food in me belly staying with you than trying my luck in Magilnada."

"Good man, good man," said Anglhan, squeezing Gelthius ever harder. The debtor-now-freeman twisted his head away as his face was forced towards the debt guardian's flabby chest and odorous armpit. Much to Gelthius' relief, Anglhan relinquished his grip and turned towards another victim.

Gelthius felt a slap on the back. Fearing another crushing, he stepped away as he turned, but it was Lepiris. The two looked at each other, smiles cracking. Lepiris grabbed the back of Gelthius' head and pulled him forwards, planting a big kiss on his brow.

"Freedom, friend," Lepiris said, his voice breaking. They stood head-to-head, gripping each other's shoulders.

"Freedom," echoed Gelthius. "Spirit-blessed freedom!"

III

The landship creaked and groaned along the dusty track as the turnsmen – all but six had chosen to stay with Anglhan – laboured at their cranks. Anglhan stood on the aft deck in his most expensive clothes – bright red shirt, cloak of black wool, red-and-blue checked trousers held by a belt fastened with a gold buckle cast in the shape of an eagle's head, black boots with the tops turned down to reveal their fur lining. Around his head he wore a green scarf embroidered with a leaf design, ending in knotted tassels that hung to his waist.

He felt magnificent. The sky was blue from horizon to horizon. The air was fresh and clear. As the landship crawled slowly up the hillside, he looked to larboard and saw the great plain of Free Country stretching between the Lidean and Minean Mountains. He fancied he could see, beneath a white cliff, the city of Magilnada, though it was no more than a smudge of black against the white, and perhaps was not the city at all.

A shout from the mast top directed his attention past the bow. A large group of armed men stood across the road ahead, bows and slings in hand. As the landship approached, Anglhan recognised Reifan, one of the rebels he had set free. The tall, lean man signalled for them to stop, but Anglhan waved for the rebel to come aboard, not wishing to stop and lose momentum whilst still on the slope.

"I was not sure you would come," confessed Reifan as Anglhan helped him over the rail. He was a gangling fellow with a mop of red hair and sunburnt skin, his cheeks darkly freckled. The rest of the rebel group fell in beside the landship, walking in lines to either side, their weapons ready.

"I don't blame you for such distrust, lesser men than I might have second thoughts about this enterprise," replied Anglhan. He returned to the aft deck with Reifan beside him. "So, where are we headed?"

"Thunder Pass," said the rebel, pointing ahead where the mountains rose higher. "There are old mines there, near Litheis."

Anglhan turned to the steersman and gave instructions to bear to larboard, leaving the road. The man called to his two mates, and all three leaned heavily down on the tiller and hauled it to the side, teeth gritted. Slowly axles turned and the landship swung in the desired direction. The tillerman and his assistants ducked beneath the boom and reversed the manoeuvre, straightening the wheels.

"We should be there a little after midday," said Reifan, shading his eyes against the sun. "Aroisius the Free is waiting for you."

"And I am eager to see him as well," said Anglhan, clasping his hands behind his back. He grinned at Reifan. "Very eager."

IV

Thunder Pass was a steep-sided valley, the walls pitted with caves and disused mine workings. Reifan guided the landship into an immense cavern not far from the entrance to the pass. Inside were hundreds of men and women, children also. Smoke from dozens of fires filled the cavern before seeping out of a fissure that ran halfway along the roof. The floor was littered with ash and other detritus. Rolls of blankets, barrels, boxes, bundles of staves, stacks of arrows and other equipment lined the uneven walls. The chamber echoed with ringing hammers and the rasp of saws, fiery crackling and shouts.

To Anglhan, who was a stickler for a neat and orderly vessel, it was quite a mess and the rebels' ragtag appearance dented his optimism a little. Reifan and his companions had led Anglhan to believe that Aroisius was well-prepared and organised. From here his "army" looked no different from the dozens of other dissident bands that had populated the mountains.

Anglhan tried to keep his smile, but Reifan must have noticed something in his demeanour.

"Don't be fooled," said the rebel. "This is just the workshop and families. Up top, it's a different story."

"Up top?"

"Don't worry," Reifan replied with a grin. "It's only a short climb."

While the crew made fast the landship, Anglhan and Furlthia disembarked with Reifan. The crew lowered blocks on ropes to chock beneath the landship's wheels and began bringing down the sail boom.

"Back to work," snapped Reifan as a considerable crowd gathered. He shoved a few of the most reluctant, and sent the children scurrying with a snarl. "You all have things to do!"

Outside, the valley was beginning to fall into shadow, while the sun shone from the almost sheer wall opposite.

The dipping valley floor was broken by scrub and rocks. Piles of boulders and scree extended out from the sides from past landslides.

"They had to give up mining because of all the cave-ins," explained Reifan as he led them up the valley. "Even slaves cost money. It's called Thunder Pass for a reason. In winter, storms sweep right down here from coldward. Really bad blizzards and avalanches."

"And you stay here during that?" asked Furlthia.

"Safest place to be," said Reifan with a wink.

The way "up top" was a winding path just wide enough for two men to walk abreast, sometimes so steep that steps had been carved into the bare stone. There was no fence or guide rope and Anglhan was happy to follow behind his guide, keeping as close to the cliff as possible. Here and there a frayed rope or bent bronze hook showed where the ore had been lowered from the higher mine workings, but most had been scavenged over the years. Occasionally Anglhan's foot scraped over ancient nails and he stubbed his toe on a thick plank jutting from under the roots of a twisted, stunted tree.

He was lathered with sweat by the time the path reached the top of the cliff, and his knees were trembling from the exertion. Heaving in painful breaths, Anglhan forced himself up the last turn of the path, Furlthia giving him encouragement from behind. With a few more panting gasps, he came to the top. Reifan extended a hand and helped him up a last steep step.

They had come to a shoulder of Mount Litheis, which stood like a sky-piercing guardian at the head of the valley. The shoulder sloped gently to coldwards and duskwards, layered with thick soil and sparse patches of grass. The plateau was easily five or six bowshots deep and extended for more than twice that length, narrowing gradually and steepening as it progressed along the valley, until it merged with the steep sides of the mountain. A ridge jutted out two-thirds of the way along, providing a natural wind barrier, and it was in the lee of this that there were pitched dozens of tents. Several hundred, guessed Anglhan, each large enough to house twenty men. The camp was strangely quiet, the wind and snap of canvas the only sounds.

"Where is everyone?" Anglhan asked.

"Hunting, getting firewood, keeping watch," said Reifan. "Some old hill tribes have villages coldwards of here, far enough from Ersua that the Askhans haven't bothered coming after them. They've always hated Salphoria too, since their ancestors were driven up here by King Arnassin. We've trading parties that go to them throughout the summer, with crops, wool and other lowland stuff they can't get hold of any way. In return, they let us stay here and give us food, wood, rope, even some of their women."

"How long have you been here?" asked Furlthia. He looked around at the camp with incredulity. "I'm surprised nobody has found you yet."

Reifan had to think for a while before he replied.

"Seven years, I think. Maybe it has been eight." He looked away, deep in thought. "Yes, eight. I'm sure of it."

As they talked, they crossed the open ground between the cliff edge and the tents. The footing was slippery with moss and Anglhan wished he hadn't worn his best boots.

"It used to be that the brigands around here would move around a lot," Reifan continued, raising his voice as the wind gusted away his words. "They were afraid that the king would send men after them. Lord Aroisius realised that was their problem; they were easy to pick off, one group at a time. Although we have raided caravans in the past, we tend to go coldwards to Ersua instead, which means the chief of Magilnada isn't really bothered by us. That means we've been left alone to gather our strength. Aroisius the Free wants to take the city before winter comes. That way, the king won't be able to do anything until next spring, by which time we'll be ready to take whatever he sends at us."

They were in the camp now, threading their way through a maze of guy ropes and canvas. Contrary to Anglhan's first impression, the camp was not deserted. Groups of men clustered around small fires. They sharpened weapons, ground grain, stirred pots of broth or skinned deer and rabbits. Here and there small corrals had been made of rope fences, holding long-horned goats.

"In here," said Reifan, lifting the flap of a tent to their left. A warm gust greeted them and Anglhan realised how chill his skin had become despite the sun. With a nod of thanks, he ducked inside.

Aroisius the Free and his chieftains sat on a circular rug at the far end of the tent, arguing. The leader was a gaunt man, even taller and skinnier than Reifan. He had a wispy beard and thinning black hair that hung lankly over his shoulders. Anglhan guessed him to be about forty years old, though he could have been older. He looked up with bright blue eyes, animated, analysing every detail of his visitors in a sweeping glance.

Aroisius stood up as far as he could and walked towards them, neck bent so that his head did not touch the ridge pole running the length of the tent. He extended a bony hand and Anglhan shook it strongly.

"What a magnificent enterprise!" declared Anglhan, wearing his broadest smile. The chieftains looked at him dispassionately, eight bearded, gruff faces. The debt guardian continued on regardless, reciting the speech he had been rehearsing to himself for several days.

"I know that at first you must think me a strange convert to your cause. Am I not one of the men that has profited from the misery of those enslaved by the cruel edicts of that spirit-cursed fiend Aegenuis? I confess to you now that I was such a man. But sometimes a man lives his life with his eyes only half-open. He sees only what he wants to see, and I am ashamed to say that I was such a man until recently.

"But if the spirits bless a man, sometimes his eyes will open full and he will see all of the world, and the true part he has to play in it. Some do so reluctantly, bowed by the burden that they see they must bear. Not I! I am, it has been said, a man of opportunity. When I–"

"Shut him up before I do," growled one of the chieftains, rising to his feet, his fingers on the haft of a small axe at his belt.

Aroisius held up his hands for silence. He cocked his head to one side and looked Anglhan straight in the eye.

"Do not think that I am an idiot because I live in a tent on a hillside." His voice was soft, cultured. "I know what it is that drives men like you: greed."

Anglhan opened his mouth to protest, but Aroisius stopped him with a raised finger.

"That was not meant as an insult, merely an observation. We all have our weaknesses. But we also all have our strengths, and it is those that interest me more. Even now, your mind is whirling with the possibilities. You are looking for the profit in this."

"I assure you, my intentions…" Anglhan's defence died away under Aroisius' unblinking stare. The rebel leader smiled thinly.

"I am sure we will come to understand each other better. For now, you should know two things. Firstly, that you are at my mercy. Your crew are being disarmed as we speak, and your Nemurians are being offered an agreement far more handsome than the one you have with them. This is not a threat, merely a statement of the measures I am taking to protect myself."

Anglhan smiled bravely, though inside his guts writhed with worry.

"And the second thing?" he asked.

Aroisius laid a hand on the landship captain's shoulder

and gently guided him to the rug. A little pressure directed Anglhan to sit, and Aroisius joined him, crossing his long legs. He gestured to one of his chieftains, who twisted around and picked up a small chest. It was passed around the circle until it reached Aroisius, who placed it in front of Anglhan.

"Secondly, you should know that whatever schemes you were concocting, I can make it far more profitable to serve me."

The rebel leader opened the chest. Inside was filled with minted gold pieces, small and triangular with a stylised face on one side and a ziggurat on the other. Anglhan stared at it. He dragged back his hand, realising that he had reached out towards the money. Something struck him as odd.

"Those are askharins," he said.

Aroisius's reply was a lopsided smile.

V

Though he could not see Anglhan's face, Furlthia could guess at his captain's expression when the gold was revealed. The first mate hung back by the tent entrance while Aroisius continued at length, talking about the need to claim Magilnada so that it could become the capital of a new state free from the tyranny of slavery. He spoke about the huge swell of support that would erupt across Salphoria once this haven was created, and how Magilnada would become the new centre of power for the Salphors.

Anglhan picked up one of the Askhan coins and examined it closely. He tapped it against a tooth and even smelt it.

"These are real," he said. "Where do they come from?"

Aroisius plucked the coin from Anglhan's fingers and dropped it back in the chest, which he shut with a thud.

"It is where some of them may end up that you should concern yourself with," said the rebel leader. "In your trove, perhaps?"

Anglhan shrugged.

"That's quite a bit of coin, but it's not enough to equip an army."

"There is plenty more, believe me," said Aroisius.

"And what sort of employment do you have in mind for me?"

Aroisius stood and gestured for Anglhan to do likewise. He led the landship master to the door of the tent.

"That is for a future discussion. Please return to your men and assure them that they are under no threat. Please also convey my regret at having to detain them at the moment. I am sure they will all become worthy soldiers in the army of liberation, but for the moment I must insist that they remain in camp."

"That applies to me as well?" said Anglhan.

"More than anyone," said Aroisius, with a smile that did not reach his eyes.

Anglhan signalled for Furlthia to leave first, and outside they found Reifan waiting for them.

"What would happen if I tried to leave?" Anglhan asked innocently as they walked back through the camp. Reifan glanced around, to the mountain and across the valley to the slope on the other side. Furlthia followed the rebel's gaze and saw more than a dozen wooden structures concealed behind branches and rocks. There were several bowmen in each covering the mouth of the valley.

"I am sure you can find your own way back," said Reifan when they reached the top of the path.

Furlthia went first so that he could help Anglhan clamber down the track. The captain was pensive for some time, saying nothing until they were almost halfway down the cliff face. As if a lamp had been lit, Anglhan's expression brightened.

"So that's the wonderful Aroisius the Free, eh?" he said. He tapped his fingers together excitedly. "I think this might turn out even better than I had hoped."

"He's an idealist," said Furlthia. "Those sorts never have a good end. The sooner we can be rid of him, the better."

"No, no, no!" Anglhan stopped and gripped the mate's shoulder tightly. "He's an idealist for sure, but he's not a fool. Sometimes a stupid man can be impossible to trick, but a man who is clever can trick himself. Aroisius thinks he has us where he wants us, and we might as well let him believe that."

"He doesn't have us where he wants us? His men got the Nemurians, the crew and the landship. That doesn't look promising to me."

"But he as much as admitted himself that he needs me for something, otherwise I've no doubt I'd have had my throat slit or been pushed over this cliff already." He started walking again, his pace as brisk as his bulk and the unsteady footing would allow. "When a man wants something, he becomes vulnerable."

"What do you suppose that could be?"

"I don't know yet, but I have a few ideas. Did you see those chieftains of his? I'm guessing that most of these rebels follow them. Half of them had hillmen blood in them, you could tell by their squinty eyes and flat noses. I'd bet you a night with my sister that they're interested in something other than the liberation of Salphoria."

"You don't have a sister."

Anglhan waved away the comment.

"Aroisius must be offering them something else, and I would think that Askhan gold has something to do with it. And what did Reifan say? They've been raiding into Ersua. Some Askhan, a rich one at that, has got his grubby little fingers all over this pretty girl, I'm sure of it. I think Aroisius is playing a dangerous game, and he might not even realise how dangerous it is."

"That doesn't sound like something we should get mixed up with," Furlthia said. "Rebels on one side, Askhans on the other, and who knows who else, and us stuck in the

160

middle? Perhaps we should just cut our losses and get out of here as soon as we can."

"Furlthia, you have such a narrow view sometimes! Aroisius isn't going to let us go anywhere until he's sure he has us on some kind of leash. And he's right about that gold; some of it should end up in my pockets. All I have to do is wait for the right moment."

"I'm giving you fair warning, that's all. I'll watch your back for the moment, but I don't want any part of any rebellion. And I want even less to do with any Askhans."

Anglhan treated Furlthia to his most paternal smile as they reached the valley floor.

"You worry like a whore that hasn't been paid yet. Stick with me, Furlthia, and I'll make you a rich man."

"And if it all turns to a pile of shit?"

"Then you'll have to run fast to keep up with me."

TEMPLE

As immobile as a statue, Lakhyri listened to the chants of his inferiors. He sat upon a chair of blood red stone, bone fingers gripping its arms, eyes closed. Around him the worshippers knelt on the stone floor, naked in their spiral-cut skin, their cadaverous bodies swaying back and forth in time to the incantation, their voices nothing more than husky whispers. The high priest's heart beat slowly in tune with the eternal rhythm, his breaths shallow, chest unmoving.

He listened; to the rasping chorus as a whole; to each of the fifty voices. His ears sought out any imperfection, any stutter or slip, any mispronunciation or variation in tone. He detected none. The flawless monotony was satisfactory.

Yet still he felt nothing. No tingle of life force in his body. No sense of the swirling energies that bound the world together. The chanting dome was empty of all except the fleeting beats of life contained within the chests of his followers. The essence of creation, the invisible force that sustained his existence and bound his immortal masters to this world, was absent.

While he listened, Lakhyri strained his mind, probed the recesses of experience and thought to divine some reason why the source of the eulanui's power was fading. His search was in vain. Never before had he encountered such a thing. It perturbed him.

The gong sounded and the chanting ceased immediately. Lakhyri did not move while his minions pushed themselves wearily to their feet and shuffled out of the hall.

He sensed the pulse of life at the doorway, a blur of heat and light in the grey existence he occupied. He opened his eyes and saw one of the younger acolytes kneeling there, eyes fixed on the ground, a clay tablet held out in one hand.

"Bring it." Lakhyri's tomb-dry voice echoed around the hall. The youth hurried across the chamber, eyes downcast, and placed the tablet in Lakhyri's lap. The boy withdrew with a quickening patter of feet.

The high priest picked up the tablet. The clay was still wet. A frown creased his leathery brow as he read the message it contained. He rose to his feet and strode out of the hall, the tablet grasped in his claw-like grip.

He ascended the winding ramp to the temple's highest level. The chamber here was small, barely fifteen paces across. Inside stood his two hierophants: Asirkhyr and Eriekh. Their eyes betrayed their worry. Between them, the youngest member of the temple lay upon an inclined stone bed. He stared at the ceiling blankly.

"Do it."

The hierophants nodded. They lifted small, wicked daggers from niches in the side of the stone slab. The boy did not flinch as Asirkhyr began his work, slicing the point of his knife into the boy's forehead. Eriekh began at the youth's chin. Blood trickled as they carved, dribbling down the boy's cheeks and neck and running in crimson threads down the table, following the rusty stains of many generations.

The hierophants cut circles and swirls into the adept's flesh, through skin and fat but never touching muscle. His face now a mask of blood, the boy continued to stare

163

straight ahead. The circles and spirals joined and flowed together, every part of the youth's face was contained within a loop or arc of the lines.

Satisfied that their work was done, the hierophants stepped back and Lakhyri approached. He placed his hand across the boy's face, palm down, covering his eyes.

"Speak to me."

Lakhyri lifted his hand. Where he had touched the boy the flesh began to shift. Blood bubbled up from the wounds and skin crawled into new patterns. The boy began to pant and his eyes were suddenly alert. There was a crack of bone and one cheekbone erupted through the skin. The boy gave a choked cry, but only his eyes moved. The cheekbone flowed like molten metal and settled back beneath the flesh. There were more snaps and splintering noises as the youth's chin and brow reformed. Tears welled up in his brown eyes until they clouded over. When the mist drained away, the eyes were darker, so dark that it was hard to tell where iris and pupil met.

Still covered with a sheen of blood, the boy's face was now that of an old man, with a patrician nose and high cheeks. The blistered lips rippled and muscles tensed.

"I am here." The voice was hoarse and had an odd metallic ring to it. Blood trickled from the corners of the mouth when it spoke.

"I have heard that the succession is under threat," said Lakhyri. He raised the clay tablet in front of the thing on the slab.

"It is nothing. Aalun has questioned the wisdom of Kalmud remaining heir. Lutaar has denied him any right to speak of it again. We work to restore Kalmud's health. It will not be an issue for long."

"The life web in which we sit is failing. Something is wrong. The succession cannot be broken. Do not forget your loyalties. If you cannot perform your duties, we will not perform ours."

"The matter will be dealt with. You have my assurance."

"Convey a message to the king. Remind him that our bargain is with him and him alone. He understands the consequences of failure."

"I will remind him."

"Go."

Flesh burned and blood boiled as the apparition withdrew. The boy, his faced restored, lurched and screamed. The hierophants grabbed his shoulders and forced him to lie back on the slab. After a while, the youth's shrieks stopped and his eyes fixed on Lakhyri.

"The first time is the worst," said the high priest. He ran a finger along the scars quickly forming on the boy's face. "Think of it as your first payment for immortality."

ASKHOR
Late Summer, 209th Year of Askh

I

Ullsaard sat on the grass and watched the wrestlers training. The evening sky was overcast but the air still kept some of the summer warmth. The two men he studied were considered the best in their classes; Huurit, a small, light man quick on his feet; Nurtut, the heavyweight favourite of Prince Aalun, a man as tall as Ullsaard, even heavier set than the general. Huurit danced circles around his opponent, catching him with kicks to the shins and blows to his shoulders, but was unable to get any firm grip on him. By contrast, Nurtut shifted very little, but his hands moved with surprising speed and twice he caught Huurit around the ankle, forcing the smaller man to spin and squirm to escape. Their mentors and coaches clapped encouragement and shouted advice from the outside of the flattened grass circle.

"Mother said I would find you here," said a voice behind him. The accent was impeccable Askhan, delivered in a precise, clear tone.

Ullsaard leapt to his feet and turned to see a youth dressed in the yellow robe of the colleges, hemmed with red and green beads in a pattern that identified him as a student of Meemis. His hair was thick, curled and blond, like his mother's, and tied back by a simple thong.

"Ullnaar!" Ullsaard declared, swamping his youngest son in a hug. The boy pulled away slightly and Ullsaard sensed embarrassment. He released his bear-like grip and stood back. He offered his hand. "Forgive your father, I forget that you are now a man."

Ullnaar shook his father's hand, his grip firm. Ullsaard snatched a hold of the boy's wrist and turned it this way and that, examining Ullnaar's fingers.

"Not a callous nor blister nor grain of dirt!" Ullsaard laughed. "To think that I would raise such a man."

"A few ink stains, that is all," Ullnaar said with a smile. "Though by the time I am your age, I am sure my back will be bent from perusing old pages and poring over tablets."

"Come on, sit with me," said Ullsaard, lowering himself back to the grass. Ullnaar followed suit, delicately gathering up his robe around his thighs before kneeling. The skin revealed was pale, almost white compared to his father's sun-tanned flesh. Ullsaard caught a whiff of glade flowers. "You're wearing a scent?"

"Just some oils they had at the baths." Ullnaar's bright blue eyes, another inheritance from his mother, quickly assessed Ullsaard, as an assayer might price a gold statue. "You are looking well. The desert has not been too unkind to you."

"It's bloody hot, I can tell you that."

"Mother says that you have been acting like a caged ailur since you came back to Askh. She told me that you can barely spend a day inside the palaces."

"You know me; born in the open air, I was."

"You are eager to get back to the fighting," said Ullnaar. Ullsaard thought he detected the slightest note of reproach from his son, but chose to ignore it.

Below on the wrestling fields, Nurtut had the other man in a front face lock, his thick arm clamped around the man's neck, forearm under his chin. Huurit pushed and twisted, using the leverage of his body to break the hold and swing Nurtut's arm behind his back. A kick to the back of the knee staggered the larger man, who flailed behind him seeking to grab his opponent.

"Aalun hasn't given me leave to return to the legions yet. He's been summoning every governor and man of influence from across the empire," Ullsaard told his son.

"So I have heard." Ullnaar picked at the grass, tossing it into the light breeze. He leaned towards his father with a self-satisfied expression. "I actually have some news for you. Allon arrived early this afternoon. That means that all of the provincial governors are now here."

"You seem to be taking quite an interest."

"Meemis has told us to pay attention to these kinds of things," said Ullnaar. "It has been more than ten years since the last time all of the governors were in Askh. There is a rumour around the colleges that Aalun has proposed some change to the laws governing the succession."

"Did he come alone? Allon, that is. It would be good if I could see another of my sons while I'm here."

"The usual bodyguard of a few hundred men, it seems. I have sent a friend to the palace to find out if Jutaar is one of them. I imagine the palace barracks are getting quite full by now."

"Nemtun brought two whole legions for some reason," Ullsaard said with a shake of his head. "He's got them camped outside the city. What a waste of men, to stand around here looking important. I don't know what he hopes to achieve, showing off like that."

"He is probably reminding the other governors that he is the only one amongst them to have led in battle," sid Ullnaar. He took on a superior air. "Things like that can intimidate lesser men."

"He certainly has a reputation to maintain," said Ullsaard, glancing at the wrestlers.

Through brute strength, Nurtut had risen to his feet and dragged Huurit around to the front again. He delivered a knee-trembling blow with his elbow to the top of the other man's head and followed this up with a swift backhanded slap across the chest. Huurit reeled away, off-balance. He had to skip quickly to avoid falling over the chalked outline of the ring. He ducked beneath Nurtut's outstretched hands as the heavyweight lunged. With acrobatic skill, Huurit snatched up Nurtut's left ankle from behind and kicked away his other foot, sending him crashing to his belly. The lightweight deftly rolled until he sat on Nurtut's back, ankle in both hands over Huurit's shoulder, bending his opponent's spine. Nurtut's hands were raised in shaking fists as he tried to fight back the pain, but he lasted only a few moments before he was slapping the grass in submission.

Ullsaard clapped loudly as Huurit sprang lightly away, rubbing at his sore head and neck.

"I would think wrestling is rather tame for a man that has shed blood," said Ullnaar.

"It's not for me," Ullsaard replied. "Luia wants a wrestler for some reason. I finally agreed just to shut her up. Noran recommended this man, Huurit. He seems handy enough."

"Buying her a wrestler?" Ullnaar was incredulous. "You know just what reason she wants him for. Why do you encourage her?"

Ullsaard looked at his son sharply. "It's none of your business. You're just barely old enough to fuck, don't start giving me advice about women."

Ullnaar held his hands up in surrender. "I was just making sure you understood the implications. You know that a champion is not going to be cheap."

"I'm sure we can afford it. And you never know, his prize money might turn a profit one day."

"That's if Urikh doesn't fritter it away on some other stupid business venture."

Ullsaard stood up and helped his son to his feet. "What are you talking about? Urikh can't spend a tin coin without the approval of Leerunin."

"That would be the same treasurer who came to me just before the solstice high day to say that Urikh has taken out a loan of fifty thousand askharins; mortgaged against *your* lands in Apili and Menesun, no less. Then the two of them disappeared to Ersua for the summer."

"Bribes perhaps?"

"For a copper deal? Is he greasing the palms of every tinker and housewife in Ersua?"

They walked back up the grassy bank towards the Royal Way. Across Maarmes on the bloodfields, workers shovelled cartloads of sawdust onto the fighting flats in preparation for the evening's contests. Ullsaard had planned to stay to watch the fights, but the news that Allon had arrived would mean the general would be required to attend the feast of greeting that night. On top of that, it was possible that his second son, Jutaar, was back in the capital.

Seeing their master approach, a small group of servants who had been sheltering in the shade of the fence jumped to their feet. Ullsaard signalled for them to approach, and pointed to Diirin, one of the youngest.

"Run back to the apartments and warn Ariid that I'll need my ceremonial gear ready as soon as I am back. Tell my wives that they'll also be required to greet Governor Allon. And tell Ariid not to take any shit from Luia this time; she's coming whether she likes it or not. If she argues, tell her from me that if she doesn't cause any fuss, I'll buy her the wrestler, Huurit."

The boy nodded in understanding and set off briskly while Ullsaard headed towards the arching gate of Maarmes at a slower pace.

"Will you join us this evening?" he asked Ullnaar. The boy shook his head.

"I have to head back to the college tonight. I was only able to be excused today because I told Meemis you would be leaving soon and this was likely the last opportunity I would have to see you."

"You lied?"

"Lawyers do not lie, Father," grinned Ullnaar. "I made an assumption."

"That's all right then," said Ullsaard, putting an arm across his son's shoulders. "You'll have time to see your brother if he's here? I'm sure Allenya will have rooted him out by the time we get back, if he is around."

"I am sure I could spare the time for a cup of wine and a small meal with you. I have already had lunch with Mother."

"I'm sorry I was not here to raise a ewer to you on your ascension," Ullsaard said. "If it's any consolation, I wasn't around for your brothers', either."

"I do not hold your absence against you. I grew up knowing that you would not be around for most of the time."

There was nothing Ullsaard could think of in reply to that and they walked back to the palaces in silence.

II

They were turning into the corridor leading to Ullsaard's apartments when a harassed-looking Ariid hurried towards them.

"I have an urgent message for you from Prince Aalun," he said. "The prince summons you to the Hall of Askhos immediately. He has had servants scouring the palaces for you!"

"Did he say what he wants me for?"

"No, master. The message said only to attend him as soon as possible."

"I'll see you later, I hope," Ullsaard said, turning to Ullnaar. He took his son's hand and shook it. "If I don't, remember that I'm very proud of you."

"Thank you. I hope all goes well with the prince."

Ullsaard dismissed the servants and headed across the palace at a swift march. Several more servants in Aalun's household waylaid him, each relaying the same message as Ariid. By the time he reached the throne room, Ullsaard was in an anxious mood.

The hall was busy when Ullsaard entered. King Lutaar paced back and forth in front of his throne, his face in a deep scowl. Udaan stood in his customary place, along with several other silver-masked senior Brothers. Each of the governors was present with a gathering of functionaries and advisors. All were dressed in white robes of office, with sashes bearing the colours of their provinces.

Nemtun sprawled on a low couch, eyes half-closed, wearing the green-and-gold of Okhar; hawk-faced Murian from Anrair hovered close to the king, his sash light blue and green; Adral, the short, grey-haired governor wearing the gold and black of Nalanor; Kulrua of Maasra, adorned with dark blue, surrounded by a crowd of shaven-headed servants taking notes on wax slabs; Asuhas from Ersua, a timid little man who stood chewing his fingernails and fiddling with his grey and green sash; and Allon, wearing the same depressed expression Ullsaard had come to know so well as First Captain to the governor of Enair, garbed with deep red.

Prince Aalun stood beside the throne, but there was no sign of Kalmud. The prince appeared to be arguing with Udaan.

"...there is most certainly a precedent for such a change," Aalun was saying. "In the reign of my great-great-grandfather, Askhos' Decree of Dominion was changed to allow non-Askhan men to attain the rank of general and lead the legions. In the time before that, the rulers of Askh first allowed women to be part-owners of their husband's trades. When King Nuurin held the throne—"

"That is enough!" snapped Lutaar. He looked down the hall and saw Ullsaard. The king's brow creased even deeper. "What are you doing here?"

Ullsaard stopped mid-step and bowed.

"I was summoned by Prince Aalun," he replied.

"Is that so?" The king's narrowed eyes swung back to his son. "What is the meaning of this?"

"Though none has used it for some time, every general of the empire is entitled to a vote on changes to imperial law," Aalun replied evenly. He looked at Udaan, who nodded, though somewhat reluctantly. "Since General Ullsaard is currently in Askh, he has every right to be included in our deliberations."

"And why is he still in Askh? One might think he has been loitering here for some purpose of yours, Aalun."

"Not at all, Father. He is still waiting for your decision on whether he is to return to Mekha or join with the Greenwater legions."

Lutaar curled his lip in irritation.

"Then he can have my decision now." The king's angry stare fell upon Ullsaard. "He is to return to his legions in Mekha immediately. Before leaving, he will receive orders for General Cosuas to take command of the Greenwater campaign. That is my decision."

Ullsaard bit back a protest and managed a nod of acknowledgement.

"I will draft the orders this evening," said Aalun, his eyes fixed on his father. "Perhaps we could return to the matter for which I have brought everybody here?"

"No," Lutaar said sharply. "I will hear no more of this idiocy concerning your brother's status as imperial heir."

"You seem to be wasting all of our time, Prince," said Adral. "The king has spoken. Unless anyone else wishes to make any remarks, I suggest we end this now and each go back to our provinces to perform our duties."

Murian cleared his throat nervously.

"I do have another point to raise, if the matter of the succession is concluded."

All eyes turned to Aalun, who waved for Murian to continue, conceding that his objections were finished.

"For the third time this year, the chief of Magilnada, Gerlhan, has raised his levy on grain coming through his city," Murian told the council. "Many of my merchants are being driven out of business. The price in the markets has been rising steadily for several years now. My citizens are very distressed by this, and I am sure my fellow governors have received similar complaints."

There were grunts and murmurs of agreement around the hall.

"What is that you propose?" asked Udaan.

"It is robbery, pure and simple," Murian said plaintively. "I wish the king to back an imperial delegation to Magilnada, to demand that Gerlhan reduce his taxes. The man is starving Askhan citizens!"

"Perhaps we could compensate by lowering the imperial tithe on Askhan grain," suggested Allon. "That would free up more of the coming home harvest to ease the demand on these expensive imports."

"Unthinkable!" snorted Nemtun. "Those tithes go straight to the legions."

"And that has nothing to do with almost a third of our grain coming from Okharan farms?" said Murian. "Farms that you own and that benefit from not only a fixed military contract, but at the growing market rate in Askh."

"I am not going to apologise for assuring a steady supply, and if you have some other accusation against me, level it more clearly."

"I have to agree," said Ullsaard. He ignored the hostility flowing from several of the governors, Nemtun and Adral chief amongst them. "There is no forage in Upper Mekha; my legions are wholly dependent upon those supplies until irrigation can be dug and farms established. That will take all of the winter, and there is no guarantee of a sure harvest next year. We need that grain."

"Now you see why it is so important that you continue to expand our hotwards border," Lutaar said. "We need more farmland."

"There is more fertile land around Magilnada, and bountiful harvests in Salphoria," said Ullsaard, sensing the mood of the governors. "With that harvest coming, it would be a better use of my legions to secure the Magilnada grain trail than scrape a few more farms out of the Mekhani desert. If nothing else, having a few legions on the road might remind this chief where he gets most of his money."

Murian nodded enthusiastically, and there was approval in the eyes of Allon and Asuhas.

"I am not going to start a war with Salphoria," the king announced, dashing Ullsaard's growing hope. "Our main thrust will continue to be along the Greenwater."

The governors fell to bickering over tithe rates and trade deals, which washed over Ullsaard's numbed mind. His fate had been decided. He would be returning to the heat and sand of Mekha.

III

Ullsaard did not head back to his apartment. He strode through the palace in a foul mood, heading for the inner gardens. Servants scurried from his path, casting nervous looks at the general as he passed. He had reached the atrium, the sun slanting through its high windows, when a call from behind brought him to a halt. He turned to see Noran. The herald caught up with Ullsaard and the pair walked into the gardens together.

"I've seen brighter storm clouds," said Noran. "It looks like someone pissed in your wine."

Ullsaard simply grunted in reply as the two of them crossed the paved border of the garden onto a close-cropped lawn. The snip of knives sounded from across the grass where three servants knelt, using their blades to trim the lawn's edge. The general was content to follow his friend to a bench beside a shallow pool. Red-scaled fish swam lazily above a multi-coloured mosaic of circles and curves.

They sat in silence for some time until Noran's patience finally wore thin.

"So, what news is so bad that you're stalking the palace with a face like thunder?"

"Cosuas is getting the Greenwater campaign," Ullsaard said between gritted teeth. Saying it out loud made the king's proclamation even harder to bear.

"I see," Noran said quietly. "So you'll be heading back to Mekha soon."

Ullsaard turned his bleak stare on his friend.

"Tomorrow."

Noran let out a sigh of sympathy. They sat for a while longer. Noran began to fidget, increasing Ullsaard's annoyance. Finally the general could hold his frustration no more.

"Fucking politics," he growled. "The empire's being run by men who can count sacks of grain but wouldn't know one end of a spear from the other. All they're interested in is holding what they've got. And those Brotherhood bastards looking over all our shoulders, keeping an eye on us like they were Askhos's own fucking guard dogs."

He stood up and took a pace before rounding on Noran.

"And all the fucking nobles as well, with their villas and their farms and their tenants, all taking their share and putting in nothing." Ullsaard saw the shock on his friend's face and he realised what he had said. He reached out a hand. "I didn't mean you, you know? I'm sorry…"

Noran waved the apology away.

"Don't fret about it, I'm not insulted. Truth be told, you're right. Most of the men with power and wealth did

176

little to earn it. Even merchants have to get up every morning and sell their wares. But what would you rather we had?"

Noran motioned for Ullsaard to sit down. The general did so, resting his elbow on his knee, chin in hand.

"I don't know. Something more than this. I was brought up with the histories of Askhos and Luriun and Muuris the Proud. Men who *did* things; carved a whole fucking empire by themselves. When did Greater Askhor stop needing men like that?"

"When we achieved peace," said Noran. "And here's the thing. You didn't grow up with the histories of those heroes; you grew up with their myths. I've read actual history, and it wasn't all the glorious victories and sunshine you think it was. Luriun? He killed his brother and raped his widow because his own wives couldn't produce a male heir. He destroyed the bridges at Narun and refused to rebuild them until the king agreed to marry his eldest son to Luriun's cousin.

"And before that, what was Muuris? Just another tribal chieftain, killing his neighbours and taking their livestock for himself. Muuris probably butchered more Askhans than all of the Nalanorian tribes did. But Askhos was clever enough to persuade Muuris that it was better for him to set off coldwards and fight there than keep shitting on his own doorstep."

"You make them sound like thugs and thieves," said Ullsaard. "What does that make me? A failed thug?"

"A civilised man," replied Noran. "You can't compare the empire as it is now to how it was born. We've taken the best of what was created and got rid of the bad parts. Well, most of the bad parts. You may not like us, but the noble families provide continuity. Like the Blood. It was my ancestors that joined Askhos and Muuris and all those other heroes; fed them with the grain from our fields, armed them with the copper from our mines, gave them our women as wives and our men as soldiers. We took no fewer risks than anyone else. We entrusted our futures to those heroes of yours, made them what they were, so don't be surprised that we're reaping the benefits now."

Though Ullsaard had to concede Noran's point, he still didn't like it. Who could say what achievements his father and grandfathers and great-grandfathers had accomplished? Yet that had not counted for anything because he wasn't a noble; he wasn't even a born Askhan.

An elderly servant hobbled across the lawn calling his name.

"What is it?" Ullsaard growled.

"Prince Aalun asks that you join him in his chambers to discuss your new orders, General."

"He can write them without me," said Ullsaard.

"He was most insistent, General."

"You best go," said Noran, standing up.

Ullsaard sighed. All he wanted was some fresh air and to spend the next few watches with his family. In the morning he would be leaving; he had no idea how long it would be before he returned. With a reluctant nod, Ullsaard waved for the servant to lead the way.

IV

The functionary took Ullsaard through Aalun's apartment to a small room filled with papers and tablets. The prince stood at a desk in its centre, a large map spread across it. He looked up with a smile as Ullsaard entered.

"Thank you, Renio, please close the door," Aalun said. He saw Ullsaard's downcast expression. "Do not be so glum, my friend. We can work this situation to our advantage."

"Really? As I see it, I have wasted the better part of the summer coming here, for nothing."

Aalun wagged his finger.

"Not at all, Ullsaard, not at all. Just after you left, my father acceded to the governors' demand that something be done about the grain problem. The king has tasked me with resolving the matter."

Ullsaard slumped into a chair beside the desk.

"Grain problem? I've been overlooked for what will likely be the best command of my life and you want me to worry about grain?"

"Stop sulking and listen to what I have to say," snapped Aalun. He visibly calmed himself. "Moving Cosuas to the Greenwater gives us an opportunity; one that will be even more to your liking."

Ullsaard leaned forward.

"I'm listening."

"The king has not said anything about how to resolve this grain problem, so I am of a mind to side with Murian. For the moment, it is impractical to continue the Mekha expansion, so I am going to issue orders for you to bring back your legions. You'll return with them to Askhor, and with their presence I will be able to put pressure on my father to change the succession."

Ullsaard rocked back.

"You want me to use my legions to threaten the king? It's unthinkable!"

"Nonsense! It was part and parcel of politics when the empire was being built. And it's not a threat, it's a reminder. I did not bring all of the governors here in the expectation that they would side with me in this argument; I did it to remind my father that though he rules Greater Askhor, he cannot govern by himself. As he has grown older he has become more convinced that the empire works simply because he says it will. The truth is the governors support him for as long as he gives them enough freedom to do what they want and gives them no reason not to support him."

"And how do my legions fit into this... reminder?"

"You have a genuine grievance to air. Two grievances, in fact. Firstly, there is the practical matter of the grain supply. If the situation deteriorates over the winter, as I suspect it will, you will be left in a very precarious position. Who can say what the legions will do if you are forced to reduce their rations? On top of that, I have been doing some reading of the old laws. Did you know that a general with one hundred thousand defeated enemies has a right to nominate a campaign of his choice for a season?"

"I didn't know that."

"Of course not; it is in the interests of the king and the governors that you remain ignorant of your powers. In fact, they've probably forgotten that right exists. It comes from when Ersua and Maasra were being conquered. There was no distinction between governors and generals back then, so to prevent it becoming a free-for-all with the legion commanders going after the same prizes, the king decided to introduce this law as a reward for those that were most successful. In short, if you followed your orders and won a few battles, the king would give you free rein for the next summer, stopping the other commanders from taking a bite out of your pie."

Ullsaard rubbed his chin thoughtfully and imagined the possibilities of being given freedom of command for a whole summer.

"I can certainly see how that would be motivating," he said. Ullsaard smirked at another thought. "And if my men were to know that was the case, you can be sure they would press me hard to take them somewhere more profitable than Mekha."

"Yes, that is a good point," said Aalun.

"But why did they stop offering this right? What was true then must still be true now."

Aalun sat down behind the desk and swept his hand over the map, encompassing the provinces of Greater Askhor.

"Your predecessors used to rule the territories they conquered in the name of the king. Whatever they could take they could keep, as long as they gave a fair share of the proceeds to the Crown. But the empire grew and new provinces had to be governed by men with minds more suited to the civic and mercantile than the military, so the king offered to buy the provinces from his commanders and appointed governors to run them. That is the reason why generals like you still have partial ownership of the lands you bring into the empire; just over a hundred and fifty years ago a contract was sealed between the Crown and the legions. That agreement is still in effect."

"And that's when the generals gave up the rights to hold a governorship? That's why I can never take civilian authority?"

"Unless you are of the Blood, like me or Nemtun," Aalun replied. He gave a lopsided smile. "The Blood can do whatever we damn well like. It is our empire, after all."

Ullsaard nodded in appreciation of what Aalun was telling him. Perhaps Ullnaar's choice to become a lawyer was the smarter career move than merchant or soldier.

"Which of your legions do you trust?" asked Aalun.

Ullsaard was insulted by the question.

"They have all sworn oaths of loyalty!"

Aalun shook his head, pushed the map to one side and placed a wax tablet on the desk.

"I did not ask which of them were loyal to Greater Askhor. I asked which of them you trust. For all of my talk of reminders and rights, let me clear what I am proposing. You are going to bring several tens of thousands of armed men into Askhor, set up camp within sight of the capital and tell the king that you want to launch a campaign into Salphoria."

Ullsaard blinked with astonishment to hear the plan put so boldly.

"I see that you are starting to understand," Aalun said. "While I might talk about 'reminders', you were more correct when you said it was a threat. If my father senses any weakness in you, he *will* exploit it, and you will be ruined."

The general took a deep breath.

"I have always been a good soldier," he said slowly. "From legionnaire to general, I have done my duty to Greater Askhor. I have held my tongue when my superiors have erred, and I have followed orders that I have known were wrong."

"All the more reason that you should now get the recognition, power and reward that is owed to you, Ullsaard." Aalun stood up and came around the desk to lay a hand on Ullsaard's shoulder. "I know this can be troubling. I have spent a considerable time and no small amount of effort to bring you this opportunity, but I would not force you into any course of action. When we are finished talking, I will sit down at this desk and write your new orders. It is your choice what they will be. If you remain unconvinced, I will simply order that you return to Mekha, send Cosuas to the Greenwater and continue your campaign. If that is what you want."

What do I want? Ullsaard asked himself. Everything he had learnt in life was about obedience: don't speak out of turn; follow orders; bring honour to the legions; respect the Crown and the Blood; do your duty to the empire. Even his mother had always told him to shut up and not ask awkward questions. What Aalun proposed ran counter to all of that, and the more Ullsaard thought, the more the prince's plan seemed like foolishness. Yet also the more he thought about it, the more Ullsaard realised that he *wanted* this. It wasn't what he thought was for the best, it wasn't the most sensible course of action, but it was what his instincts told him he *needed*. Aalun was handing him an opportunity on a plate. He would never get another chance like it.

"The Fifth and Tenth are both Enairian legions," he said slowly. "They'll follow me anywhere. I raised the Thirteenth myself and they'll do the same. The Eleventh and Fifteenth are Cosuas's men. Ersuans mostly. You should send them with him to the Greenwater."

"Good, good," said Aalun. He sat down and started scratching notes on the tablet with a bone stylus. "What about the Twelfth and Sixteenth?"

"Mixture of Okharans, Maasrites and Anrairians. Most of the First Captains are men promoted by me, so they'll follow happily enough. I think the legionnaires will follow their purses more than anything else."

"They certainly have something to gain from this," said Aalun, still writing.

"I have a concern," said Ullsaard. The chair beneath him creaked loudly as he leaned back, his enthusiasm evaporating. "I can't march over thirty thousand men from Mekha to Askh without being noticed."

"You will be following orders, plain and simple," said Aalun, waving the wax tablet at Ullsaard. "If anybody tries to stop you, tell them to piss off and mind their own business; and that includes Nemtun and any of the other governors."

Ullsaard's eagerness was drying up quicker than a puddle under the Mekha sun.

"If I do all this, and the king says no, what then?"

Aalun dropped the tablet on the desk in a gesture of irritation.

"My father cannot say no," he said. "He cannot simply ignore you. That leaves him with two options: submit to your lawful rights or break the law."

"He could change the law, take away those rights."

"Stop worrying about things that will not happen." Aalun laid his hands flat on the desk and looked straight at Ullsaard. "This might seem new and devious to you, but men in your position, men in all positions of power, have

183

been doing this sort of thing for generations. Take Murian today, for example. His point about the grain shipments through Magilnada was an implied threat. He might well have said 'Don't forget that I can starve half the empire if I choose, so help me out with this problem.' The king needs the grain supply, and he needs the loyalty of the legions as well. He has more to lose by refusing you than by indulging you."

Though Ullsaard found it hard to accept this reasoning, he trusted Aalun to know about this sort of politics. There was only one other thing that caused him to hesitate.

"You know that I could never raise a weapon against another Askhan," he said.

"Of course not!" said Aalun. His look of revulsion would have been no greater if Ullsaard had suggested the prince perform a sexual act on his sickly brother. "Implied threat, Ullsaard. *Implied*."

Finally satisfied, Ullsaard stood up. He shook hands with the prince and turned to leave. As he grabbed the door handle, he looked back at Aalun.

"Is this politics or plotting?" Ullsaard asked.

The prince looked at him with surprise.

"Is there a difference?"

V

That night, Ullsaard slipped into bed beside Allenya. She rolled over and stroked his arm.

"You are tense," she said.

Ullsaard said nothing. He planted a long kiss on her lips. His attentions moved to her neck as his hands cupped her breasts. He stroked them gently and lowered his head to kiss them. Allenya giggled as his beard tickled her stiffening nipples. She threw an arm around his shoulders and pulled him closer, her other hand moving to lightly scratch the back of his thighs with her long nails.

He continued downward, ducking beneath the covers to kiss her belly before moving on to her thighs, placing delicate kisses in a trail from waist to knee. Allenya's hands pushed through his hair, tightening as his tongue delved into the bush of hair between her legs. His hands lifted her up, always strong but gentle, caressing her buttocks, running along the outside of her legs.

She pulled him up, rolling onto her back so that he could enter her. His lips found her mouth as he slid inside, and she clasped him tighter, pulling him down onto her. They embraced as he began to thrust slowly, her hips moving in time to his. Allenya felt his measured breaths on her cheek as he moved his head to kiss her shoulder. She planted her hands on the small of his back and urged him to go faster, wrapping her legs around him.

Harder and faster he thrust, still planting kisses on her; on her breasts, on her chin, on her forehead. With shuddering sighs they both reached the point of climax. Ullsaard clasped onto Allenya, holding her tight, until he was soft inside her. He rolled to his back and stared at the ceiling. She took her hand in his.

Not once had Ullsaard looked Allenya in the eye.

"You are leaving," she whispered. His only reply was a tightening of his grip on her fingers.

FREE COUNTRY
Autumn, 209th Year of Askh

I

It was a pretty model, Anglhan had to admit. Using little more than bits of wood, pebbles and old frayed rope, Aroisius had cobbled together a scale representation of Magilnada. The miniature city sat on a hummock of dirt and rocks, just as the real Magilnada squatted on the slope of Mount Gellian. Anglhan had been to the city more than two dozen times, and all of the winding main streets, the marketplace, towers and barracks were where they should be.

Aroisius the Free, self-declared rebel leader and hope for future generations of exploited Salphors, explained how his army would capture the city.

"Two hundred men could easily take the coldwards tower by climbing down the cliff face above the tanneries and across to the wall." Aroisius dangled a few pieces of string down the corresponding rock face. "When the tower is in our hands, the garrison will have to move up from the wall barracks in the merchant quarter, along the wall here. An attack at the gatehouse will trap them between two forces."

The chieftains squatting around the model grunted and nodded in appreciation.

"How would you get enough rope?" asked Barias, a round-shouldered man with a hook for his left hand.

"Rope isn't difficult to buy or steal," replied Aroisius. "The cliffs around the camp will allow our men to train on similar terrain. I am confident that the descent can be done in darkness and at speed. The tower guards will have no time to react."

"What about the militia house over here?" asked Griglhan, a lean Salphor brigand with pock-marked skin inflicted by some past disease. "What's to stop the militia coming along the cartway from the duskwards wall?"

Aroisius peered at the model with a slight frown and rubbed his chin.

"Burning arrows across the wall targeted at the millhouse beside the river," he said confidently. "That would keep the militia busy enough until we have control of the dawnwards wall."

He looked at the chieftains, but they had no more questions.

"Good," said Aroisius. "I'll find someone to procure more rope, and we'll begin selecting the soldiers who'll train from the cliff climb. I want to attack before the eve of Serinalia. After that, the weather will quickly worsen and the climb might be impossible. We take the city by the start of winter, and the Salphors cannot respond until spring. Is everybody agreed?"

There were nods and words of assent. Anglhan cleared his throat loudly. Aroisius and the others turned to look at the debt guardian-turned-rebel standing leaning against the cave wall with crossed arms.

"You have a comment?" asked the rebel leader. Anglhan nodded.

"How many men do you have?"

"Two thousand full fighters," Aroisius answered. "Perhaps the same again of elders and boys."

"And how many soldiers defend Magilnada?"

Aroisius shrugged.

"Perhaps two thousand as well. Mostly militia, poorly trained."

"I see," said Anglhan, pushing himself away from the cave wall. "Do you expect any of the city's people to take up arms in defence of their homes?"

"Why should they? There'll be no looting or raping. We'll be liberators, not conquerors."

There were a few bemused noises from the chieftains at this announcement. It was Lubrianati – oldest of the chiefs, a wiry, bearded dwarf of a man – who voiced their dissent.

"The men will want some compensation for risking their lives," he said.

"And they will have it," replied Aroisius. "When I become lord of Magilnada, every man who fights with me will be granted a home in the city and deeds to lands outside."

The chieftains exchanged dubious glances but said nothing. Anglhan had noticed the divided agenda before; Aroisius was so possessed of his goals that he was blind to the nature of the men he had recruited.

"A worthy reward indeed," Anglhan said with a smile. "They will, of course, be keeping any arms you give them."

Barias erupted with a snorting laugh.

"A few bows and pikes? Pot hats and bucklers? That's not a lot to take home."

"I have men out trying to find more supplies of weapons," Aroisius said quickly. "I understand that our equipment might not be the best, but it is the heart behind a sword that counts for as much as the sharpness of its tip."

"I am puzzled by something else," said Anglhan. "I have been with you for the best part of fifty days, and you have yet to tell me what my part I can play in this war for our freedom."

"Yes, I am coming to that." Aroisius stood up, annoyed. "I want you to spy for me. Take the landship into Magilnada a few nights before we attack and scout out the city to make sure there is no call for last-minute alterations."

"Your spies seem to be doing a good job already," said Anglhan, pointing to the mock city. "I don't see how I could help further."

Aroisius looked a little uncomfortable and darted a look at the chieftains before he answered.

"As a debt guardian you have access to sources of news that are currently beyond my men: the chieftain's council and their households; captains of the militia; armourers and such."

"Oh, you want me to use my contacts?" said Anglhan, grinning broadly. "Of course I can do that! In fact, I was hoping that was what you were going to ask me to do. You see, I think I can do more than just bring you some news. I know several merchants in this area. That rope you were talking about? I'm sure I could get you fifty casts of the stuff for a good price within three days."

He turned his attention on the chieftains.

"And weapons? Armour? I know just the man who could sell us what we want."

"What sort of weapons?" asked Barias.

"Proper ones," said Anglhan, crouching down in front of the sitting chieftains. "Javelins, knives, scimitars, arrowheads, spear tips. And proper armour too. Bronze breastplates, helms with cheek guards, light mail shirts. The sort of thing those militia boys in Magilnada will be wearing."

"Such things would be very useful," said Lubrianati, looking up at Aroisius. "Our boys could match that militia for sure with that sort of kit."

"Well, if you tell me who your contact is, I can send a delegation," said Aroisius. He raised a warning finger. "If you think I am prepared to let you just go off on your own, you must think the spirits shat me out of the sky yesterday."

"On my own?" Anglhan feigned surprise. "I wouldn't know where to begin judging the quality of weapons. I'm more of a barley and wood man, myself. No, I was going to take Barias here with me. And other than a few men with essential ship skills, I was going to let you pick my crew. If any of them think I am up to no good, they can stick a knife in my gut."

Aroisius' face betrayed his distrust.

"Why not simply give me the information you have, and I will broker the trade."

Anglhan shrugged apologetically.

"Because that knowledge is the only thing I have left that stops you from killing me. We will have to learn to trust each other, and I am sure we will. Until then, I think we can agree that mutual interest will keep us both honest. As a sign of my support for you, I will even purchase the weapons with my own money, and when I return you can pay me for half of them."

Aroisius's mouth opened and closed a couple of times as he sought some fresh argument to Anglhan's proposal.

"That seems good, boss," said Barias. "I'll make sure he doesn't pull a fast one."

"We need those weapons," added Lubrianati. "Quality gear would make all the difference in a close fight."

The rebel leader sagged and looked at Anglhan.

"All right. We will organise this trade mission on the terms you have laid out. If you betray me, I will make it my life's work to hunt you down and stake you out for the crows to peck out your eyes and guts. Am I clear?"

Anglhan performed a gracious bow.

"I only wish to see your cause succeed, Lord Aroisius the Free."

II

"You're tying a line, not wrestling a whore!" Furlthia bellowed.

He ran down the deck and snatched the rope from the hands of a man struggling with one of the sail cables. For what seemed like the hundredth time, he showed the rebel how to properly secure the line through the starboard grommets and returned to his watchful position on the aft deck.

"Sorry," said Anglhan, joining the first mate from where he had been loitering at the aft rail. "Aroisius wouldn't let me keep more than ten men."

"Bunch of idiots," muttered Furlthia. He glanced over his shoulder. "At least he let us keep some decent steersmen."

The landship steadily shook with the clatter and rumbles from the cranks below, trundling along at a steady pace. It had been slow-going at first as Aroisius' men had been unaccustomed to the slow but methodical rhythm maintained by a good turnsman. The journey had been made all the longer by a diversion that took them further coldwards from Magilnada than would normally have been the case; Anglhan had been adamant that they keep clear of the city until they were ready to enter.

"We're going to Carlangh, aren't we?" said Furlthia. Anglhan nodded. "You're going to do business with Meaghran! I told you we shouldn't have anything to do with that dogfucker."

"There's no need to get personal," said the captain. "You really shouldn't pay heed to rumours."

"Rumours?" laughed Furlthia. "My cousin was there, he swears it by the spirits. Meaghran fucked a dog for a bet when he was drunk."

"He could have fucked a dozen dogs, he still has what we need," replied Anglhan.

"I still think this is madness," said Furlthia, keeping his voice quiet. He looked around the ship for Barias. The chieftain sat at the forward hatch, chatting with some of his men. "I can't believe you actually volunteered us for this nonsense. You're dragging us deeper into the shit, you realise that?"

"We were in the shit already, friend," said Anglhan, his voice also low. "We just have to keep paddling for the moment."

"And I suppose you have a scheme for getting us out of it later?"

"I think 'scheme' would be an exaggeration. I'm playing for time. At the moment this can end one of two ways. Either Aroisius's attack succeeds and he kills us because he doesn't need us anymore; or, the attack fails and we're hunted down and killed as rebels."

"Thanks for the encouraging news."

Anglhan gripped Furlthia's arm lightly, but kept his gaze ahead, looking at the crew.

"I have to make sure Aroisius doesn't attack before winter. His current plan is half-arsed and doomed to failure."

"So? Just let him fail, and we'll take our chances. The longer we're mixed up in this, the harder it's going to be to get out. Why supply him with weapons? We'll be flayed and our guts ripped out as soon as we get caught."

"Weapons are a means for bargaining," explained Anglhan. "You've seen how poorly equipped that 'army' is. They have numbers, but little else. Aroisius has his chiefs convinced that he can deliver what they want. When I return with a hold full of spears and shields, they'll start to realise that he can't give them shit compared to me."

Furlthia was horrified. He fought to keep his voice down, his next words coming out in a strangled squeak.

"You want to take control?"

Anglhan's grip on Furlthia's arm tightened painfully.

"I want to be in the position that I *could* take over if I need to. I've got no need of a ragtag army, but being in charge is better than not being in charge, which is where we are at the moment."

Furlthia pulled his arm away and shook his head.

"I don't think you've thought this through. You've got to convince the dogfucker to sell you some of his weapons. And if you manage that, the rebels will get them and they'll be more ready than ever to launch their attack. You're right when you say you don't have a plan."

Anglhan looked at his first mate with disappointment.

"I never said I didn't have a plan," the captain said, tapping the side of his nose. "Let's just make sure we survive until the winter. You never know what might come up."

III

The rattle and thud of chains and manacles hitting the deck sounded across the landship. Anglhan sighed deeply and tilted his head back, letting the light rain patter onto his face. Having regained his composure, he looked at the group of surly men in front of him. Behind them, the dawn sun was just lighting the pale roofs of Carlangh.

"You're meant to be debtors," he said, slowly and purposefully. "You all look too well-fed as it is. If anyone comes aboard and sees that you're not shackled, we'll be found out for sure." He turned to Barias, who stood beside him, a grin splitting his bearded face.

"He's right, lads," rumbled the chieftain. "It'll be just for a few days."

"I swore I'd never wear one of these again!" said one of the men, holding up the ankle bindings. "Why don't you put it on?"

"I've got to go with the captain, see?" Barias replied with a shrug. "Make sure everything goes down proper."

With more grumbling and muted protests, the rebels filed belowdecks. The click of locks continued for some time before Furlthia reappeared. He handed the bunch of keys to Barias.

"Like we agreed," said the mate, with a sideways glance at his captain. "You can set them free anytime you like."

Barias took the keys and stuffed them into a pouch at his belt with a nod.

"All right," he said. "Let's get moving."

Furlthia bellowed a few commands down the hatch and the landship slowly got underway. The rising sun revealed the plains of Salphoria; an expanse of grasslands stretching from the mountains to coldwards all the way to the distant horizon. Herds of cattle roamed the grassland, watched over by groups of men with long spears and bows, with small boys running around the beasts with thin rods.

Ahead Carlangh rose out of the grass, on the gentle slopes of a broad hill. The river Briensis meandered hotwards down the mountains, watering the plains, before turning duskwards just before it reached the hill of Carlangh. Around the town a wide swathe of grass had been cleared in generations past, replaced by rows of cereal. It was harvest time and large numbers of women were already working in the fields, reaping the crop and piling it onto the back of carts drawn by laughing bands of children. A small procession was already making its way towards the town and the landship joined the back of the harvest parade.

The outer town consisted of a few dozen roundhouses built from mud bricks around wooden frames. It was little different from any other Salphorian farming town, save for one feature; at the brow of the hill stood a wooden fort. Its wall of sharpened logs, carried some distance from the forests in the foothills to coldwards, followed the contours of the hill in a rough circle, broken at even intervals by six towers. It covered an area far larger than the group of buildings outside its wall, which had spread out of the protective enclosure in past years because the growing population could no longer be contained.

This was the most dawnward extent of Salphoria proper. Though the king had an historical claim to the Free Country, he had signed an agreement early in his reign with the king of Askhor to grant Magilnada and its territories a neutral status. To all intents, Carlangh guarded the border of Salphoria. This had attracted families to make new homes here, marrying into the Carlanghians or simply bringing everything they had to the town. The expected boom in trade from Carlangh's new status never came, leaving the people scratching an existence out of the grassy plains while trade continued to go dawnwards through Magilnada, never coming within a day's travel of the old fort.

Rather than pass through the town, the crop wagons circled around the hill, following a winding track into the fort on the far side. Anglhan ordered the landship to do the same. As they approached, the captain saw a large number of armed men gathering on the rampart behind the sharpened logs of the wall. There were some nervous whispers from those rebels still on deck.

"Relax," Anglhan told them. He winked at Barias. "We're just here for a bit of trading. Nothing out of the ordinary."

"Get the water butts out of the hold," said Furlthia. "We might as well fill up from the river while the captain does his business."

In this way the majority of the rebels were kept busy while the landship entered the Carlangh fort. A group of warriors waited in the square just inside the gate. They wore brightly striped woollen trousers and padded jerkins sewn with rings of bronze for protection, and pointed helms popular amongst the Salphorian tribes, decorated with crests of boar hair. All were armed with long spears and bronze-edged bucklers. They were headed by a broad-shouldered chieftain marked out by the bearskin cloak he wore.

"Probably fucked the bear too," Furlthia whispered out of the side of his mouth.

Fighting back a laugh, Anglhan raised a hand in greeting to Meaghran.

"Hello, friend! The spirits' blessings upon you!" he called out, but received nothing save a blank stare in return. The captain looked at Barias and Furlthia. "Wait here until I signal for you."

Anglhan clambered over the side and lowered himself to the ground as the landship came to a creaking halt. He hurried across the packed dirt of the square, palm still raised. Reluctantly, Meaghran raised his palm in return.

"You're the last person I expected to see out here," the commander said gruffly, before remembering his manners. "The spirits' blessings on you too."

Anglhan looked around at the fortified town, noting the patched canvas roofs on the granary stores, the frayed hems on the tunics of the guards and the sun-whitened wood of the buildings.

"Prospering as ever, I see," said Anglhan.

"Very funny," said Meaghran. "I suppose you're going to tell me that you've got a proposal I can't afford to ignore."

"The spirits themselves must have brought you my thoughts in the night, Commander. The very words I was thinking."

"All right," Meaghran said with a sigh. He gestured with his head for Anglhan to follow. "Come on; let's go to my rooms and discuss it."

The captain turned and waved for Furlthia and Barias.

"Who are they?" Meaghran asked as the pair shimmied down the ropes hanging down the landship's hull.

"My first mate and my storemaster," Anglhan replied quickly. Carlangh's commander eyed Barias with suspicion but said nothing.

They followed Meaghran across the square. He led them into a low building under the rampart of the wall, still swathed in shadow. Inside were two sparsely furnished rooms. In the first were a few guards who sat on the floor, eating from bowls and chatting. Meaghran ignored them and carried on through to the next room. The floor was covered with scattered straw, which to Meaghran's credit was fresh. He gestured to some low wooden stools and the four of them sat down.

"You came from dawnwards," said Meaghran. "Just been to Magilnada, yes?"

"I have," said Anglhan.

"Any news?"

"Nothing remarkable. The usual stuff. Prices are up, trade is down."

Meaghran nodded with little enthusiasm.

"Same here. The town's bigger than ever, the harvests better than ever, but you try getting a half-decent price... Someone's making money somewhere, but the spirits take me if I can work out who it is."

"I'm avoiding grain at the moment," Anglhan said. "Like you say, it's a bad market."

Meaghran stretched out his long legs and folded his arms.

"If it's not grain you're after, why are you here?"

Anglhan coughed twice and spat to one side.

"Sorry, my throat's a little dry."

"I see," Meaghran said with a smile. "That's how it is?"

He bellowed out of the door for someone to fetch beer and cups. A soldier returned shortly carrying a tray of jugs and mugs.

"Don't you have a slave for that sort of thing?" asked Barias. Anglhan's heart skipped a beat but he kept a smile on his face.

"Had to sell them all," confessed Meaghran as he poured the amber-coloured beer. "Too many families now to have folk standing idle while we feed extra mouths."

Anglhan raised his mug in toast before Barias could say anything else.

"With the blessings of the spirits, I think my coming here may solve your problems," he announced. "Well, some of them."

They all drank from their mugs, signalling that business could start in earnest.

"Weapons," Anglhan said, seeing no reason to delay. Meaghran's eyebrows rose in surprise. Anglhan plunged on. "I wasn't being entirely honest when I said there was no news from Magilnada. Rumour has it that rebels have been gathering in the mountains."

Barias shifted next to Anglhan, but he ignored the chieftain and continued.

"Speculation, there's nothing like it for good business. I would guess that you've got a few things in your armoury doing nothing but getting in the way. I could help you clear some space."

"You want to buy weapons from me? Who are you going to sell them to? I'm sure as the sky is blue that Gerlhan can equip his troops just fine."

"You're right, my friend. But the good citizens of Magilnada, they're not all that confident in their militia. And the freeholders in the farms outside the walls, well, they are getting very nervous."

"They're not really mine to sell," said Meaghran, without much conviction. "They were given to Carlangh by the king, to defend his lands."

"You're not selling them for yourself," said Anglhan, his voice as slick as oil. "You'll just be holding the money until you find someone to take it to Carantathi."

Meaghran looked at Anglhan for a long time and shook his head.

"No, it's too dangerous. You wouldn't pay what I would ask for, to cover the risk."

"I am happy to negotiate."

"No," said Meaghran. He stood up and offered a hand to Anglhan. "I'm sorry, but it'd be my skin on the line."

Anglhan took a small tin wafer from his belt and put it into the commander's hand.

"I really didn't want to do this," said the landship captain. "I'm happy to pay the price you name."

Meaghran looked at the token in his hand. It was no bigger than his thumb, stamped with three things: the seal of the king, a sum of money, and a name. On seeing the last, Meaghran's face flushed red.

"My son?" he snarled. "You've bought my son's debts?"

Meaghran lunged for Anglhan, grabbing the front of his jerkin. Barias hooked an arm around the commander's waist and hauled him away, the pair of them falling into the straw. Furlthia leapt up, putting himself in front of Anglhan.

"Calm down!" said Anglhan.

Meaghran tried to wrestle Barias aside but the chieftain shifted his weight, pinning down one of the commander's arms with a knee. Meaghran spat and threw the debt token at Anglhan.

"You filthy slavefucker! You dirty, lying bastard!"

Anglhan stood very still, his expression calm.

"I am doing you a favour, you stupid arse," he said slowly.

"Taking my son into slavery? What did the stupid prick do? I can't believe it!"

Anglhan stooped and picked the token out of the straw. He held it up between two fingers.

"It doesn't matter," Anglhan said. "Something to do with wool trade with the Fetea. Your son is in a cell in Labrias. I saw his token and bought it before anybody else could. I thought being a prisoner for the moment was better for him than the alternatives. If it wasn't for me, he'd be mining copper, panning salt or worse. You can have him back if you sell me what I want. Take this token to Labrias and the Fetea will hand your lad over without a problem."

The debt guardian picked up Meaghran's mug from the floor, dropped the tin token inside and filled it with beer. He proffered it towards the commander. Meaghran's shoulders sagged and he sank back into the straw with a groan.

"That stupid little shit. I knew it was a bad idea to send him away, but his mother insisted." He banged a fist against his forehead. "Shit."

Anglhan nodded Barias aside and helped Meaghran to his feet. The commander straightened his cloak and dusted down his trousers with sweeps of his hands. When he was done, he sat back on his stool, glaring at Anglhan.

"So what is it you want?"

"Why don't we have a look in your armoury and see what you have," replied Anglhan as he handed over the mug of beer.

IV

The crew heaved up bundles of spears, shields and swords to the landship, while Furlthia kept a tally of everything being loaded on a wax tablet. When the last box was being hoisted up, filled with bronze mail links, the first mate handed the tablet over to Meaghran.

"What's this?" the commander asked.

"We'll need your mark on this so that we can take the cargo into Magilnada," replied Furlthia. "Just to avoid too many questions. What happens after that won't be your problem."

Meaghran slipped a heavy ring from his left hand and pressed its embossed design into the wax. He handed the wax slate back to Furlthia. Anglhan joined them as the commander was putting the ring back on.

"This is yours," said the debt guardian, placing a sack of coins in Meaghran's hands. He glanced at the Carlanghian warriors who had gathered around the landship and raised his voice. "I've put in a little extra for your men; a thanks for their help in loading."

Meaghran growled in irritation.

"I could have my men take you prisoner right now," he

said. "It'd be a justice if I did."

"Why don't you?" Anglhan asked innocently.

Furlthia edged a little closer to his captain, fingers on the handle of the knife at his waist. He looked over his shoulder and was pleased to see most of the landship crew were done with the loading. They lined the side of the deck, wiping their sweaty bodies, winking and waving at the local women. A few suggestive calls rang around the square. Several of the men lounged close to one of the spear throwers, the sharp point of its bolt aimed towards Meaghran. Barias was with them. The chieftain grinned at the group on the ground.

"We're not brigands," Meaghran said between clenched teeth. "Get out of here. May the spirits shit in your mouths while you sleep."

Furlthia followed his captain up the side of the landship and puffed with relief when the chocks were stowed and the beat of the drum sounded. The vessel turned laboriously around the square and headed back out of the gate, followed by several dozen warriors. The landship headed towards the river.

"I don't think you'll be coming back here in a hurry," said Barias.

"I don't think we'll be back here, ever," said Furlthia.

"Oh, I don't know," Anglhan said with a smile. "I'm sure Meaghran and me will be doing business again sometime."

"He'll cut open your guts for sure," said Furlthia. Anglhan plucked the ship manifest from his mate's fingers and planted a light kiss upon it.

"Not while I have proof that Meaghran sold weapons to escaped slaves," he said with a wink and a satisfied chuckle. "Never let a fish out of the net unless you have to, my friends."

V

The weather was worsening by the time the landship returned to Thunder Pass. Twice on the journey back flash floods had swept across the mountains, bringing deluges with them. Light rain pattered on the deck and splashed from the sail as the crew steered the landship along the rutted road leading up the valley.

A large congregation of rebels waited for them outside the caves, Aroisius and his lieutenants at the front. Anglhan was eager and scrambled down the side netting before the landship had rumbled to a halt. He crossed the rocky valley floor almost at a run, a broad smile on his face.

"Success!" he cried out. "The spirits have blessed our endeavours. I bring you a cargo more precious than gold or rubies or iron. I bring you freedom!"

There was a ragged cheer from some of the assembled rebels, but Aroisius's expression remained stern. He eyed Anglhan carefully.

"You have my gratitude," said Aroisius. "How much did you pay?"

Anglhan had expected suspicion, but he was prepared for it.

"It is of no matter. Consider this equipment my gift to your cause."

"That is not necessary," said Aroisius. "I will cover half of the payment, as we agreed."

"Certainly not," said Anglhan in his most insistent tone. "We have the weapons already. Those askharins of yours can be put to far better use than simply swapping between our pockets. Think of the welcome you will have in Magilnada when, as the new lord of the city, you are able to show your generosity with a few well-placed donations to the local shrines and elders. What I have brought you might be the means to take the city, but it is only you that will be able to keep it."

Anglhan saw Aroisius's stern demeanour flicker as he imagined the scene, a hint of a smile at the corner of his lips. It passed in a moment.

"Start unloading," barked the rebel leader. He bent close

to Anglhan as the rebels swarmed towards the landship. "I know that you are not doing this out of belief in my cause. What is it that you hope to gain? Where is your profit going to come from, slaver?"

Anglhan quickly considered his alternatives and decided that a protestation of innocence would fall on deaf ears. The truth would be better at this stage. Or a half-truth.

"You're right, Lord," he said conspiratorially. "My profit will come when you control Magilnada. You'll need someone to help run the city, taking care of the boring day-to-day affairs. A man in that position receives all sorts of attention; gifts from those who want his ear, business from those who want his favour. There's no reason for us to be at odds over this. I want you to rule the city; you want to rule the city. We both get what we want. I've already given you my ship, my debtors, and now a sizeable cargo of weapons. What more can I do to persuade you that I want you to succeed?"

"If you remain loyal, and useful, I could include you in my council," replied Aroisius. "I know you think I am blinded by my lofty ambitions, but do not think that I see the world as a child. I know how power works. Just remember not to get greedy. That can get a man into trouble."

"It certainly can," said Anglhan.

VI

There was a mood of celebration around the rebel camp that night. The fires were banked high and the rain passed in the early evening so that everyone was outside the tents and caves. Jugs of ale were passed round and those that had served on the landship told their tales to the rebels that had stayed in camp. Anglhan found himself beside the main fire, sitting between Barias and Lubrianati. The two chieftains stank of untreated hide and stale sweat as they talked across Anglhan.

"The lord says that with these weapons, we're ready to go," said Lubrianati. "We'll be going at the half-moon."

"That's about six days, isn't it?" said Barias, rubbing his hands cheerfully. "Seven nights from now, we'll be in Magilnada, drinking their beer and fucking their women."

"You heard the boss," warned Lubrianati. "This isn't a raid. We'll be staying. That's hard to do when someone is after you for having your way with his sister."

Barias's unconvinced expression was all the answer he needed to give. Anglhan spied Aroisius approaching through the camp. The self-appointed future lord of Magilnada stopped to speak with some of his men. They were joking and laughing, excited by the prospect of the coming attack. That didn't suit Anglhan well at all. He turned to Lubrianati.

"So, it's your men that are going to be storming the gate, right?" Anglhan said. "I would bet they're pleased they've got some decent weapons and armour."

"Most of the new stuff is going to Griglhan's men," said Barias, which Anglhan already knew to be true. "They'll be climbing down the cliff."

"Oh," said Anglhan. He furrowed his brow. "Hmm."

"What?" asked Barias. "Why the frown?"

"Oh, it's nothing. Just ignore me."

"You think that my men should get more of the weapons?" asked Lubrianati, pulling Anglhan towards him.

"It doesn't matter what I think," replied the landship captain. "I'm just a trader. Aroisius is your leader. I'm sure he knows best."

"If you have something to say, slave-man, just say it," said Barias. "What's wrong with the boss's plan?"

Anglhan snatched his jerkin from Lubrianati's grasp and stood up haughtily. Out of the corner of his eye, he saw Aroisius getting closer, just at the edge of the light on the far side of the fire.

"Nothing," Anglhan snapped. "I would have thought the best gear would go to the men doing the most dangerous job, which as I see it is those making the assault on the gate."

Anglhan stalked away before they could ask any questions. He slipped past the closest tent and stopped in the shadows to watch what happened. Aroisius waved a greeting to the two chieftains and sat down close to them.

"I've been thinking about who gets the new weapons," Lubrianati said gruffly.

"We should have another think about the plan," added Barias.

With a smug grin, Anglhan turned away and headed across the camp.

VII

The next day, news circulated around the camp that Aroisius had decided to split the weapons between Barias and Griglhan. Anglhan wondered what hold the rebel leader had over his subordinates that he could get them to agree swiftly with his commands. Was the promise of Magilnada enough to get these rebels, brigands and hillmen to put aside their rivalries? He decided to find out how much control Aroisius really had over his army.

An idea came to him as he wandered into the main storage cave. Inside he saw Cannillan, second-in-command of Urias's gang. The shaven-headed lieutenant's back and upper arms were criss-crossed by whip scars, and his wrists and ankles bore the telltale marks of long-time bondage.

"I bet you don't have much time for the likes of me, do you?" Anglhan said solemnly as he joined Cannillan. "I know it's worthless, really, but I hope my gift goes just a little way to atoning for my past greed."

"What are you talking about?"

"You know, my gift? The weapons and armour? I hear that Aroisius is sharing them out amongst the groups to

205

make sure everything is fair. Now that he's decided not to give them all to one group, I'm sure he's stopped any hard feelings."

"He's splitting them between Griglhan's and Barias's mobs, that's all."

"Oh, I must have misheard. I thought he said he was going to give them to those that needed them most. You know, the most important leaders, the best warriors. I thought that sounded like a sensible plan. I mean, no point giving a nice sword to some pig-fucking hillman who doesn't know one end from the other. And after all, my gift really is for those who have shared the burden of debt that I have helped spread, not for a bunch of opportunists who've just come down from the mountains for a bit of fighting and looting."

Cannillan's eyes narrowed and his brow creased.

"Sorry, you look busy," said Anglhan as he backtracked towards the cave mouth. "I didn't mean to interrupt."

VIII

The wrangling over who got the new weapons took another three days for Aroisius to settle. The rebel leader was forced to split the cache amongst the chieftains, in proportion to the number of men each led. The chieftains were free to distribute the weapons amongst their own bands as they chose. With just two days before the rebels would break camp and move towards Magilnada, Anglhan knew he had to find some way to stall the attack quickly.

Sweating despite the chilling wind, Anglhan hauled himself up the cliff path to the tented camp. Most of the rebels had left on their daily forage and hunt, leaving Griglhan and his warriors to practise their climbing on the cliffs above the campsite. Anglhan found the bandit leader at the base of the rock face coiling rope while his men laboured up the cliff.

"I feel the spirits' blessings today," Anglhan said cheerfully. He picked up the end of a length of rope and began idly knotting it.

"What are you so happy about?" asked Griglhan, not looking up from his task.

"No reason," Anglhan replied airily. "Good to see that rope I got you is strong stuff. Wouldn't want any of you falling down that cliff. I'm just glad the rain's still holding off. Let us hope the spirits see fit to give us a dry sky when we attack. I'm sure you and Aroisius will make the proper sacrifices and such, just to be sure."

"I hadn't thought of that," said Griglhan. "We should get a boar or something."

"That would be wise. You and your lads have got the most dangerous job, it's only right that you have the spirits on your side."

"What's that?" Griglhan pointed at the double-loop of rope in Anglhan's hands.

"This?" Anglhan replied distractedly. He acted as if he wasn't even sure for a moment. "It's a sling knot. We use it for hauling cargo aboard."

Griglhan took the rope and inspected the knot, tugging at it roughly.

"A man could slip his arms through those loops," the bandit muttered. He looked at Anglhan. "Would that be safer than having it tied around your waist?"

Anglhan looked for a moment as if he didn't understand the question and peered up at the men clambering across the rocks.

"When it's windy, the men at the mast top use that knot for their safety lines. If you fall with that around you, you might dislocate a shoulder, but if you fall with it around your waist, you could snap your back. I think that's it, but I might be confused. I'm not a terribly practical man."

Griglhan leaned towards Anglhan, staring at the knot.

"Teach us how to tie these," he demanded.

"I'll have Furlthia and some of my old crew show you," Anglhan replied. "They'll do it better than me, be sure of it."

"Thank you."

"No problem. I figure you'll need every help you can get. You boys certainly don't lack courage, do you? Climbing down in the dark, on wet rocks? I've got men that don't think twice about hanging from a sail boom that wouldn't do that."

"It won't be that dark," Griglhan said with a shake of his head. "That's why we've picked the night of the half-moon."

"Ah, yes, very clever. Although…"

"Although, what?"

Anglhan had to hide his delight. Why, he wondered, did such a simple trick work so often?

"It seems to me that the lighter it is, the more chance you'll be seen from the wall and tower."

"We have to have some light so that we can see where we're climbing."

"Good job you've got the best armour, that's what I say. I mean, if your men don't get on to the wall, the whole attack is going to fail. It's good to know that Aroisius is putting you first in his priorities."

"Lord Aroisius made it clear that nobody is to argue about the new weapons," Griglhan said. "He said that we have to stop squabbling like children with a piece of sweet-cake."

"Very right he is too," said Anglhan, rocking back on his heels. "He's the one in charge, after all. We can trust him to have considered everything."

Griglhan nodded.

"It's the small things that he's so good at, isn't it?" Anglhan continued. "It's smart to have everything prepared, like what to do if it's cloudy, or rainy, or if it isn't cloudy."

"You're not making sense."

"Well, if it's cloudy, it might be too dark for you to climb. And the cloudier it is, the more chance of rain making your job more difficult."

"So? I'll tell Aroisius that we aren't doing it unless we get a clear night."

"That's for you and our fearless leader to sort out, nothing to do with me." Anglhan smiled and clapped Griglhan on the arm. "We can't fail with men like you!"

IX

Later that day, Anglhan found Lubrianati and his men returning from their forage. Using the same sort of arguments that had worked on Griglhan, he convinced the chieftain that it would be absolute suicide to attack the gatehouse of Magilnada with anything less than total darkness. As he flopped down onto his cot in the landship's main cabin, he wondered how long it would take Aroisius to sort out this dispute, with the lives of both men at stake.

The rebel leader's solution was both swift, sensible and exactly what Anglhan wanted. Aroisius announced that the attack would be delayed until the night of no moon, so that there would be total darkness to cover their approach. The fires would be set in the mill before the climbers started down the cliff. If the rain was too heavy for the flames to catch, the attack would be called off.

Six days after this pronouncement, after the attack would have taken place if the original plan had been followed, autumn storms hit the mountains. Wind and rain almost destroyed half the camp on the plateau and the rebels had to take shelter in the caves. New rivers poured through cracks and crevasses in the rocks, soaking many of the supplies that had been carefully hoarded over the summer. The hillmen amongst the army wagged their chins and warned that the seasons had turned. The spirits of summer had lost their annual battle, and now the spirits of winter were in the ascendancy.

As gloom fell like a shadow over the camp, Aroisius was forced to make a reluctant announcement: there could be no attack until spring. Anglhan remembered just in time to look suitably disappointed.

NUMBER
Autumn, 209th Year of Askh

I

The bridge shivered with the tread of abada as Ullsaard rode across the Nakuus River, his servants on the wagon a short distance behind. A little way upstream work was underway building the stone crossing, though the legionnaires broke from their labours to wave and cheer for their returning general. The camp had changed dramatically, many of the tents replaced with low wooden buildings with steeply sloped roofs of dried grass. Smoke billowed from chimneys, drifting across the midday sky.

The guard companies formed up by the coldwards gate to welcome Ullsaard, clattering spears on shields and shouting praise. As he rode between the two lines of soldiers, he saw that many bore bandages and other signs of recent wounds. Cosuas waited for him inside the camp, his face heavily tanned and wrinkled. Ullsaard dismounted and they greeted one another wrist to wrist.

"Decided to come back, did you?" said Cosuas. "I thought you'd stay in Askh."

"You have no idea," Ullsaard replied with a rueful shake of the head. "I wondered if I'd ever get to leave."

The two walked side by side towards the centre of the camp-town. Ullsaard noticed a number of women and children; families of legionnaires that would be the first settlers of Mekha. A large barn had been erected behind the duskwards wall and Ullsaard remembered the growing problems with the grain markets.

"How are we for supplies?" he asked.

"Steady, but that's about it," said Cosuas. "I've been trying to stockpile as best as I can, but we're running low on fodder. There's barely a blade of grass for the abada, and getting meat for the kolubrids is proving difficult. I've sent a few companies duskwards along the river to see what they can find."

They continued to discuss the logistics of the growing settlement as they walked along the streets, some of them now fixed with cobbles bedded into the dirt. Water cisterns rose on stilts above the remaining tents and the earth embankment beneath the wall had been replaced with brick foundations.

They reached Ullsaard's pavilion by early evening. He strode inside, thankful to be in the shade after several days' riding from the Greenwater. Everything was as he left it, even the sand trails across the rugs in the main chamber.

"Looks like you've seen some action," he remarked as he slumped into his chair.

"Two Mekhani attacks in the last three weeks," Cosuas told him as he took a seat to Ullsaard's left. "Night attacks, both of them. Last one was three days ago; shame you weren't back just a little earlier."

Ullsaard wasn't sure if this was a genuine regret on Cosuas' part or a veiled accusation. He decided it was the former – Cosuas' threats and accusations were rarely veiled.

"What's the current head count?" Ullsaard asked.

"Not too bad. We've lost just over a thousand to infected wounds, disease, food poisoning and other attrition. About two-and-a-half thousand dead from fighting. Kulrua, Haarin, Lokirna and Menuan have died. I've promoted

Jutiil to camp captain, and Nemenis to First Captain of the Eleventh."

Ullsaard nodded as he absorbed the information. Two of the mute Maasrites entered carrying a chest between them.

"Open it," Ullsaard called out, pushing out of his chair. He crossed the tent as they set the bronze-bound box down on the rugs. Amongst the clutter inside, Ullsaard found the orders Aalun had written. He waved the servants away and returned to his campaign throne.

"Prince Kalmud is unfit to continue in command of the Greenwater campaign," he told Cosuas, tossing the rolled parchment to his fellow general. "Aalun has put you in charge."

Cosuas's eye widened with surprise.

"He's picked me to take over?" A smile spread across Cosuas's face, a rare sight in Ullsaard's experience. Cosuas looked at Ullsaard and the smile faded. "I'm sorry. I know you've had your eye on this command for some time."

Ullsaard waved away the apology.

"Don't feel too bad; Aalun thinks it's your last chance for some real glory." Ullsaard winked at Cosuas. "I'll still be around when your ashes are drifting on the breeze."

"That's true," said Cosuas. He unrolled the parchment and read the contents, one finger following the characters slowly. The finger travelled back a few lines and traced them again. Cosuas looked over at Ullsaard with confusion. "I'm taking the Eleventh and Fifteenth with me?"

"That's right. That'll still leave me with more than thirty thousand legionnaires; more than enough to defend our new town."

"Unless the Mekhani unite again," said Cosuas.

"It'll make the supply situation easier as well," added Ullsaard, ignoring Cosuas' warning. "Just for the winter, I think. Aalun's been talking about raising some new legions from Ersua and Anrair."

"It says here that I'm to tell Kalmud's men not to expect his return. Is it that bad?"

"He'll probably live a good while yet, but he can barely breathe or stand. Unless the Brotherhood have something up their black sleeves we've never seen before, I wouldn't expect to see the prince in armour again."

"And I'm to leave straight away…"

"No point waiting around for winter. You should take a couple of days just to get everything straightened out. Take what you need in terms of equipment and food; I made sure more are on their way right now."

Cosuas was not known for being easily vexed, but he took a few paces back and forth, obviously nonplussed.

"It's an honour, accept it for what it is," Ullsaard told him, guessing what might be occupying his thoughts. "You deserve it."

Cosuas nodded uncertainly and left. Ullsaard sat brooding until it was growing dark outside. He did not like deceiving Cosuas in this way. Yet for all his guilt, the general knew it was the right thing to do. Cosuas was loyal to Lutaar in every muscle and bone, and any hint of dispute would bring him to the king's defence. It was better for Ullsaard and Cosuas that the aging veteran was gone, out of harm's way, when this dispute came to light. He heard the watch captains calling Dusk and pushed himself to his feet. Cosuas was not the only man who had a long march to prepare for; the difference was that Cosuas did not have to hide his plans.

II

Silence filled the pavilion following Ullsaard's announcement that the army was packing camp and leaving to march coldwards. His five First Captains, each a legion commander, looked at each other in amazement.

"Coldwards?" It was Anasind, the burly Enairian First Captain of the Thirteenth that voiced the question they were all thinking. "Where are we going?"

"Somewhere a lot better than Mekha," Ullsaard replied. He did not want to go into the details of the plan; it sounded far too much like lawyer talk for him to be comfortable.

"But what about the town?" asked the Sixteenth's commander, a lean, short man called Luamid.

"Just another camp. We'll take what we can, burn the rest. No point leaving anything for the Mekhani to plunder."

"And the settlers?" This was from Donar, leader of the Fifth. His wife and three children were amongst those that had travelled hotwards to populate the town.

"We'll be travelling with full baggage. Any civilians come with us as far as Okhar. After that, it's up to individual families. They might as well return to their previous homes; we will be going on campaign again later in the year."

"That sounds good. I'm sick of all this sand." This was from Rondin, another sturdy Enairian, who had been born in the same town as Ullsaard. Though Rondin was half his general's age, they got on well.

"Keep this to yourselves for the moment, but if what I have in mind comes to pass, we can look forward to a summer in Salphoria!" Ullsaard said. The First Captains goggled at the significance of this, but Ullsaard held up his hand to silence any further questions. "You have your orders. Dawn tomorrow, I want to be ready to leave. That includes all families and non-legion persons. Let them know that stragglers *will* be left behind."

The First Captains raised their fists in salute and filed out, chattering like fish wives. Jutiil, Twelfth's First Captain, stopped at the curtained doorway.

"The king must think very highly of you, to give you such a command," he said.

Ullsaard could think of nothing to say and merely nodded before waving away the officer. When the First

Captains had gone, the servants came in and began to re-move the furniture, carefully breaking down the panels and rolling up the rugs. Ullsaard plonked himself in his chair, arms folded across his chest. Normally at a time like this he would be out in the camp, ensuring that everything was proceeding properly. Today he could not bring himself to show his face for fear that he might betray the uncer-tainty that had gripped him during the three days since Cosuas had departed. It had been one thing to discuss this whole affair in the comfort and privacy of Aalun's cham-bers; it was another entirely to issue orders that set him on a confrontation with the king.

III

A groom stood close by, holding Blackfang's reins. Dust swirled in the air in a cloud raised by the tramp of thou-sands of marching legionnaires. The last of the companies filed from the town, where smoke was already rising from dozens of fires. The rearmost legionnaires carried kegs of oil with them, which they splashed onto the bridge as they crossed. Jutiil came with a lit torch and handed it to Ull-saard. Normally the general would have been at the head of the column, but he had decided that he would perform this simple act.

It was nothing unusual in itself; Ullsaard had ordered the destruction of bridges before. It was common Askhan practice to deny such infrastructure to the tribes not yet under the sway of the empire. Today was different. Today Ullsaard knew that he was figuratively as well as physically burning a bridge. He and Aalun had set in motion a se-quence of events that was about to become unstoppable. From this point on, there would literally be no way back.

"Would you like me to do that, General?" said Jutiil.

"No," replied Ullsaard.

He took a step and flung the torch out onto the bridge. The oil caught quickly and the flames spread along its length and lapped up the rails. As the wood caught, dark billows swirled within the roiling cloud of dust. Ullsaard watched for a short while, hoping that his ambitions, his career – his whole future – wasn't going up in smoke as well.

He mounted Blackfang and turned to Jutiil.

"I want a full march, no delays. No point wasting time."

TEMPLE

The silence that had so often acted as bedrock for Lakhyri's thoughts now threatened his equilibrium. Each moment seemed inexorably long, a sensation he had not felt since his youth. The silence was symptomatic of his worries; no sound from the masters and no word from his outside agents. Too long had passed since he had instructed Udaan to deal with the issue of the Askhan succession. His usual patience was wearing thin.

The only evidence of this disturbed mindset was the tapping of Lakhyri's finger on the arm of his chair. It was a slow, measured percussion, barely making a sound, but in comparison to his normal immobility, it was the same as another man running around in a screaming panic. Lakhyri's followers sensed his unease and cast worried glances at each other. They too felt the absence of the eulanui; usually so reassuring in their oppressive, otherworldly presence, now strangely distant.

The situation was intolerable. Lakhyri was loath to act, but it was now plain that he needed to take steps to ensure things progressed as outlined in the Great Plan.

He stood, causing a tremor of surprise to flutter through the worshippers around him. He looked at Asirkhyr and Eriekh, who nodded in understanding. Asirkhyr beckoned to a youthful acolyte and the three of them followed their master from the circular hall.

The group ascended the stairs that wound up through the centre of the temple, keeping pace with Lakhyri's slow, measured stride. Upon reaching the upper tier, they turned left through a square archway into a small, roofless room. Above, the dusty air swirled, the sky yellow and sickly. The boy was directed to lie on the stone slab. Eriekh whispered an enchantment, his fingers weaving patterns in the air in front of the adept. The boy's look became glazed and his body relaxed, arms flopping to his sides.

Asirkhyr took a stone box from a shelf on the wall and lifted off the lid. Reaching inside he pulled out a small ingot of gold, which he passed to Eriekh. He took out several small pins, with which he fastened the youth's eyelids open. When this was done, he produced a needle-thin blade, one end wrapped with cured skin for a handle. He gave a similar instrument to the other hierophant, though this had a flattened tip like the nib of a pen.

Asirkhyr turned to the boy on the slab.

With tiny, precise movements of his fingertips, Asirkhyr drew the tiny blade across the surface of the boy's eyes. He carved miniscule lines and coils around the pupils while Eriekh placed the gold into a small clay crucible, which he handed to Lakhyri.

The high priest clasped the crucible in both hands and muttered words of alignment and power. The scars and tattoos across his skin heated, the faded grey ink releasing wisps of smoke that coiled around the high priest's body forming awkward, unnatural sigils. The crucible began to blacken and crack while the gold bubbled.

Dipping his knife-pen into the gold, Eriekh hunched over the boy and allowed the shining liquid to dribble into the fine tracery of lines on the acolyte's eyeballs. The gold flowed in hair-thin curves and cooled to form an intricate web of lines and symbols.

When the gilding was complete and the tools restored to the stone box, Asirkhyr said a few more words and passed his hand over the boy's face. With a panting screech, the youth returned to awareness.

His golden-flecked eyes roved around their sockets, seeing nothing.

"Where am I?" he asked in a shrill, panicked voice.

"What do you see?" said Lakhyri. The high priest's voice soothed the boy's mood and he lay back.

"Clouds. Storm clouds."

"Where do you see them?"

"Over mountains. I see a city, girded by a wall, on the face of a cliff."

"Magilnada," said Asirkhyr, earning himself a piercing glare of annoyance from Lakhyri.

"The city slumbers," the boy continued. "The rains sweep across the slate roofs. There is something else. My eye is drawn to it."

"Do not fight it. Let your eyes see what they must see." Lakhyri's tone was as monotonous as ever but the boy seemed comforted.

"In the mountains, a hidden rabble. I see a cave. Many caves. They bicker and swear at the weather."

"Tell me of Askh," said Lakhyri.

The boy's eyes roved fro a while before focussing again.

"The sun still shines, but the trees bend in the strong wind. I see the precincts of the Brotherhood, and the palace. There is a chariot race on the circuit. There is nothing to see here."

"See what must be seen," said the high priest, leaning closer.

"I fly towards the desert. There is flame and smoke."

"A battle?" asked Lakhyri.

"No battle. The soldiers have left. I see them now, a day's march coldwards of the fires. They are the legions of Askhor."

"Who leads them?"

"A large man rides a grey and black cat. He has a short beard and carries a spear of gold. I count five icons, five bearded faces of gold. They march at speed. Wagons follow them, with women and children on their boards and walking beside. Some are unhappy, others have smiles."

The boy fell silent. At a gesture from Lakhyri, Eriekh removed the pins from the boy's skin, allowing him to blink. The acolyte looked at the three priests as if seeing them for the first time. He reached out towards Lakhyri.

"So bright," he whispered. He met Lakhyri's cold gaze. "Such a web of colours."

"You may go," said the high priest. "Send another acolyte to us."

The youth nodded and left with a glazed look and a half-smile.

"What does this mean, master?" asked Eriekh.

"I do not know. Perhaps Udaan can give us some answers."

ASKHOR
Late Autumn, 209th Year of Askh

I

An Askhan column on the march was the epitome of efficiency. From Enair to Maasra, every legionnaire and officer was ruthlessly inculcated with the routine of war. Whether the army was a small patrol of five hundred men or, as Ullsaard now led, five full legions numbering more than thirty thousand, daily life was always the same.

At the call of Dawnwatch the men would breakfast, feed the animals and begin to break down the camp. Every company would begin by dismantling their tents and stowing them with the baggage. Each was assigned a sector of the camp wall to dismantle. The guard companies, a tenth of the army, stood ready to respond to any threat while the rest of the force carried out its tasks. A legionnaire worked in his armour and was forbidden from ever being more than ten paces from his shield, helmet and spear. Infractions were always applied to the whole company – usually in the form of extra rotations on the most demeaning duties such as digging and filling the latrines, or extra stints on the guard duty just before dawn, known as Gravewatch. This meant that the legionnaires were always watching out for the discipline of their comrades, and any who brought the company into disrepute could expect a severe beating from his fellows.

Breaking camp took two hours, half an Askhan watch, after which the whole force would be ready to move out. Like all other duties, the task of vanguard and rearguard was cycled through the legions and each would move out in its appointed place, their baggage gathered in a single train at the centre of the column. Kolubrid-riding scouts fanned out ahead and to either side of the advancing column, alert for danger.

The army marched without pause, through the rest of Dawnwatch, Low Watch and Noonwatch, ten Askhan hours. At the prescribed pace the army would cover twenty-five Askhan miles over this time, a mile being one-tenth the distance a legion could cover in a full watch. Ullsaard pushed his troops hard each day, so that by the time High Watch came about in mid-afternoon they had instead covered forty miles. When High Watch was called the scouts reported suitable camping sites and the legion would erect their temporary town over the course of the next four hours, until Duskwatch was rung in. By this time, the tents would be erected, organised by company and legion; wooden walls were built, either from locally cut wood if available or timber brought with the baggage if lumber was sparse, with ditches around them. The cook fires would be burning, the transportable forge lit and the night duties detailed out to the companies.

Families and other non-combatants that were often left behind by the pace of the march caught up with their soldiers in the evening and made their own rough camp outside the walls – no closer than a bowshot to ensure their tents and carts did not provide cover to an attacking foe.

In the event of enemy action, the gates would not be opened for them, so these folk camped nearby woods if they could, which would allow them to flee if they were set upon during the night. Wives and children of legionnaires that had served for many years were no less disciplined than their husbands and fathers, and the life in the civilian camp was a strange mirror of the military routine, with families from the same companies and legions sticking together, organising their own food and sentries. Ullsaard had always marvelled at this spirit, a true demonstration of the discipline and organisation that bound the Askhan people with their empire.

From Duskwatch to Howling the legionnaires were at their leisure, food being served company by company, repairs made to equipment, the animals foddered. Small amounts of beer were allowed, carefully rationed by the captains – drunkenness was punishable by death. Depending on the locale, companies would also be sent to forage in the surrounding area, and often the kolubrid companies would set out to hunt for fresh meat.

Any infractions from the day would be dealt with by the officers, and the men would be sent to their blankets at Howling, save for those companies that were called for guard duty. These guards spent one watch patrolling the walls and garrisoning the gate towers while their companions slept. Midnight Watch and Gravewatch passed the night until Dawnwatch when the whole machine set to action again.

Hour by hour, watch by watch, day by day, Ullsaard's legions marched coldwards towards Askh. Even when they had crossed into the more civilised lands of Okhar, the routine did not change. Though there was little threat of attack, the ritual of life on the march was adhered to. Under hot sun, through driving rains and gales, a legion would always be the same, the familiarity of the life bringing the men together in bonds surer than simple friendship.

Ullsaard kept to himself for much of the time, either in the vanguard or at the head of the main column as his daily mood took him. Some mornings he woke up eager and he wanted to be at the forefront of the advance, every step bringing him closer to realising his ambition of a campaign against Salphoria. Other days he woke filled with nerves, worried by the prospect of dispute with King Lutaar. On those days he lost himself in the daily matters of his army and stayed with the bulk of the legions, discussing the running of the army with his First Captains. It was easy to drown out the doubts with endless questions about supply, punishments, promotions and the other distractions of a commander.

It was a source of some pride for Ullsaard that none of his officers questioned his orders as they continued towards Askhor. It was another worry of his that something might happen to test that loyalty and he did his best to treat his First Captains well, gently reminding them individually and as a group that he had their best interests at heart.

II

Forty-seven days of hard marching brought Ullsaard back to the Askhor Gap and the Wall. He could have reached the border sooner, but had chosen to avoid the main road along the Greenwater, instead heading almost directly coldwards from Mekha before turning dawnwards to cross the Greenwater between Paalun and Narun. They had entered the foothills of the Askhor Mountains and marched coldwards again, coming upon the Askhor Gap across a wide ridge that extended out to duskwards from the foot of the mountains.

Ullsaard's feelings on seeing the Wall were mixed, just as they had been in the summer. Beyond was Askh, which held the key to his future, for good or bad. From his vantage point he stared across the flat plain of the Askhor Gap and saw nothing amiss. Lines of carts moved along the road, meaning that the gate was open. If Lutaar had suspected anything, he would surely have closed the gate and stopped Ullsaard from approaching the city.

Feeling a little more confident, Ullsaard summoned his First Captains. He tried hard to keep any sign of his nerves from his demeanour, hoping to exude confidence and make his subordinates believe that they were perfectly entitled to march into Askhor whenever they pleased.

"I'm going to split the column once we are through the gate," he told them. "Donar, I want the Fifth to make their camp ten miles inside the gate. There's a large hill hotwards of the road that you should use. The rest of the legions are coming with me to Askh. We should be there in two days' time. We'll set up camp and I'll go to the city."

"Wouldn't it be easier to keep the legions outside the Wall rather than marching them in and back out again?" asked Jutiil.

"Winter's almost here," Ullsaard replied. "We'll not be going anywhere until spring, so we might as well enjoy the shelter of Askhor."

There were nods of agreement. Ullsaard sent the commanders back to their legions and pulled himself up onto Blackfang's back. He sat there for some time while the order of march was barked out to the companies. He stared at the Wall, arms crossed, part of him dreading that the gates would be closed against him when he approached; part of him hoping for the same thing because that would mean it wasn't his fault if he turned around and headed back to Mekha.

Ten abreast, the army wound down the side of the ridge towards the road. Seeing the approaching legions, bearing their polished icons, crests on their helms, shields gleaming, the people on the road made way, beating their abada to pull their carts out into the fields, shooing families from the legionnaires' path.

Ullsaard smiled to himself, pleased with the conduct of

his men. As he rode along their lines he saw that were all in step, spears held rigid, backs straight. They knew they marched into Askhor, many of them for the first time. He could feel pride emanating from rank after rank, their foot-falls a thunderous beat as they headed for the gate.

Ahead the gatehouse loomed across the road, still open to traffic. Ullsaard saw men gathering on the ramparts, their speartips shining against the overcast sky. For a mo-ment he thought they were mustering to defend the gate and he reined Blackfang to a halt, suddenly terrified. He expected to hear the splashing of water and grinding of gears at any time; to see the square of light between the towers narrow and disappear.

Anasind fell out from his company and approached, marching stiffly across the road.

"I guess they want to see what real soldiers look like, eh?" he said, looking towards the Wall.

"I think you guess right," replied Ullsaard, hiding his re-lief when the standards of the vanguard passed into the shadow of the gatehouse without incident. "Not since Nemtun's triumphs have these walls seen legions return-ing from battle."

"Do you think we'll be receiving honours, General?" asked Anasind.

"What's that?"

"I know you've been quiet about why we've come here, but we think we know what you're up to, General."

"You do?" Ullsaard studied Anasind's face for some sign of disapproval. There was none. "And what do you think that is?"

"You've organised us city honours, we reckon. You know, like legions used to get after a conquest."

Ullsaard remembered the tradition, though no city parade had been held in more than twenty years. Victorious legions were granted leave to enter the city, march along the Royal Way, circle the palace and leave. At the palace, the king would hang honours on the standards of the legions, which would be carried proudly for the rest of their existence.

Honours were the last thing Ullsaard expected from Lutaar, though perhaps next year if they did well in Salphoria the king would recognise their efforts.

"We'll see," Ullsaard told Anasind. The First Captain winked knowingly and headed back to his subordinates.

With mixed hope and fear, Ullsaard urged Blackfang into a trot and headed towards the gate.

III

Ullsaard decided to walk into Askh, leaving his legions to make camp a few miles outside the city walls. Undoubtedly word would have already been taken to the king of the presence of so many soldiers, so Ullsaard hurried up the road with Luamid, Rondin and fifty legionnaires from the Thirteenth in tow.

As with crossing the Wall, their entry into Askh was not barred in any way. Sentries at the gate stared incredulously at the general who a season earlier had been welcomed with a full parade, now hastening along the Royal Way with a relative handful of men. Ullsaard could imagine the rumours already spreading through the city; the camp was clearly visible from the road and walls, and such an appearance was sure to cause comment.

Though there was no cheering crowd this time, Ullsaard felt he was the centre of attention as he marched up the mound toward the a palace, garbed in his campaign gear. Workers fixing walls and roofs downed their tools to stare, drovers allowed their herds to wander while they gazed at the imposing general and his entourage. Ullsaard could see the street vendors gossiping with their customers, shielding their mouths with their hands while their eyes fixed on him. Amongst them he saw the black robes of the Brotherhood, their eyes watchful in the shadows of their hoods. He did not glance behind, but fancied that a growing number of people were following, drawn by the spectacle.

He wondered for a moment if he should stop and address the forming crowd. It occurred to him that the sympathy of the common people would be no bad thing in the dispute he knew was swiftly coming. He dismissed the thought. He wanted to present himself directly to the king, under the full right of the law, not arrive as some rabble-rouser.

He had wondered how he would feel, this close to confronting Lutaar. He realised that he was enjoying the thrill of it; he felt the same way he did before a battle. Every step he took closer to the palace filled him with more confidence. The difficult part had been done: deciding on this course of action. Setting the scheme in motion had been the hard part, all he had to do now was hold his nerve and tell the king what he wanted.

It was what he deserved, as Aalun had pointed out. More than that, it was his *right* by Askhan law. As they turned onto the road encircling the palace, Ullsaard conceded that while he had been a little underhanded in bringing his legions here, their presence should be no argument against his legal claim.

His thoughts were broken by a shout from behind. He looked over his shoulder to see that several hundred people had gathered on the Royal Way no more than a spear's cast behind him. He sensed some hostility, and could see anger in the eyes of those at the front of the mob. Black hoods moved through the crowd, no doubt whispering words of encouragement.

"I don't like this," said Luamid. The First Captain put his hand to the hilt of his sword, but Ullsaard grabbed his wrist to prevent him drawing his weapon.

"Let us just get to the palace quickly," said the general, picking up the pace of his long strides.

Around him the legionnaires looked confused, as people

gathered under the trees lining the road, their arms crossed in disapproval, scowls on their faces.

They reached the gate and found a company of palace guards barring their path. They stood with spears held to salute, shields lowered, but there was no doubt that they had been ordered to stop Ullsaard from entering. Though he had hoped that such a thing would not come to pass, he had been prepared for this eventuality.

"Wait here," Ullsaard told his men as he pulled a roll of parchment from his belt.

He strode up to the captain of the guard and thrust the scroll towards him.

"These are my orders, directing me to report to Prince Aalun as soon as I reach the city," Ullsaard growled. "If you attempt to impede me or my men, you will be disobeying a command from one of the Blood. The penalty for such an offence is death by hanging."

The captain did not spare a glance at the parchment. The officer looked away from Ullsaard's fierce stare and stepped back.

"Let them pass," he muttered.

Ullsaard strode straight towards the lines of legionnaires, who bumped into one another and trod on each other's feet as they parted before the general. Taking his lead, Rondin and Luamid waved the bodyguard onward and they plunged through the widening gap made by their leader. A few of Ullsaard's men jeered and snarled at the palace guards until Rondin silenced them.

Boots and sandals slapped on stone as they jogged up the stairs. The doors to the palace had been closed when they were at the bottom, but opened up as Ullsaard reached the upper steps. The widening doors revealed a worried-looking Noran. He raced across the hall and grabbed Ullsaard by the arm.

"What by Askhos's hairy balls are you thinking?" Noran demanded.

"I am here to claim my rights," said Ullsaard, shaking off his friend's grip. Noran followed him inside, like a dog at its master's side.

"Your rights?" said the herald. "What right have you got to claim a change to the succession?"

Ullsaard stopped on the spot, Rondin almost walking into him. The general rounded on Noran.

"What did you say?"

"I warned you not to get caught up in politics, but you wouldn't listen. You just had to back Aalun's claim, didn't you?"

"I don't understand. Tell me what's happened!"

"Prince Aalun has told the king that he has your support to be named heir, and that your legions stand ready to swear loyalty to him and him alone."

"He's done what?" Ullsaard's bellow echoed from the corridor walls as he grabbed the front of Noran's tunic and hauled the herald to the tips of his toes. The herald wrested himself free and straightened out his clothes with an indignant look.

"Prince Aalun says that your legions are loyal to him and support his claim to be made heir over Kalmud."

Ullsaard turned away and stalked down the length of the corridor. The serving staff scurried from his path like mice bolting from a cat, disappearing through archways and ducking into doorways hidden by wall hangings. The clatter of the general's bodyguard followed him up the hall as he thrust open the door at the far end.

In the hall beyond he was confronted by more legionnaires, more than a company of them. Three senior Brothers regarded him through the eye slits of their faceless masks. They stood between the general and the doors leading towards the throne room. No words were spoken, but their intent was clear. Ullsaard cut to his right, quickening his pace even more, and headed towards the royal apartments, his men and Noran jogging after him.

"Where are you going?" Noran asked breathlessly.

"To find Aalun!" Ullsaard snarled.

IV

The prince's apartment was in tumult. The door was opened wide.

"Wait here," Ullsaard told his bodyguard before he marched in, Noran tagging along behind. Every chamber and hall and corridor bustled with servants filling chests and sacks with Aalun's possessions. Ullsaard grabbed one of the men.

"Where is your master?" he demanded. The servant waved uncertainly towards the rear rooms. Ullsaard let go of him and continued down the main passageway, glancing through arches and doorways for a sign of Aalun. He found the prince in the windowed rotunda facing the gardens. Aalun stood with one foot up on a bench, staring out of a window.

"What have you said?" barked Ullsaard as he strode into the room. Aalun turned sharply, surprised.

"You made it!" he said with obvious delight. "I knew you would come."

Ullsaard stopped just a pace from the prince, fists clenched. Aalun held his ground. The two stared at each other.

"I am still a Prince of the Blood," Aalun said quietly.

Ullsaard met his gaze for a while longer before stepping back, averting his eyes. Aalun sat down with a long sigh.

"Those cretinous governors have turned on me," he said. "Despite promises and bargains, they've sided with my father and called for my exile for disputing the succession. Even Murian! I don't know what my father has offered them for their support, but they've all fallen into line."

"And why is it that I find my path barred by Brothers and legionnaires?" said Ullsaard.

"My father does not want to grant you an audience," replied the prince. "If you cannot make your petition in person, you cannot claim your personal campaign. Now that you have your legions here, things might be a bit different."

"I don't see how," said Ullsaard. "The king has obviously decided to call our bluff. There's not a lot we can do now."

"Don't be so defeatist, Ullsaard. This is just a setback. We'll be able to turn the governors around. It will just take some time, that is all."

"But you are leaving now?" asked Noran.

Aalun looked past Ullsaard, seeing the herald for the first time.

"I am exiled," the prince said quietly. "Banned not only from the city but from all lands within the Wall. I've wrangled and argued just to remain here long enough for Ullsaard to arrive. If I stay any longer I will invite even more trouble. No, it will be best to leave for the time being and let things cool down. We will regroup in Nalanor and consider our options."

"And what is to happen to me?" said Ullsaard.

"Well, my father's edict does not name you, but it does extend to all so-called conspirators and agents of mine. I think the implication is clear."

"Exile? I'll lose my command. I'll lose everything!"

"That will not happen," Aalun assured, grabbing Ullsaard by both shoulders. "If we stick together, we can still make this happen."

Ullsaard tried to understand this turnaround in events. Less than an hour ago he had been steeling himself to make his claim to lead a campaign into Salphoria. Now he was on the brink of ruin. The king would take everything he had: his generalship, his legions, his lands, his...

"My family!" He pulled away from Aalun and headed for the door.

"They are safe!" Aalun called after him. The general swung back to face the prince.

"How do you know?"

"I feared my father would use them against you, so I had your wives moved to one of the houses I own in the city. We can take them with us when we leave."

"Where? Which house? What about my sons?"

"Ullnaar is protected by the sanctuary of the colleges," Aalun said. "Jutaar is still in the guard of Allon, far away. As for Urikh, nobody knows where he is. Somewhere in Enair, it seems. There is nothing to worry about."

Noran spoke from the doorway.

"There is no reason to believe the king would harm them. Can I speak with you for a moment, Ullsaard?"

There was something in the tone of his friend's voice, urgent and insistent. With a glance toward Aalun, who nodded his assent, Ullsaard followed Noran out of the apartment into the corridor. Luamid and Rondin had positioned the bodyguard at either end of the passage, where several harassed officials were demanding to be let past. The First Captains saw Ullsaard leaving the apartment and started towards him, but he held up a hand to stop them.

"This is not your fault," Noran said. The herald was quiet but firm. "The king's dispute is with Aalun. Why would you ever think you could change the succession?"

"I didn't come here to change the succession!" hissed Ullsaard. "I just want to state my right to lead my legions on a campaign of my choosing."

"You want to do what? What madness is this?"

"It's not madness, it is my right. Aalun explained it to me. I came to Askh to petition the king to accept my right to command a campaign against Salphoria."

"Oh." Noran seemed disappointed that his friend had not been a conspirator in the quiet but bitter power struggle between Aalun and his father. "Oh! Aalun has played you for a fool. The king thinks you are here to enforce his claim to the succession. You should send Lutaar your promise that you have no intention of doing that. Though there may be some repercussions, there is no reason to be caught up any more than you already are."

"I can't abandon Aalun," Ullsaard said. "A fine way to repay the favour he has shown me, to let him be thrown out in this way."

"Don't get involved in something this big," warned Noran. "You were right before, it is not in your nature."

"Perhaps I need to make it part of my nature. It seems to me that service and loyalty are not enough to earn a man the rewards and recognition he deserves. Sometimes he has to demand them."

"Don't do anything hasty. Take Aalun and your family out of the city. I'll have a nose around to see what I can find out and I will come to you tomorrow. Promise me you won't do anything rash."

"Promise you? Why didn't you send me a warning of how Aalun was using my name? Why did you wait until I was at the palace?"

"I did not know that you were planning to come to Askh, of all things. Aalun kept that secret to himself. When messengers arrived two days ago that you were at the Wall, the whole palace was in uproar and that was the first I knew of it. What do you plan to do now?"

"Just as both you and Aalun suggest. I'll leave Askh with the prince, and I'll wait for you in camp. I am sure we can work this out."

Noran looked unconvinced.

"Your plan is to wait and see what happens?"

"Just for the time being. If need be, I'll withdraw my legions beyond the Wall and return alone to speak with Lutaar. Perhaps he'll be more reasonable if he doesn't feel threatened."

"You've already marched here with an army, that's a clear signal of intent, my friend. But you may be right. Maybe."

"Do you have a better suggestion? I would be happy to hear it."

"That depends on what it is you want to achieve."

"I want to lead my legions on a worthy campaign, not fuck about in the desert chasing savages. I want what is mine by right."

Noran pursed his lips, something he was prone to when agitated. "Then I have no ideas for you."

"I'll see you tomorrow," said Ullsaard. "I hope you bring me good news."

Noran nodded and turned away, stepping quickly through the legionnaires. At a wave from Ullsaard, Luamid and Rondin approached.

"We are going to form an escort for Prince Aalun," the general told them. "I don't like the look of that mob that was forming outside. The Brotherhood are up to something. Don't let anyone in or out of this area."

Rondin saluted and turned away, leaving Ullsaard with Luamid. The First Captain of the Sixteenth smiled ruefully.

"No honours then, General?"

Ullsaard couldn't help but smile as well.

"Not at the moment, Captain," he replied. Luamid saluted sharply and headed off towards the other end of the passage.

Ullsaard walked back into the prince's chambers. Travel chests and boxes were piling around the door. Aalun was in a banqueting hall, directing his servants to remove the wall hangings. Ullsaard called out to him.

"Is your armour packed?"

Aalun nodded and pointed to a box in the hallway.

"Take that and one chest of clothes," said Ullsaard.

"What do you mean? I can't live with just one chest of clothes."

"If all goes well, you can send for more of your gear later. If it doesn't... Well, a change of clothes is going to be the least of your problems."

V

It was two hours into High Watch when the prince was ready to leave. The legionnaires formed up, thirty in front, twenty behind, with Aalun, Ullsaard and the two First Captains between. Several porters carried three chests between them – Ullsaard had relented slightly and allowed the prince to bring a number of maps, scrolls and other important documents from his library.

"What about Meerina?" Ullsaard asked Aalun when all were gathered outsider the royal apartments.

"Who?" Aalun was distracted, obviously unhappy at the circumstances of his departure.

"Your wife, Princess Meerina," said Ullsaard. "Is she not coming with you?"

Aalun considered the possibility for a moment and then shook his head.

"No, I think not," said the prince. "As tempting as it is to have her around to fuck, I could do without her fawning and gossiping. She'll be safe enough staying here."

At a nod from Ullsaard, the group set off.

They marched along the halls of the palace without hindrance, and the doors were opened for them. Outside, the guard company still waited, their captain eyeing Ullsaard sullenly as he passed, though he raised a fist in salute to Aalun. Ullsaard bit back his anger and let the insult pass.

At the palace gates, it was a different matter. A sizeable crowd had gathered outside, several hundred strong, and at the sight of Ullsaard's entourage they erupted with boos and shouts. The gates swung inwards and the frontmost members of the crowd were thrust a few steps into the palace grounds. They staggered to a stop in front of the shields and spears of the legionnaires, suddenly hesitant.

A Brother emerged from the mass, his pale face hidden by the great fold of his hood. He raised his arm, black sleeve falling back from a bony hand, and pointed accusingly at Ullsaard.

"Traitor," the Brother said in a matter-of-fact tone. The crowd's baying increased in volume.

"Stand back for the Blood!" Luamid shouted above the noise, but the crowd would not give way. He looked to Ullsaard for instructions.

At that moment, a stone flew over the heads of the mob and crashed into the brick courtyard inside the gate. Other missiles – eggs, vegetables, stones and clay pots – sailed through the air. The legionnaires closed protectively towards their charges, raising their shields. Small objects clattered and bounced around Ullsaard.

"What are you waiting for?" Aalun snarled. "Clear a path!"

Ullsaard looked at the wall of angry faces and heard the jeers. He could still see the black cowls of the Brotherhood amongst their number, and slowly the mob was creeping closer, pushed by the weight of those at the back.

Ullsaard tapped Luamid on the shoulder.

"Do it," said the general. "Use your spears if you have to."

Luamid gave a nod of resignation and drew his sword.

"Legionnaires of the Thirteenth!" he bellowed. "Clear a path for your general and prince!"

Having been pelted with rocks and filth, the soldiers were happy to oblige. With a throaty roar, they lowered their shields and aimed the tips of their spears towards the mob. The protestors at the front backed away, fear in their eyes. Urged on by Luamid, the legionnaires pressed towards the crowd, advancing slowly and in step.

"Lock shields!" ordered the First Captain. The front rank of legionnaires followed the command, tightening their formation with the ominous clatter of shields being drawn together. "Full march!"

With every pace, the soldiers let out a shout. As those at the forefront of the mob turned to run, they found their path blocked by more people pushing towards the gates.

The people coming through saw what was happening and tried to stop, panic rippling back through the crowd.

The Brother who had pointed at Ullsaard disappeared from sight into the mass. A moment later an old man stepped up, puffing out his chest.

"We're citizens of Askh!" he declared boldly. "You would not raise your weapons against us."

The small phalanx continued on regardless of the protest. A legionnaire at the left of the line thrust his spear, taking the old man in the gut. He fell with a cry and suddenly the murmurs of disquiet turned to screams of fear. As easily as the speartip had pierced the man's stomach, the knot of legionnaires drove into the mob. Following behind, Ullsaard splashed through puddles of blood and had to step over contorted bodies and the writhing wounded.

Like a flock of birds startled by a hunter, the crowd scattered, running in all directions as the legionnaires pushed relentlessly ahead. The path to the gate was clear and Luamid gave the order to break shields and advance at the double. Trotting along the Royal Way, Ullsaard was shocked by how quiet the city had become. Fearful faces peered from doorways and windows as the soldiers ran along the street.

"Where are my family?" Ullsaard asked Aalun.

"The Grain Way, at the bottom of the hill," said the prince. "It is a house with a red wall and a mural of Askhos conquering the Maasrites."

"Did you hear that? You know where that is?" Ullsaard said to Rondin. The First Captain nodded. "Take twenty men and escort my wives to the camp."

"Yes, General," replied Rondin.

"Luia, the dark-haired one, may give you trouble. Tie her up and drag her if you have to."

"I will, General," Rondin said with a grin, though Ullsaard did not feel like smiling.

Rondin peeled away with his contingent, vanishing along a side street. The main group followed the Royal Way down towards the main city gate. Wondering whether gates would be closed against him had become a recent habit for Ullsaard, and he was pleased to see that his exit from the city was not barred. The general called for his men to slow to a march.

"We're an escort of the Blood, not fugitives," he growled to the legionnaires. "Let's bloody act like it."

Keeping step, Ullsaard and his soldiers marched out of the gate with straight backs and shouldered spears. The guards on the towers to either side looked down with surprise as the entourage passed beneath them, but no challenge was called. A dozen paces later Ullsaard was out of Askh and on the road duskwards.

He called the group to a halt half a mile from the gate, where he waited anxiously until he saw the shields of Rondin's men emerge from the city. They pulled a hand-cart on which Luia, Meliu and Allenya were sitting, amongst piles of hurriedly bundled clothes and small boxes. The legionnaires slowed and the cart trundled to a stop next to Ullsaard.

"Hello, husband," said Allenya. Though her expression was stern, Ullsaard could see amusement glittering in her eyes. "It is a good time to get some country air."

"Yes, it is. The country in autumn can be beautiful.

"You have caused quite a fuss."

"Sorry, my love," Ullsaard replied, eyes downcast. "I didn't mean for this to happen."

"Of course you did not, husband," Allenya said softly. "I am sure you will sort everything out for the best."

"I will."

VI

Ullsaard said nothing as he heartily attacked the venison on his plate. It had been a terrible day and he was happy to occupy his mouth with eating rather than talking. Ullsaard had donated his pavilion to Prince Aalun, and had taken Rondin's tent instead. The First Captain had moved his gear in with Anasind without complaint, though Ullsaard would find some way to reward them both for the sacrifice.

Allenya did her best to keep the mood around the table congenial, talking about everything and nothing: the prices of clothes in the market; hiring a new kitchen maid; the unseasonal warm weather; the embroidery on the walls of the pavilion; the quality of the meat. She did not chatter, but spoke quietly and calmly about these things, as if they were back in their palace apartment.

Meliu picked idly at her food, avoiding Ullsaard's gaze. Her eyes were still rimmed red from crying. Luia stared daggers at her husband throughout the meal, and did not eat. Ullsaard was not sure what she was more annoyed by – their eviction from the city, or the fact that Ullsaard had ordered his legionnaires to escort her tame wrestler from the camp. He had also instructed Anasind to quietly pass the word around the army that any man found consorting with Luia would be flogged and beheaded; the last thing he needed was to waste time worrying about the disruption that would be caused by his wayward wife's sexual appetites.

When they were done, the Maasrites silently entered and cleared the table, bringing wine and water in earthenware jugs. At this, Meliu brightened slightly and insisted on pouring Ullsaard's drink. He noticed her measure of wine to water was very generous and suspected that she was trying to get him drunk.

He drank sparingly, wanting to keep his head clear, and said nothing, until even Allenya's supply of gossip and observations ran dry. The tent walls flapped in the wind and ropes creaked outside. The call of the sentries split the night air and the bell sounded the third hour of Duskwatch.

241

"This is ridiculous!" snapped Luia, standing.

"Sit down," Ullsaard said. She stopped, sneered and was about to turn away when Ullsaard growled. "Sit down!"

She locked eyes with him, and he stared back, daring her to speak out of turn. She broke from his unflinching glare and sat down with a pout, thudding her fists on the table. Ullsaard took a moment to calm before he spoke.

"I did not intend for this to happen," he said. "I thought that a campaign in Salphoria would be the best way to guarantee the future of this family. The new lands, th–"

"Liar," said Luia. "You were not thinking about this family at all. You were thinking about the glory and prestige you would have."

"Glory and prestige that would be a legacy for my sons," Ullsaard answered coolly, forcing himself to keep his temper in the face of his wife's scorn. "The name Ullsaard kon Salphoria would carry more weight than Ullsaard ad Enair."

"A title?" Luia laughed. "You think you can battle your way into the nobility?"

"Why not? Every noble family name in Askhor was once just a normal family name. Wealth, prestige, these things can be grown over generations. History does not forget the names of great men. Perhaps your ambitions for your granddaughter would not be so far-fetched if her grandfather was known as the conqueror of Salphoria. That's a claim that could entice even the Blood into a union."

Luia opened her mouth to argue and stopped. She bit her lip and tapped her fingers together as she considered this. Then her expression darkened again.

"That would have been well and good, but all you have managed to achieve is shame, and your name will be remembered with ignominy. What sort of legacy is that?"

"All is not yet lost," said Ullsaard. He took another sip of the strong wine. "When we have found out what Noran can tell us, I will ask him to take a message to the king. I will offer my deepest apologies and regret for the turn of events, and ask for his forgiveness. In my experience, the Blood find humility hard to resist. I'll swear my oaths of loyalty again, at his feet if necessary, and vow to uphold Kalmud's right to become king."

"You would distance yourself from Aalun?" asked Allenya. "He has been your ally and patron for a long time. He will not take such a move kindly."

"Sister, you are right," said Luia, and her eyes were distant, narrowed in calculation. "The king is your enemy for the moment, but he will not live forever. When he is gone, what power will Kalmud have to protect his succession against Aalun? It is more likely that Aalun will become the next king, and you would be better to have him as a friend than an enemy."

Ullsaard lowered his head into his hands and massaged his temples.

"I feel like I've opened a box of snakes and I don't know which one to grab," he muttered. "What was I thinking?"

"It does not matter," said Allenya. She walked around the table and laid an arm across Ullsaard's shoulders. "What has happened cannot be changed. Right or wrong, we are where we are."

He put an arm around her waist and pulled her closer, planting a kiss on her belly, feeling her soft woollen dress on his lips. Allenya stroked his hair.

"Nothing can be done until the morning," she said. "Why not get some rest?"

This seemed like a good idea. Ullsaard took Allenya's hand in his and stood up.

"I have a few duties around camp," he said. "I'll be back soon."

At that moment, a captain from the guard company announced his presence outside the tent. Ullsaard told the man to enter.

"General, Noran the herald is at the camp gates," the soldier announced.

"So soon? Let him into the camp and send word to Prince Aalun of his arrival."

"Yes, General," the captain said with a brief salute before hurrying out of the tent.

"This cannot be good," Ullsaard said, sitting at the table.

Allenya summoned a servant and instructed him to prepare hot tea.

"I am sure Noran would like something to drink," she said, sitting opposite Ullsaard.

"Always the perfect hostess," the general replied. "Perhaps I should have you with me all the time."

"You are not dragging us around on your campaigns like common camp followers," said Luia. "You may choose to live in ditches, but I will not."

Meliu gave a sob and buried her hands in her arms.

"This is so awful," she moaned. She lifted her tear-streaked face. "Where will we go? What about my darling Ullnaar? He'll be all alone! You've made us the mockery of all Askh."

Ullsaard had no time to reply. The tent door swirled open and Noran strode in. Behind came two women, one about twenty years of age, her belly swelling with child, the other a little older.

"Neerita!" squealed Meliu, launching from her chair towards the pregnant woman. Ullsaard's youngest wife swamped Noran's with a hug and a shower of kisses.

"What is g—" began Ullsaard. He was silenced by Noran's fist catching him flush on the chin.

"You fucking selfish cunt!" the herald raged while Luia laughed behind Ullsaard. "Of all the pig-headed, fucking stupid things you have done, this is the worst! You utter m—"

Ullsaard's return punch caught Noran square between the eyes, knocking him to his backside.

"Don't ever raise your hand to me, friend or not," Ullsaard said, rubbing his chin.

Noran blinked with disbelief, slightly cross-eyed. Ullsaard reached out and helped Noran to his feet.

"Let us leave you two alone," said Allenya, hustling Meliu, Neerita and Anriit towards the back of the tent where canvas screens had been hung to create separate rooms. Luia lingered a while longer, hoping that Noran would hit her husband again. When it became clear that this would not happen, she huffed disapprovingly and joined her sisters.

"Perhaps you should start again," suggested Ullsaard. He lifted the wine jug and Noran nodded and sat down at the table. Noran scrunched his nose a few times.

"Is it broken?" the herald asked.

"Not even bleeding, you weakling," Ullsaard replied, placing a mug of undiluted wine in front of Noran. "Drink this and tell me what's happening. Why so upset?"

Noran took a large swig from the mug and fixed Ullsaard with a resigned stare.

"Because I brought you to Askh on the prince's orders, Lutaar has accused me of being in league with you and Aalun. Members of the Brotherhood came to my apartment, but my servants held them off until we managed to get out through the window. Imagine it!"

"I'd say you've had plenty of experience of hasty window retreats over the years," chuckled Ullsaard.

"This isn't fucking funny."

"No, it isn't. Sorry. Carry on."

Noran drank some more before continuing.

"There is not a lot more to say. We slipped out of the palace grounds, managed to pick up a few things from Neerita's old house and then left the city before the gates closed at Howling. Here I am."

"Did you manage to find anything out before you were chased off?"

"Yes, but it would be better to tell you and Aalun together. Where is the prince?"

"Let's go and see him." Ullsaard downed the contents of his cup and Noran did the same.

As they left the tent, Ullsaard beckoned to one of the legionnaires on guard with a crooked finger.

"Ask First Captain Jutiil if he'll give up his tent for Herald Noran and his family. He can share with Luamid."

The legionnaire headed off into the flame-broken night.

"That's kind of you," said Noran as the pair set off in the opposite direction, towards the centre of camp.

"It's the most I could do," Ullsaard joked. "I do feel partly responsible for your predicament."

"Partly?" Noran's voice rose an octave with incredulity.

"You're the one who decided to flee the Brotherhood. You could have stayed and explained what happened."

"With everything that's been going on these last couple of days, I panicked, all right? No one in the palace is open to reason and explanation at the moment. And that *is* your fault."

"More Aalun's than mine. He started all of this."

"And without you going along with him, he wouldn't have dared be so bold."

Ullsaard was too tired to argue any more. When they came to the grand pavilion, Aalun was sitting in Ullsaard's campaign chair dictating a letter to a scribe. He looked up, waved the attendant away and signalled for Ullsaard and Noran to approach. Ullsaard bit back a comment about being invited into his own home and took up a stool in front of the prince. Noran did the same and briefly recounted what he had told Ullsaard. Aalun looked at Noran with sympathy.

"My father's unreasonableness about this whole affair is beyond comprehension," said the prince.

"You don't understand your father's 'unreasonableness', not yet, Prince," replied Noran. He looked at Ullsaard. "He has instructed the Brotherhood to declare you traitor to the empire. I heard about the trouble you had trying to leave. Now the Brothers are dragging your name through the dirt across the city, from the hill to the goat quarter."

Ullsaard absorbed this without comment and Noran continued.

"On top of that, messages were sent to Nemtun more than a week ago. He has gathered two legions from Okhar, will pick up another in Nalanor and is marching here right now."

"More than a week ago?" said Aalun. "That's before Ullsaard even entered Askhor."

"Someone must have sent word," said Ullsaard. "I kept from the main routes, but you can't avoid everybody when you're marching with that many men."

"It's a rare rumour that travels faster than a legion," said Aalun. "And when it arrived, I heard nothing of it."

"Probably the Brotherhood again," said Noran. "Some reckon they used trained crows to carry messages between the precincts."

"It doesn't matter," said Ullsaard. "Nemtun surely knows he can't threaten us with two less legions, and untested ones at that."

"That's the other bad news," said Noran. "I spoke to a clerk in the treasury, who confided in me a letter sent to Kulrua in Maasra. It authorised the governor to release monies from the imperial vaults for the hiring of Nemurian mercenaries."

"How much money?" asked Aalun.

"At the going rate, enough for five thousand at least."

Ullsaard let out an explosive breath of air.

"Five thousand Nemurians? Nemtun needn't bother with his legions."

"But they'll take time to get here," said Aalun. "Nemtun will probably be trying to keep us here until the mercenaries arrive."

"I don't think I've ever heard of so many Nemurians in one place," said Ullsaard, unable to shake the picture of rank upon rank of massive dark-scaled bodies clad in iron armour. A nervous tingle ran down at his back at the prospect of facing such a force. "Best that we don't allow Nemtun to trap us."

Aalun called for the servants – borrowed from Ullsaard – to bring in more lamps while he delved around in his chest of scrolls and parchments. He produced three maps and laid them out on the rugs. One showed Narun and most of Nalanor; another covered more of Nalanor and the lands to duskwards; the third was a broad map of Greater Askhor as a whole. The three of them knelt down beside the broad sheets.

"So, once we get past the Wall, where do we go?" the prince asked.

"Wait a moment, that's a big assumption," said Ullsaard. "It seems to me that the men at the Wall were given orders to let us in, so that we would be trapped in Askhor. Getting out might not be a foregone conclusion."

"In which case we might as well not bother planning any further," said Aalun. "Just humour me, Ullsaard."

"Couldn't we head dawnwards to the coast and take ships instead?" asked Noran.

"Maybe *we* could," replied Ullsaard. "Getting the other thirty thousand men transport would be nearly impossible. We would need at least four hundred ships. We could start building right now and they wouldn't be done before the Nemurians show up. No, if we're going anywhere, it's through the Wall."

Aalun looked at the other two men, his expression asking whether they had finished interrupting. He pulled the Narun map to the top of the pile.

"The Greenwater is our next big obstacle," the prince said. "If Nemtun keeps to the duskward bank, he could contest any crossing we make. Our numbers would not count for much in that case."

"Narun's the worst place to cross, no matter what Nemtun decides to do," said Ullsaard. He retrieved the Nalanor map and spread it out in front of the prince. "We turn coldwards once we're outside the Wall. Head into the foothills. The river's faster there but not so wide. The autumn floodwaters won't start for another thirty days at least, so we should find safe crossing. Also, that puts us even further away from Nemtun, who'll be coming up the river from hotwards."

Noran and Aalun both nodded in agreement.

"What then?" asked Noran. "We can't stay in Nalanor. Head duskwards into Anrair, or Ersua?"

"Enair," said Ullsaard.

"You just want to go home," Noran said. "There's barely anything up there."

"Exactly," said Aalun, smiling at Ullsaard. "We need a sanctuary over the winter. Nemtun won't be able to chase us too far into Enair before the weather turns really bad. And the king won't want to pay the Nemurians for the whole winter. If we go to Enair, what do you think Nemtun will do?"

Ullsaard looked at the map, and located a small town on the intersection of the borders of Nalanor, Ersua and Anrair.

"He'll make winter quarters at Parmia," the general decided. "There's enough forage, not too far from supplies along the Greenwater, and he's placed to move in any direction come the spring."

"You know Enair better than any of us," said Aalun. "Where would you stay out the winter?"

"As far duskwards and hotwards as possible without being too close to Parmia. Somewhere near the coast."

Aalun pored over the map, his finger tracing the duskward coastline of Enair down to the Ersuan Mountains. "What about this place? Luurastin?"

Ullsaard shrugged.

"As good as any. Fishing town. No problem with food, woods in the nearby foothills for timber. Not a lot of livestock around there, we'd have to slaughter the kolubrids; can't feed them grass or grain."

"Anything else?" asked Noran. "You seem rather pleased."

"I raised most of the Thirteenth from that area. A lot of them still have family there. We can disband the legion over the winter and muster them again just before spring breaks. We could probably do the same with some of the Fifth and Tenth, as long as they don't go too far dawnwards."

Aalun straightened, his face serious.

"I have to ask you this again, Ullsaard: will your legions follow us? It is one thing for them to abandon Mekha, another for them to march into exile."

"Well, I won't tell them we're marching into exile, will I?" Ullsaard replied. "I'll tell them we're going to Enair to raise another legion ready for the Salphorian campaign."

"You would lie to your men like that?" said Aalun. "What will happen when they find out the truth?"

"Winter is a long time, Prince," Ullsaard replied as he stood up. "A lot can happen. Let's not get too far ahead of ourselves. For the moment we have two things to plan for. First, getting past the Wall. Secondly, the march to Enair. I suggest that we spend tomorrow preparing for the first. Then set out the day after. The quicker we can be on our way, the less chance of running into trouble with Nemtun."

"I'm sure I can leave it in your capable hands," said Aalun, also standing. He shook Ullsaard's hand, and Noran's. "I think it is time we all got some sleep."

VII

As Noran and Ullsaard walked back across the camp, the herald was agitated.

"What's bothering you?" asked Ullsaard.

"Apart from the obvious? What are you going to do if the Wall is held against you? Will your men attack?"

Ullsaard smiled.

"You didn't see them with that mob earlier today. Soldiers love fighting. They don't care if it's some Mekhani red-faces, Salphor mud-eaters or other legionnaires. They spend their lives marching around, making camps and eating shitty food. Any opportunity for a fight is a relief from the boredom. Don't worry about that. They'll be more than happy to deal with anyone that tried to get in our way, including Nemtun's legions."

The sentry at Ullsaard's tent informed them that Noran's wives had gone to Jutiil's pavilion. Ullsaard and Noran parted company without another word spoken and Ullsaard entered with a long yawn and a stretch. Only a single lamp lit the inside of the tent, and he cracked his knee against a chair as he headed towards the sleeping quarters that had been erected at the back.

A curtain ruffled and Meliu's pretty face appeared in the candlelight.

"I am afraid," she said softly. "And lonely."

Ullsaard allowed her to take his hand and pull him into her bed area. She disrobed him quickly and threw off her dress. Her hands found his stiffening member and massaged him to a full erection. The tiredness he had felt disappeared as he cupped an ample breast in one hand and plunged the fingers of his other between her legs. She continued to work her hand along his shaft, nipping the hairs on his chest with her teeth.

Though he longed to extend the anticipation, her moistness on his fingertips unleashed his full lust. He pushed her back onto the bed, she giving a girlish shriek as she landed amongst the blankets, legs splayed. He fell on top of her and grabbed an ankle, opening her legs even wider.

"Fuck me," she whispered, and he did as he was told, pushing himself down on top of her, one hand around her throat.

Ullsaard watched her face reddening as he pounded inside her. She gasped between gritted teeth and he placed a hand on her cheek. She pursed her lips for a kiss, but he pushed her face sideways into the pillow so that she was not looking at him.

Adjusting his grip on Meliu's leg, he pushed himself into her as far as he could, his climax exploding through his body. Her nails dragged down his chest as she bit the pillow, muffling a whimper, whether of pain or delight he did not care. Ullsaard pulled himself out and squeezed out the last few drops of his seed onto her belly.

Meliu reached an arm around his neck but Ullsaard pulled away, pushing her back to the bed. He looked down at her heaving chest and the glistening between her thighs. He saw desperation in her eyes and suddenly he felt sickened by what he had done. He turned away.

Meliu scrambled across the bed and grabbed his wrist.

"Get some sleep," he said, wrenching from her grip.

He pushed out of the curtain and turned into the next compartment. Allenya lay in bed pretending to sleep; he had watched and listened to her enough times to know when she was truly asleep. He mentally thanked Allenya for the kindness of her silence and slipped under the covers beside her.

He rolled over towards Allenya, ignoring the soft whimpers coming through the canvas screen from Meliu.

VIII

"What do you reckon?" asked Noran.

The former herald sat on his ailur with Aalun and Ullsaard beside him – the prince's followers had smuggled the war beasts out of the city the previous night, along with several chests containing Aalun's belongings, including a large amount of gold askharins. The three of them looked at the distant Askhor Wall trying to discern if the gates were closed. It was impossible to tell in the morning haze.

"I think we have to assume the worst," said Aalun.

"I agree," said Ullsaard. "I cannot see Lutaar going to the trouble of giving Nemtun his generalship back and hiring mercenaries if we could just walk out."

"We need to detail companies to the forests to collect timber for machines and ladders," said Noran. "That is going to take some time."

Both Aalun and Ullsaard laughed.

"What is so funny?" demanded Noran.

"You," said Ullsaard. "Trying to think like a military commander."

"You'd be right about the siege engines and ladders except for one small thing," said Aalun.

Noran thought for a moment, wondering what he was missing. He had read enough about the sieges of Parmia, Leruin, Geehd and other towns to consider himself fairly knowledgeable on the subject.

"I do not know," he admitted. "What do your keen military minds know that I do not?"

Aalun and Ullsaard exchanged a glance and smiles.

"Shall I tell him?" asked Ullsaard. Aalun nodded. "We're *inside* the Wall, Noran. There are *steps* on this side."

Noran covered his face with a hand and shook his head in shame, feeling like an idiot. He looked up and gave a pragmatic shrug.

"Perhaps I should leave the generalling to you two," Noran said.

"That would be for the best," said Aalun.

"But there is something you can do for us," said Ullsaard.

"Yes?" Noran was eager to be useful. He had a feeling that the coming days would take him far out of his element.

"You see that caravan there?" said Ullsaard, pointing to a ring of wagons camped beside the road roughly a mile away. "Ride down there and find out what you can from the merchants. I want to know if they've heard anything about Nemtun or the Nemurians, what's happening outside the Wall, and when they came in."

"Not a problem, General," Noran said, banging his fist against his chest in salute.

"Good for you," Ullsaard said with a smile. "You could make second captain with an attitude like that."

"By Askhos's balls, I hope not," Noran said with a grimace. "I decided at a young age that I was not cut from military material."

"You can stay on as special advisor," laughed Aalun. "How does 'First Gossip-gatherer' sound?"

"I think 'Chief of Intelligence' will suffice," Noran replied stiffly. He steered his ailur down the road and urged her into a trot.

As he rode towards the merchant encampment, Noran considered his options. It was all well and good for Ullsaard and Aalun to make fun of his military inexperience, but Noran refused to be patronised. If it had not been for him, they would have known nothing about the Nemurians or Nemtun.

The prospect of spending a winter stuck in Enair with an army did not fill him with hope. He wondered if it would be better taking Anriit and Neerita and heading for the coast. He had enough money with him to book passage hotwards to Maasra and from there it would be easy to travel to his villa in Okhar. He could keep his head down, wait for this political storm to blow over, and when it was settled they could return to Askh. He could easily put his case as an unwitting servant of the prince and beg to be returned to his former position. If it came to the worst, living out his days amongst his vineyards would not be such a bad fate.

That certainly seemed like the more prudent route, and Noran had no illusions about his own strong feelings regarding self-preservation. But even as he considered fleeing for the countryside, he knew he could not do it. Though an able commander and a strong man, Ullsaard would be powerless against Aalun's manipulation without Noran to guide him.

If things got as bad as Noran suspected they would, he was sure that most of the blame would fall on Ullsaard if Aalun had his way. For better or worse, Noran realised he could not bear the guilt of letting that happen without trying to help.

And if the situation got *really* bad, he could always flee with his wives later.

IX

Ullsaard and Aalun had gathered the First Captains in the main pavilion and were discussing how to assault the Wall when Noran returned. The nobleman's serious expression told Ullsaard all he needed to know about the situation at the Wall.

"The gate was closed two nights ago," Noran said, helping himself to a cup of water that had been holding down one corner of the map. "The merchants bribed the gate captain to let them in at dusk yesterday, but all other traffic was sent back to Narun."

"Are we really going to attack?" asked Anasind. "Up to now, all we've done is kill a few peasants. Some would say this was treason."

There were discontented mutterings from the other First Captains.

"Leave us," Ullsaard said sharply, flicking a hand at his subordinates. "Don't go far though."

The First Captains withdrew and as soon as they were gone, Aalun spoke up.

"They have a point," said the prince. "Perhaps there is no need for this to become a physical confrontation. If we

255

attack the Wall, we are attacking the legionnaires of the Crown; we will be waging war against our rightful king. I am not sure that is a step I want to take."

"And the alternative?" asked Ullsaard.

"We relinquish command of the legions, send word to my father that we accept exile and bide our time. In a few years' time, sooner probably, my father's death will create a new platform to challenge Kalmud's suitability for the Crown."

"And if Kalmud recovers?" asked Noran.

Aalun spread his hands on the table and his tone was earnest.

"I know that you think this is my personal ambition, but I assure you it is not. I genuinely worry for the future of Greater Askhor should my brother become an infirm ruler; worse still if Kalmud dies and the Crown passes to Erlaan, who is far too inexperienced."

"He has a point," said Ullsaard, looking at Noran.

"For himself, maybe," Noran replied. He directed his attention towards the prince. "I have no doubt what you say is true. I agree with you for the most part, even if your methods up to now have been faulty."

Aalun opened his mouth to speak but Noran raised hand.

"Let me finish, Prince, if I may. I think that if you were to dissolve the army and retreat for a while, you would be all right. The king exiled you personally." Noran turned again to Ullsaard. "But you, my friend… You have been declared a traitor to the empire by the Brotherhood. Seizure of all your lands, your family, and a gruesome death come with that. Aalun may walk away from this intact, but you will not. Lutaar will want your head on a platter for what he thinks you have done."

Noran began to pace, but kept his eyes on Ullsaard.

"No comfortable exile for you, General." Noran jabbed a pointed finger towards Ullsaard. "You would have to leave not only Askhor, but flee the empire entirely. Your reputation is already in tatters; your sons will be ruined and made paupers. People will spit in the dirt when your name is mentioned, and should you ever be caught, your flayed remains will be paraded around the empire as a warning to anyone who thinks they can defy the king of Askhor."

Ullsaard's expression grew grimmer as he listened to Noran, until a deep scowl creased his brow.

"I'll not let that happen," said the general. His hard stare moved between Noran and Aalun. "You can both leave now if you want no part of this, but I will be ordering my men to break through the Wall, and they will obey my order."

"I'm with you, friend," Noran said immediately. Aalun did not answer for some time, and when he did it was with a heartfelt sigh.

"If this is the way it must be, then so be it," the prince said eventually. "We must force this issue to a conclusion."

"Good," said Ullsaard. "Noran, I have another favour to ask of you."

"What do you want me to do?"

"Ride down to the Wall with a message for the gate captain. Warn him that if he refuses to open the gate for me, I will have no choice but to attack. He can avoid the deaths of his men if he does not interfere with our leaving Askhor."

"Is it wise to forewarn them?" Noran asked.

"I have thirty thousand men camped five miles away from the Wall. I think the gate captain already has a good idea of what we intend to do. Let's give him a chance to do the sensible thing."

Noran headed for the tent flap.

"And could you send my captains in again?" Ullsaard called after him. Noran raised a hand in acknowledgement without turning around and left the pavilion.

The First Captains stood around a fire not far away, deep in conversation. Noran passed on Ullsaard's message and stood looking into the flames when the legion commanders were gone.

This is it, he thought. A few days ago he would never have imagined he'd be in a legion camp, about to start a war with his own king.

"Bollocks," he muttered. "Shit and bollocks."

X

Outnumbered by three to one, the commander of the Wall had chosen not to meet Ullsaard's army on the hills around the Wall, but had drawn in his entire garrison to the rampart and towers around that massive gatehouse. Though the majority of the war engines defending the Askhor Gap were pointed outwards, a few of the spear throwers had been dismounted from their positions and turned around to face inward. Kolubrid scouts had returned to report that only skeleton garrisons had been left to defend a few towers to coldwards and hotwards, no more than a thousand men out of the Wall captain's force.

Armed with this information, Ullsaard sent Donar coldwards with his Fifth Legion. They were to take possession of the Wall three miles coldwards and march along the rampart to the gatehouse. From the back of Blackfang, Ullsaard watched carefully as the Fifth's trumpets rang out signalling the advance and Donar's companies wheeled off to the right.

There was no movement in the gatehouse. Clearly Ullsaard's opponent was not willing to weaken his defence of the gate. Ullsaard wondered what he would do if he had been in his enemy's boots. It was not an enviable position. I'd probably have opened the gates and waved goodbye and good riddance, Ullsaard decided.

The air was filled with a fine drizzle of rain, the clouds low over the hills. Droplets dappled Ullsaard's armour and the bronze mask of his ailur. The wind was low, the company standards of his army hanging lank on their poles. With each passing hour, the footing was getting muddier, but the road was too narrow for all of the legions to attack along. All things considered, it was a miserable day for a battle, but things would get worse if they waited. Noran had reported no sightings of Nemtun or the Nemurians, but the lack of news did not comfort Ullsaard.

He despatched kolubrid messengers to his First Captains, telling them to prepare for the advance. Companies trotted into position around the general, their armour clinking dully in the rain, the shouts of the third captains distant and muffled.

The left wing was held by Jutiil and his Twelfth. Their orders were to swing left and draw some of the defenders towards the closest hotwards guard tower. To their right Ullsaard had positioned the Tenth under Rondin, their companies organised into broad phalanxes six men deep. On the far right of the line, now that Donar had departed on his mission, the Sixteenth held the flank. Ullsaard had saved the prestigious centre position for his own Thirteenth, standing in tight, square formations beside their general.

Ahead of them, a little under a mile away, stood the Wall. Ullsaard knew that it had not been designed to withstand attacks from the Askhor side, and the advantage of numbers was his, but nonetheless it would not be an easy task. The enemy had the advantage of their elevated positions and doubtlessly would have barricaded the tower stairs with whatever they could find to hold back Ullsaard's assault while they poured arrows and spears into their foes. Ullsaard had neither the equipment nor the inclination to force the gate itself. He had to take control of the gate mechanism and open the gate, and all his attention was focussed on that goal.

When he estimated that the Tenth would be close to beginning their assault, Ullsaard turned to his signalmen and raised a hand. They brought up their drumsticks as the rain pattered on the skins of their instruments.

Ullsaard dropped his hand and a long rolling drumbeat sounded across the army. *Advance!*

Ullsaard felt a growing dismay as not a single legionnaire stepped up. He twisted in his saddle and snapped at the musicians to signal the advance again. They did so, with equal effect.

The general looked for Anasind, and saw the First Captain of the Thirteenth running towards him, his staff officers trailing after.

"What the fuck is going on?" Ullsaard demanded once Anasind was in earshot.

"I don't know, General," the First Captain confessed. "The men are just ignoring the order. They don't look too happy. Should I have the company officers make a few examples?"

"That won't be needed," said Ullsaard, dismounting. He handed Blackfang's reins to an orderly and his spear to another. The ailur turned her head towards him, apparently confused by his absence. She sniffed the air and twitched her tail, sensing battle.

"What are you going to do?" asked Anasind, following behind Ullsaard as he strode towards the front rank of the Thirteenth.

"This isn't mutiny, it's uncertainty," Ullsaard said. "Let's just show the boys that we mean business."

The worried eyes of the legionnaires followed Ullsaard as he walked along the line just in front of the Thirteenth legion's front rank. He came to a stop a few paces from the first company, whose captain, Venuid, held the legion icon.

"I know you are not sure why you must fight today," Ullsaard said, his voice a shout that could be heard by the distant companies. "You wonder why we raise our spears against our fellow Askhans. The reasons are many and tedious. All you need know is that today we fight for our

260

rights as soldiers and men. The king has refused to treat with us as the law demands, and he seeks to quell our spirit with threats of violence.

"It is not we that start this war, but King Lutaar, who refuses to acknowledge my rights, and through me, your rights. He would have us waste our time choking on dust and sand while his favourites earn rich spoils elsewhere. No more! I came here to demand what we are entitled to, but he will not even see me. Today we do not fight against the soldiers of a just ruler, but against the lackeys of a tyrant who ignores his own laws."

Ullsaard paced back and forth and saw anger on the faces of some of the men, but most were still confused. He would need to give them something more to fight for. He strode up to Venuid and took the Askhan icon from the captain's grasp. He held it up so that all of the Thirteenth could see it.

"This is the symbol of the Thirteenth!" Ullsaard roared. "I gave it to you when I raised you. On it, you swore oaths of loyalty, and you took the coin from my hand and the wisdom from my lips. You are my Thirteenth, who have been like brothers and sons to me. You have fought for me, bled for me, and died for me. Today I ask you to do that again."

Ullsaard stalked away from the line, still holding up the icon. He stopped about twenty paces from the front rank.

"Are you going to let your icon fall to this bunch of boys and dogs?" Ullsaard bellowed. "Are you going to let this rabble of pigfuckers kill your general?"

With that he turned away and marched along the road towards the gatehouse. He heard shouts of dismay and anger behind him.

"Thirteen!" a voice cried out. He recognised it as Anasind.

"Thirteen!" several thousand throats roared in response.

The legion advanced as one, splashing through the rain after their leader and standard. To their left and right, the other legions followed suit, none wanting to be shamed by the enthusiasm of their rivals.

Ullsaard heard a splash of sandaled feet behind. Venuid caught up with him, his round face split by a wide grin.

"I think I could carry that for you, General," said the captain.

Ullsaard thrust the icon back into Venuid's hands with a wink. The general stepped to one side to allow the first company to catch up with their captain. As they reached him, Ullsaard raised his shield above his head.

"Thirteen!" he cried and received the answering call.

"Thirteen!"

XI

About a quarter of a mile from the Wall, the spear throwers hurled their bolts down into the Thirteenth. Their shields gave little protection against the heavy missiles and men were flung back through the ranks with harsh cries. Ullsaard had joined the front rank of the first company at the head of the attack.

"Keep moving! Fast advance!" bellowed Ullsaard as a spear flashed past him only a few paces away, punching through a legionnaire's shoulder to send him spinning to the ground. The other soldiers quickly stepped in to fill the gap. Speed would be their best defence.

Drummers sounded the order and the legion, company by company, broke into a trot, spears on their shoulders. More bolts crashed through the ranks but the legionnaires ignored their dead and wounded and pressed onwards with their general.

A cloud of arrows flew up from the rampart ahead. The second captains bellowed commands to form a shield wall and the legionnaires closed in around Ullsaard. The front rank held their shields to the front, while the men further back created a roof with theirs. Though this provided greater protection against the arrows, it slowed down their advance. Ullsaard winced as shafts thudded around and above him, a few finding gaps to bite into flesh. Volley after volley descended on them as they tramped towards the gatehouse, leaving a trail of injured men.

An arrowhead split the wood of Ullsaard's shield and cut his forearm. Blood dribbled from the slight wound, dripping down the inside of his shield onto his leg. He ignored it and glanced around the side of his shield to see how far they were from the gatehouse.

Less than two hundred paces.

"Sound the charge!" he roared. Around him, the shield wall fell apart and the company broke into a run.

The horns sounded the order. This was no barbaric sprint into combat, but a controlled increase of speed. The legionnaires loped along at an easy pace, mud churning up beneath their feet, keeping to their ranks while more arrows whistled overhead.

The first company angled their run towards the gate tower to the right, while the second company split to the left. Ullsaard kept his focus on the archway at the base of the tower. He could see crates and timber had been piled onto the stairs within. More arrows fell on them as they reached the foot of the wall and burst towards the open archway.

"Clear this shit out of the way," rasped Anasind, a little to Ullsaard's right. The First Captain turned to shout at the third company who were following behind. "Shields up!"

They hefted up their shields to form a protective barrier over the heads of the first company, while those legionnaires began to pull apart the impromptu barricade. Planks and barrels were passed from man to man beneath the shield roof, to be thrown out to each side to keep the path clear. Archers stationed inside the tower loosed their shafts into the men clearing the debris, but those that were injured quickly withdrew to allow others to continue, while the bodies of the dead were tossed out of the way like any other junk.

Behind the assaulting companies, others were defending the lava-throwers. Protected by the shields of their covering companies, the crews worked their machines and unleashed gouts of black and red fire at the ramparts above the gates. The charred corpses of bowmen fell from the Wall to crash into the mud while the hideous shrieking of the survivors rang down the tower steps.

"Push on!" Ullsaard ordered, clambering over pieces of broken furniture and bundles of ragged bedding. "No duties for ten days for the company that takes the tower!"

Though the path was not fully clear, the first company surged into the tower, the second company eagerly on their heels. Ullsaard raced up the steps, flanked by two legionnaires. They were met halfway by soldiers coming down, spears jabbing at the attackers.

Ullsaard used his spear to batter away the weapons of his opponents and leaped up the steps two at a time, crashing into the opponents ahead with his shield as a battering ram. He dropped his spear and pulled his sword out to blindly hack left and right. Caught between the swordsman in their midst and the spears of the first company, the Wall garrison were forced to retreat up the steps, but Ullsaard would not let them create the space they needed, following up with hacking swings that shattered the shafts of their spears and left rents in their shields.

Ullsaard could see the sky behind the press of men ahead and knew he was not far from the rampart. He took another step but the enemy came towards him, pushed down the stairs by more men pouring into the tower from above.

Ullsaard was forced back two steps, and his foot slipped from under him in a puddle of blood. He swung his sword wildly as he fell, catching one of his foes across the chin with its tip before he rolled down into the feet of his own men. Two legionnaires helped to him his feet as the rest pressed ahead, forming a solid wall of shields across the narrow stairway.

Panting, Ullsaard leaned back against the wall and let more men rush past to take up the fight. In the scrum of the melee he spied Anasind. The First Captain looked worried, but Ullsaard raised his sword to show that he was unhurt. Anasind nodded his understanding and disappeared into the throng of legionnaires, bellowing encouragement.

Shouts of alarm echoed from the top of the tower and Ullsaard guessed that Donar's men had reached the rampart to coldwards or the other gate tower had been taken. Whatever the cause, the defenders' resistance collapsed as they turned to run.

With triumphant shouts, the Thirteenth boiled up the stairwell onto the rampart, stabbing anyone left in their path. Ullsaard pushed through the crowd of soldiers as they spread coldwards along the Wall, finishing off the wounded their enemies had left behind. Ullsaard stepped to the inner edge of the rampart and looked hotwards to see the second company were fighting hard but had gained the rampart. Beyond them, further along the Wall, Jutiil's men advanced towards the gatehouse with spears ready.

Some of the defenders threw down their shields and weapons in surrender, but they were cut down mercilessly. A great many jumped from the Wall to escape, most of them landing with bone-cracking impacts. They too were swiftly despatched by the rear companies; the few lucky men that survived the jump were allowed to limp away with laughs and jeers ringing in their ears. Ullsaard could imagine his men thought it bad form to cut down a man who had survived such a death-defying leap.

XII

As pairs of legionnaires tossed the bodies of the dead off the rampart, Ullsaard called for Luamid and Rondin. The two First Captains shouldered their way through the press of soldiers occupying the gatehouse.

"Raid two towers cold- and hotwards and see what supplies you can get. Don't take too long. And remind Anasind that First Company took the gatehouse. They'll appreciate ten days of soft duties!"

The captains saluted and left, leaving Ullsaard alone amidst the maelstrom.

"General?"

He turned to see a legionnaire holding Ullsaard's golden-headed spear. The man's face was streaked with grime and sweat, his left eye closed by a vicious bruise. His good eye was wide with reverence. "You left this behind, General."

"What's your name?" Ullsaard said, taking the weapon. "Which company?"

"Cobiunnin, General," replied the legionnaire. "Third Company. Thirteenth."

"Thank you, Cobiunnin. Tell Captain Anasind that Third Company is excused camp duties for the next two days. Make sure you tell your friends why."

"Thanks, General!" Cobiunnin replied with a broad grin. He headed back towards his company, shouting the names of his friends. Ullsaard watched as Cobiunnin announced the news. The other legionnaires clapped their comrade on the back and raised their spears to Ullsaard in thanks.

Ullsaard felt tired. He took off his helmet and rubbed a hand through his sweat-soaked hair. Out of the corner of his eye, he caught sight of the golden-threaded banner of Aalun. The prince rode through the Askhan dead with Noran by his side, a bodyguard of kolubrid riders in a circle around him. The two men tugged hard on the reins of their mounts when they stopped to sniff or paw the corpses.

Ullsaard turned his back to Aalun, to Askh, and looked out across the hills to duskwards, pushing everything else from his mind. The rain fell steadily, obscuring the distant mountains in murk, and nothing could be seen of the Greenwater and Narun.

It didn't matter. Out there was open country. Nemtun would never catch them before winter. Ullsaard was pleased. Victory in the first battle of a war was always a good omen. He took a deep breath, savouring the air, tinged with blood and sweat and all the sweeter for it.

After allowing himself this moment, he put on his helmet and bellowed for Anasind. There was a march to be organised.

ENAIR
Early Winter, 209th Year of Askh

I

Though Noonwatch approached, the ground was covered with frost that crackled under the wheels of the abada cart as it trundled along the rutted road. The branches and needles of the surrounding forest were equally rimed with ice. Above the treetops smoke rose in thin columns from a small cluster of buildings.

The village stood on the bank of a narrow river, the water's edge laced with fronds of ice. The single storey cottages were constructed from hewn logs, sealed with muddy mortar, roofed with several layers of branches tightly woven together. The road petered out into a muddy open area where swine and fowl wandered freely under the watch of several children, sitting on a low stone wall beside the river. A brick bridge was the only sign that the Askhans had ever come to this backwater, everything else was unchanged from the way the Enairian tribes had lived for centuries.

This was Ullsaard's home.

He clambered down from the first of three wagons and stomped his feet to get some feeling into his chilled toes. Wrapped in a heavy coat of goatskin lined with fur, boots of the same, his beard unclipped for several weeks, the broad-shouldered general looked like a beast of the forests. His breath came in clouds as he clapped together his gloved hands and grinned at his wives, who sat on the second wagon.

"This place is so much nicer in winter," Ullsaard declared.

"If you say so," said Luia, little more than a cold-reddened nose poking out of a thick fur shawl and woollen blankets. "I think I prefer it in the summer."

One of the cottage doors opened and an elderly, rotund woman in a plain red dress and high boots emerged. Her generous cheeks were flushed from effort and steam billowed out of the door behind her.

"Lord Ullsaard!" she exclaimed as she trotted across the mud and frost. "Ain't never expected to see you at this time of year."

"Hello, Freyna," the general replied. "How about some hot drinks?"

Freyna, the local loremother, looked past Ullsaard and saw the three women bundled up on the back of the cart. She scowled at the general.

"Shame on you for bringing your lovely ladies out in this weather," said Freyna. She hurried over to the wives' cart. "Come on, dears, let's get you warmed up inside."

One by one, the Askhan women lowered themselves from the wagon and waddled after Freyna, swathed in their cloaks and blankets. Freyna was chattering away, asking after their health and news of their families. Ullsaard was content to leave them to their gossiping for the moment and wandered over to the river. Behind him the third wagon trundled onwards, carrying four servants and the luggage, heading through the village towards Ullsaard's house a mile further up the road.

Ullsaard took a deep, cold breath and grinned to himself. He remembered a dozen winters here in Stykhaag, chopping trees, fishing through ice holes in the lake a couple of miles to duskwards, hanging the holly wreaths from the trees to keep the frost spirit at bay. There was nothing like it in Askhor, where the ancient, misguided tribal beliefs that had held sway before Askhos had risen to power had been purged by the Brotherhood.

He looked around and saw the telltale signs of the old wards around the village: the crossed nails on the lintels; holly ropes threaded into the branch roofs; the rune charms carved into the logs of the cottages. It didn't matter how many times the Brotherhood came here and chastised the people for their superstitions, the old ways still remained in some fashion.

To coldwards the bald hill known as the Crow Mound loomed out of the forest, the snow and ice covering the burnt earth and charred timbers on its summit. Not in Ullsaard's lifetime had anyone gone up there, but in generations past every equinox and solstice had seen the flames dancing high as the loremothers and the lorefathers had led the people in their rituals of sacrifice to appease the spirits of sky and earth and forest.

Yes, Ullsaard thought, it was misguided nonsense. A life in the legions had taught him that well-placed bronze and a bit of luck had more sway over people's destiny than imaginary spirit folk. But for all his pragmatism, there was something real, something genuine about the old celebrations and ceremonies which Askhan pomp could never capture.

"Here you go."

Ullsaard found Allenya behind him with a steaming mug in her hand. Ullsaard took it with a smile and sniffed: chicken broth. He took a gulp, enjoying the warmth of the soup as it flowed down into his gut.

"Why did we stop here?" Allenya asked. "We are only a mile from your mother's house."

Ullsaard nodded towards the river wall, where there was one less child than before.

"To give my mother some warning," he said. "She's a

stickler for certain things and she'll be annoyed that I didn't send word that we were coming. This way she can get everything in order before we turn up."

"You are a considerate man, Ullsaard."

"Not really. If I was considerate, I would have sent her a letter before we left the camp."

"Do you think Nemtun really has given up for the winter? He chased us all over Nalanor and through Ersua."

"He knows that we can't go anywhere else," replied Ullsaard. "He has nothing to gain by coming after us in this weather, and everything to lose. He'll be sitting tight in Parmia, I'm sure of it, giggling to himself as he imagines my men deserting in their dozens."

"Do you think they will? Desert, I mean."

"Some, perhaps, but not many," said Ullsaard. He finished the soup and flicked the dregs out of the mug into the river. "They'll either all go, or none of them. The men know it'll be bad for them if someone deserts their company, so unless they all decide to quit together, they'll keep the troublemakers in order."

They walked back towards Freyna's house.

"And if they all decide to go?"

"They won't. At the moment, they're aggrieved men. They think they've been cheated out of something and they want it. Don't underestimate a man's stubbornness when greed and justice overlap. They'll stick out the winter for sure, just to see what the spring brings. If it doesn't go well after that, that's when we'll start losing them."

"I wish we could stay with you," said Allenya.

"It's better that you stay here, out of the way. Having you around distracts me, and I need to think like a commander, not a husband."

"We understand."

"I'm sure you do, and I think Luia will be glad to have more comfort. I don't know about Meliu. She always takes everything in the worst way possible."

They were at Freyna's door. The smell of cooking wafted out in the steam and smoke and Ullsaard was uncomfortably aware that the soup had whetted his appetite rather than sated it.

"There'll be time enough for chatting," he called inside. "Let's get you up to the house while the skies are clear. I smell more snow coming."

"He's right, my ladies," Freyna's voice came from a back room. She emerged into the main chamber with a lid-covered pot, which she handed to Meliu. "You should get up to the house to settle in. Now, dear, just boil that in some water and you'll be fine."

As they were leaving, Freyna grabbed Ullsaard's sleeve and pulled him into the cottage. She spoke in a stern whisper.

"Urikh arrived here not more than three days ago," said the loremother. "Rode straight up to the house without so much as a hello. Now, I don't know much, but I does know that something is up when the both of you are here in the middle of winter. You don't have to tell me what's going on, but I might be able to help, you never know."

"There is something going on, Freyna, but there's no help you can give me. Urikh's here? I didn't know that."

Ullsaard gave her a kiss on the cheek and turned towards the door when something occurred to him.

"When was the last time the Brotherhood were here?"

"Not since summer, collecting tithe," Freyna replied. "Why?"

"If you see a Brother, or anyone not local, send word to Allenya as soon as you can."

"Are you in trouble?"

"Yes," Ullsaard said. He left it at that and crossed back to his wagon.

Freyna waved from her doorway as the two carts creaked into motion, the abada grunting under the switches of the drivers. Once they were past the few cottages the road reappeared, two winding lines of mud that followed the course of the river.

The grounds of Ullsaard's house were nothing grand, though he had paid for a stone wall around the cleared space of forest, and brought some of the mountain flowers and bushes from Askhor for his mother to tend. In the summer, the villagers came here to hold games and there was a wide hedge-bounded lawn on the hotwards side of the house, now just a muddy field.

The lower storey of the house was of grey stone like the enclosing wall, the upper floor made of strong Enairian timber. The windows even had blown glass panes, small though they were, and the roof was covered with slate from the Ersuan hills. By local standards it was a veritable palace in size, though it had only ten rooms in total – fewer than Ullsaard's apartment in Askh.

The servants Ullsaard had sent ahead were waiting in the courtyard, along with a member of the house staff whose name the general couldn't remember. They helped Luia, Meliu and Allenya down from their wagon. Ullsaard joined his wives and the four of them headed for the main doors while the carts were taken away.

The entrance hall was warm and lit by a fire in a deep hearth opposite the door. The floor was covered with thin strips of wood, each carefully lacquered and interlaid to present a herringbone pattern. Two housemaids appeared to take the arrivals' travel cloaks and blankets and Ullsaard was glad to be free of his heavy coat as he rubbed his hands in front of the fire.

"The mistress is in the sitting chamber," one of the maids told Ullsaard.

The young girl led them to the right through a wooden arch, into a carpeted room where another fire blazed. Narrow windows showed the frost-caked lawn and the outer wall, the trees of the Enairian forests looming beyond. There were several couches and chairs and a slab of green and grey marble that served as a table. Lamps on the walls combined with the firelight to give the room a comfortable glow.

Sitting by the fire in a low, stuffed seat was a woman in her late sixties, her straight grey hair bound in a tight braid, her lined face staring towards the flames. As they entered, she looked up at Ullsaard, her flint-hard eyes betraying nothing of her thoughts.

"Welcome, son," she said, standing. Pretaa looked at the women and smiled. "And my daughters."

"Are you well?" asked Ullsaard.

"As well as could be hoped," she replied, receiving kisses on the forehead from Allenya and Luia.

"You look wonderful," said Meliu, hugging her tightly. She pulled back and stroked Pretaa's hair. "You look the picture of health."

"Thank you, child, you are such a dear," said Pretaa, waving them to the couches around the table. Jugs and bowls steamed and there were plates of nuts and preserved fruits. "I thought you might prefer an informal meal. We can have something proper this evening when we have time to prepare."

Ullsaard understood the gentle rebuke and whispered an apology as he embraced his mother.

"I hear that Urikh is here," said Ullsaard.

"Really?" said Luia, looking around the room as if her son were hiding somewhere.

"He will be back this evening," said Pretaa. "I am sure he would have been here to greet you if he had known you were coming."

Ullsaard gave his mother a look of warning not to push too far and she smiled thinly.

"It is good to see you all, even if the circumstances are not to our liking."

"What have you heard?" asked Ullsaard as he sat down and spooned venison stew into a bowl.

"Only what Urikh has told me," said Pretaa. "You have had a falling out with the king, and now you have been chased into Enair."

"It was not quite like that," said Ullsaard.

"I would say it is exactly like that," said Luia. "Which part is wrong?"

Ullsaard ate his stew and said nothing while Pretaa performed her mother-in-law and grandmother duties, asking after the health of the family and goings-on in Askh. He sensed disapproval from his mother, but knew better than to ask. She would make her opinion known when she wanted, and not a moment sooner.

When they had finished eating and the servants had cleared away, Pretaa invited the women to retire to their rooms for some rest. Ullsaard watched them leave with a sense of foreboding. When he was alone with Pretaa, a mug of beer in his hand, he gave her a long look.

"Just say what you want to say," he said heavily.

"Whatever do you mean?" said Pretaa, moving to sit next to the fire, her back half-turned from Ullsaard. "You are always welcome here. After all, you built this house for me. It would be ungrateful to turn you away."

"You have always been welcome in Askh, you've just chosen not to come," said Ullsaard.

"It seems that neither of us is welcome in Askh these days," she said with a sigh. "I knew that something like this would happen one day."

Ullsaard sat in the other fireside chair and leaned towards his mother.

"What do you mean? You barely know what has happened."

Pretaa would not look at him. She gently shook her head and folded her hands in her lap.

"It was a mistake telling you to go to Askh," she said quietly. "No good can come of being around the Blood and their kind. The Blood calls to itself and brings out the worst."

"I don't understand what you are talking about. What have the Blood got to do with any of this? If you mean Prince Aalun, he has been nothing but a friend and an ally. Though he is in part responsible for what has happened, he could have easily broken his ties with me and left me to the mercy of his father."

"That is exactly what I mean," said Pretaa. "Why did you get involved at all? The Blood has a power of its own. It makes men hungry for power, makes them selfish."

"That may be true of Aalun, but my ambitions have nothing to do with the Blood. I have come so far, achieved so much, I can't let all that effort simply fade into nothing, can I?"

"No, you could not, though you should have done. I cannot see what good will come of this. You should have been content. You have three fine wives, three fine sons. You have everything a man could want from his life, but for you it is not enough! I should have known that this would happen."

Ullsaard studied his mother. There was a haunted, distant look in her eye that he had never seen before.

"What is it?" he demanded. "How could you know anything like this would happen? Tell me what you're keeping secret."

"It does not matter." Pretaa's words did not match her behaviour.

Ullsaard had seen the same before, from officers who wanted to confess a break of regulations, or when one of his sons had misbehaved whilst he had been away and wanted to tell Ullsaard before he found out by other means. Something was on Pretaa's mind that she could not bring herself to tell him but knew she should.

"If it has anything to do with what is happening now, it is better that I know."

Pretaa glanced at him and when she spoke she continued to look into the fire.

"Do you know why I have never been to Askh? I am scared that I will be recognised."

"I don't understand. Recognised by who?"

"I am Askhan, born and bred. Not from a noble family, but one that was well enough off that I spent time in the palace."

"I always knew you were not Enairian; that much is obvious. What does it matter that you are Askhan?"

"I was something of a slut, I suppose. I was always bedding some soldier or servant or other. I was pretty then, as well. No shortage of men wanted to bed me. It was just some fun, at the time. So I thought."

She sighed again and picked at the heavy wool of her dress, eyes downcast.

"One of those soldiers was a young captain called Cosuas."

"You slept with Cosuas? What are you telling me?"

"Not what you think, though it is what he believes. No, Cosuas is not your father."

"But he thinks I am?" Ullsaard could not quite comprehend the importance of this. "Why has Cosuas never said anything about this?"

"Because I asked him not to. I did not want him to lie to you, though I lied to him. When Cosuas was a captain in the palace I used to visit him often. On one occasion I caught the eye of another man, a powerful man, and he took me to his bed. With any other man, that might have been the end of the story. Not for me. The man I slept with was Prince Lutaar, now the king."

Ullsaard was aghast. A dozen questions crammed into his mind but he could not voice any of them before his mother continued.

"There is a dark secret kept in Askh, one that few know about. Any woman bedded by one of the Blood, not their wives, is taken away to the Brotherhood. It is to ensure that there are no bastards trying to claim the throne.

277

What the Brotherhood do with them, I have no idea. We'd hear whispers of some young woman or other going missing now and then, but we would just assume they had been sent somewhere else. Maybe they are, I don't know."

"So what happened? What did the Brotherhood do with you?"

"They never laid their hands on me. Cosuas was ordered to keep me under watch until the Brothers came for me. I didn't tell him what had happened, but I confess I used all of my wiles to twist his heart to my side. He helped me to escape before they came for me, and then faked my death just outside Askh. I fled and headed here to Enair to live out my life in secret." Her face told the sad story of what followed more than any words. "Cosuas was meant to follow, but he did not."

"So you are a fugitive?" Ullsaard almost laughed. "That's why you cannot go back to Askh? This all happened a long time ago, I am sure that nobody remembers you."

"It matters not whether they remember me. When I arrived here, I learnt that I was pregnant with you."

"Another chance encounter on the road?"

"I have not slept with another man since leaving Askh."

Ullsaard thought about this for a moment.

"But you said Cosuas isn't my father."

Pretaa nodded. Ullsaard flew to his feet, sending the chair flying backwards.

"No, you have it wrong! How can you be sure Lutaar is my father? How many different men did you sleep with? How can you know Cosuas really isn't my father?"

"Look at yourself," Pretaa snapped. "Tall, strong, intelligent, powerful. Certainly it was not Cosuas's Ersuan seed that made you, though he deludes himself it may be. You have the Blood in you. Aalun recognises it, even if he does not know it. That is why he has been drawn to you, and why you have risen so far so fast with his help. Perhaps your father feels it in you as well and that is why he is afraid of you."

Ullsaard walked away, waving his hands in denial.

"No, no, this does not make sense. The king is not afraid of me. I would be no more than a second captain without Aalun's help. There is not one drop of the Blood in me."

"How else does an Enairian of no name marry into Askhan nobility? How else does an ignorant coldlander become a celebrated general of the legions? You have never courted power until now, and yet throughout your life you have gained it. Most men of ambition achieve half of what you have."

It was Pretaa that now stood. She grabbed Ullsaard's hands and held them between hers. She looked up at her son's distressed face with a fierce expression.

"I have always been so proud of you, but I could never tell you why. To lead others, to fight, to command, it is in your nature. You have said it to me in the past; you feel alive in battle like at no other time. That is the Blood, its blessing and its curse."

"I cannot talk about this," said Ullsaard, whirling away. He stalked from the room and back into the entrance hall. He stopped and marched back into the room where his mother looked at the door. "Tell nobody else this!"

He grabbed a heavy cloak and left the house, setting off towards the woods to think.

II

Though it was barely two hours into High Watch when Ullsaard returned to the house, the sky was darkening quickly. The narrow windows upstairs were slivers of yellow against the black of the building, the setting sun beyond obscured by heavy cloud. Ullsaard tramped through the mud to the gate, where one of his mother's retainers waited with a lantern. Ullsaard recognised him as Illsaard, a man a little older than the general. The two of them had grown up together, and Ullsaard could not help but think how differently their lives had turned out. Perhaps there was something to what his mother had said about the power of the Blood.

"Has Urikh returned yet?" Ullsaard asked as Illsaard opened the wooden gate.

"Not yet, general."

Ullsaard nodded and continued into the house. His mother was waiting for him where he had left her, sitting by the fire. There was no sign of Ullsaard's wives.

Pretaa stood up as he entered. She said nothing, but there was a question in her look.

"It doesn't matter; you were right," Ullsaard said. "You will never speak of this to anyone else."

"You understand why I did not tell you before?"

Ullsaard kicked off his muddy boots and threw his coat over the back of a couch.

"The Blood changes nothing. I was raised without a father and I will die without a father."

Ullsaard left and headed upstairs, seeking Allenya. He found her in the bedroom set aside for her visits, sewing by the light of a lamp. She put the piece down and stood when she saw his taut expression.

"Is something wrong?"

"No," said Ullsaard. "Nothing new, anyway. Don't let me interrupt. What are you making?"

Allenya held up her work; a cushion cover half-embroidered with a forest scene.

"It's nice," said Ullsaard, kissing his wife on the forehead. He slumped on to the bed and laid back, arms behind his head. "Have I been selfish? Greedy?"

"Is it greed for a man to want the most from life?" said Allenya. "If a man has no ambition, he leaves the world with what he had when he entered it: nothing. You know I will always be here for you, no matter what happens. I do not know if what you have done is right or wrong; it is

280

done and cannot be changed. Now is not the time to doubt yourself, my love. You have chosen a path, you have to follow it all of the way to the end."

Ullsaard stared at the white ceiling, stained with smudges of lamp soot.

"You are right, as usual," he said quietly. "What's done is done. It's too late now for regrets."

III

The family were just finishing their evening meal – a fine banquet of game and fish – when the banging of the main door heralded Urikh's arrival.

"In here!" Pretaa called out. "I have other guests now."

Urikh strode into the dining chamber and stopped dead in his tracks upon seeing his father and mothers. He was in his mid-twenties, with Ullsaard's height but Luia's slimness. He had thick, dark hair cut at the shoulder, bony cheeks and a narrow chin. His thin lips parted in surprise.

"Don't standing there gawping like a simpleton," Luia said as she stood. "Greet your family properly."

"Hello," said Urikh. He gave Luia a peck on the cheek, and did the same for Meliu and Allenya. He hesitantly extended a hand towards Ullsaard. "Father. I did not expect to see you so soon."

Ullsaard gripped his son's hand and clapped him on the shoulder.

"Better sooner than later," said the general. "There's still plenty left to eat. Join us. Tell us what you've been up to."

Urikh sat down between Ullsaard and Pretaa and loaded food onto his plate.

"I've been trying to find out just how much trouble you have got us into," he said amiably. "If I'd known, I might have been able to help. Actually, I think I still can help."

"Really?" said Ullsaard. "If I need any copper kettles, I'll be sure to let you know."

"Fine!" declared Urikh. "If you don't want to hear what I have to say, I won't pester you."

The young man ate fastidiously, cutting away all fat and gristle from his meat, ignoring his father's scowl. He poured himself a cup of wine and looked across the table at Luia.

"I wouldn't stay here too long, if I were you," he said casually.

"Why's that?" asked Ullsaard. "What have you heard?"

"So you are interested?" Urikh made no attempt to conceal his smugness as he slowly chewed his food. His amusement grew in proportion to Ullsaard's impatience.

"You've made your point," snapped the general. "What do you know?"

"Nemtun's joined forces with Allon, just outside Khybrair," Urikh said. "The two of them are marching this way right now. At a guess, I'd say they were about seven days dawnwards."

"In winter?" Ullsaard took a large gulp of wine. "That makes no sense. Why would they do that?"

"What about Jutaar?" asked Allenya, her hand raised to her cheek in dismay. "Does he march with Allon?"

"How am I supposed to know?" Urikh replied with a shrug. "I just hear talk, that's all. I don't have a spy in Allon's army!"

"Allon will defer to Nemtun, he isn't a natural commander," said Ullsaard. "The king wants this settled quickly. How many men do they have?"

This last question was directed at Urikh, who shrugged again.

"I just talked to a grain merchant fresh from Ersua, and I've told you everything he told me."

"I have to warn Aalun. We need to move the army, or we'll be trapped against the sea."

"Where will you go?" asked Pretaa. "Hotwards into Ersua?"

282

"Where will we go, you mean," said Ullsaard. He looked at his mother and wives. "I can't leave you here, it isn't safe. If Nemtun gets to you, he'll use you as hostages against me."

"I'm too old to go anywhere in winter," said Pretaa. "Leave me here. I can look after myself."

"No!" This was from Meliu. "We can't let that horrid Nemtun get his hands on you. I hear he is a beast in all regards."

"Surely if you are so worried about us, the last place we should be is with your army," said Luia. "I'm sure Urikh can find us somewhere to hide for a while."

"No," said Ullsaard, cutting off Urikh's answer. "If you can't stay here, I want you close by where I can protect you."

"Protect us?" Luia's voice rose to a shriek. "We wouldn't be in danger if it was not for your stupidity!"

"No more," said Ullsaard. "I have made my decision."

"I will come with you," said Urikh. There was a snort of derision from Meliu. Urikh darted a sour glance at her. "Not for my protection. If it is Ersua you're heading for, I know a few folk who could be useful."

"I'm sorry," said Ullsaard, standing up. He walked around the table and stood behind Pretaa, his hands on her shoulders. "I wish you could have spent the winter here."

Pretaa patted his hand and looked up at Ullsaard.

"We will manage, dear," she said. "Do what you think is best."

Ullsaard saw sadness in Allenya's eye. He guessed it was worry about Jutaar more than her personal circumstances. Ullsaard wanted to promise her that everything would be all right, but he knew such a promise would be empty. He had no more idea what the future held than the rest of them.

"Get everything packed again this evening, we'll leave at Low Watch," said Ullsaard. He squeezed his mother's shoulders. "I'll have the servants ready travel chests for you. Let them know if there's anything particular you want to take."

Ullsaard nodded for his son to join him in the next room. Urikh brought his wine with him and settled on the edge of a couch near the small fire.

"I don't know what started this, but I am with you all the way," said Urikh. "Kalmud has always been jealous of your success, and we both know that Mekha was a means to keep you busy and out of the way."

"When we leave tomorrow, I want you to find out as much as you can about Nemtun's army, and see if you can also find out what's happened to Jutaar," Ullsaard said. He looked his son in the eye. "You always have your best interests at heart, I know that. Whatever it is that you are planning, however you think you can exploit this, I don't want to know about it. Just make sure it doesn't risk the safety of your family."

Urikh had the good grace not to pretend offence. He simply smiled.

"And what about my safety?"

"You've never had problems looking after that, I don't expect you to start now," said Ullsaard. He fixed Urikh with an earnest stare. "Thank you for your help. I need it."

"Yes, you do," Urikh replied with a short laugh. "You need all the help you can get."

FREE COUNTRY
Winter, 209th Year of Askh

I

It was by far the most miserable winter Anglhan had ever experienced. Normally he would have been far to hot-wards, trading between the Caelentha, Deaghra and Orsinnin tribes duskward of the Lidean Mountains. He found the biting wind intolerable and the frequent mountain blizzards a nightmare. His clothes stank, the food was terrible and the company stupid and predictable. Even thoughts of the chest full of gleaming askharins failed to cheer him up.

The debt guardian-turned-revolutionary spent as much time as possible in the caves, usually sitting beside a meagre fire with a cup of honey-sweetened hot ale and a blanket over his shoulders. He had cut three new notches into his belt on account of his thinning waist, and his hair was a straggly mess that hung past his shoulders. His crew had been all but disbanded, its members abandoning him for one chieftain or other. Only Furlthia and a few, older hands like Gelthius and Lepiris had decided against throwing in their lot with the brigands or hillmen.

For the moment at least, he told himself. Soon even they would desert him, he was sure of it.

Anglhan did not let his sedentary lifestyle affect his politicking. Out of habit more than any specific aim, he continued to keep the chieftains uneasy with each other, though he was always vocal in his support of Aroisius. Having bought himself the time he wanted, he was at a loss to know what to do with it. He had hoped something would occur that would provide him with an opportunity, but through the short, cold days and long, colder nights he began to doubt the wisdom of joining with the rebels.

When he confessed as much to Furlthia one night, his ex-mate was less than sympathetic.

"What did I say, before all this started? I warned you not to get involved and now we're up to our necks in shit. Come the spring, it'll be all hands on deck for an attack on Magilnada, and then where will we be left? You know Aroisius will do away with you the moment he thinks you're a threat or useless."

"I know, I know," Anglhan said with a sorrowful sigh. He looked past the fire to the snow-filled night beyond the cave entrance. Now and then a swirling gust brought a shower of white further into the cavern. The darkness and cold had gnawed away at his resolve and he wanted nothing more than to be far away, where the sun was still shining. "I took a gamble, that's all. I never said you had to come with me."

"And I'm even angrier at myself for sticking with you."

"Really?" Anglhan's expression showed the deep hurt he was feeling. Furlthia relented and patted Anglhan on the arm.

"Yes and no," he said. "I know you've always done right by me and you didn't mean nothing bad to come of this. I just wish you had listened to me."

The two of them sat in silence for some time; Furlthia poked the fire with a stick, Anglhan nursed his mug until the steam stopped rising from it.

"You should find out where Aroisius is going," Furlthia said.

"What? Aroisius is leaving?" Anglhan straightened up from the doze that had been settling over him. "How do you know?"

"I heard some of the others talking about packing for an expedition. I didn't hear where. They're leaving tomorrow."

"This won't do at all," said Anglhan, heaving himself to his feet, the blanket falling to the rocky ground. "I can't have him going off without knowing where."

The landship captain finished off his cold ale with a wince and tossed the empty mug to Furlthia. He looked around the cave, wondering where to start his investigations. There was the usual mix of cretins: escaped debtors; flat-faced hillmen; former turncranks from his crew; haggard womenfolk and noisy children. Not one of the chiefs could be seen. Time was short, so Anglhan decided that the direct route would serve him best.

With a huff of trepidation, he pulled his cloak tighter and ventured out into the snowstorm. His ears were burning within moments, eyes watering and cheeks reddening. He turned right, towards the head of the valley, and forced himself through the flurries of snow.

He passed two cave entrances glimmering with firelight and stumbled on, almost losing his footing on a snow-buried rock. It was another fifty paces to his destination and by the time he reached the shelter of the cave mouth, his whole face was numb and his boots wet. He barely noticed, such was the allure of fresh activity.

The cave was much smaller than the one Anglhan had left, connected to many others by mine workings that delved deeper into the mountains and to internal galleries above. He had explored a little of their workings, but such was their extent he doubted any of the rebels had fully mapped them. He had, during his deepest misery, toyed with the idea of trying to navigate his way through the depths to find another way out of the valley, but had been put off by the thought of spending so much time in the lifeless, confined tunnels.

A few of the chieftains' lieutenants lounged around a fire near the back of the cave but there was no sign of their masters. One of them looked up, his face pitted, one eye obscured by a drooping eyelid, and pointed to a tunnel branch off to the left, guessing Anglhan's intent. The captain waved his thanks and set off in the direction indicated.

Inquiries with the men in the next cave led Anglhan up a set of shallow steps into a long, narrow cavern. The weapons he had bought had been confiscated from the men and were stacked against the walls; to protect them from the elements and keep them out of the hands of the squabbling rebels until they were needed.

The next chamber contained the last of the preserved meat, which was carefully rationed out by the chieftains every few days. As he passed the barrels, Anglhan reckoned there to be only enough for a few more meals. After that, it would be stew made from tough roots and whatever was left of the dried grain. It was a prospect that fuelled Anglhan's desire to get out of the mountains even further.

He found Aroisius in the next chamber, with half a dozen of his chieftains. The cave was dimly lit by a handful of stubby candles, yet Anglhan's eye was immediately drawn to a small chest just behind the rebel leader; the one that contained the Askhan gold. Aroisius frowned at Anglhan as the captain ducked through the low entrance with a smile.

"You're not an easy man to find," Anglhan said.

"Not for you," replied Aroisius. "What do you want?"

"Wherever you are going, I want to come with you," Anglhan said. He was aware of the squelching his boots made as he crossed the cave to sit down next to the others.

"Really? And what makes you think I want you to come along?"

Anglhan blew on his cold fingers, his breath steaming in the cold air.

"To keep an eye on me, perhaps," he said.

"I do not think there is too much trouble you can cause here," replied Aroisius, though he smiled at Anglhan's honesty. "You do not even know where I am going."

"I can make a guess," said Anglhan, tapping the money chest with his toe. "You have friends who want to know why we aren't drinking your health in the beer halls of Magilnada."

Aroisius's smile disappeared.

"You are far too clever for your own good, Anglhan," said the rebel leader. He sat for a moment staring at the landship captain, one finger stroking his bottom lip.

"He's handy to have when you're bargaining," said Barias. "You should have seen him with that Salphor bastard with the weapons."

"Yes, you might prove useful," Aroisius said. "You have a way with persuasion that might be needed."

"Anything I can do to help," Anglhan said with a grin. "Just get me out of these spirit-cursed mountains. Even if it's just for a day!"

II

Anglhan was groggy as the party set off down the valley midway through the following morning. He had spent a restless night, mind abuzz with possibilities. Aroisius had offered no clue as to where they were going or why, but Anglhan felt it in his waters that they were meeting the rebels' Askhan sponsor.

There were eight of them in the group: Anglhan; Aroisius; Barias; two other chieftains called Gedderik and Stal; a pair of hillmen guides, Dulkan and Gerril; plus the red-headed Reifan. The snows had lightened but the sky was filled with clouds that hung low across the mountains. Anglhan was soon out of breath keeping up with the hillmen's brisk pace along a narrow goat trail that meandered down the dawnwards slopes towards Ersua. By the time they called a break mid-afternoon, the landship captain's feet were sore, his back and legs ached and he was sure he was developing a fever.

They pressed on relentlessly as the snow thickened again towards evening, eventually making a rough camp in a stand of pines. After the wind and snow, the peace within the trees leant the place an air of sanctuary. Anglhan flopped down into the carpet of needles covering the ground, and rested his head on his travel sack. Within moments he was asleep.

III

He woke the next day with the smell of cooking meat in his nostrils. Suddenly aware that he had not eaten the night before, he sat up to find himself covered by a thick blanket lightly dusted with snow. The smell came from a small fire to his right, where four hares were roasting. Reifan sat close by, turning the meat. Beyond, a large canvas had been tied between two trees to create a windbreak, and in its lee Aroisius and the chieftains talked quietly with the two guides.

Anglhan yawned, stretched and stood up, sweeping the blanket from his lap to his shoulders. Reifan looked over at him with a gappy grin.

"You looked dead on your feet," said the rebel. "I wondered if you would wake up this morning."

"I have you to thank for this?" said Anglhan, lifting up the corners of the blanket.

Reifan shrugged as Anglhan joined him, squatting next to the fire to warm his hands.

"No point letting a man freeze to death. I was going to have to wake you; we need to set off soon."

"After breakfast?" Anglhan said hopefully.

"These are for later," said Reifan. He turned and rummaged through a bag, pulled out half a loaf of hard bread and tossed it to Anglhan. "We've already eaten. Toast that and catch some of the dripping juices."

Anglhan did as suggested, moistening his mouth from a cup filled with meltwater. It was rough fare, but it stopped the rumbling protestations of his stomach. No sooner was he done than Aroisius was calling for everybody to pack up their gear. Anglhan had taken nothing out, and so helped Reifan damp down the fire and wrap the cooked hares.

They set out with the guides in the lead, heading through the trees to emerge on a steep hillside dotted with dark boulders jutting from the snow.

"Be careful of drifts," warned Gerril. "You could sink past your head and we'd never find you."

Step by step they forged their way down the slope using staves cut from branches. At the base of the hill, a half-frozen stream trickled from coldwards and they filled their canteens. Turning upstream, they followed its course until a large rock provided a means to jump across to the other bank. Ahead the shoulder of the mountains jutted across their path, rising up behind the white humps of the hills. Anglhan did not enjoy the prospect of tackling the steep obstacle and it was with some relief that they turned dawnwards just after noon, following a much wider river as it rushed down from the mountains towards the Ersuan flats.

Anglhan ached from scalp to toes and had neither the breath nor the inclination for conversation, despite his continuing ignorance concerning their destination. Though the others fared better than he did, little was said as each man concentrated on keeping his footing as the snows continued to fall on the highlands. With only the wind and the scrunch of feet in snow to break the stillness they forged onwards, their route taking them lower and lower.

IV

The snows had turned to a steady drizzle of rain the day before. The perils of slippery ice and deep snow had been replaced by spongy turf, sucking mud and deceptively deep puddles. Anglhan floundered on occasion, his trousers soaked through from wading through heather and ferns, his boots thick with mud. His makeshift walking staff had proved invaluable a number of times, and Reifan had twice heaved him out of briars that ripped Anglhan's jacket and scratched his face and hands.

For all Anglhan's difficulty, six days of walking had put the worst behind them. While the weather remained bad, this was compensated by the flattening of the terrain. The hills became shallower and the firs of the mountains gave way to leafless woods and mossy heaths. They spied the occasional goatherd or group of hunters, and by the time they were looking for a campsite on the sixth evening they saw the telltale smoke from scattered farms not far to dawnwards.

They erected their canvas sheet beneath the overhang of a small cliff, and nestled down between lichen-covered rocks. After a small meal of field fowl caught earlier in the day, Aroisius called them together. He revealed a stoppered bottle of an Okharan spirit called arish, often known further afield as throatburner. They each took a nip from the bottle to warm against the strengthening wind while Aroisius explained what was going to happen next.

"Tomorrow we'll reach Thedraan, a market town on the Parmian Way. I have a contact there who will send word to our sponsor, who will be arriving shortly if he hasn't got to Thedraan before us."

"At last! That'll be at least one night with a proper roof over our heads!" said Anglhan, rubbing his hands together with anticipation. "Soft beds, hot beer and proper food."

"Don't get too comfortable, we will stay only until I've met with my ally." Aroisius's warning did little to dampen Anglhan's excitement at reaching civilisation after so much time in the wilds.

"So, what are you going to tell the big man?" asked Dulkan, combing his fingers through his thick beard. "He'll want to know why we didn't attack."

"I have a better question," Anglhan said before Aroisius answered. "What exactly is your partner getting out of this? And another question – why do you need him?"

"I could not say for certain what my ally is seeking; he has placed no demands upon me," Aroisius said. He tugged the bottle from where it had lingered in Barias's possession and shoved it back in his pack. "I think he's an Ersuan stirring up trouble for rivals in Anrair. He's probably some greedy grain merchant hoping to hike the prices by causing instability in the trade between Askhor and Salphoria. Or perhaps he hopes that with me in charge of the city he'll be able to strike some preferential deal."

The rebel lord looked at the three chieftains when he spoke next.

"We need his money for a number of reasons. To bribe some of the hillmen elders to allow us to hunt on their lands and make our camps; to buy food and equipment; and to purchase information from associates I have in Magilnada and Anrair."

"He must be looking to make a lot of money, judging by the amount he's willing to give you," said Anglhan. "Do you think you could ask him for more?"

"What do I need more money for?"

Anglhan looked at Aroisius as if he had asked what he needed air for. The landship captain leaned back against a rock, hands on his rapidly diminishing belly, and smiled.

"There's always something you can do with more money. The question isn't why you would want more; it's why you *wouldn't* want more! The odd bribe to a militia here and there, the purchase of a few carts, maybe give a bit more to your hill chiefs for more than just permission to hunt, and getting into the city could become a whole lot easier."

"And more dangerous," said Reifan. "So far we've survived through secrecy. The more folk get involved in our plans, the greater chance we get found out."

"That is the truth," said Aroisius. "Also, as you would put it, the more hands in the pot, the less meat for everybody."

"That's a good point," said Anglhan. "No need to share the spoils with more people than necessary."

"I am not interested in financial gain," Aroisius said firmly. "I wish to create a new Magilnada, to provide refuge for those brave souls evading captivity and drudgery. And with Magilnada I will be able to exert influence over the Salphorian king and his nobles to do away with their draconian debt laws."

Anglhan accepted this with a slight nod. Reifan's eyes were wide with adoration, while Barias and the other chieftains exchanged hidden smirks. Certainly the hillmen were looking for a profit in all of this, on top of a chance to get one over on their ancient Salphorian enemies. But it was not them that intrigued the former debt guardian. The real power here was the mysterious Askhan providing the funds. That he might meet this unknown person filled Anglhan with excitement as he arranged his bedding in the shelter of the overhang.

As he drifted off to sleep, the chieftains muttering amongst themselves on the a short distance away, Anglhan's mind bubbled with possibilities.

V

Thedraan was a typical Ersuan town consisting of round stone houses with domed roofs of thatch, about fifty in all.

The wide square at the town's heart was empty, nothing more than a broad muddy patch criss-crossed with footprints and littered with goat droppings. Around this the market barns yawned empty, the wind whistling through their rafters, the rain pooling inside their open doors. But for all Thedraan's dismal, quiet appearance, to Anglhan it was the embodiment of luxury after so long in the mountains.

The group had no difficulty finding lodgings with an old widow, who was willing to rent out her dead husband's house for a fraction of the price she would have charged in the summer. Grateful for this unexpected business, she packed a few belongings and moved in with her son next door.

Anglhan's first mission was to get himself a decent meal, and was soon ensconced at the table surrounded by plates of goat meat, cheese, late harvest pears, pickled vegetables and assorted game. He set to this feast with considerable focus, not sparing a breath to speak to the others until his belly was aching as much as the rest of his travel-weary body. Finishing off his feast with a jug of ale, he declared Thedraan to be the most civilised place in the known world. He retired to bed and did not leave it until the following evening, except to fetch a brief luncheon from the leftovers.

While the town would have been heaving with farmers, traders and drovers during the summer, in these cold days nothing much at all happened. The arrival of Aroisius and his party had caused a few raised eyebrows, quickly dismissed by a story of woe concerning brigands on the Salphorian border; doubts were eased further by the coin Aroisius clearly possessed. It took Anglhan no more than half of the morning following his day of bed rest to find out everything there was to know about Thedraan: who were the important locals; how the year had been; what the townsfolk knew of wider events.

So it was that he came to be sitting next to a small fire in the headman's house, talking to an elderly couple called Rainaan and Thyrisa, sharing a bowl of thick soup. One snippet of gossip had intrigued Anglhan and he wanted to know more.

"I hear there's been some trouble dawnwards," Anglhan said casually, dipping a spoon into his broth. "Some disagreement between Lutaar and one of his sons, isn't it?"

"That's what the last of the traders was saying back in the autumn," said Thyrisa. Her husband grunted in agreement. "Some even claimed there was fighting! Course, we ain't heard nothing since. The Brothers what came through collecting the harvest taxes told us it was all rumour and nonsense, course, but they obviously knew something they weren't telling. Usually you can get good news from their sort, but not this year."

"Our son moved out to Parmia two years ago." Rainaan's voice had a nasal quality to it and his accent was thick enough that Anglhan had to concentrate to understand him. "He's a friend what came through on the last goose drove, and he said that the legions marched through Parmia just before the rains came. Nemtun hisself, mark you. Nobody knows where he was going, but them all headed coldwards without stopping, headed up into Enair I reckons."

"Figure that, eh?" Thyrisa continued. "That old goat Nemtun putting on his marching kilt and armour again. I reckons them Enairians have been kicking up a fuss again, like what they did when my grandma was alive. They've always been a feisty lot, them coldlanders. Isn't that right, my sweetheart?"

"Couldn't say, my precious, ain't met a whole lot of Enairians," the headman replied. He picked up his bowl and licked it clean, talking between slurps. "Only thing they've got to sell is timber, and most of that comes by way of the Ersuan traders, and not much comes this way."

Rainaan pushed his dish away, dragged himself slowly to his feet and hobbled over to the fire. Wrapping the long sleeve of his jacket over his hand, he pulled a pot from over the flames and dumped it onto the table. Steam wafted in Anglhan's face, the heat making his eyes water.

"Try some of that," said Rainaan, dipping a small cup into the pan. Anglhan took the drink and sipped it. He spluttered at the heat of it, but soon his discomfort was washed away by a pleasantly sweet flavour.

"Good stuff," Anglhan said, drinking some more. The headman laughed, raised his own cup in toast and knocked back its contents in one draft.

"I can sell you the recipe, if you like," Rainaan said with a wink. Finishing his cup of hot spirits, Anglhan realised he was not going to get any more information from this pair.

"Some family secrets are best kept that way," he said, standing up. He gave a bow and wink to Thyrisa and shook hands with Rainaan. "Thank you for your time."

Anglhan returned to the house to ponder this news. He said nothing to Aroisius and the others of what he learnt, though the rebel leader could not have failed to hear some of the rumours in the town. Anglhan suspected Aroisius didn't much care what the Askhans were up to as long as it didn't interfere with his plans, and the landship captain was happy to let him continue in that belief.

VI

Six days after Anglhan had arrived, Thedraan was startled by the arrival of another group of travellers, this time arriving from coldwards. This small party consisted of a young man of obviously noble bearing and wealth, accompanied by a handful of servants. Before he encountered this stranger, Anglhan spent a little while around the town listening to the stories being told. Nobody knew the noble's name, but he had come here previously, for a few days at a time for the past two seasons. Many suspected he was thinking of buying the town for himself. Anglhan was pleased to find out that the man had taken over one of the winter-empty shops on the main square. At least he would know where to find this enigmatic sponsor.

Despite his arguments to the contrary, Anglhan was not invited to join Aroisius when he met his "ally". Annoyed by this snub, Anglhan did his best to talk to the noble's attendants, but was disappointed to find the only ones he could meet were both tongueless Maasrites. Cursing the spirits for abandoning him at this important moment, he returned to the house and brooded into the night.

Sleepless with irritation, Anglhan finally abandoned any hope of rest. He threw on his clothes and sneaked out of the house, determined to meet this stranger. Nothing stirred as he hurried along the muddy street, lit only by the occasional glow through the slats of shuttered windows. It began to rain again as he splashed across the square towards the nobleman's lair.

Lamps burned through the shop windows and Anglhan saw a pacing figure on the upper storey, though whether it was the man himself or one of his servants keeping watch he could not tell. He stopped just outside the rear door of the shop and asked himself what he was hoping to achieve. Unfortunately, Anglhan did not have any answers to that question, but was simply filled with the burning desire to meet with this mysterious foreigner.

He realised subterfuge could only get him so far, so he softly knocked on the door. It was opened almost immediately by a bleary-eyed, bald Maasrite. The servant frowned, made a shooing gesture, and tried to close the door. He was prevented from doing so by Anglhan's foot wedged next to the frame. Anglhan pushed the door firmly open and spoke in an urgent whisper.

"I have to speak with your master, immediately! I have news for him. He cannot trust the man he was seeing today!"

The Maasrite looked at Anglhan dubiously but nodded and waved him inside. Despite Anglhan's efforts at stealth, two more servants came into the back hall and regarded him with suspicion. Anglhan studied them in return, and noted the way they held themselves straight, the hard look in their eyes. They were obviously body-guards, but lacked the casual thuggishness Anglhan had seen in other such men. He was convinced they were sol-diers more than servants, though neither man looked old enough to be a retired legionnaire.

The Maasrite reappeared and beckoned to Anglhan to follow. The servant led him up a short flight of steps and motioned for him to climb up a ladder to the second storey. Pulling himself up to the floor above, Anglhan found himself in a bedchamber that filled the whole of the upper floor. Seated on a stool next to the narrow bed was the Askhan noble, arms and legs crossed, his expres-sion one of marked displeasure.

"Greetings, Lord," Anglhan said with a bow. "My name is Anglhan Periusis, an associate of Aroisius."

The noble's expression did not change; his dark eyes bored into Anglhan. The landship captain took a deep breath, ideas whirling through his head, and plunged on.

"I have come to warn you, Lord. Aroisius is going to be-tray you!"

VII

"Really?" The noble uncrossed his legs and leaned closer, arms on his knees, his penetrating gaze never leaving An-glhan. Standing with his hands clasped in front of him, alone with this powerful man, Anglhan felt like a hare that had been spotted by an eagle and it took all of his compo-sure to meet that hard stare without flinching.

"Yes, Lord, it is true."

"Why should I believe you?"

Shit, thought Anglhan. He was ready for any number of questions: what was Aroisius planning? Why would he renege on their deal? Anglhan hadn't expected his integrity to be doubted. The stranger had a sharp mind, and that worried Anglhan.

"What would I have to gain by lying to you?" Anglhan replied as quickly as he could.

"You might be a rival," said the noble. His eyes never relented for a moment. "Perhaps you hope that I will help you oust Aroisius from power."

Spirits abroad! cursed Anglhan, this man has me figured already. Under that unnerving stare he felt the urge to confess everything, but resisted the temptation. Anglhan plunged on with the lie, ignoring the question.

"Once he has control of Magilnada, Aroisius plans to stop all grain trade between Salphoria and Askhor. He wants to starve the Askhans and cripple the treasury of the Salphorian king."

Had he guessed right? Was Aroisius's belief that this was about the grain trade true? Anglhan suppressed a tremble as he searched the man's face for any sign of his thoughts. There was nothing; Anglhan would have had an easier time trying to discern the ponderings of a statue.

"You have not answered my question," the noble said. "What do you gain by telling me this?"

"I'm a merchant by nature, Lord, and my first thought is always for profit, I admit."

"You want paying for this information?"

"Not at all, Lord! I have associated myself with Aroisius in the hope of getting a cut of the Magilnada taxes. If there's no trade, there's no tax, and no money for me."

A half-truth was always better than an outright lie, Anglhan had always thought. It is far easier to convince another man to believe selfish motivations over selfless acts. It appeared this belief still held true: the Askhan straightened on his stool and smiled.

"What do you propose I should do about this?" he said. "Should I send my men to cut off his head for this act of betrayal? Perhaps I should entrust you with my money to complete this business?"

Anglhan smelt a trap; the stranger's proposal was far too convenient for Anglhan.

"I wouldn't do that, Lord. Without Aroisius, this ragtag army of his will vanish in a few days. Your money could convince the hillmen to stay, but Aroisius has a sway over the rebels and debtors. Neither have any respect for me."

The noble thought about this some more before speaking.

"You are right, Anglhan. Killing Aroisius would favour nobody, and would mean I have wasted a great deal of effort and money."

Anglhan edged forward with a hopeful expression.

"What do you plan to do, Lord?"

The man looked at Anglhan with a flicker of annoyance.

"Why the fuck would I tell *you* what my plans are?"

Anglhan retreated two steps, shocked. As he recovered his composure, he found himself feeling a mixture of respect and awe for this man. There was a streak of ruthlessness about him that Anglhan admired.

"You do not have to tell me anything, Lord," Anglhan muttered. He looked earnestly at the Askhan. "But if there is something I can do to help, please tell me."

The noble examined his fingernails for a moment as if he had not heard the offer. He looked up sharply at Anglhan, as though an idea had just come to him.

"There is one small thing you can do for me, Anglhan. How well do you remember your journey here?"

Anglhan wrinkled his lip and shrugged.

"Most of it, Lord."

"So you could find your way back to your camp?"

"To the general area, yes."

The noble stood and walked around the foot of the bed to a bronze-bound strongbox against the wall. He lifted the lid, revealing a mess of scrolls and wax tablets. He pulled out a map and tossed it to Anglhan.

"I am sure this would help," the Askhan said with a lop-sided smile.

Anglhan looked at the map and at the noble's cruel amusement, realisation sinking in.

"If I am to guide you to our camp, I would like to know something first."

"Yes?" The Askhan showed surprise for the first time.

"Your name, lord. If I am to betray Aroisius, I would like to know the name of my new master."

"Of course you do," said the noble, and for a moment Anglhan thought he was going to be denied an answer. The Askhan stepped across the room with a hand out-stretched.

"I am not a lord, so you can forget all of that," he said. "Just call me Urikh."

ERUSAN FOOTHILLS
Winter, 209th Year of Askh

I

A haze of fine rain swathed the camp as bells rang out the start of High Watch. There were muffled calls from the walls as the guard companies changed. The clatter of hammer on metal, the shouts of the third captains drilling their men, the slap of canvas in the wind blurred with the constant patter and splish of raindrops.

Noran hurried across mud-spattered wooden walkways with his cloak drawn over his head, stopping when he reached the awning of his pavilion. Shaking the wet from his clothes, he turned inside. Neerita sat in a low chair wrapped in blankets, her pale face shivering among layers of blue and red wool.

"The Fifth's surgeon gave me this," said Noran, holding up a fistful of dried leaves. "He said I should boil them for half a watch, and then use the water to make you some porridge."

Neerita nodded hesitantly inside the hill of cloth. She flipped back the edge of a blanket and rubbed her swollen belly.

"I wish there was a loremother," she said. "It is coming soon."

"You mean *he* is coming soon," said Noran. He tossed

the medicine onto a small table and knelt beside his wife, his hand on hers. Neerita chuckled.

"A little Noran, that would be perfect," she said. "Have you decided on a name yet?"

"I though perhaps my grandfather's – Noridan."

"And if it is a girl?"

Noran shrugged and stood up.

"If it is a girl, you can choose the name," he said. The herald stopped and listened for a moment, hearing nothing. "Where is Anriit? She should be here with you."

"My sister is asking Allenya if we could have one of Ullsaard's maids." Neerita struggled to get to her feet. Noran sprang to help her. "We'll need all the hands we can get once the baby is born."

"I should have thought of that," Noran muttered as he put an arm around Neerita's shoulders and helped her into the screened-off bed area. He lowered his wife onto the bedding – more blankets piled atop each other – and kicked off his boots. Throwing his cloak over a stool, he settled beside her on the bed and smoothed her hair.

"You'll be a wonderful mother," he said quietly. Neerita reached out and stroked his cheek with the back of her hand.

"And you will be a fine father," she said. Noran snorted.

"A fine father it is that brings a child into this," he said, waving a hand to encompass the tent and, by extension, the camp beyond and everything else that had happened of late. "Our son should be born in Askh, with a loremother and a dozen servants to hand; not in a grubby field surrounded by soldiers."

"It was not your fault," Neerita said, not for the first time. "Things will settle down, you'll see. It will be a great story to tell him when he is older."

Noran kissed her lightly on the lips and pushed himself to his feet.

"I should get to work on that herbal porridge," he said.

"See? Who needs servants around when I have you? You are doing a wonderful job."

Noran snorted again, unconvinced.

"Making porridge is one thing; looking after a newborn is something else!"

"The common people manage it just fine without servants, we will as well," Neerita said sleepily.

Noran stayed at the doorway watching his wife until her eyes fluttered closed. He went back into the main compartment and snatched up the leaves.

"Right," he muttered. "Porridge. Where can I find a pot?"

II

Ullsaard continued to stare at the map, but no matter how long he looked at it, the situation never changed. If they moved further hotwards they would come too close to Parmia; dawnwards and coldwards put them closer to Nemtun, now camped no more than thirty miles away.

The only choice if Nemtun continued to advance would be duskwards, into the mountains. Ullsaard was desperate to avoid that. Keeping thirty thousand men and their baggage together was hard enough under the best circumstances; in the mountains it would be all but impossible to find somewhere to camp them all. He'd have to divide the legions, and that ran a greater risk of desertions and attack. There was the problem of the hillmen – an offshoot of the old Ersuan tribes that still had many villages in the mountain passes. An Askhan column and supplies might prove too tempting for them to ignore, even with the bad weather.

He studied the map yet again, wondering if they could double back on their route and head coldwards again, slipping between Nemtun and the Enairian coast. It was a possibility, and if such a plan worked, they would have the whole of Enair stretching dawnwards to move into.

But if Nemtun found out…

Ullsaard and Aalun's army would be trapped against the sea with nowhere left to run. They had no clear idea of the size of Nemtun's force, whether he still had Nemurians with him and how many, or of the quality of the troops they would face. Ullsaard had avoided a confrontation with Nemtun not because he was afraid of defeat, but because it would be yet another escalation from which they could not back down. Prince Aalun still hoped that he might come to some agreement with his father that would end hostilities in the spring.

Ullsaard's thoughts were broken by the stamping feet of the sentries outside the tent. He heard a brief exchange and Urikh entered, looking pleased.

"You've been gone a while," said Ullsaard, sitting down behind the map table. Urikh grabbed a chair and sat opposite his father. "I don't understand how you can think of business at a time like this."

"I have some good news, and it is all because of my business," said Urikh. "I have found somewhere to stick out the winter."

"Is that so? Where is this sanctuary?"

"In the mountains," said Urikh, planting a finger on the map.

"I've already considered that," Ullsaard replied. "It's a refuge of last resort."

"What if I told you that there was already a camp, which could house all of our men and baggage until the spring?"

"My men," said Ullsaard.

"What?"

"These legions are *my* men. Not ours. Don't get grand ideas."

"Are you interested in this camp or not?"

Ullsaard drummed his fingers on the table and studied his son. Urikh seemed genuinely excited by what he had to say, in stark contrast to his usual chilly disposition. No doubt this plan was not solely for Ullsaard and Aalun's benefit.

"All right," Ullsaard sighed. "Tell me."

So Urikh related the whole story; how he had been sponsoring Salphorian rebels to attack grain shipments coming past Magilnada to drive up the prices; how he had paid the hillmen to team up with those rebels for an attack on Magilnada in return for preferential trade; and how he now knew where the rebel camp was.

Ullsaard stared in disbelief as Urikh unveiled this plot, as casually as if he had been describing what he had eaten for breakfast.

"So, what do you think?" asked Urikh. "The rebels could easily accommodate us until spring."

"Wait just a fucking moment," Ullsaard snarled, surging to his feet, fists balled on the table. "By Askhos's giant prick, what do you think you've been doing? Are you trying to start a war with Salphoria?"

"Well, you are," Urikh snapped back.

"With the full support of the king and the whole fucking empire!"

"And how is that going, eh? Besides, I have the king's support. Half the damn loan I took was guaranteed by Lutaar."

Ullsaard slumped back in his chair, stunned.

"You've got a deal with Lutaar?" The general struggled to comprehend the implications of this revelation. "The king? The same man that currently wants to cut off my balls and feed them to me?"

"This started a long time before all of that happened," Urikh said calmly. "It was his idea, for the most part. He provided me with some extra money to cause trouble for the Salphors. He has his own plans for duskwards."

Urikh spread his hands and leaned back in his chair.

"You know, if Aalun hadn't twisted you into his own plotting, you might have been successful in asking for a campaign."

Ullsaard growled and grumbled wordlessly at the thought that Urikh was right. He thumped a fist onto the map.

"That still doesn't explain what in Askhos's name you thought you were doing, getting involved in something like this."

Urikh shook his head, stood up and took a few paces, wringing his hands in front of him. He spun back to face Ullsaard.

"Stop avoiding the issue with excuses," Urikh said. "The rebel camp; do you want to know where it is or not?"

"It's not just for me to decide," Ullsaard replied, pushing his concerns about Urikh's schemes to the back of his mind. "It is Aalun's decision as much as mine."

"Well, let's find the good prince and see what he thinks," said Urikh, heading for the door.

"Wait!" Ullsaard rose to his feet again. "*I'll* talk to the prince; *you* can stay here and wait for me."

"But…" Urikh said with a pleading expression.

In that moment, Ullsaard was reminded of the many occasions his son as a young boy had protested his innocence against some accusation or other, or had tried to persuade his father to allow him to do something that he had expressly forbidden. Urikh's scowl had never changed, nor his habit of squeezing his hands into tight fists when he was being denied. The years slipped away, and Ullsaard saw again the bright, conniving Urikh, shaped by Luia's scheming, craving his father's approval, yet showing him no respect.

"Urikh, listen to me," Ullsaard said sternly. The effect was instant; his son's hands dropped to his sides in surrender. "It is best if Aalun hears this from me, and the less he knows about your involvement, and his father's, the better it will be. Trust me, son."

Urikh flopped onto his chair with a reluctant nod, pouting, his hair falling across his face. Ullsaard bit back a laugh and patted his son on the shoulder as he walked past. As he reached the door, Ullsaard looked over his shoulder.

"And sit up straight; you're not some lazy fucking poet."

III

Servants moved around the main chamber of the pavilion lighting the oil lamps hanging on the wooden partitions. Ullsaard finished explaining the situation and sat back to wait for the prince's response. Aalun's answer was immediate.

"No."

Aalun lifted his cup and took a sip of wine, his eyes following one particular servant. Ullsaard waited for an explanation or a counter-proposal, but none was forthcoming.

"I think you should consider this," said Ullsaard, choosing his words carefully.

"It is unthinkable," said Aalun, turning his attention back to the general. "I am a Prince of the Blood, and I am not about to start scraping around in the mountains with a ragged bunch of dirty Salphors and hairy hillmen. What would you have them think of us, running for their help with our tails between our legs? This is an Askhan affair, it has nothing to do with foreigners."

"Do you have a suggestion for what we should do next?"

"We stop running, Ullsaard," said the prince. "It is about time we face up to Nemtun and look him in the eye. He will back down, I am sure of it. I have always said we should make a stand rather than let ourselves be chased all over Greater Askhor."

Ullsaard knew Aalun had never said anything of the sort, but opted for discretion.

"Nemtun wants to prove he's still the big man, an army commander," said Ullsaard. "He doesn't give an abada's turd about the consequences, he'll attack just out of spite for me."

"We will stay here, build up the fortifications. Even Nemtun will think twice about attacking five legions in a strong position."

"I think you misjudge your uncle's desire for renewed glory. He'll happily send his men to the spear just to prove he's still got what it takes."

"Not all of the men are his," Aalun said, wagging a finger in disagreement. "I shall send messages to Allon."

"And what will your messages say, Prince?"

"Allon is a nobody, Ullsaard. He is governor of Enair, the arse end of the empire, and at the moment Nemtun and my father make him feel important. I shall offer to transfer his governorship to somewhere more to his liking when I become king." Aalun smiled at a thought. "Probably Okhar if Nemtun continues to push his luck."

"But that depends on Allon believing you can deliver on your promise. What if he thinks you're already on the losing side? What can you bargain with?"

"Enough with the 'ifs' and 'buts', man!" Aalun stood up, fists on hips. "I have told you my decision. I thought you were a general of Askhor! If Nemtun wants a fight, you should give it to him. Unless you think you cannot beat him?"

It took all of Ullsaard's resolve not to bite on the bait. He stood up slowly, pressed his fist to his chest in salute and left. The evening routine occupied the camp as he stepped out of the pavilion. A few soldiers gave him odd looks as he marched stiffly back to his tent, keeping his boiling temper in check.

Inside, Urikh was still waiting for him, joined by Luia and Pretaa. Ullsaard almost left again at the sight, but refused to be chased out of his own place by his family.

"It looks like you don't approve of whatever Aalun had to say," said Luia. Ullsaard darted her a foul look but she continued. "Urikh has told me everything he has been doing. It is most enterprising."

"The prince wants us to stay and wait for Nemtun," Ullsaard said, flopping down into his chair. He looked around for something to drink but the table was empty. "Bring me some wine!"

"When did Aalun become commander of your army?" said Luia. "He sits in your tent, is served by your household, and now he gives the orders."

"Hush, Mother, Aalun is one of the Blood," said Urikh with a mocking tone. "We have to do what he says."

At this remark, Ullsaard's eyes met his mother's. Her thoughts were easily guessed. A servant appeared at Ullsaard's shoulder with a jug and cup, and he was glad to look away. Taking the drink, he focussed on Urikh.

"How many of these rebels and brigands are there?" Ullsaard asked.

"Oh, few hundred, maybe a thousand," Urikh replied. "From what their leader tells me, they have plenty of space. They are holed up in some caves just above Magilnada, easily defended if Nemtun is stupid enough to come after us."

"If you defy Aalun, are you sure your men will follow you?" asked Pretaa. "That is what you are thinking, isn't it?"

"There is no reason why that should be a problem," Urikh said quickly, cutting in before Ullsaard could reply. "Aalun is not as all-powerful as he might like us to think; not away from Askh, at least. He needs us more than we need him, for the moment."

All eyes turned to Ullsaard, expectation on the faces of Luia and Urikh, concern on Pretaa's. He drank more of his wine, collecting his thoughts. He looked directly at his mother when he spoke, though his words were addressed to Urikh.

"You're right, we don't need Aalun." Ullsaard tugged at his bottom lip, still thinking. "His succession is worth less than piss to me. There are other ways we can force the king to deal with us evenly."

"He could still cause us problems," said Luia.

At that moment Meliu entered the tent with Neerita. The two were chattering gaily until they felt the others staring at them.

"What is the matter?" asked Meliu. "Why does everyone look so glum?"

"Nothing to worry you, sister," said Luia. She glanced at Pretaa, who smiled warmly and stood up.

"Come with me, sweethearts, I have a few things to tell you that I cannot say in the company of men," said Pretaa, ushering the two women towards the back partitions. "Childbirth makes them squeamish."

"Is there any chance you could force Aalun to agree with your plan?" Luia continued in a hushed voice when they had left. Ullsaard shook his head.

"He's a stubborn bastard, I can't see him changing his mind."

"Sounds like someone else I know," muttered Urikh.

"It's probably best if I just kill him," said Ullsaard. Luia's eyes widened with shock, but Urikh simply nodded in appreciation.

"Direct," said Urikh. "I like it. But if you just stab Aalun in the heart it will turn some of the men against you. For all my jokes, Aalun really is one of the Blood."

"So am I," Ullsaard said quietly.

The shock of Urikh and Luia seemed to silence all noise across the camp. Mother and son stared at Ullsaard, utterly taken aback.

"I'm Lutaar's bastard," Ullsaard said, answering the question that was doubtless in the minds of the other two. Ullsaard glanced back towards the bed compartments from where his mother's voice could just about be heard. "I did not know until recently."

Even sharper than his mother, Urikh was the first to make the next leap.

"That means I am of the Blood as well! I am your *heir*!"

Ullsaard recognised too well the look of greed and calculation that came over his son. The general grabbed Urikh's arm tightly and pulled him close.

"Tell nobody of this!" Ullsaard hissed. "Do not even tell Pretaa that you know!"

Urikh nodded and tried to pull his arm free, but Ullsaard's grip was unmoveable.

"Swear to me," the general growled. He shifted his glare to Luia. "You too! No one is to know this until I am ready to announce it."

"You have my word," said Urikh, struggling against his father's grasp. "Not a hint to anyone."

Ullsaard released his hold and sat back, face flushed.

"I can see why we do not need Aalun," said Luia. "You could take the throne for yourself!"

"Do not think that for a moment," said Ullsaard, alarmed at the suggestion. "I just want the king to listen to my demands for a Salphorian campaign. What I want hasn't changed."

"You cannot openly challenge Aalun unless you are prepared to reveal who you really are," said Urikh.

"I cannot simply slit his throat in his sleep," replied Ullsaard. "Such an act would turn the legions against me."

"Leave it with me," said Urikh.

"What do you plan to do?" asked Ullsaard.

"Do you really want to know that?"

Ullsaard saw the look in his son's eye and decided that ignorance would be better.

"You're right," he said. "Whatever it is you do, if you get caught you're on your own."

"You cannot say that," said Luia. "Urikh is your son."

"It is all right, mother," Urikh said. "I can look after myself if I need to. I had to in the past, I see no reason to stop now."

A piercing scream broke the stillness of the night. The shrill wailing continued, rousing the whole camp. Ullsaard woke immediately and was on his feet in a heartbeat, dragging on his kilt and a thick tunic.

"What is it?" Luia asked groggily from the bed behind him. "Where's Urikh?"

"I don't know," said Ullsaard as he pulled on his boots. Another ear-splitting scream cried out.

Ullsaard dashed outside to find the camp in uproar; sentries shouted from the walls; captains bellowed at the companies spilling from their tents; legionnaires babbled to each other. When the scream sounded again, Ullsaard located it. It was close at hand, not far to his left. Turning that way, he saw Noran stumbling half-naked through the mud, his hands and chest covered with blood.

"What is it?" Ullsaard demanded as Noran grabbed hold of him.

"There's something wrong," Noran said between sucking sobs. "She's bleeding! There's so much blood!"

Ullsaard realised with horror that Noran was talking about Neerita. He collared a second captain running past, almost hauling the man off his feet.

"Send for the surgeons!" Ullsaard ordered.

"Which one, General?" the startled captain asked.

"All of them!" Ullsaard shoved the man away and followed Noran back to his tent.

Anriit appeared like a bloodstained ghost in the doorway, her light gown ripped and stained. Ullsaard realised the screams had stopped, but he did not know if that was good or bad news. Anriit held up her crimson-coated hands and looked at Noran with blank eyes.

"She's dead," said Anriit.

"No, she can't be," wailed Noran. He tried to push his way into the tent, but Ullsaard grabbed him and dragged him back.

"Best not to see," Ullsaard said quietly. Noran lunged towards the tent again but Ullsaard did not let go.

"Bastards!" shrieked Anriit, ripping at her hair in madness. She looked venomously at Ullsaard and turned her wild gaze on the other soldiers gathering around them. "Murdering bastards!"

Her eyes fell upon Noran, half-collapsed in Ullsaard's arms.

"She should never have been here!" Anriit leapt at Noran, her fingers clawing at his face. "You killed her!"

Noran raised a weak arm to defend himself, but blood streamed from scratches across his cheek and brow. Ullsaard tried to push Anriit away, but she stormed at him, kicking and screaming. He grabbed her by the throat and with one swing of his arm tossed her to the ground.

"Get this crazy bitch away from me," he growled, looking at the legionnaires close at hand. They dropped their shields and spears and wrestled Anriit away from their general.

"She's right," sobbed Noran, sinking to his knees. He looked at his blood-soaked hands and back at the tent. His voice was a choked whisper. "She needs a loremother… She needed proper attention… The cold, and the wet…"

There was another shrill cry from behind Ullsaard and he turned to see what new horror had been visited upon him. Meliu ran barefooted between the tents, her hair streaming, robe open at the front, belt trailing behind her. Ullsaard made no attempt to stop her as she plunged into Noran's tent. He heaved Noran to his feet and almost carried him away.

"Let's get you some clothes and a drink," Ullsaard said. "There's nothing to be done here."

V

Smoke spiralled through the light rain, the flames of the pyre hissing and spitting as they consumed Neerita's linen-wrapped body, her arms arranged around a tiny bundle of cloth and flesh. Noran felt nothing as he watched the flames crawling across her body and listened to the cracking of bones and the popping of fat. He was dimly aware of Ullsaard's bulk next to him, and felt his friend's hand on his shoulder.

"It was a boy," Noran said softly. "Noridan. He was called Noridan."

Ullsaard said nothing, which Noran was vaguely grateful for. He had suffered through the platitudes of Prince Aalun that morning, who had lost his own family years before; and the mewling pity of Meliu and Allenya. Their words were meaningless; nothing could be said that would bring back his wife and son. Anriit's scorn had been the most honest response.

"We should go back to the camp," Noran said dully.

"We can stay here as long as you need," replied Ullsaard. "There isn't any hurry."

Noran slipped from Ullsaard's touch and walked back towards the army camp, half a mile away. He looked at the ditch and banked earth walls; the small figures of sentries making their rounds; the guards at the open gate as companies filed back in after a morning's foraging. The legions were unchangeable, their routine regulated by the drip of water clock and flicker of watch candle.

He didn't know what to think and his thoughts churned between desolation and resignation. Last night his wife and child had died, and the legionnaires kept to their schedule as if nothing had happened, uncaring of events. But there was also reassurance in that timeless discipline; men who walked hand in hand with death every day who knew that, until their time came, life went on.

"I don't know if I can stay," Noran said as Ullsaard caught up with him.

"I don't think it's a good idea to be on your own right now," said the general. "But if that's what you want, I'll do whatever I can to help; protection, supplies, servants."

Noran plodded on with Ullsaard at his side, pulling his cloak tighter as the drizzle soaked into his clothes and chilled him. A respectful distance behind them, a guard of legionnaires followed with a jingle of armour and splash of sandaled feet.

"What a waste!" he exclaimed. "What a vanity it is, that we aspire to change kings and forge nations, but we can't stop a woman from dying. It's all so fucking pointless."

"We have one life to lead, friend," said Ullsaard. "Our achievements are all that we can lay claim to. Men are born and die, but their actions live on down the generations. History is only the tales of the lives of men that came before us."

"And what history do I write?" Noran was bitter, his words snarled between gritted teeth. "What achievements have I? I could not even bring a son into the world. I have not even given that small gift to the future."

"You are not dead," Ullsaard replied, quiet but stern. "Your life goes on. You can choose to abandon your dreams now, or you can be strong and strive for them again."

"I do not know if I have the strength," said Noran.

"Only time will judge that," said Ullsaard, gripping Noran's arm. "Do not let this misery destroy you. What has happened is sad, but to throw away the rest of your life because of it would turn sadness to tragedy. You are better than that."

Noran said nothing and the pair of them walked on in silence. Behind them, the flames burned higher.

VI

Though camp life continued as normal for the next two days, Ullsaard was aware that the death of Neerita had cast a gloom over his army. It was difficult to understand, for few in the camp had known the woman, and accident and disease were no strangers to army life. The general noted

317

the subdued mood as he made his morning rounds. The men saluted sharply enough as he passed, but he heard the mutterings, saw the look in their eyes; the inactivity was giving them time to think, to wonder what was happening, to ponder the future. In short, the legions were bored, and bored soldiers could be dangerous.

Ullsaard summoned Anasind to his tent to discuss the matter.

"They're not sure what they're doing here," the First Captain said. "And soldiers are a superstitious lot. They think the woman's death is a bad omen. It's a bad mix, making uncertainty become fear. They're not sure who the enemy is, who they're meant to fight or if they're meant to be fighting at all. It's no surprise they're restless."

"I want the companies on double-drill, and longer foraging," said Ullsaard. "Keep them busy, keep them sharp, stockpile more supplies. Make it look like something is happening; that we're not just sitting around with our thumbs up our arses."

"Is something happening?" asked Anasind. Ullsaard realised that the First Captain had been talking about the upper ranks' uncertainty as much as the common soldiers.

"Soon, I hope we'll be able to tell the men some good news," Ullsaard said. "I won't mind if a few rumours start spreading that we might be moving out. That'll keep their minds off the cold and the bad omens."

"I understand, General," Anasind said with a slight smile. "If I'm asked if there are any new orders, I'll firmly deny anything is happening."

"That's the trick," Ullsaard said with a wink. "There's no better way than going around saying nothing is happening to convince soldiers that something definitely is!"

When Anasind had gone, Ullsaard set off into the camp to find Urikh. His son was throwing dice with a bunch of second captains from the Twelfth Legion.

"Don't gamble with this one," Ullsaard said as the ring

of men looked up from their game. "He'll own your wives and mothers by nightfall!"

As the men laughed, Ullsaard motioned for Urikh to join him.

"You can keep your womenfolk for the moment," Urikh said as he stood up. "Your tin and salt is worth more."

Light-hearted jeers followed them as Ullsaard led Urikh back through the camp.

"Whatever your plan is to deal with Aalun, how soon can you do it?" Ullsaard asked in a hushed tone.

"As soon as need be," replied Urikh.

"Then do it as soon as you can. I don't know how long we can hold things together here, and the weather in the mountains isn't getting any better."

"By this time tomorrow, Aalun will no longer be a problem."

VII

As in every other part of camp life, Prince Aalun had a precise routine, which Urikh knew well. Every morning at the third hour of Gravewatch, Aalun walked and groomed his ailur, Destiny. It was probably a habit of many years; growing up in the palace, learning how to look after the beasts. Though Urikh had never owned one of the prized cats himself, he knew enough that regular contact was needed to reinforce their loyalty, and Destiny was no exception.

So it was that a little after the second hour of Gravewatch, Urikh made his way through the camp. It was still dark, but the blackness was broken by torches on the distant camp walls and braziers every ten tents along each row. Even at this hour there were plenty of men up and about; the guard companies walking their patrols; kitchen masters gathering breakfast from the stores; armourers stoking up their forge for the day's labours.

Urikh made no attempt to hide; such behaviour would arouse more suspicion. Instead he sauntered along streets of wooden planks sunk into the mud, heading for the stretch of latrines close to the dawnwards wall – downwind of the prevailing breeze from the mountains. He relieved himself into the deep trench, whistling tunelessly.

Leaving the latrines, he headed back by a different path to the low, black tent covering the ailur corral. A quick glance around assured him that nobody was paying the slightest attention, and he slipped inside. The three ailurs were sleeping, deeper shadows in the gloom, but they stirred as he entered. Heavy chains clinked as they moved in the darkness, against a backdrop of heavy breathing.

Urikh found the barrel containing the offal and bones from the kitchens and prised off the lid. With a grimace, he pulled out a handful of deer guts, while he opened a pouch at his belt with his other hand. From this he produced some shredded leaves, which he rubbed into the guts. The ailurs were now on their feet; he could hear them padding around in the darkness, the tent filled with pants and loud sniffing.

Destiny was the closest. Urikh tossed the meat towards her, but it landed short; the ailur strained at her chain to reach it, kept in check by a long pin driven into the earth. With a grunt of annoyance, Urikh picked up the drugged food and threw it closer. Slurping and chewing followed. Urikh sank to his haunches and waited for the soporifics to take their effect.

When the blotch of darker shadow that was Destiny no longer moved, Urikh approached cautiously. He prodded her with a foot, but there was no response. Now came the most dangerous part, and Urikh's heart was thumping in his chest as he edged closer.

With trembling fingers, he found the riveted straps holding the ailur's face mask in place. With a small knife, he prised off the rivets where they attached leather to bronze. He did this twice more, so only a single strap remained in place.

Retreating quickly, he put the lid back on the barrel of food and wiped his hands on a rag. Taking a deep breath, he sauntered out of the tent and headed back to his bed.

VIII

Dawn was still hours away as Aalun stepped sharply through the camp, a loop of reins in his hand. He nodded in return as legionnaires and officers saluted him. As he reached the ailur tent, he unhooked a lamp hanging on the pole inside the door and lit it from a nearby brazier. Ducking inside, he turned to his right, where the tack and grooming tools were hung on a wooden rack.

He heard a growl from behind him but thought nothing of it as he placed the lantern on top of a box. Uncoiling the reins, he turned towards Destiny, who was lying facing away from him. The ailur growled again, and he stopped, wondering what had agitated her. She was pawing at her face. Sitting up, the ailur turned towards him, and something glittered in the darkness.

At first Aalun took the light to be a reflection from the lantern. He stepped a couple of paces and stopped. The glimmers in the gloom were like two tiny fires; flickering horizontal ovals of red and orange. Perplexed, he took a closer look; the tiny flames hovered just in front of Destiny's face.

With a cry of realisation, he straightened. The flickering glow came from Destiny's unmasked eyes.

Aalun had taken no more than a quarter-turn towards the door when the ailur attacked.

Destiny leapt through the air, chain snaking behind her. The ailur's forepaw caught the prince on the side of his face, claws ripping through skin and tearing out an eye. With a scream he fell, clasping his ruined face. Destiny jumped onto his back, pushing Aalun to the ground as her long teeth sank into the muscle of his shoulder, biting through to the bone.

Blackfang and Thunderbolt rose to their feet, sniffing the air and snarling. They strained at their chains but could not reach the blood they could smell.

With another cry, Aalun tried to crawl to safety but the ailur was too heavy for him to throw off. Releasing her jaws, Destiny raked her claws down his back, shearing through tunic, shirt, skin, fat, muscle; right the way down to his ribs. She drew back and pounced again, clamping her teeth into the back of his neck. Tossing her head from side to side, Destiny snapped the prince's spine, leaving Aalun's limp corpse dangling like a doll.

With her prey killed, Destiny settled down beside the corpse. Soon the tent was filled with the crack of snapping bones and the wet sounds of flesh being torn.

IX

Aalun's cremation was a far grander affair than Neerita's. The officers and first companies of all five legions stood in attendance at the pyre, their spears lowered in tribute, five golden faces of Askhos reflecting the flames.

Beside the great pyre burned five smaller fires; the bodies of the first legionnaires who had investigated Aalun's dying screams. It had taken numerous arrows and spear thrusts to slay Destiny, who had attacked the soldiers with unearthly, almost feminine shrieks. The incident had unsettled the whole army, not least because it had happened so soon after the death of Neerita. That one of the Blood had been slain in their midst gave the men grave concerns, and the whisper around the camp was that the Brotherhood had cursed them.

Ullsaard and the First Captains had done what they could to quell the growing dissent, but Ullsaard could sense that he was in danger of losing control of his legions. It was with much trepidation that he addressed the funeral guard. He began by speaking at length on the qualities of Aalun, impressing upon the men that they should be proud to have served under one of the Blood. He reminded them of their duty to Askhor, and to their companions.

"Though one of our champions has fallen, our call for what is ours cannot fall silent," Ullsaard said, arms folded across his broad chest, rain pattering from his ceremonial armour, wind tugging at crest and cloak. He looked at the rows of expectant faces, and knew that what he was about to say would make or break his ambitions.

"When one of our own has died, we say we have a lost a brother, for the legion is family. It raises us, nurtures us, teaches us discipline and respect, feeds us and gives us purpose. For me, the loss is greater than that, for I have truly lost a brother. Aalun was my prince, my mentor, my friend; but we also shared a father."

The announcement was first greeted by astonished silence, but soon ripples of chatter spread through the ranks, while the First Captains looked at each other in disbelief. Ullsaard held up his hands for quiet, but the disturbance continued. There were some who laughed, thinking Ullsaard's proclamation was a joke.

"Listen to me!" he bellowed. "I only tell you this now so that you may know that the Blood has not abandoned you. Our cause, for justice, has not changed. Though the Blood runs through my veins, though but for circumstance I might be called prince, you need know only one thing: I am still your general. The legion is still my family, and you are still my brothers. Today we take the next step on the path to glory and riches!"

Ullsaard snatched up his spear from where it had been driven into the mud. He strode along the line to stand in front of the Thirteenth's first company and lifted the weapon above his head.

"If I command, will the Thirteenth follow?"

The legionnaires replied with an approving roar, lifting their spears in salute. Ullsaard turned to his right.

"If I command, will the Sixteenth follow?"

The company cheered, adding their voices to the Thirteenth.

"If I command, will the Twelfth follow?"

Ullsaard marched along the line repeating the same call, until all five companies were shouting. He looked at his First Captains and they had their spears raised, joining in with the roars of their men.

The crackling of the pyre intruded into Ullsaard's thoughts and he spared a glance towards Aalun's burning body. He felt a flicker of guilt, but it was soon washed away by thoughts of what he could achieve without the prince to hold him back.

He was one of the Blood too, and power was his birthright.

FREE COUNTRY
Midwinter, 209th Year of Askh

I

The cold permeated the caves, a leeching chill that constantly numbed the toes and fingers. Gelthius blew on his hands and rubbed them together to get the blood flowing as he attempted to splice two lengths of cord. He sat cross-legged on the main deck of the landship, back against the larboard rail, while a steady cold breeze wafted over him from the cave entrance. Next to him, Lepiris filled lamps with oil, cursing occasionally as his shaking hands dribbled the flammable liquid onto his clothes.

"I'll have t–" Lepiris stopped as a muffled shout echoed into the cavern from outside.

Gelthius and the other remaining crew put down their work and took up the rough cudgels they had been given – metal-ringed clubs no more useful in a fight than a belaying pin. Others stirred in the cave and groups of rebels drifted towards the entrance, called by the cry. Gelthius slipped down the rope ladder and dropped to the cave floor, Lepiris close behind him.

There was a commotion to the right as Anglhan pushed his way through the gathering crowd, Furlthia just behind him. The snow had stopped outside, but the valley floor was covered in a thick layer of white. As he reached the cave entrance, he saw Lord Aroisius and a handful of his chieftains coming down the valley from the right. In the mid-afternoon light, two figures approached from the valley mouth, walking calmly between the cliffs as the cries of the sentries followed their progress.

Gelthius wondered what was happening; Aroisius and his men had their hands on the hilts of their swords, but had not drawn their weapons. The rest of the rebels crowded in behind their leaders, restless and bemused. The two strangers marched through the snow without pause and stopped a dozen paces away from Aroisius. Gelthius shouldered his way to the front of the mob for a better view.

His eye was drawn first to a big man in Askhan armour. He was larger than even the biggest chieftain, and carried a round shield and golden spear. His breastplate and helm glimmered with water droplets as he planted his spear butt-first in the snow and took a couple of steps closer to Aroisius. Beside him walked a much younger, slimmer man, though as tall as his companion. He held up a hand in greeting, and directed his words towards Lord Aroisius.

"There is no call for alarm," the man announced. "Are we not friends, Aroisius?"

Gelthius glanced at the rebel leader, who eyed the new arrivals with suspicion. The ex-debtor caught sight of Anglhan close by, watching the meeting with interest, his gaze alternating between Aroisius and the strangers. Gelthius watched his master closely; instinct told him that Anglhan's attention was more than casual.

"What are you doing here, Urikh?" said Aroisius. "How did you find this place?"

There it was: a flicker of worry on Anglhan's face before he masked it. Gelthius sidled closer to his captain, cudgel in hand.

"We have quite a lot of maps, Aroisius," Urikh, the younger man, replied. "It was not too difficult to work out possible hiding places for so many men."

326

"Who is this with you? Why are you here?"

Urikh looked at his burly companion with a smile.

"This is General Ullsaard, of Greater Askhor," Urikh said. "He and I have a favour to ask of you."

Aroisius was already shaking his head, perturbed by the arrival of the two men. Gelthius could feel tension; the sudden disturbance of an existence that had been routine for many days. The hillmen in particular were unnerved by the presence of an Askhan officer; for generations their tribes had raided into Ersua and Anrair, lands that had belonged to Askhor for most of the hillmen's lives.

"We want to share your lodgings," Urikh said. "It looks as though you have plenty of room here, and our men do not take up too much space."

"Your men?" Aroisius's eyes narrowed as he looked around the valley, empty save for his own people. "What men?"

"They will be with us shortly," said Urikh. "We thought it better to come ahead and make sure they had a suitable welcome."

"How many?" demanded Aroisius.

Urikh looked towards the towering general beside him. The man was full of confidence.

"I'd say about thirty-two thousand," said Ullsaard. "Plus camp followers."

Aroisius gawped at this news while there were laughs from some of his chieftains. A disturbed muttering rose up from the crowding rebels. Still watching Anglhan, Gelthius saw the landship captain whisper to Furlthia, who shook his head in reply, frowning.

"That is impossible!" said Aroisius. "We cannot house and feed that many men until spring."

"There won't be a need to," said Ullsaard, stopping just a couple of strides from Aroisius, a satisfied smile on his face. "We'll be in Magilnada long before spring. Plenty of beds and food there."

"What?" Exclamations of surprise came from both Urikh and Aroisius. Urikh stared at Ullsaard, brow creased.

"I never said anything about Magilnada," said Urikh.

"It's not your decision," replied Ullsaard. The general turned his eyes upon Aroisius. "Do we have a deal? We'll share camp for a while and I'll help you take Magilnada."

One of the chieftains, Lubrianati, strutted towards Ullsaard.

"My blood will be cold before I share air with Askhan dogs," Lubrianati growled. "Let's kill these bastards and have done with it."

Gelthius saw Anglhan wince at this outburst and shared the captain's opinion. All eyes were on the Askhan general. Ullsaard did not even look at Lubrianati. He folded his arms across his chest, his full attention on Aroisius.

"It is my belief that you are in charge here," said Ullsaard, his words softly spoken. "You should keep your men in order."

"I have no need nor desire for Askhan aid in taking Magilnada," Aroisius said slowly.

"My fucking money was good enough, though?" snapped Urikh. "You would not even have an army if it was not for me."

Both Aroisius and Ullsaard darted looks of irritation at the younger man and returned to looking at each other.

"Wait, wait!" Anglhan called out, stepping from the crowd. "Did you not hear them? They have thirty thousand men!"

"I doubt it!" laughed Barias. "Any man would be a fool to march so many men in winter."

"Thirty thousand, a hundred thousand, it makes no difference," said Aroisius. "We will reclaim Magilnada for true Salphors without your help. I will return your money, what is left of it, and we will continue without your support."

"Are you breaking our deal, Aroisius?" Urikh hissed. "You spend my money and expect to give nothing in return?"

"What is this madness?" exclaimed Anglhan. He turned his words to the assembled rebels. "Who would turn down such allies? If we wish to take Magilnada, this would seem to be to our fortune."

There were laughs and shouts of derision amongst the crowd, though Gelthius heard most of it coming from the rebels. The hillmen were oddly quiet, despite the outburst from one of their chieftains. They watched guardedly, trying to guess at the outcome of this confrontation.

A pointed silence ensued, Urikh and Ullsaard facing down Aroisius and his men. A sound startled all except the two Askhans: the distant beats of a drum echoing along the valley. It sounded a quick march, and as it rolled along the cliffs another noise could be heard, a constant rumbling. This soon resolved into the tramping of feet; thousands upon thousands of feet.

The shouts of the sentries were filled with alarm as a line of armoured men appeared at the mouth of the valley, marching in step to the drum. Fifty abreast, rank after rank of legionnaires entered the pass behind their golden icons, spears shouldered, shields held up.

Gelthius watched the reactions of those around him: fear in the eyes of the rebels, save Aroisius, who glowered at the oncoming army; surprise and delight from Anglhan; a mixture of worry and anger from the hillmen and their chiefs; and Ullsaard standing calmly in front of Aroisius with a slight smile.

"Would you like to reconsider your position?" the general said. "There is no reason we cannot be allies."

"Listen to him," said Anglhan. "Our quarrel is not with the Askhans, but with those toads that would squeeze the blood from Salphoria. What does it matter how we take Magilnada? We are strengthened by this alliance!"

Aroisius rounded on Anglhan, his face a mask of fury.

"You reward my trust with betrayal, you wretched thief!" snarled the rebel leader. "Has this been your plan all along? Usurper! You have not a single fibre of honour or decency in your whole body. You are a traitor to Salphoria."

Anglhan did his best to look offended.

"I swore to do all that I could to put Magilnada into your hands, Lord Aroisius," he said. "What better way to deliver the city than with the help of these men?"

"Save your lies, you treacherous, spirit-cursed oath-breaker."

"See sense," said Ullsaard. "Listen to your friend."

"He is no friend of mine," rasped Aroisius. The rebel leader stared directly at Ullsaard, spittle flying from his mouth. "There is no alliance here. Take your men and leave."

Ullsaard's hand moved so fast, Gelthius barely saw the general rip free his sword. In one motion, blade left scabbard and connected with the side of Aroisius's head, splitting skin and skull. As the rebel leader fell back with a cry, Ullsaard followed up, chopping his blade into Aroisius's neck, blood spattering across the general's face and breastplate.

Gelthius glanced down the valley; the legionnaires were barely two hundred paces away.

Lubrianati stepped up with a shout, but his sword was barely out of its sheath when Ullsaard's shield smashed into his face. The Askhan lunged with the tip of his sword, driving it into Lubrianati's left armpit, deep into the chieftain's chest. Lepiris moved out of instinct, but Gelthius grabbed his arm and hauled him back. Ullsaard dragged his sword from the body of Lubrianati and stood at guard, Urikh backing behind him, casting glances over his shoulder towards the advancing column.

"No fighting!" roared Anglhan, stepping in front of Ullsaard to face the rebels; out of weapon reach of both,

Gelthius noted. "Do not throw away your lives. This is a hopeless battle. We cannot win!"

"Listen to your man!" bellowed Ullsaard. "No harm will come to any man that does not raise his weapon against me. Any that choose to fight will be shown no mercy."

The sight of the two dead men at the general's feet, and the massed ranks advancing behind him, quelled any immediate attack. The legionnaires stopped at the command of their captains, barely fifty paces from the line of rebels that stretched from one side of the valley to the other. Ullsaard, Urikh, Anglhan and Furlthia stood between the two lines, watching warily.

Gelthius tugged at Lepiris's jacket and the two of them melted away towards the closest cave entrance. Others were doing the same, Anglhan's old crew and bands of hillmen mostly; the line thinned as the chieftains raised their open palms and ordered their followers to stand back. With their numbers growing smaller by the moment, most of the ex-slaves and Salphor brigands threw down their clubs and spears, hurling insults and disgust at those that had backed down.

Calm descended. Ullsaard wiped his sword on Lubrianati's jerkin and sheathed the weapon. He passed his shield to Urikh and placed his fists on his hips, regarding the rebels and hillmen impassively. The general's gaze turned on Gelthius, who froze, gripping Lepiris's arm tightly.

"You!" barked Ullsaard, pointing at Gelthius. "Are you prepared to swear an oath of loyalty to me? Will you become a legionnaire of Greater Askhor?"

Gelthius looked along the two lines of men. To his right stood the rebels, with their leather jerkins and mauls, their ragged trousers and bent-shaft spears; to the left waited the Askhan legionnaires, with their broad shields, their bronze-tipped pikes, their polished armour and their gleaming standards.

"It's the legions for me, right enough," Gelthius replied in a quailing voice.

"Good man!" Ullsaard replied with a grin. Still smiling, he took a deep breath and spoke to the others. "Any man not willing to join me will not be forced to. Those that wish to leave, step forward and make yourselves known."

There was no movement at first, but then Barias strode up to Ullsaard and spat at his feet. In ones and twos, half of the chieftain's warriors joined him. Others drifted from the crowd, alone or in small groups, until there were several hundred men in the dissident group. Ullsaard nodded and walked back to his army, where his officers met him and they spoke for a short while. At the shout of "Split column!" the legionnaires divided their line, opening up a space down the middle of the valley.

"Off you go!" Ullsaard shouted cheerfully, waving Barias and the others towards the mouth of the pass.

With glances back to those they were leaving behind, the dissenters walked down the valley, passing between the lines of legionnaires. A few more men broke from those that had stayed behind, running to catch up with those that were leaving. When the last of them had caught up, Ullsaard turned to his army and raised his fist.

At this unspoken command, the captains bellowed the order to attack.

Like the jaws of an ailur closing, the legionnaires turned on the men in their midst, bearing down on them with shield and spear. Realising their plight, Barias and a few others drew their weapons, but it was too late; line after line of bronze spearpoints surrounded them, rank after rank of soldiers bore down on them.

The clash of weapons and shouts lasted for only a brief time; all along the valley silence fell. The rebels were dead, only the legions of Ullsaard remained.

MAGILNADA
Midwinter, 209th Year of Askh

I

The only traffic on the road leading to Magilnada was a solitary two-wheeled cart drawn by a plodding abada. Cold sleet rained down on the wagon, whose driver and companion sat huddled in their cloaks beneath an improvised awning of stretched canvas. Water caused the sheet to bow, so that now and then the driver reached up with a stick to poke the awning, sending ice-cold water sloshing over the sides.

"Still, better than snow, eh?" said Gelthius. His passenger, the Askhan noble called Noran, replied with a doubtful look.

"I like snow, in moderation."

"What's 'moderation' mean?" asked Gelthius.

"Not too much," Noran told him with a sigh. Gelthius absorbed this piece of knowledge with a nod, and stored it with the other long words he had learnt on the journey from the camp.

They carried on, the cart rocking slowly from side to side, the wind bringing gusts of spray into their faces.

"Ever seen Magilnada before?" Gelthius asked. Noran shook his head.

"Not in person," said the noble. "I have seen drawings."

"It's a mighty city, right enough," said Gelthius. "A mighty city indeed."

"I was born in Askh, the greatest city in the world," said Noran. "It takes a lot to impress me."

They rode on for a while longer, until Gelthius spoke again. It had been the same for the whole journey: Gelthius trying to pass the time with chat, Noran answering only reluctantly.

"Pardon my saying, but you don't seem all that happy to be here," said Gelthius.

Noran didn't reply straightaway. He drew his hood tighter to his face and stared up at the mountains. Gelthius thought the noble was going to ignore him, but then Noran spoke. His voice was quiet, his mood sombre.

"Bearing all things in mind, I would rather be in Askh. I have a large house there, and a lodge in the hills I can visit if I fancy some mountain air. I would travel in a covered carriage, out of the wind and rain. Servants would attend me at my slightest word, bringing me good food and splendid wine.

"Instead, here I am on the board of an open wagon, in the pissing rain, my belly half-empty, my clothes soaking to the skin. And what am I about to do? Ride into the city my friend, your general, is about to attack, at no small risk to myself."

Gelthius pondered this for a moment.

"So, why are you here?"

"Because I am an idiot, my odious companion. An idiot who thought he could help a friend."

Gelthius decided not to ask what "odious" meant, though he might guess at its meaning. The cart hit a particularly deep rut in the road and sent the pair lurching to one side. Gelthius grabbed the wagon seat to stop from toppling from the board. Noran reached over and hauled him upright.

"Careful there. There is no point getting hurt before we

even reach Magilnada." Noran directed a sour look at the wagon and the beast pulling it. "Besides, I have no idea how to drive this thing."

The abada had almost stopped at the commotion. Gelthius prodded it with his long stick and it lumbered on again, the traces tightening as it picked up speed. Soon the cart was rumbling and swaying.

"Seems to be you don't want to be here, right enough," said Gelthius. "Me, I can't go nowhere else. I been a cattle thief, a shoemaker, a farmer, a debtor, a rebel and now I'm an Askhan legionnaire. I got food in my belly and clothes that ain't full of holes. I reckon I'm doing all right at the moment. If you've lost so much, why don't you just go back to Askh? Putting aside friendship with the general and all that."

"Go back to what?" Noran's wistfulness grew into bitterness. "The king has exiled me. My family has probably disowned me. My estates are no longer mine."

Noran grew even quieter. Gelthius struggled to hear his words over the noise of the cart's axle, the splashing of the wheels and the pattering of rain on the awning.

"Nothing to go back to; nothing to take back. Neerita's gone. No son. I have nothing left."

Noran stared bleakly ahead, eyes fixed on something else. Gelthius said nothing. He recognised a foul mood when he saw it, and knew that any attempt to cheer up his companion was likely to end in anger. They rode on in silence until the walls of Magilnada could be seen through the rain.

Grey and brown like the mountains from which its stones had been carved, the semi-circular outer wall curved from a cliff face that rose far above the plain. Square towers broke the wall every quarter of a mile, and there was only one gate, protected by fortifications twice as high as the rest of the wall. In the summer, when Gelthius had seen the city before on his three visits as one of

335

Anglhan's turncranks, there had been a second city of tents outside, filled with traders, craftsmen and other visitors. Now the city was surrounded by a flat stretch of muddy grass, in places turned to bog by the rain. Little could be seen of the city within; a haze of smoke from forges and hearths hung over the city.

The stone-strengthened track they were on curved around to coldwards and joined a straighter road; paved with giant slabs, though now much cracked and overgrown with plants. To either side stretched the fields that fed the city, the flat expanse broken by clusters of low farmhouses and long barns. The landscape was still, the only movement the empty branches of scattered trees swayed by the strengthening wind.

Weighed on by such dismal surrounds and Noran's sombre mood, Gelthius tried his best to be happy. He was a free man, in reality and by the law of Salphoria. He had talked to his new comrades in the Thirteenth, and Gelthius had come to the conclusion that life in an Askhan legion was certainly not the worst thing that could have happened to him. And this current job, meeting others in Ullsaard's army that had sneaked into Magilnada, looked to be safer than what the future had in store for his fellow crewmates and rebels.

II

A group of twenty or so warriors stood guard at the gates, which were open. Obviously bored, they waved to Gelthius to stop the wagon and quickly surrounded it, peering into the bundles on the back and looking at the two men aboard with suspicion.

"What's your business here?" one guard asked. He was of typical Magilnadan stock, with the wiry frame and dark hair of a Salphor, and the flat nose and wide chin of a hillman.

"Trade," Noran replied quickly. He made no attempt to mask his accent; such a thing would have been pointless considering his narrow features, fair hair and long limbs easily identified him as Askhan to the bone.

"It's still winter," the guard replied. He walked to the back of the cart and prodded around for a while. He would find nothing other than Noran's personal belongings. The guard came back to the front of the cart. "You ain't got nothing to sell, and you couldn't carry much out of here in this, if you're buying."

"Contracts," said Noran. The man frowned and he continued. "You know, an agreement for a sale? There has been fierce competition for the grain come trading season again, what with everything that has been going on. While my rivals are warming their feet by their fires, I will be getting one step ahead of them."

"There's been some strange folk coming to the city of late," said another guard. "Never seen so many visitors at this time of year. What's going on out dawnwards?"

Gelthius felt his stomach tighten at so many questions. He kept his gaze firmly fixed on the hindquarters of the abada and let Noran do the talking.

"Oh, the usual sort of thing," said the noble. "Generals falling out with each other, governors trying to wriggle for position and power. Nothing to be worried about. Say, I hear there has been some trouble with rebels around here. Is that true?"

"Trouble?" said the first guard. "Nah, not so much. A few caravans get attacked and suddenly every merchant and his son thinks there's an army in the mountains waiting to pounce on them. "

"They've been quiet since the weather set in," added the third warrior , stroking grimy fingers through his forked ginger beard.

"Another good reason to get my business concluded as quickly as possible," said Noran.

"No need to hurry away too soon," said a fourth man. "We're always happy to welcome visitors with some coin in their pouches. If you're looking for lodgings, there's rooms at my cousin's place in the tanners' district. Good price too. Ask around for Helghrin."

"I will be sure to look into it," said Noran.

The guards stood around for a while longer. When they were convinced that this fancy Askhan merchant would provide no more entertainment, they waved the cart through the gate. Gelthius gratefully prodded the abada into motion and they passed into the city of Magilnada.

III

The shrine gardens had become the regular haunt of Noran and the rest of Ullsaard's infiltrators. Most days, the noble could be found sitting in the overgrown park at the centre of Magilnada, talking to one or more of his conspirators. While they swapped information regarding the city, the people of Magilnada went about their business, leaving small sacrifices or paying homage at the small altars dotted around the gardens, each dedicated to one spirit or another.

Thirty days had passed since Noran had entered the city, and he was now one of a hundred and fifty of Ullsaard's followers tasked with spying on the Magilnadans. Every few days, one of them would leave with a short report penned by Noran and another would return several days later with requests and questions from the general: asking about the dispositions of the guards; their numbers and equipment; names of prominent locals and chieftains; locations of barracks and armouries; sentry rotations; standards of alertness and discipline. Noran gathered all of this through the network of followers in the city, and through the odd bribe or conversation with locals.

On this particular day, Noran met with Gelthius again. The ex-debtor had secured himself a position in the craftsmen's league, on the back of his experience as a cobbler. In the short time he had been in the city, Gelthius had learnt the names of the most important tradesmen and the supplies they provided to Magilnada's chieftains and warriors. Today he had nothing new to report, and was about to leave when Noran told him to stay.

"What do you think our chances are?" said Noran. "You are a Salphor, you know how these people are likely to react once we take over."

"The men I talk to won't care one way or other," said Gelthius, sitting on the wooden bench beside Noran. He kept his voice low, nervous of the people walking past just a few paces away. "In fact, if the general comes in and starts buying up gear and such, they'll be happy. Magilnada's always been a strange place. These people are from all over – Ersuans, Salphors, hill folk, Anrairians. It's a place unto itself and I don't think they're bothered by who sits in the lord's hall."

He jabbed his thumb over his shoulder towards the artificial hill that rose up beneath the cliff behind Magilnada, where the largest houses and richest inhabitants of the city could be found.

"Salphoria ain't one people, besides," Gelthius continued. "I'm Linghar, then there's the Hadril, the Cannin, the Vestil, the Hannaghian, all sorts. You call us all Salphors, but Salphoria's just the land we live in, it ain't who we are. The king's just the most powerful chieftain, nobody special."

"What are you talking about?" asked Noran.

"I heard things in the camp," admitted Gelthius. "This ain't about Magilnada. The general's promised his men the chance to have a go at Salphoria. They're all excited about it, which is why they've stayed. All I'm saying is, even if you beat the king, it don't mean all the Salphorian tribes'll just fall into line. Same's true here. If you get the chiefs on your side, the city's yours. If they decide to make a fight of it, it could get dirty.

"The tribes fight amongst themselves three days out of four, but if you lot march in and start telling everyone what to do, that's a sure way to get them to join forces. I hope the general's got plenty of gold to throw around, that's all, cause that'll get him the city surer than any number of spears."

Noran smiled.

"Gold that is offered at spearpoint tends to have a brighter gleam, though," he said. "It will be harder for these chieftains of yours to negotiate with a few thousand legionnaires staring at them."

Gelthius shook his head and sighed.

"What?" asked Noran. "What is the matter with that?"

"You ain't heard what I said," Gelthius told him. "If rebels take over Magilnada, or some rival chieftain gets rich enough to stake his claim, the tribes wouldn't give two rotten apples for it. But if you Askhans start sticking your golden faces all over the walls and prancing about like you own the place, that's the best way to get them angry and fighting together. Magilnada's part of the Free Country, which means it's fair game for any Salphorian tribe – for everyone 'cept the Askhans. Your kings made an agreement, and breaking promises is a sure way to make the tribes hate you even more."

Noran considered this opinion with a frown.

"We cannot start a war in Salphoria," he said. "Not until everything back in Askh has been smoothed out."

He stood up, and Gelthius did likewise. Noran was clearly agitated and he glanced around the gardens with a faint look of distaste.

"I think I have to make some suggestions to your general. If he comes in here with his full legions, he will be starting something he cannot finish yet." Noran clasped Gelthius's shoulder briefly. "Thank you. You have been a great help."

As he watched the Askhan stride off through the gardens, Gelthius was left wondering just how much help he wanted to be. It had been one thing to join up with the rebels; he had never really believed they had a chance of taking the city. It was another matter to hand the city over to Askhans. Askhans, he thought, that wanted to use the city as a position to launch attacks on the Salphorian tribes.

Troubled by his conflicting allegiances and expectations, he wandered through the long grass and leafless bushes until he found the shrine to the spirit of justice. It was a low, broad slab underneath the naked branches of a short, twisted tree. The stone was covered with coins of low value, stubs of candles and dishes of smouldering leaves that gave off a sweet odour. Thin strips of material hung from the tree limbs, covered with writing that Gelthius could not read – the invocations of petitioners scrawled by the shrine's priestess. She sat on one of the tree's roots, an old woman, her eyes bound with rags. She turned her craggy face towards Gelthius as he walked across the mat of rotting leaves.

"The spirit of justice calls out to you," she crooned. "Make your offering and let it guide your hand and your words."

Gelthius looked at the shrine, tapping a finger on the pouch of coins given to him by General Ullsaard. He saw the rags on the branches waving in the wind and wondered how many favours the spirit of justice had granted people over the years, and how many they had ignored no matter how great the sacrifice to them was. He thought about his own life – the years lost aboard Anglhan's landship – and realised that the spirits, of justice and everything else, had abandoned him a long time ago. The Askhans did well enough without them, perhaps it was time he looked to a different power to look after him; the power of the Crown and the Blood, the power of the legions.

"Not today," Gelthius said, and walked away.

IV

Noran paced restlessly, cursing the backward inhabitants

of Magilnada for having neither water clocks nor watch candles. How in Askhos's name did anybody here know what the time was? They had some sundials, but they were crude and altogether useless at night, and it was sometime after Midwatch.

And time was important.

He ceased his striding and forced himself to sit down on a low wall that ran along the side of the street. The clouds obscured stars and moon, and all he could see were the torches on the gatehouse at the bottom of the road, and the flickering fire and candlelight from the windows of the small houses on each side of the street. Looking coldwards, he saw the glow of the huge bonfires lit in the garden of shrines, and the wind brought the shouts and chants from those celebrating the Midwinter festival of spirits.

He was aware of other people in the dark; thirty fellow infiltrators gathered close at hand, most pretending to be drunk. They were all Ersuans from the Fifteenth, picked because they looked the most like Salphors. They swigged from beer jugs and wine bottles and laughed and chatted. Noran thought a few of them were just a bit too convincing and wondered whether they were pretending at all. Then he remembered they were legionnaires, and they were under orders. Their company code would mean that none of them would be allowed to get the others intro trouble by actually being drunk.

Over half of them wore swords at their belts; not the short and easily recognisable blades of Askhor, but the clumsy, curved weapons Anglhan had bought for the rebels. Noran had to admire Ullsaard's attention to detail. Once Noran had passed on Gelthius's wisdom, the general had quickly agreed that Magilnada had to be overrun by rebels, not Askhan legionnaires. Having access to the stores of the genuine rebels helped in this regard, but he had also been careful to send in only those men not obviously from one of the more distant provinces of Greater Askhor.

342

Likewise the legion he had assembled to attack the city was drawn from across the army, leaving out Okharans, Enairians and Nalanorians who would be immediately identified as men of Greater Askhor. Nobody in the city was to realise that their new "liberators" were anything other than disaffected Salphors and their hillmen allies, with a few Ersuan and Anrairian opportunists thrown in.

Details, thought Noran.

Details like choosing the festival of spirits for the assault, when people were on the streets so that Noran and the others could move around with freedom; a night when most of the city's warriors and militia would be drunk, even those supposedly on duty.

Details such as the carefully drawn maps of Magilnada handed out to the captains in the legion waiting outside, so that they knew exactly where to go once they were in the city.

Details like the small box of gold coins Noran had in his room, melted down from the askharins Urikh had provided and smelted afresh as more debased, local coinage.

Details like choosing one hour after Midwatch, after careful observation of the guard routine on the wall; the watch changed around midnight, and so Ullsaard had allowed just enough time for the new men on duty to get comfortable.

Other details Noran had spotted, telling the men not to fall into step with each other whenever they were in a group; or the way the legionnaires acted around the handful of officers that had come into the city with them; or their altogether un-Salphorian attention to personal cleanliness. Noran had almost been forced to order the men to piss in the street like everyone else in the city because they had chosen to designate a particular back alley as their latrine and would visit it in shifts like they were still in camp.

But they had all missed one detail.

"How the fuck do I know when to start things?" Noran muttered.

Over towards the dawnward wall, another group of men were waiting with oil and tinder to set a fire as a distraction. When that was blazing, Noran and his band would take the gatehouse, as stealthily as possible, and at that moment Ullsaard and his makeshift legion would be appearing out of the darkness ready to walk straight in and claim the city.

All of this was to begin at the second hour of Midwatch, but Noran had no idea when that would be. If they took the gatehouse too soon, they would have to hold until Ullsaard arrived; if they took it too late, some sharp-eyed sentry might spot the approaching troops and raise the alarm.

Ullsaard was used to his legions acting in concert according to his orders, every part combining to bring victory. If all went well, Magilnada would fall with hardly any blood being shed – another detail Ullsaard had been keen to emphasise once he had decided that he could not just storm the city and force everyone inside to submit.

But Noran gnawed at a nail as he considered the risks. Doubts troubled his thoughts. What if the firestarters got caught before they could set the blaze? What if the fire did not catch well and fizzled out in the damp night air? What if nobody noticed it until it was too late? And even if that diversion worked well, there was no guarantee that Noran and his band would secure the gate.

"This is the shit part," said a figure, appearing out of the smoky gloom.

It was Nidan, a second captain from the Sixteenth. He had been sent into the city because, unlike many lower officers, he was literate. He was a squat, bow-legged man who had grown a drooping moustache to blend in better with the Magilnadans. As he sidled up to Noran, the smell of stale sweat and strong ale came with him.

"What is the shit part?" Noran asked, wrinkling his nose at the stench.

"Waiting," replied Nidan, slumping against the wall a few paces away. "Done it a dozen times. There you are, all geared up, ready to chop some bastard's head off. You can see the enemy, a mile away maybe, looking back at you. You've got your orders, all the boys are ready, but it's not quite time for the off.

"Or the night before you know there's gonna be a battle. That can be a real fucker. Those long hours, the bells ringing in the watches and you just know that in a day's time you could be dead."

"How do you deal with the fear?"

"Fear? I'm talking about the boredom. No need to be afraid. Do your job, kill the other son of a whore first and you don't have to worry about anything. Although... I do end up pissing quite a bit on those long nights. I don't know if that's important."

"Easy as that, is it?" said Noran. He glanced up and down the street and considered sending the runner to the other group with the order to start the fire; better, Noran figured, to be early rather than late.

"You should send Lihrin off with the word, I reckon," said Nidan.

"Do you think it is time?"

"We're a bit behind, really."

"What?" Noran jumped off the wall and looked around, searching for some sign that the plan was going wrong. "How can you tell?"

"Three patrols." Noran looked at Nidan with confusion. The second captain pointed towards the gatehouse. "The guards time their watch by the number of patrols from the gatehouse along to the next tower and back – twenty before a change. I've been keeping an eye on them, and they make twelve patrols in one of our watches, so that's three in an hour. The third patrol came back across the gatehouse just now."

Noran held the second captain on either side of his face and planted a kiss on the surprised man's forehead.

"Nidan, you are a fucking credit to the legions!"

Noran signalled to the runner, Lihrin, who set off up the street at a steady trot. Nidan gave Noran a wink, and headed back to his troupe of pretend drunkards. The noble realised how lucky he had been that the officer had chosen to talk to him at that moment.

Noran corrected himself with a further realisation; he was not lucky, he was an idiot. Nidan had talked to him precisely because he knew the runner was late being sent, and had even shown the good grace not to remark on Noran's ineptitude.

Noran checked that his sword would come out of the sheath easily, and glanced around at the other men. Now that the plan was set in motion, all his anxiety was gone. His eyes turned towards the dawnwards walls while he waited for the first bloom of the fire.

V

Cities stink, thought Gelthius. Not the natural smell of cattle dung or the musk of sweating turncranks, but the rotting stench of refuse, the smoke from a thousand fires, and the accumulated waste of too many people living in such a small place. The tanneries, where he was crouched in an alleyway with three other men, stank of the piss used to treat the leather.

Since coming to Magilnada, he had decided that he didn't care for cities, not one bit. Magilnada was too crowded and everybody living there considered themselves far more important than everybody else. Part of him wished that the fire he was about to set would spread out of control and eat up the whole wretched place in a glorious blaze.

But that wasn't the plan, so he and the others would be careful to set the fires closest to the stone wall, and they would raise the alarm quickly before disappearing into the night. When Gelthius had first heard of the distraction the general wanted, he had thought about the poor tanners that would lose their businesses. They had families to feed. The guilt did not last long, not when he considered the huge amount of trade that would come their way once the city was in the general's hands.

The padding of running feet drew his attention to the street. Lihrin appeared out of the darkness, emerging like a shadow from the lingering smoke that blanketed the city from the festival fires.

"We're on!" Lihrin said, waving for the group to join him.

Checking that nobody on the city wall was looking down on them, they gathered at the side door to the closest tannery. It was not barred; the owner and his family would be at the celebrations. Gelthius was the first inside, the gloom within the low stone building no darker than the unlit street. He fumbled around with the flint of his firebox and managed to strike a small flame into life. Lighting a candle from the small bag hanging at his belt, he found himself in a side chamber. The noxious reek of the tannery was even stronger here, and Gelthius wondered how anybody could live so close to such a stench.

"Let's just do this and get going," whispered Grendlin, pulling a flask of lamp oil and a rag from his sack.

Gelthius and the others soaked their rags with oil and stuffed them between vats and barrels. They splashed more oil onto the piles of treated leathers, and on the frames where the stretched skins were hanging. Their work done, all but Lihrin retreated back to the door. Lihrin walked backwards after them, dribbling a trail from his flask. Gelthius checked outside and, seeing that no one was nearby, tossed his lit candle onto the slick stream of oil on the floor.

They bolted out of the door one after the other as flames licked in a line across the room. None of them was sure how quickly the blaze would take, but their orders were to raise the alarm only when the fire was large enough to take considerable time and effort to put out. They headed back to the alley where they had been hiding before, and watched smoke wreathing from the windows and around the doors. A distinct orange glow could be seen through the slot-like windows, and the wooden planks of the roof began to smoulder. Pops and crackles could be heard from inside.

"Do you reckon that's big enough?" asked Gelthius. "Should we start shouting?"

"Let's just give it a f–"

Lihrin's reply was interrupted by a huge sheet of flame that shot up through the boards of the roof, scattering smouldering planks into the street. As the debris clattered down onto the stone, Lihrin turned to the others with a jubilant grin.

"I think that's going well enough," he said. Lihrin ran out into the street and headed towards the tower on the wall, hands cupped to his mouth.

"Fire!"

VI

Noran and his men staggered towards the gate as a clamour of shouts and banging swept through Magilnada. The thick smoke from the tannery fire billowed across the roofs of the buildings and the dull glow from bonfires was engulfed by the towering flames that reached up higher than the curtain wall. There was a commotion at the gatehouse as warriors poured out onto the wall to see what was happening, while others came out of the arched doorways of the flanking towers.

"What's happening?" Noran slurred his words as he draped his arm across the shoulders of one of the guards and looked dawnwards toward the pillar of flame.

"That's the tanneries!" the warrior shouted up to the wall.

"It's spreading into the city!" came the reply.

An argument ensued between several of the guards, regarding whether to abandon their posts to help fight the blaze or to stay at their posts. Many of the warriors did not wait for permission and streamed up the street towards the centre of the city, calling out concerns for homes and families. Unseen, the group of "drunks" sidled closer to the towers and gate.

Noran saw that there was nobody at the door of the closest tower and slipped inside. Treading lightly, he walked up the wooden stairs within. He turned on a landing and came face to face with a bearded warrior heading the other way.

"What are you doing?" the guard demanded.

"Better view from the wall," Noran replied and pushed past, not giving the man any time to refuse.

The guard looked as if he would stop Noran for a moment, but ignored him and carried on down the steps. Noran found a steep flight of steps at the top of the tower and pulled himself up to the battlement of the wall.

There were more than a dozen men on the stretch of rampart between the towers, all of them looking into the city at the flames spreading from building to building. From this vantage point Noran could see hundreds crowded into the streets close to the dawnward wall, while chieftains in long cloaks waved swords around and ordered groups this way and that to fetch water or rally more people.

Noran glanced over his shoulder, out of the city. He could see nothing in the dark, but he knew that out there somewhere was Ullsaard and his legion. They could surely see the fire now and would be on their way.

The thud of footsteps heralded the arrival of Nidan and half-a-dozen of the men at the top of the wall.

"You can't be up here," one of the guards said, shouldering past Noran to berate the new arrivals.

Nidan drew his sword and plunged it into the man's throat.

Behind Noran, the guards shouted in alarm and readied their spears and shields. The noble threw himself aside and skulked at the bottom of the parapet as the guards ran towards Nidan and his soldiers. The Magilnadan warriors didn't give him a second glance as they pressed towards the armed men coming out of the tower. As soon as they passed him, Noran rose to his feet, sword in hand.

He ran to the edge of the wall and looked down at the gate arch. Bodies littered the ground; he recognised a couple of them as his own men, but most were guards cut down by the surprise attack, dead before they could even raise a shout of warning. Certain that nobody down there was going to be calling for help, he turned his attention to the men fighting the legionnaires.

He thrust his sword into the back of the nearest guard and was struck by how unlike the measured, ceremonial duels of the bloodfields the hack and slash really was. Another man turned to see what had happened to his falling companion, to be greeted by the edge of Noran's sword in his face. The man fell back with a scream and Noran leapt after him, stabbing and stabbing, driving his swordpoint into the man's chest and gut over and over, even after he had fallen to his back and lay still.

A guard swung backwards with his shield as he fought, unintentionally smashing it into Noran's shoulder. Noran stumbled and lost his grip on his sword, the weapon clattering beneath the feet of another guard. Noran back-stepped quickly as the Magilnadan turned on him, but the threat was short-lived; Nidan's sword took the man across the shoulder and darted back into his groin with a splash of blood. The second captain stepped over the twitching corpse, stooped to pick up Noran's sword, and handed it to him hilt-first.

A quick glance confirmed that the only living men at the gatehouse were Noran's. By the flickering light of torches stretching left and right along the wall, Noran could see nobody else.

He peered out into the night, waiting to see the first sign of Ullsaard's approach.

VII

With Furlthia in tow, Anglhan walked through the gate of Magilnada, feeling very much like the conquering lord though he had not had to strike a single blow himself. Once he was through the gate, he entered one of the towers and skipped up the steps as quickly as his heavy build would allow, and was panting by the time he pulled himself up onto the stones of the wall. Noran was there with a few others that had opened the gate; he seemed surprised by Anglhan's arrival.

"Where is Ullsaard?" said the Askhan.

"Down there somewhere," Anglhan replied, waving a hand towards the city, "having some fun with his troops."

"It looks like utter chaos," said Noran.

Anglhan could see all the way across Magilnada, now illuminated by several fires, the largest being the one started in the tanneries. Groups of Ullsaard's men roamed the streets with spears and flaming torches, herding the inhabitants this way and that. The greater part of the attacking army had pushed through the streets to the Hill of Chiefs and was busy battering at doors and throwing brands onto thatched roofs. Atop the wall to either side, other companies had fanned out, taking prisoner or killing any guards they encountered. In the square behind the gate, several companies guarded the streets to make sure nobody in the city could leave.

"It's a great deception," Anglhan told Noran. He pointed to their right, where a cluster of men were standing around a number of sizeable buildings not far from the

351

marketplace. "It looks like a bunch of rebels running amok, but it's all been carefully worked out. That's the grain stores secured. Others have taken the armouries, the treasuries. See how none of them have entered the shrine gardens? That's all part of the plan too. And the chieftains are being rounded up. Ullsaard's got a list of names of those that are likely to cause the most trouble; they'll be killed in the fighting. Those that will be helpful, they'll be taken captive if possible."

It was a remarkable sight. The Askhans were everything Anglhan had hoped they would be, and in many ways much more. Two hundred years of expansion had honed their conquering skills to the sharpest edge; two hundred years of the legions had turned bands of individual warriors into a something far more dangerous, capable of overwhelming anything and everything they had been sent against. Even now, masquerading as incompetent rebels and with poor equipment, the legionnaires were unstoppable. Dawn was still several hours away, and yet the city was already in their hands.

And that power was something he had helped guide. He had never known such a thrill, and he envied those Askhan generals and nobles who had such resources at their call every day. The swift taking of Magilnada was proof to Anglhan that the future was with the Askhans, and that it was far better to be on their side than against them.

"What are you thinking?" asked Furlthia. "You've got that look in your eye that I don't like. It's the same one you get when you've lined up a deal with a healthy profit, or when you've picked up a dozen debt tokens for half their value."

"Today Magilnada falls," replied Anglhan, "who knows what tomorrow will bring?"

"Funerals," Furlthia said. "Tomorrow there will be a lot of funerals."

"I mean all of the tomorrows to come, not just the day after this one."

"I know," Furlthia said, his mood grim. "And they will bring a lot of funerals too. The Askhans were never going to be a problem for us, not in our lifetimes, but now you've let them in you know they'll never be gone. It's what they do; take what they want, kill those that fight to protect what is theirs, and send the survivors from their homes to build new towns and cities."

"Ask the Ersuans, or the Enairians, or the Nalanorians what they think," said Anglhan. "I'd bet a herd against a calf there's not one of them that wouldn't want to send a message back to their forefathers, telling them not to fight, telling them that things would be better if they just accept the Askhan way. The Maasrites, now, they were the clever ones. Look at them now. But nobody learns, do they?"

Furlthia's expression was one of disgust as he tore his eyes from the city and looked at Anglhan.

"The only voice you're hearing is the sweet songs sung by gold. I hope that whatever you get is worth the price those people are paying. I'm done with this, and I'm done with you."

The former mate stalked off back into the tower, leaving Anglhan alone with Noran.

"Progress can be a harsh mistress," said Noran. "Many more people before yours have learnt that lesson, but now benefit from her sweet attentions. Ignore your man; he has a narrow, selfish view."

"You're right," said Anglhan. He rubbed his hands together and chuckled. "It's fools like him that have been holding me back for many years. Idealists like Aroisius; petty-minded merchants with no ambition; thuggish chieftains and bullies. It is time they woke up and realised the world is changing. Well, this old captain can smell which way the wind blows and I've never tried to move against it."

"What are you going to do now?" asked Noran.

Anglhan looked at the city and did not see the fires and the screaming mobs. He saw streets and markets not ankle-deep in shit; gleaming palaces of stone and gold; lines of merchants and farmers passing through the city. And through and under and above it all he saw taxes, his taxes as lord of Magilnada – chest upon chest of gold and silver, naked and lithe serving boys, fruits from Maasra, exquisite Askhan murals, hot baths and all the other delights of Askhan life he had heard about from the men in the mountains.

That was his future.

VIII

They had arranged to meet in a small house in the middle of the crafts quarter, seemingly stuck at random between a kiln and a forge. Dawn was just creeping over the city wall and Magilnada was quiet, cowed by the aggression of the disguised legionnaires. Ullsaard sat in the main room beside a dimly glowing firepit and waited for the others to arrive. He felt uncomfortable, and not just in mood. He was wearing the trousers that Salphors preferred and they chafed at his legs. He also wore a heavily embroidered shirt, the heavy red material patterned with blues and white. It was too fancy for his liking; Ullsaard preferred the clean cut and plain colour of his own wardrobe. He wanted to be in his armour, as befitted his new status as ruler of Magilnada, but he knew it could not be known that he was an Askhan general.

And that was why he was here, waiting for Anglhan and Noran. In the next room, watched over by several men, the previous ruler of Magilnada, Gerlhan, waited to learn his fate. The lord of the city had surrendered to Ullsaard's troops the moment they had come to Gerlhan's hall. Gerlhan had been smuggled through the city to this place so that the future of Magilnada could be discussed, but first Ullsaard wanted to straighten his own thoughts on the matter.

The door creaked open and Noran and Anglhan arrived together, behind them an escort of a half-company of legionnaires wearing a mishmash of clothes and carrying an assortment of weapons. Noran whispered something to their captain and the soldiers assumed a more mob-like appearance, breaking the lines they had naturally formed in the street,

"I bet you wish you had never trained them so hard," said Noran, crossing the room to slump into a chair behind the table. He looked even more haggard than when he had entered the city. There was water and beer, and he helped himself to the latter. "Good habits are as hard to break as bad ones."

"I think they're enjoying themselves," said Anglhan. "It isn't often they get to lounge around, drink and behave badly."

"As long as they don't lounge, drink and behave badly too much," said Ullsaard. "We're only here for the winter."

Anglhan stood at the firepit and warmed his hands, though the room was quite warm. He looked at the flames as he spoke.

"So that's still your plan, is it?" he asked, trying to appear nonchalant, but Ullsaard detected the slightest edge of expectation in the man's voice.

"It's never been my intention to stay here," said the general. He leaned to one side and grabbed hold of a low stool onto which he swung his feet. Ullsaard pushed his chair back on its rear legs and put his hands behind his head. "Somewhere nice to wait out the winter before we tackle Nemtun and Allon."

Ullsaard stopped as he heard raised voices outside. He recognised one as Urikh's.

"Let him in!" the general bellowed, half-turning towards the door. He hadn't invited his son to the meeting, but he had expected him to learn of it.

Urikh hurried inside, wearing a hooded cloak which concealed his face.

"What do you look like?" said Noran.

"An arse," said Ullsaard. He glared at Urikh and pointed to a chair on the opposite side of the fire. "Sit down and don't interrupt."

Urikh was about to argue, saw the look in Ullsaard's eye and thought better of it. With a curled lip, he settled into the chair and glared back at his father.

"As I was saying," the general continued, "the campaign begins again in the spring. As soon as the weather turns for the better, I'll be marching into Anrair with the legions. Murian is a coward; hopefully Nemtun hasn't got to him first. Anrair has the Third and the Fourth stationed along the border with the Free Country. I can find a much better use for them."

"So what happens here?" said Urikh, earning himself a frown from Ullsaard, which he ignored. "You don't plan on giving the city back, surely."

"Of course not," said Ullsaard. "When I have things sorted back in Askh, it will make a wonderful base to launch a campaign into Salphoria. Taking the city now saves us time later."

"Which means that you'll need to leave somebody in charge whilst you are leading the army," said Anglhan.

"And you think that should be you?" laughed Urikh. "Out of the question!"

"I nominate Noran," said Ullsaard. Both Anglhan and Urikh looked at the general in amazement. Noran said something, too quiet to be heard.

"What was that?" said Ullsaard.

"I do not want it," Noran said. "I am not staying here amongst these oafish barbarians while you run around doing whatever it is you want to do. Whoever is left in control will have to have eyes in the back of his head,

356

and I am not one for looking over my shoulder like that."

"Noran doesn't want it," said Anglhan. "And for all your son's credit in starting this whole thing with Aroisius, he clearly isn't old and experienced enough to run a city."

"And you are qualified?" scoffed Urikh. "A half-literate slaver with pretensions to grandeur?"

"I was a debt guardian, not a slaver," Anglhan replied softly. "And I am fully literate and numerate, thank you. I even speak a little Nemurian. Do you?"

Urikh seemed about to protest further when Ullsaard lifted up his legs and let his chair thud to the floor.

"I need you for other things, Urikh," he said. "You'll be coming with me. If Noran doesn't want the job, why don't I just keep Gerlhan in his position? It would certainly stop some of the problems we might have."

"What 'things' have you in mind for me?" said Urikh, straightening haughtily. "I am not one of your captains to be ordered around as you please."

"No, you're my son, which means your duty to me is even deeper. You will do what I tell you to do or I will disown you and cast you out, and that bitch of a mother you have. I no longer have to worry about what Aalun and the nobles think of me, I have no reputation to protect, so I'll do as I bloody well please. If you have a problem with that, you can leave now."

Urikh became the centre of attention as he squirmed in his chair, caught between his dislike of his father and his dependence on him.

"For my mother's sake, I shall remain," he said, folding his arms angrily.

"You can't leave Gerlhan in charge," said Anglhan. "He has too many connections with other chieftains across Salphoria. He could cause a lot of trouble."

"Your greed clouds your reason," said Noran. Anglhan whirled towards him.

"I have never lied about my ambition to rule the city. Well, not to you. It was my intent to betray Aroisius and take control, but that is no longer needed. I understand this city better than any outsider, and I know how the Salphor mind works."

Anglhan paced across the room as he set out his vision for the city.

"This place can become a tribute to the ideals of Askhos under me. We will make Magilnada an icon of civilisation again, lost these past two hundred years since the decline of its founders. Salphor and Askhan will be welcome together and the peoples that live duskward of here will see that there is nothing to be lost by accepting Askhan values into their lives. We can show them the benefits of being part of Greater Askhor, and when I am done the people in the city, the people who trade here and travel through Magilnada will be your best spokesmen."

Noran and Ullsaard looked at each other. The noble seemed impressed and gave a slight nod. Urikh was still sulking.

"Words are all well and good, but can I trust you?" Ullsaard asked.

"I have no reason to turn on you, Ullsaard." Anglhan sat on the stool in front of the general, his face earnest. "I am a man who has enjoyed meagre fortune and made the most of it through my life. You think I am greedy, but I am not. I will take my share of the city's dues, and I will rule it in my name for your cause."

Anglhan placed a hand on Ullsaard's knee.

"I have everything to lose by betraying you, and nothing to gain. Leave a thousand of your men here, under one of your best captains. They are loyal to you and you alone. They would be your guarantee of my good behaviour."

Ullsaard considered this for a while, rocking his chair

back and forth.

"Very well," he said. "I agree to your terms. You will increase Askhan influence in the city until it can be brought into the empire willingly."

The general stood up and bent over Anglhan, dwarfing him with his massive frame.

"And remember that if you fuck around with me, I will come back and not only kill you, I'll burn this whole place to the ground. Is that understood?"

Anglhan kept his composure well and simply nodded.

"Good," said Ullsaard, straightening up. "What should we do with Gerlhan? Do you need him?"

Anglhan shrugged.

"No point keeping him in the city, he'll do everything he can to undermine me."

Ullsaard nodded and strode to the door leading to the adjacent room. He opened it and signalled to the legionnaires standing guard over the former chieftain. As Ullsaard turned back to the others there was the sound of a brief struggle, ended by a gurgling cry and the thud of something heavy hitting the floor.

"Well, that is all sorted," said Urikh. He looked at his father with raised eyebrows. "Just what are you going to do come the spring to convince the king to call off Nemtun and allow you to lead your legions into Salphoria?"

"I'm not going to convince the king of anything," said Ullsaard walking to the door that led onto the street. "It's gone too far for any negotiation."

"What do you mean?" Noran called out as Ullsaard opened the door. "What are you going to do? What is the plan?"

Ullsaard turned around to face them, one hand on the door frame. He looked at Anglhan, Urikh and his gaze settled on Noran. His next words were spoken in a matter-of-fact tone, the same way he would tell an officer to prepare a provisions list or name the men on punishment duty.

"I am going to be the next king."

ANRAIR
Early Spring, 209th Year of Askh

I

"What if they put up a fight?" asked Rondin.

"We kill them," said Ullsaard.

The general looked down the road winding through the foothills. The first caravan of the season headed towards Talladmun; more than thirty wagons laden with timber and ore, smelted bronze and quarried stone. There were probably three hundred people, perhaps more. Some of them pulled handcarts; others walked next to the wagons or rode on them. Ullsaard could see the covered carriages of the richest merchants, and the bodyguards that protected them. Most would be ex-legionnaires, drawn back to a violent life for any number of reasons. Here and there a Nemurian towered over the humans; no more than half a dozen, for which Ullsaard was thankful. His army, hidden just below the ridge behind him, numbered twenty thousand of his men and was more than a match for anything the mercenaries could offer, but Nemurians fought to the death if paid and would take a toll in Ullsaard's soldiers doing so.

He looked further dawnwards, towards the Nalanor border. He could see the rising sun glinting from the weapons and armour of Luamid's men, a detachment of five hundred that would close in on the rear of the caravan to stop any fleeing back towards Askh.

"Let's show ourselves," said Ullsaard, raising a hand.

The hills came alive with the rustle of men moving, the jangle of armour, the thump of sandaled feet. As the first ranks of the legions came into view, hurried shouts from the lead wagons warned the rest of the caravan. Drivers pulled their abada to a stop and pointed towards the hills, at line after line of armed soldiers spread along the road.

While shock pulsed back through the caravan, a few groups tried to turn their wagons around. Carts became entangled with each other in the panic, while women started screaming and children wailed. A few cowardly souls broke altogether, leaping the ditch that flanked the road to sprint away across the hills on the other side. Ullsaard was happy for them to go; he wanted people to know what he was doing.

With the general leading the advance, the greater part of Ullsaard's legions marched down the ridge, descending on the caravan in a bronze, red and black wave ready to sweep away all in its way. Families clustered around the menfolk, while the unruly snorts of the abada and cries of other animals added to the commotion.

Ullsaard headed for a particularly elaborate covered wagon a little from the front of the line, judging it to belong to the caravan's master. The men who stood guard beside the wagon warily eyed the general and his bodyguard as the legionnaires drew up into a block just in front of them. A short, chubby man with heavy rings on his fingers and a few stray locks of hair plastered over his bald scalp peered nervously from under the canopy.

"Is this your caravan?" Ullsaard asked. The man nodded uncertainly, and climbed down from the wagon at a wave from the general.

"You're the renegades, aren't you?" the merchant said, gulping heavily with fright. "Are you going to kill us?"

"Not unless you want us to," replied Ullsaard. He looked up and down the line of wagons filling the road, while other traders approached cautiously to hear what was happening. "I'm buying all of your stock."

"You're... buying our stock?"

Ullsaard nodded and waved his men on. They climbed up onto the wagons, shoving drivers from their seats. There were fierce shouts from up ahead. A harassed-looking second captain came hurrying along the line and saluted Ullsaard.

"There's a man refusing to give us his wagons," the officer reported. "What should we do?"

"Kick his cunt in," said Ullsaard.

"General?"

"Rough him up, but don't kill him, that should stop trouble spreading," Ullsaard growled. The captain nodded in understanding and set off. Ullsaard turned his attention back to the caravan master. "We're not robbing you, unless you refuse to sell us what you have."

"You have money?"

"Of course," laughed Ullsaard. "Why wouldn't we?"

"I heard you were all starving in the mountains," said the merchant.

"Homeless vagabonds, that's what Nemtun called you lot," added another from a safe distance. "Cowards and traitors, too."

Cries of pain cut through the hubbub from the head of the caravan, punctuated by snarled curses and sounds of a thorough beating. A sobbing call for mercy ended with a snapping noise that caused the gathering merchants to wince in fear.

"We're doing you a service," said Ullsaard. The merchant captain cringed as the general leant an arm on the shorter man's shoulder and smiled. "You should know that Salphorian rebels and hillmen are running amok in the mountains coldwards of here. *They* would rob you; we

363

won't. As long as you give us a fair price, of course."

"A fair price?" This came from a young man not far to Ullsaard's left. "What do you think is a fair price?"

Ullsaard straightened, strode over to the dissenting merchant and rested a hand on his sword.

"We'll start with your lives and work up from there, eh?" said the general with a pleasant smile. "But don't get too fussy, I have no stomach for haggling."

The youthful trader retreated a few steps and looked at his fellow merchants.

"They warned us about this!" he said. "I said we should have brought more men, but you were all worried about the cost. 'Shut up, Lenruun,' you said. 'We can handle a gang of half-arsed ruffians,' you all said. Look where that's got us. I hope you're Askhos-damned happy now, you bunch of misers!"

"And you're taking our wagons!" protested another voice from the crowd.

"We'll pay for those too," said Ullsaard. He pointed back along the road. "Leskhan is only two days' walking that way, stop complaining."

There was an impromptu conference amongst the senior merchants, whose heads bobbed and beards wagged as they discussed the situation. The caravan master approached Ullsaard, urged on by approving glances from his companions.

"All right, renegade," he said. "We'll give you everything at seventy sindins on the askharin. That's nearly a third of market value. That's a good price."

Ullsaard leisurely folded his arms and shook his head.

"Sixty?" offered the merchant.

Ullsaard looked over his shoulder towards a nearby phalanx of legionnaires. They booed and shook their heads. The general's gaze returned to the merchant, who sighed heavily.

"We can't go lower than fifty."

"Half price will be fine," Ullsaard said with a smile. "Pass the word to your men not to interfere, and make sure the Nemurians don't start anything. Take any personal belongings with you. I'm not paying for anything not on your ledgers."

The merchants gave reluctant nods and dispersed back to their wagons and families. Rondin approached Ullsaard, cocking an eye at the merchants.

"I still don't understand why we're paying for stuff we could just take," said the First Captain. "This lot wouldn't even make the boys break a sweat."

"We're going to need all the help we can get if we're to beat Nemtun and the king," Ullsaard said quietly. "The last thing we need is word spreading that we're murderous, thieving bastards. We forage what we can, pay for what we take and act like proper legions. Lutaar would love to paint us as lawless brigands, let's not give him the chance. Things are going to be difficult enough as it is without having to worry about every common man and woman in Greater Askhor hating us. If we get them on our side, we've half-won the war."

"And what's going to win the other half?" asked Rondin.

"We'll starve Anrair and Enair into submission, and then chop off Nemtun's head. That should do it." Ullsaard slapped a hand to Rondin's shoulder. "Let's get these wagons off to Anglhan before any of these idiots start having second thoughts."

II

Wandering along the clean, paved streets of Talladmun, Gelthius was again convinced that he had made the right choice siding with the Askhans. Magilnada aside, there was nowhere in all of Salphoria that could match the size and achievement of an Askhan town. Gelthius had never seen one before, and it was amazing to him that only twenty years earlier, Talladmun had been little more than a fishing village on the Ladmun River. He guessed there must be thousands living here now, in stone and wood buildings, brought from quarries and forests at least a dozen days' travel away. In contrast, even Carantathi, capital of Aegenuis, Salphoria's current king, looked like a dishevelled collection of rough barns and mud-brick hovels.

It'd be easy, thought Gelthius, to slip away into the town and hide until this all blew over. He could be a shoemaker again. Even Askhans needed shoes. He was not young, but Gelthius was sure he could find another wife; he still had it in him to raise another son or two. He could start all over; put the cattle thievery, the debts behind him. Nobody would care, nobody would know.

But Gelthius couldn't bring himself to slip away. He wasn't much for thinking, he was the first to admit, but he hadn't survived in an uncaring world by being slow-witted. The general was a man with an idea, and that sort of person, once started, was hard to stop. And Gelthius had no doubt that if he abandoned his current mission he would end up getting caught out in the end. Somehow, Ullsaard would find him and make him pay for any disobedience. If there was one thing above everything that he had learnt in his time in the Thirteenth, it was the price of failure.

There was something else that nagged at him as he walked along the main road that led to the town's central district. He already had a wife, two sons and a daughter. It would not be right for him to forget them while he enjoyed the comforts of this Askhan life. If he wanted this, it was only right that he shared it with them.

Family was important to Askhans: legionnaires got pensions, farmers got money from the king when their crop failed; even a middle-aged shoemaker could expect the odd bit of trade thrown his way by the legions or governors if he really needed it.

He crossed the street, nimbly stepping between two lumbering abada, as he caught sight of the distinctive black robe of a Brother amongst the growing crowd of townsfolk. He was in two minds about that lot. The other men in his company had told him how the Brotherhood was the glue that kept the Askhan Empire stuck together. A word from a Brother could make or break a man, but they couldn't be bribed, couldn't be flattered, couldn't be tricked. They were, as third captain Leagois had put it, "straight as the Royal Way," whatever that meant.

The Brotherhood upheld the law – even governors and kings had to obey it. They collected the taxes, but did so without favour, and sometimes they even paid people money if they could prove they had suffered a bad year. They wrote lots of things down, Gelthius had heard. Who was born and who was dead, who was married and who had what jobs. They arbitrated disputes between merchants and families, judged those who broke the law and kept everything working.

It was a huge difference from the chieftains and their cronies who ruled the Salphorian tribes, from the king on down. Gelthius had long ago accepted that his betters would be self-serving bullies, until he had met the Askhans. If Gelthius had a complaint about Naraghlin, chieftain of his people, there was nothing he could do but shut up and bear it. If he had something to say about Captain Leagois, he could speak to the second captain, Aladaan. Not that any legionnaire ever did make a complaint, but they could if they really wanted to.

But the Brotherhood made Gelthius uneasy. He glanced over his shoulder as the black-robed man disappeared down the road. For everything they did, the Askhans never liked talking to them, and for Gelthius there was something deeply wrong with a whole bunch of men who claimed to know the will of a man dead for two hundred years and who denied the existence of the spirits. That denial scared him more than anything. He had realised in Magilnada that he owed the spirits nothing for the woes he had suffered under their gaze, but that was a long throw from going out of his way to insult them by pretending they didn't exist.

Caught up in his thoughts, Gelthius wandered into the path of a patrol of legionnaires. There were twenty of them with heads of ailurs painted on their shields, from the Second Legion commanded by Nemtun. Seeing the soldiers reminded Gelthius of his mission – and of several dozen other men sent by the general – prompting him into action.

Unslinging a small bag from his shoulder, Gelthius tripped in front of the soldiers, spilling its contents. Bunches of spring berries scattered across the paving slabs in a shower of red and purple. He fell to his knees and hurriedly gathered them up, with a glance of apology at the patrol's officer.

"Morning there, Captain," said Gelthius. He noticed the men looking at the fruit he scooped back into the sack. "I'll be out of your way in a moment."

"Where'd you get those?" the captain demanded, pointing at Gelthius's bag.

"These?" Gelthius replied innocently. "Picked them meself, I did. You boys look hungry. D'you want some?"

He proffered the bag towards the legionnaires, who stepped up with arms outstretched until their captain barked at them to stay in line.

"Where you from, stranger?" the captain asked. "You talk funny."

"I do talk funny, Captain. I'm from the Free Country, thought I'd try to see if things were better up here. Things haven't been going so well since the rebels took Magilnada."

"The renegades have taken Magilnada?" This was from

a young, round-faced legionnaire. He stepped back into line as the captain rounded on him with a snarl.

"Keep your fucking mouth shut!" The officer turned his temper on Gelthius, grabbing him by the scruff of his jerkin. "What do you know about the rebels?"

"Not your rebels, captain," Gelthius said as he squirmed in the captain's grip. "Some other lot. Took the city to spite King Aegenuis, I reckon, and now they're raiding left and right without a care in the world. It's been hard, there ain't nothing coming from duskwards, I tell you. Not a piece of tin, nor a plank of wood nor drop of beer. Still, I'm sure you boys'll be all right. Got your own stores and everything, right enough."

The captain shoved Gelthius to one side.

"Mind your own business."

"I was lucky, got saved by one of your legions when I thought I was done for," Gelthius continued. "Drove them rebel bastards back into the hills quick enough when they came for us. Like the spirits of vengeance themselves they came down on them brigands."

Gelthius threw the bag of fruit to the captain, who caught it awkwardly out of instinct.

"You boys saved my life; I reckon you should have these more than me."

"We didn't save anybody's life," said the captain, his anger replaced with confusion. "What the fuck are you talking about?"

"I told you, legionnaires what chased off the rebels in the hills. I saw them meself. Black shields, red crests."

"That's the Thirteenth, Captain," muttered one of the legionnaires.

"I know that," said the captain, forgetting to admonish the soldier for speaking out of turn. The officer bore down on Gelthius once again and grabbed him by the collar. "You fucking idiot, the Thirteenth *are* the rebels. How did they look, how many of them were there?"

"Thousands of them, and they was hungry for a fight. Butchered them thieves good and proper, the ones what they caught."

"What about their gear?" the captain continued. "How did that look?"

"Bright and shiny as a new askharin, I'd say. Not that I've ever seen an askharin, but I can imag–"

"Where was this?" The captain let go of Gelthius, looking worried.

"Somewhere between here and Magilnada, Captain. We kept walking for quite a time before we got here."

"How long? How many days?"

"Sorry, Captain, I can't remember rightly and I'm not so good at counting. I'd say more than less."

"You're no fucking help," said the captain. He waved his men to continue, the sack of fruit still in hand.

Gelthius watched them go and chuckled. The Second's legionnaires were getting all sorts of news about their enemies, and none of it matched up. The general had given each of those sent to Talladmun a different story to tell, some putting him far to hotwards, others claimed he was just a couple of days' march away. Some of the tales had the legions as a bedraggled remnant of their former glory preying on whoever they could find, while others spoke of an army numbering fifty thousand well-equipped soldiers. Gelthius guessed all of the bad information was really Anglhan's idea; it smelt like the sort of thing he would think up.

It was a mean trick to play on men already missing their first three supply shipments, intercepted by Ullsaard's legions before they reached Talladmun. Hungry and confused, after a rough season quartered in the Anrairian cold and rain, the legionnaires would be dispirited.

No doubt the patrol Gelthius had just met would enjoy their fruit back in camp; unfortunately for them it was laced with canaris juice, which made it pretty much certain

370

they would be throwing up their guts before the end of the watch. Gelthius had been assured that he wouldn't be poisoning anyone, just making them ill for a few days. The aim was to get the Second to refuse orders or disintegrate by desertion. Gelthius didn't really care whether they drifted away or fell down dead, as long as it meant there were less spears pointed at him when the Thirteenth had to face them.

Pleased with his first success, Gelthius turned back towards the house he shared with some of the others, to get another bag of fruit.

MAGILNADA

Early Spring, 209th Year of Askh

I

The city bustled with activity. Every market square was filled, and men at the gates claimed never to have seen so many people coming to Magilnada. Anglhan stood on the long balcony at the front of the old lord's hall and looked over *his* city. The wind was still fresh down from the mountains, and the sky was overcast, but he was warmed from within by a deep glow of satisfaction.

Everybody was happy, and that was the key. Anglhan had lowered the taxes – not by much but just enough – and had emptied the city's coffers to make some much-needed repairs and improvements. The fire-damaged buildings had been torn down and were being replaced by new houses and businesses. Anglhan had also made generous offerings at the garden of shrines on behalf of the city, which had confused his Askhan underlings, but been well-received by the citizens of Magilnada.

When he had bought his first debt, Anglhan had realised that in order to make money it was necessary to spend some, and he had taken that philosophy with him through life. Back then it had been half-a-dozen debtors and two handcarts, his caravan growing in size each year until he had enough money for the landship. That had been an extravagance; he could have just as easily been a caravan captain and moved as much cargo. But the pleasure had been in the ownership of such a vessel, of knowing that he was in charge and answerable to nobody.

He had left the landship in the mountains. He wondered if it was being looked after or mouldering into ruin, or had been pulled apart and used for firewood. He felt no pangs of guilt about abandoning the landship to its fate; he had a far greater domain to control.

And the spending had worked, as he had known it would. Everything from Salphoria had to come past Magilnada; between Ullsaard's legions and the hill tribes in the general's pocket, that meant everything stopped at Magilnada. Anglhan had been building new storehouses as quickly as possible, and almost every room in the city was filled with guests or paying visitors. The shrine attendants were happy, the craftsmen were happy, the traders were happy, and that meant Anglhan was happy.

"Admiring your own little empire?" asked Noran as he joined Anglhan.

"Certainly," Anglhan replied. "It's important to enjoy the benefits of our labours."

Noran laughed but there was no mirth in his expression.

"Labours? What labours have you done to earn this?"

Anglhan turned a smile upon his companion.

"Only last night I had to endure a meal with three chieftains from the Vestil, who could talk about nothing except pig farming and fucking. And I'm not sure they realised there's a difference between the two."

"A terrible hardship, I am sure," said Noran, leaning against the balcony rail, eyes on Anglhan. "I have no idea why Ullsaard trusts you."

"You're a fine one to talk about hardships," said Anglhan, his mood spoilt by Noran's accusations. "I pulled myself up from the filth of my parents' village to make myself the man I am today. Who the fuck are you? An

Askhan noble who has never known a day's hard work. You've been given everything you ever wanted; I had to take what I needed. Don't talk to me about what I've done to earn this."

"The price levied on me for this winter can never be repaid," said Noran. He glowered at Anglhan and left, the door slamming behind him.

Anglhan looked at the city again, at the crowds meandering through the streets and gathering around the wagons in the markets. He missed Furlthia and wondered if his old mate was still in the city somewhere, or if he had really left.

The lord of Magilnada sighed and wandered back into the hall, pushing aside his glum thoughts with a dream of golden pillars and serving boys.

II

Noran shoved his way through the crowds, ignoring the shouts of annoyance that followed as he plunged through the streets towards the house he shared with Anriit and Ullsaard's family. He knew why he was in such a foul mood; the deaths of Neerita and his son still hung over him; and when he thought about this whole ludicrous enterprise, their deaths seemed entirely pointless. Noran had said nothing, but Ullsaard's claim to become the next king of Askhor was clearly insane. He had no chance of taking on an empire and winning, no matter how clever he thought he was or how great his legions were.

As he cut down an alley between two low halls, Noran kicked out at a stray dog eating scraps from the gutter. The mongrel yelped and scurried away. Noran felt a sudden pang of guilt at his becoming so thoughtlessly cruel. His self-loathing ignited his simmering anger again and by the time he reached the modest house where he lived, he was in a mood to kill someone, or himself, or both.

The servants opened the doors as he approached and he strode inside, fists and jaw clenched. He knocked aside a tray carrying a cup of water, sending the servant reeling back, the cup smashing on the floor. He stomped up the stairs and flung open the door to his bedchamber, where Anriit sewing sat by the narrow window.

She looked so much like Neerita at first glance, but there was nothing save disdain in her expression. It was a harsh reflection of the face of his dead wife, full of malice and accusation. Anriit had never liked him, but every glance and word from her since Neerita's death was filled with hate.

"Get out," he snapped, pointing to the door.

"Get out yourself," Anriit replied.

Noran crossed the room, snatched the canvas and thread from his wife's hands and tossed it out of the window.

"Out!"

She refused to move until he grabbed her by the arm and dragged her to her feet. She clawed at his face but he swatted away her arm and switched his grip to her hair, pulling her shrieking to the door. With a final thrust, he propelled her onto her knees on the landing. Anriit hissed at him over her shoulder as he slammed the door

Noran flung himself down on the bed.

Exhausted, he tried to rest. There had been few nights when he did not wake up in a sweat, plagued by dreams of his bloodstained wife, the ruin that had become of her and his son. He lay there with his eyes closed, trying to picture Neerita's welcoming eyes and full lips instead of Anriit's scowls; the two kept merging so that he saw the face of his dead wife twisted with anger.

He heard the slamming of the main doors and breathed with relief that Anriit had left. Noran lay for a while longer trying to relive happier memories, but his vision kept coming back to that bloody night in the camp.

There was a knock at the bedroom door a moment before it was opened a crack.

"It is me, Meliu. Can I come in?"

Noran sat up but said nothing. The door opened further and Ullsaard's youngest wife crept in, eyes wide with apprehension.

"I can leave if you wish," she said, her worried gaze fixed on Noran. Being angry at Meliu was worse than kicking a dog and Noran felt no desire to berate her for intruding.

"Come in," he said with a deep sigh and a wave. "I am sorry. I did not mean to frighten you."

Meliu closed the door behind her and slipped over to the chair where Anriit had been sitting. In the slanting light from the window her straw-blonde hair shone and Noran realised just how beautiful she was; except for the sorrow in her eyes, that was hard to bear.

"What is the matter?" Noran asked.

Meliu looked out of the window, the pale sun on her face.

"I am lonely," she said. "I miss Ullsaard, and Neerita."

"I miss her too," said Noran. "But there's no need to be lonely, I will keep you company."

Meliu's grateful smile reminded him so much of Neerita that Noran had to look away. He heard Meliu cross the floor and sit on the bed beside him. He looked at her.

"Nobody to gossip with? It must be hard."

Meliu playfully punched him on the arm.

"We did not gossip," she giggled. "It is important to know who is doing what with whom. I am sure Neerita helped you more than once with something about one of the other noble families."

"That she did," Noran said with a sigh. "Amongst all the bed-hopping there was usually something about whose farms were doing well, who was looking for a wife or husband, who had no heirs. That is the sort of thing you can make business plans around."

"I am very sorry she is not here," said Meliu, laying a hand on Noran's arm. "And so sorry about your son."

"Let's not talk about that," replied Noran, taking her hand in his.

"Luia says Ullsaard treats me like a whore, but I still miss him so much," Meliu said, her voice a whisper. "At least he likes me, which is more than he does Luia. There is nothing wrong in enjoying a bit of attention, is there?"

"Nothing wrong at all in a wife that wishes to please her husband," Noran replied. "Neerita was always accommodating in that way."

Meliu sniggered again.

"What?" asked Noran, catching her infectious laugh. "What are you thinking?"

"Neerita and I used to talk about, well, you and Ullsaard," Meliu admitted. "You know, your prowess…"

"Compared notes, eh?" Noran had always suspected as much. The two of them had talked about other people's sex lives so much it was unthinkable that they did not do the same about their husbands. "I hope the reports were good."

"Oh yes!" Meliu became more demure and looked away. "She said you were always very considerate."

She fell silent and Noran put a hand on her cheek and turned her face towards him. Her eyes were moist.

"What is it?" he asked. She shook her head. "Tell me."

Meliu's words came like a spring flood down a river.

"I know that Ullsaard doesn't love me, not the way he loves Allenya, and Luia's right, he does treat me like a whore sometimes, and I am grateful that he chooses to bed me, but sometimes I wonder what it must be like, to share something more with someone, and I know it's ridiculous because I know he wouldn't look twice at me if Allenya wasn't my sister, so I should be thankful that he does, but it would be nice if…"

Her voice trailed away as Noran leaned across her, planting a gentle kiss on her lips.

"Stop talking so much," he said.

His hand moved from her cheek to her breasts, massaging them through the cloth of her dress. They kissed again, a long, sensuous meeting of lips and tongues. Meliu pulled back with a gasp.

"What?" Noran asked. "Did I misunderstand something? I'm sorry if I–"

It was Meliu's turn to silence the chatter, reaching a hand into Noran's trousers to caress his stiffening member. They lay down next to each other, kissing and touching, their hands exploring each other's bodies through and inside their clothes. With an impish smile, Meliu broke off from a long kiss and, pulling Noran's woollen trousers to his knees, lowered her mouth onto his shaft. He gave a grunt of pleasure at the touch of her lips and tongue and stroked the thick curls of her hair as she worked back and forth.

It was almost too much, but Meliu pulled away with a parting lick before Noran's pleasure burst forth. She giggled as he rolled to his back and lifted her onto him, pushing her dress up above her waist. Cupping Meliu's buttocks, Noran steered her into position and she lowered herself towards him, but stopped short, brushing the tip of his member but no further.

Meliu grabbed his wrists and pushed his hands behind his head as she wormed her way up his body.

"Your turn," she said, placing a warm thigh on either side of his head, lowering herself onto his face. Intoxicated by the scent of her, he thrust his tongue out, pulling his hands free so he could grip her backside again, dragging Meliu further onto him as she ground her groin back and forth across his mouth.

Meliu's breath came in short pants and squeals. Noran felt her fingers clamping onto the top of his head and for a moment he was worried that her nails would draw blood, so tight were their grip.

This time Noran pushed her away, sitting up so that she fell to one side, her face and chest flushed with red, one breast protruding from the top of her dress. For a moment in the dim light, he swore she looked like Neerita, so happy with him, so eager for more. The sensation passed with a twinge of guilt, but that was easily swamped by Noran's desire to finish the act.

With Meliu still on her side, he lifted her upmost leg and pushed himself slowly inside her. There was a real hunger in Meliu's eyes as she looked over her shoulder at him, almost pleading with him. He could resist no longer and started with quick thrusts, each made deeper by her movement back against him.

His climax built swiftly and strongly, and Meliu's wild eyes betrayed her own approaching moment of fulfilment. Every muscle tightened in Noran's body as he reached the highest point, all of his lust and grief and anger and loss condensing into a feral shout as it burst out of him into her. The whole world stopped for a few spasming heartbeats, his ears hissing with blood, barely hearing Meliu's shriek of pleasure.

As he sank back into the bed covers and pillows, Noran enjoyed the calm that washed over him. But the bliss would not last, something nagged at him: Meliu's tight grip on his arm, digging into flesh, pinching the hairs on his skin.

"What is it?" he asked, opening his eyes and turning his head slightly to look at Meliu. Her stare was fixed on the door. Noran lazily rolled over to see what she was looking at.

Luia stood in the open doorway, hand on the frame, one eyebrow raised in amusement.

"You were at the jewel market!" Meliu snapped in accusation.

"I am back," Luia replied quietly. She slowly shifted her eyes from Meliu to Noran. "My sister is a brainless slut, so I can understand her part in this. You? I thought you would be wiser. You have a wife for this sort of thing."

"Have sex with Anriit?" Noran laughed. "My cock and balls would freeze off before I was finished."

"You seem to find this situation amusing," Luia said.

She walked stiffly across the room and sat on the end of the bed. Meliu straightened her dress and pulled the covers over Noran's bare legs in an attempt at decency.

"You've fucked more men than the female population of this city, who are you to judge your sister?" Noran said.

"That is true," said Luia, smoothing a hand across the blankets. "I would not think twice about this squalid little tumble between you. In fact, if I had known you were looking for some bedroom action, I would have helped you myself."

"So why are you looking so smug?"

"My husband expects the least from me," Luia said, leaning back with all the contentment of a cat with a rat. "I am not sure he would be so forgiving of my sister. And I never sleep with any of his friends or subordinates."

Meliu's expression was of growing realisation of what they had done and her voice broke into sobs when she spoke.

"Ullsaard will kill us," she said.

Noran dismissed her worries with a shake of the head.

"No, not for this." He turned back to Luia. "And besides, he is not going to find out, is he?"

"If you are worried about him finding out, then you are worried about how he will react," said Luia. "You are close friends, but Ullsaard is a territorial man, used to being in command. He does not like it when his wishes are disobeyed, and more importantly he gets very angry when his expectations are not met. You know this. And he is a violent man by nature."

Noran leapt out of the bed and lunged for Luia, but she skipped away and he tripped on his falling trousers, landing flat on his face. Luia's laugh filled the room.

"What are you going to do to silence me? Kill me? That is not going to work, is it? Threaten me? You cannot, there is nothing you know that is as damaging as what I know."

"For the sake of your sister?" suggested Noran, awkwardly hauling himself back onto the bed. "She will be blamed as much as me."

"Meliu is safe because she is also Allenya's sister. Ullsaard will beat her, severely I would say, but he knows she is dim-witted but harmless, and he will suspect you of seducing her. If he hears the story from the wrong person..."

"What is it that you want from me?" asked Noran as he secured his trousers and tightened his belt. "Money?"

"I do not know... Yet." Luia approached Noran and he flinched as she reached a hand out towards his groin. "Perhaps it is you I want."

"No, no, no!" Noran backed away. "To sleep with one wife might be forgiven, but I am not repeating the mistake."

"This was a mistake, was it?" There was a brittle timbre to Meliu's question and Noran had to choose his words carefully.

"It was a mistake to be caught, but what happened between us was not wrong. We needed each other and found each other at the right time. That is all."

"Shameful!" laughed Luia. "You show no remorse at all for fucking your friend's wife. Does Ullsaard mean so little to you now? Perhaps I would be doing my husband a favour by telling him of your disdain. Betrayal can grow so quickly, you know. First you take one of Ullsaard's wives, next you will be heading back to Askh to gain favour with the king by hanging Ullsaard out to dry."

"I would never do that!"

"A year ago you would never have slept with me," said Meliu, jumping from the bed. Noran dragged his gaze away from her swinging breasts and looked at her distraught face. "Was this some way of getting at Ullsaard? Were you going to use me?"

Noran had to laugh with the shock of it all, a bitter snorting that threatened to engulf him.

"You really are a stupid cow if you believe this bitch."

"I think you had better leave," Meliu said primly. "Urikh will be back shortly."

"It might be best if you leave the city altogether," said Luia. "To avoid the temptation of a second performance. I have to protect my sister's reputation."

Noran looked at the two women, who were now standing side by side. He tried to comprehend what was happening, but found no reasonable explanation. Noran was forced to conclude that the pair of them had either conspired to trap him, or were most certainly insane. Leaving the city sounded like a fine idea.

"I shall pack my things and leave before dusk," Noran assured them. "I will go to Ullsaard and explain to him what has happened. If he chooses to kill me, so be it. It might even be a relief."

Noran hurried from the room, confused and angry. Luia's laughter followed him down the passageway. He stopped on the landing, turned around and strode back into the bedchamber.

"Get out!" he snapped at them. "This is my room!"

ANRAIR
Spring, 209th Year of Askh

I

A town's mood was like the weather; you could sense when it was changing. Gelthius knew what it was like to live in a place where the harvest had failed, or the local chieftain had died to be replaced by a better or worse man. He could sense the mood of Talladmun in the quiet of the markets; the nervous manner of people in the streets; the houses left empty by families that had fled.

The town knew war was coming soon.

"There he is."

Gelthius looked at his companion, the general's eldest son, Urikh. He was pointing at a third captain standing with a company of legionnaires at the duskward road leading into the market. The officer was tall and thickset, with a flat face and straight-cropped hair poking out from under his helmet. Urikh passed Gelthius a folded piece of parchment sealed with a blob of wax.

Gelthius headed across the market with the message, ambling through the thin crowd looking at the wares on display. It was meagre fare. Only those farms within a couple of days' of the town had brought their winter stores. Everybody farther afield was too scared to travel, though whether it was the renegade legions or the hillmen brigands that frightened them more Gelthius couldn't say.

He stopped at one wagon laden with limp spring cabbages and listened to the farmer asking for far more than they were worth. The woman shopping shook her head and walked away. It was the same all over the town. No ore meant the forges had gone cold. No food meant prices were rising so quickly only the governor and his legion could buy anything, and often they did, taking all of the available food, leaving the people of the town to go hungry.

Crossing the open pavement to where the third captain stood, Gelthius performed his "tripping up" routine. Rather than shouting at him as usually happened, the captain stepped up to help Gelthius to his feet. Surprised, the Salphor almost forgot to slip the message to the captain. He pushed the parchment into the officer's hands with a whisper.

"Read it later, in private."

With that, Gelthius staggered away, leaving the confused Askhan captain looking dumbly at the letter for a few moments before he carefully folded it and pushed it down into his breastplate.

"My brother is an idiot," Urikh muttered when Gelthius rejoined him. "Let us just hope he has not forgotten how to read."

II

Urikh had sent word that Nemtun had definitely left Talladmun with half the legions, chasing a rumour of Ullsaard encamped five days to coldward in the Enairian forests. Governor Allon had gone with him, leaving the cowardly Murian in charge of the army protecting Talladmun and the road to Parmia.

Ullsaard had not had things all his own way, and his forces had been depleted by raiding parties, escorts and diversionary forces, and the thousand men still posing as rebels in Magilnada. In all, he had about three and a half legions at hand, more than enough for the two dispirited legions Urikh claimed were stationed in Talladmun.

It was a bright morning, full of the promise of spring. Twenty thousand legionnaires marched along the road to Talladmun, which could be seen nestled in the foothills a few miles away. Ullsaard's army made no attempt to hide its approach. The general wanted the opposition to have as much time as possible to get scared. If Urikh and the others had done their jobs properly – and he had no reason to doubt they had – the mixture of Murian and Allon's men would be more than nervous about the army bearing down upon them.

A mile from the town, Ullsaard faintly heard the warning horns. He called the army to a halt on a low, long hill overlooking the farmlands outside Talladmun; each phalanx took its position in a line that stretched for half a mile, clear to see for every soldier on the walls. After nearly two seasons spent running away, hiding in the mountains, posing as rabble and beating up innocent merchants, Ullsaard was looking forward to having a proper battle. Part of him hoped that his clever plan would not work and he would have to fight for the town.

He did not have to wait long.

A column of armoured soldiers snaked from the town's closest gate, about five hundred men. They carried with them their golden standard and Ullsaard could see a figure riding an ailur at their head: Governor Murian. Ullsaard signalled to his own bodyguard from the Thirteenth and urged Blackfang down the slope.

The two delegations met half a mile from the town wall, and the contrast between them became clear. Proud and confident, Ullsaard swung down from Blackfang and strode up to his opponents while Murian hunched in his saddle, surrounded by guards. The governor's eyes never strayed from Ullsaard and he fidgeted with a piece of parchment in his hands.

"You got my letter?" Ullsaard called out lightly. Murian held out a hand, the parchment shaking in his fingers. "Good. Do you have any questions?"

"The king will have me skinned and then boned like a fish if I do what you ask," Murian said. "I cannot hand over my soldiers and the town without a fight!"

"The king is not here," said Ullsaard, stopping a little way from Murian, arms crossed. He fixed the governor with his best stare, perfected over years of command and fatherhood. "I am."

"But this is outrageous!" Murian swallowed hard and tried to rally some confidence. "We can hold the town until Nemtun returns with the rest of the army."

"No, you can't."

"What makes you so sure? I have enough men to hold the walls, and supplies for more than ten days."

Ullsaard moved his gaze from Murian to the captain just behind him: Jutaar. Ullsaard's son met his eye and nodded.

"Allon's men will not defend the walls," said Ullsaard. "They've had a better offer. That leaves you with just one legion."

"You seem very certain of that." Murian's nervousness was quickly becoming indignation. "I think this is just a ruse to get me to surrender. Do you think I am that easily fooled?"

"No ruse, no fooling," said Ullsaard. He looked again at Jutaar.

With a shout, Jutaar drew his sword and lunged at the officer next to him, cutting down Murian's First Captain. From behind Ullsaard, the Thirteenth bodyguard surged forward as Allon's men turned on Murian's with a crash of shields and spears. Murian tried to bolt, kicking his heels into his ailur's flanks but Ullsaard reacted quickly, leaping to snatch at the heavy reins.

Digging his heels into the dirt, Ullsaard wrenched back with all his strength, pulling the great cat off balance,

386

bringing her sliding to her flank in a cloud of dirt. Murian was thrown clear as the ailur righted herself and leapt at Ullsaard, fangs and claws bared. Ullsaard dodged to his left, but a paw caught him in the shoulder, sending links of mail scattering in a shower of bloody droplets. The ailur thrashed her head, almost wrenching Ullsaard's arms from their sockets.

"Give me a behemodon any time," the general snarled as he hurled himself between the beast's outstretched forelegs.

His shoulder slammed into the ailur's armoured chest. With a grunt, Ullsaard straightened his legs as claws raked down the back of his armour. Linking his fingers through the ailur's mane, Ullsaard twisted to his right and swung his legs, putting all of his weight on to the animal. She buckled with a roar and fell forwards. In an instant, Ullsaard had his knee on the ailur's throat and his hands were wrapping the reins around her slashing forelegs. Once he was confident she was hobbled, Ullsaard jumped back out of harm's way. The ailur struggled to right herself, but fell down twice and gave up, lying panting in the flattened grass.

"There's a good girl," Ullsaard said.

He spied Murian trying to crawl away and went after him, grabbing the governor by the ankle, twisting until Murian rolled to his back. The vicious shouts and ringing metal of the fighting legionnaires was already growing quieter as those loyal to Murian were overwhelmed. Ullsaard hated wasting good fighting men in this way, but it was the only method to be sure the others would fall into line. Just like ailurs, legions needed to be shown who was in charge.

Ullsaard grabbed Murian by the front of his jerkin and hauled him to his feet.

"Do you surrender?" the general snarled. Blood trickled down his cheek from a claw scratch.

Horror filled Murian's expression as the screams of his men died down. He looked at Ullsaard with abject submission, shoulders slumped, legs trembling. The governor of Anrair nodded fitfully and swayed where he stood. Ullsaard thought the man was going to faint and reached out a hand to stop him. Murian shrieked as if attacked and fell to his knees.

"Fuck Nemtun," Murian whispered. "And fuck Lutaar."

"That's the spirit!" Ullsaard said as he pulled the broken governor back to his feet. "Don't worry. I'll look after you."

MAGILNADA
Spring, 209th Year of Askh

I

A rough shaking woke Anglhan. He prised open a weary eye and saw Furlthia beside the bed. For a moment the lord of Magilnada thought he was dreaming and rolled to his side, away from the apparition. A hand grabbed his shoulder and pulled him back. As his senses came to him, Anglhan could hear shouting from outside the hall.

"Is that you, Furlthia?" he asked.

"It is. Come on, get up and get dressed. We have to get you out of here."

Anglhan slapped away Furlthia's hand.

"What are you talking about? I'm not going anywhere. And what's all that racket?"

"That's why I'm here. Come on, see for yourself."

Anglhan threw back the covers and slipped ponderously from the bed. His time as ruler of Magilnada had not been wasted and he had taken a good share of the food coming through the city, so that not only had he replaced all the weight he had lost in the mountains, he had added some more. Hands massaging his flabby gut, still sleepy, he crossed the room to the window, bare feet slapping on the tiled floor.

Throwing open the shutters, he looked out at his city. It

was barely dawn, but in the haze he could see a group of armed men approaching up the steps to the lord's hall. They were garbed as Askhan legionnaires, and he recognised Jutiil at their head.

"What does he want?" Anglhan muttered. "And why is he in uniform?"

"They all are," Furlthia said as he busied himself around the room, pulling a chest from beneath Anglhan's bed and filling it with clothes. "All the Askhans are in full gear. I think Ullsaard has turned on you."

"No, there must be some mistake. I've done everything he wanted. Really, I have. There must be some other reason." Anglhan stopped and fixed his eye on Furlthia. "What are you doing here? I thought you had abandoned me."

"There's some of us didn't trust the Askhans, so we've been keeping an eye on them," Furlthia explained as he dumped an armful of shirts into the chest. "Not causing any trouble, but just watching what they've been about. There's been a lot of shipments coming into the city these last couple of weeks that seemed to disappear. Looks like Ullsaard was sending in weapons and armour for his men.

"Just before dawn, they came together and stormed the guardhouses and the homes of the chieftains we left alive last time. They've killed several hundred men already, some of them rebels we brought from the mountains."

There was a pounding on the hall doors and Jutiil's voice called out, demanding entry. Furlthia froze, apparently gripped with sudden fear.

"We can escape out the back," said Furlthia, slamming the chest shut. "Grab the other end of this."

Anglhan shook his head and stood with his hands on his hips.

"I'm not being driven out of my hall like vermin," he declared. "I'm going to find out what's going on."

"They'll kill you," snapped Furlthia.

"Nonsense! If Ullsaard wanted me dead, he's had plenty of opportunities before now."

Feeling a little more in control again, Anglhan dragged on his trousers, slipped a shirt over his head and sat on the end of the bed to pull on his boots, tucking his trouser legs into their tops. Furlthia hovered like a frustrated fly.

"Thank you for the warning," Anglhan said. He stood up, stomping his feet a couple of times to get his boots on fully. "Don't worry, friend, I'll take care of this."

"How?"

Anglhan shrugged.

"I'm sure something will come to me when we find out what's happening."

The thumping on the door had ceased and there was a clattering downstairs. Evidently one of Anglhan's men had succumbed to the demands, or else was in league with the Askhans. Anglhan shooed Furlthia towards the door.

"Go down and tell Jutiil I'll be with him shortly. Make sure nobody does anything stupid." Furlthia hesitated until Anglhan shoved him towards the doorway. "That includes you. Go on, make our Askhan allies welcome!"

Furlthia darted Anglhan a doubtful look, but complied. When he was gone, Anglhan busied himself at the dresser, pulling on rings and hanging a broad chain of gold around his neck. He picked up a polished bronze mirror and smoothed his hair as best he could.

Now he felt like the lord of Magilnada, and looked the part too. Cinching his belt a little tighter, he left the bedroom and marched down the stair to the main hall with a confident swagger. Jutiil stood with a hand on the hilt of his sword, a shield in the other, backed up by half a company of legionnaires. The shutters on the hall windows had been thrown open and the dawn light cut ruddy bands through the gloom.

"Good morning, First Captain," Anglhan said cheerily. "What can I do for you?"

"By right of conquest, General Ullsaard of the Greater Askhan Empire claims the city of Magilnada as his dominion," Jutiil intoned solemnly. He was about to continue when Anglhan interrupted.

"Save the official speech, Jutiil, and just tell me what Ullsaard is up to. Are you planning to kill me? And what's with the fighting in the city?"

For a moment it looked as if Jutiil was going to continue with his bombastic pronouncement, but he stopped, suddenly deflated.

"The general has decided to make his presence in Magilnada official," said the First Captain of the Twelfth. "There were a few objectors we had to deal with, nothing serious."

"And me?"

"Ullsaard wants you to be governor, with Magilnada as a province of Greater Askhor. If you agree, then we have no problem."

"And if I disagree, you'll cut me down like a dog?"

"That's pretty much it, yes." Jutiil smiled. "If it comes to that, the general will put Urikh in charge of the city."

"I'll be fucked by an abada before I let that happen!" Anglhan declared with a snort. "Of course I'll be Ullsaard's governor. What's the rush? What happened to the plan of slowly converting the city to the Askhan ideal?"

"General Ullsaard needs more men and equipment," explained Jutiil. "Your first job as governor will be to raise two more legions for him. We've got smiths and armourers who'll be teaching your lot how to make proper kit. You're also to open up the stores you've stockpiled. It's time to let trade flow again."

"Why now? What's brought all of this on?"

"Things are going well for the general," Jutiil said with a grin. "With Murian defecting to his side, Allon of Enair and Asuhas of Ersua have thrown in their lot as well. Nemtun's now the hunted one and has fled into Nalanor.

To gain more support, General Ullsaard has bravely stormed the rebel city of Magilnada and will be sending the supplies he has captured for the relief of those poor folk who have been so deprived since the start of spring."

"So Ullsaard gets to masquerade as conquering hero and saviour," Anglhan said with a chuckle. "I admire his balls. For a dumb brute, he has thought about this a lot. Was this always his plan?"

"You can ask him yourself."

"What? Ullsaard's coming here?"

"He'll be in the city in a couple of days. As a governor of Greater Askhor, you have to be properly invested with your powers."

Anglhan thought about this as he wandered across the hall to the open doors. Daybreak spread across Magilnada and Anglhan could see the distinctive silhouettes of legionnaires already on the walls to dawnwards. Whatever he felt about the change, it was done and he could do nothing about it.

With all things considered, being an Askhan governor would be even better than the city's chieftain. Backed by the power of Askh, and more importantly by its legions, Magilnada would consolidate its hold on the Free Country. Anglhan would rule not just a city but a whole province.

Despite Furlthia's panic, this was the best news he could have heard. However, a doubt crept into the mind of the governor-to-be. Anglhan's future prosperity now depended upon a simple but important fact: Ullsaard had to succeed in his bid to become king. Posing as a rebel lord of Magilnada would have been preferable. If Ullsaard failed, Lutaar would not stand for allowing Anglhan to remain in power. Ullsaard's fate and that of Anglhan would be inseparable from this point on, and it was up to the former debt guardian to do everything he could to ensure the general's bid for power did not fail. Ullsaard was proving to be anything but a simple soldier and Anglhan knew he would have to watch his step even more carefully.

The lord of Magilnada turned back to Jutiil with a clap of hands and a smile.

"That all seems agreeable. I shall ensure that your men have every cooperation they need, and I shall put out the word that under the protection of General Ullsaard the merchants will be safe to travel into Ersua and Anrair. The treasury will be opened and you can begin recruiting your new legions after my investiture."

"That's good to hear," said Jutiil. "I have to attend to a few other matters in the city. I suggest you stay here for the next day or two, until the general arrives. I'll be leaving my men here for the time being, for your protection, of course."

"Yes, for my protection," said Anglhan, knowing the legionnaires would be gaolers as much as guardians.

Anglhan left the main hall for a side chamber which he had turned into a secluded office. Furlthia followed him in and closed the door.

"Are you mad?" Furlthia said in a low voice.

Anglhan ignored the question and sat behind a table littered with parchments and scrolls. He cleared a space and leaned on his elbows, chin in one hand.

"Listen to me, friend," said Anglhan, gesturing for Furlthia to sit down opposite. "I need your help as much as I ever did. You know that if I don't take this governorship, Ullsaard will have me killed and will thrust that bastard Urikh into the position. Whether you like it or not, you have to admit I'm the better choice."

Furlthia did not sit. He paced back and forth, shaking his head.

"I don't like it one bit. I told you before; I don't want to be an Askhan. Aegenuis isn't going to like this one bit either."

"Aegenuis can go fuck his mother," snapped Anglhan. "He hasn't got the will or the money to retake the city by force, not against a legion or two. Give it a few more days, everybody here will get over the shock and it'll be business as usual. If I'm in charge we can make sure the Askhans don't do anything excessive."

Annoyed by Furlthia's pacing, Anglhan walked around the table, grabbed his friend by the arms and thrust him into a chair. A question occurred to him.

"How did you get into my bedroom?"

"Your headman, Lenorin, is one of our group. He tells us what you've been up to."

"You've been spying on me?"

Furlthia shrugged.

"Even when I was your first mate you didn't tell me everything that was going on, why would that change?"

"True enough," said Anglhan, slumping back into his chair. "This group of yours, who else is in it?"

"I'm not saying. People here and there; some came with us, some lived in the city before. Folk interested in making sure the Askhans don't get out of hand."

"Well, you can add me to that list," said Anglhan. "Ullsaard thinks he can make me his creature, tame me like an ailur, but I'm not going to simply roll over for him. I'll need your eyes and ears, friend. It's situations like this when you need to know as much as possible. Can you do that for me?"

Furlthia looked uncomfortable and rubbed his forehead in thought. He took a long look at Anglhan, weighing him up.

"All right. If I hear of anything you need to know, I'll pass it on. But let's be clear about something: I'm not your man any longer. I don't like you, I don't work for you."

"But still you came to warn me, to take me to safety…"

"Yeah, I did. I hope I don't regret it."

II

Ten thousand legionnaires formed a guard of honour for Ullsaard and Anglhan as they paraded along the narrow street through the centre of Magilnada. Ullsaard wanted to put on an impressive show and Jutiil had not failed him. The men looked pristine and a good crowd had been turned out, although the reception of their new governor veered towards the sullen rather than celebratory. It didn't matter to the general; the whole point of the investiture was to make it plain to even the dullest Magilnadan that Anglhan was in charge, backed by an Askhan general with a large number of well-trained soldiers.

Ullsaard glanced across at the new governor as Anglhan waved to the crowd, a beaming smile on his face. The general knew that inside Anglhan's mind gears were turning like the machinery of a mill, looking at every possible means to gain an advantage. He was a slippery ally at best, but he was also the most useful one Ullsaard had at the moment, out of a very slim choice.

In a way, Ullsaard had Murian to thank for his recent success. If it hadn't been for the governor's complaints about Magilnada, Ullsaard might have never realised the importance of the city to the duskward and coldward provinces. While Nalanor, Maasra and Okhar were self-sufficient, the newer regions were still developing their irrigation and their farms, clearing space for settlers. It took several generations to get a province into full working order, and that vulnerability had given Ullsaard his chance.

With the half-hearted shouts of the Magilnadans ringing from the high buildings alongside the street, Ullsaard wondered if he'd been lucky so far. Was it luck that Urikh had been involved in an insurrection against Magilnada's rulers? Perhaps there was an element of fortune about it, Ullsaard decided, but he was sure that what had come next had come about from good planning and hard work. Provinces didn't capitulate to a general because of luck.

They reached the steps that led to the first level of the richer residents' houses, where a wooden stage had been built overlooking a wide plaza. Behind a cordon of armed soldiers, the people of Magilnada followed the procession and filled the square.

Was it luck? The question continued to irk Ullsaard. If he had been lucky so far, that made the future that much more uncertain. It was certainly luck, or fate, that Kalmud had fallen ill, but Ullsaard had been well-positioned to exploit the opportunities as they arrived.

He ascended the steps to the stage behind Anglhan, shield and spear in hand, and stood to one side as the governor moved to the front and raised a fist above his head. The assembled legionnaires beat spears against shields and raised such a shout that the square was filled with noise.

Anglhan motioned for silence and the legionnaires quit their clamour immediately. Ullsaard allowed his thoughts to wander further as Anglhan launched into what would undoubtedly be a long and tedious speech. Ullsaard was a more direct orator and believed in three simple things: inspire the men, tell them what you want, and tell them what they get out of it. Anglhan was of that breed of men who loved the sound of his own voice, and Ullsaard listened vaguely as the governor went on at length about a new age of prosperity, a dawn of renewed civic pride and the welcoming of a time of plenty for all.

Suppressing a yawn, Ullsaard tapped a marching beat on the haft of his spear. The sun was bright, the sky cloudless. It would be a great day for a battle, and Ullsaard wished he was many miles away in Nalanor, hunting down Nemtun. He had left Anasind in charge of the legions, camped three days duskwards of the Greenwater. There was no point in moving any further towards Askh until Ullsaard knew where Cosuas and his legions could be found. To advance without that knowledge was asking to be trapped. It was also the reason Ullsaard wanted to move full legions raised from Magilnada, so that should it come to a straight fight against Nemtun and Cosuas, Ullsaard could at least match their numbers.

But nothing had been heard of Cosuas since he had left Maasra. No soldier, no farmer, no trader had heard anything of the legions fighting to hotwards. Perhaps the king had underestimated Ullsaard initially and ordered Cosuas to stay on campaign, but that seemed increasingly unlikely. What worried Ullsaard was the idea that Cosuas had found some route back into Greater Askhor, perhaps circling hotwards of the Mekha desert and coming back through the mountains duskwards of Okhar. Even now, Cosuas could be marching on the rear of Ullsaard's army.

Though the general's instinct was to go for the killing blow now, he was reluctant to strike while Nalanor, Okhar and Maasra were still loyal to Lutaar. As it was, Ullsaard controlled half of the empire, but by far it was the poorer half. If he delayed too long, more legions would be raised against him in an escalation of armies he couldn't hope to match, but if he acted too swiftly, his blow might fall astray; and he reckoned he would have only one chance at victory. Any significant defeat, any hint of weakness, and his support from Murian, Allon and Kulrua would evaporate quicker than an Enairian morning mist.

With some relief, Ullsaard realised that Anglhan had just about finished his inaugural speech. He was announcing three days of celebrations, more donations to the shrine gardens, and ended with a general call to all men of strong arm and fair mind to enlist in the new legions.

"Imagine the glory that awaits such men," said Anglhan. "The first of a new breed of legionnaire, a place in history. The Askhan legions have proud traditions and they pay good gold for those that place their lives in danger for their fellow men. Such are the benefits of the Askhan way – food and a livelihood for you, money for your families. No longer will you have to toil in field or workshop for little reward, only to be asked to put down your hammer and scythe for a spear. You will be numbered amongst the most powerful army in the world, the Magilnadan First."

Ullsaard shifted uneasily at this announcement. Legions belonged to all of Greater Askhor. Even though he defied the king and waged war against other legions, Ullsaard was still firm in his belief that he did so for a better Askhan future. Anglhan's two legions were to be the Nineteenth and Twentieth, raised and trained and equipped by legal means, not the private army of Magilnada.

Ullsaard cleared his throat meaningfully and stepped up beside the governor. Anglhan glanced at the general and brought his speech to a hurried close. Ullsaard lifted his spear above his head.

"Magilnada, I salute you!" he cried. "For generations you have laboured under the tyranny of weak kings and self-serving nobles. This day things change. This day you become Askhans. To be an Askhan is to be proud of where you were born, but also to put the good of all above the wants of the few. I am an Enairian and also an Askhan. I grew up in a small village in the forests coldwards from here. Only in Greater Askhor could I have dreamt of becoming who I am today. Each of you can hold that same dream. To be master of your destiny; to raise your children without fear; to feed your families every day.

"I too have suffered from the cruel indifference of a distant king. I am not a meek man, and so I do not sit at the table and grumble into my wine about it. No, I am a man of action more than deeds, and I will march to Askh and take the Crown of the Blood from the head of a man who does not deserve to wear it.

"I can make a promise to you today. Every man of Magilnada who joins my legions and marches with me through the gates of Askh will have done his duty. I will give him a house and a farm, and money for crop and livestock. One year with me guarantees freedom and prosperity for the rest of your lives!"

This announcement drew a far greater reaction than all of Anglhan's long-winded endorsements. The legionnaires began to chant Ullsaard's name, and their enthusiasm spread into the crowd. Raising shield and spear high, Ullsaard turned to the left and right, basking in the growing cries of adulation. Out of the corner of his eye he saw Anglhan looking on with jealousy. Ullsaard directed a cocky wink towards the new governor as a reminder: the power is mine, not yours.

III

Anglhan's new reign as governor of Magilnada began with a feast, and the lord's hall was packed with as many tables and benches as could be found; the former laden with food, the latter filled with dignitaries who had begged, borrowed or stolen an invitation. Music formed the backdrop to the ceaseless chatter and, much to Anglhan's delight, naked serving boys waited on the tables with Askhan wine and Salphorian ale. He sat at the head table with Jutiil to his left and Ullsaard to his right. Midst the hubbub, Anglhan had to raise his voice to have a simple conversation.

"You might have the hearts of the solders and the common people," Anglhan said to Ullsaard, "but I have the purses of the chieftains, the craftsmen and the merchants."

"Which is why we will make such a powerful pairing," replied the general, raising his cup of wine. "Just don't forget that all of the money in Magilnada can't stop a spear tip."

"And I am sure you will always remember that a simple bronze spear tip is the difference between a soldier and a man with a long stick."

Ullsaard laughed deeply while Anglhan lifted his own mug in salute.

"You've made me governor of Magilnada, and I am grateful," Anglhan continued. "When I help make you king of Greater Askhor, I am sure the favour will be more than returned."

"And I am sure the favour will not be a cheap one," said Ullsaard, his expression losing its humour.

"You can be sure of that," replied Anglhan.

NALANOR
Late Spring, 209th Year of Askh

I

The camp outside Parmia rivalled the largest towns in Greater Askhor. It was one of three such camps, spreading hotwards from the town, each three days from the Greenwater. The legionnaires had dubbed it Ullsaardia, the others being Jutiilia and Donaria after the respective First Captains. Officially they were simply Parmian Barracks One, Two and Three, but Noran preferred the soldiers' names.

The marching camps Noran had witnessed during the winter were nothing compared to the construction of these garrisons. Each housed between fifteen and twenty thousand men and their families, in endless rows of canvas tents around a few wooden buildings such as the First Captains' headquarters, the baths and the armouries. Wooden walls protected the camp, with five rows of stake-lined ditches spreading out like ripples outside them. The forge chimneys billowed smoke day and night as the weapon smiths forged more armour and weapons, fed by a steady stream of ore now coming from the Midean Mountains and the peaks coldwards of Parmia. Supply caravans arrived almost daily, with fresh slaughtered cattle and goats, barrels of salted meat and the first shipments of spring grain from Salphoria. Noran was used to such industry on the outskirts of Askh, in Geria and other cities, but here in a temporary camp in the middle of the Nalanor farmlands it seemed incredible.

Having fled the wrath of Luia, Noran had avoided Ullsaard, despite his promise to confess all to the general. It had not been so difficult; Ullsaard had been busy marshalling his forces throughout Ersua and Nalanor, gathering the legions of Murian, Asuhas and Allon into three army groups to guard against attack from Nemtun on the other side of the Greenwater, and the possible arrival of Cosuas. Noran had kept himself distracted by becoming an unofficial ambassador to Ullsaard's governor allies, and spent more time with them than in the camps. He was far more comfortable dealing with the governors' continual manoeuvring than army logistics, and certainly the accommodation in their palaces was far more to his liking.

But for all the insight Noran was gaining into the governors' motives, expectations and likely ambitions, he could not hide from the fact that he was dreading a confrontation with Ullsaard. The matter became more pressing when Noran learnt that Ullsaard had travelled to Magilnada for Anglhan's investiture. That same night he had considered fleeing, maybe to Maasra. Though the desire to save himself from Ullsaard's inevitable wrath was strong, there was a part of Noran that knew he deserved whatever punishment was coming to him. Grief was no excuse for his betrayal, and that he had betrayed the memory of Neerita added to his burning shame.

He had tried strong wine to wash away the feelings of guilt, but drunkenness just left him in an uneasy fog, leaving him more vulnerable to bursts of depression. He wondered how it could be that he had once been free to leap from bed to bed of any women who took his fancy, yet one natural, grief-driven indiscretion now left him feeling hopeless and scared.

When news came that Ullsaard was returning to Nalanor, Noran knew that it was time for him to make a decision. He wondered whether he could deny the act, but his past was against him; while Ullsaard might doubt Luia's motives for making such a claim, the general would surely believe innocent Meliu. Noran hoped that Ullsaard was not too harsh on his youngest wife. Having already dismissed self-exile, Noran was only left with the option of facing up to what he had done and begging Ullsaard to forgive him.

Most likely it would mean a meeting on the bloodfields, where men of honour resolved their disputes. Noran was no slouch with a sword, but he knew Ullsaard would butcher him in moments.

It was with such dark thoughts that Noran heard the horns sounding Ullsaard's return early one evening. Seized by a sudden doubt, Noran packed a few belongings into a sack in case his nerve failed him and he chose to bolt for safety. He could not decide whether to approach Ullsaard and throw himself on his friend's mercy, or wait to be summoned by the general.

As the tramp of the column thundered across camp, Noran waited in his tent, biting his nails and fidgeting with his bag of clothes. He heard the officers calling out the halt and could picture Ullsaard saying a few words to his men before dismissing them.

Would Ullsaard send for Noran straight away, or would he deal with his other business before attending to personal matters? Unable to contain his worry, Noran began to pace, rehearsing what he would say over and over. Muttering to himself, he tried to find the words to express how much he regretted what he had done, but they felt empty. They were excuses, not reasons. Had he been a man at all, had he been a true friend, he would have kept his lust in check and sent Meliu away.

An odd light of hope filled Noran's thoughts as he lingered at the tent door, awaiting the summons. What if

Ullsaard really didn't care? Meliu had said it herself that he didn't love her and simply desired her body. There was a chance that Ullsaard would be annoyed by Noran's indiscretion, but would understand the desires that can sometimes cloud a man's judgement. If Noran admitted his misdeed there was the possibility that his honesty would earn a little favour.

Back and forth, Noran wrestled with his decision, but no matter which way he looked at the situation, there was no easy route out.

"You're an idiot," Noran told himself sharply. "You fucked the man's wife; of course he is going to care."

The hour bell rang and Noran realised it had been half a watch since Ullsaard had returned. Wrapped in his woes, he had lost of all sense of time. What was keeping the general so busy?

Tired of gnawing at his fingers, feeling his balls shrinking with fear, Noran strode to the tent flap, determined to see Ullsaard and declare everything. He gave a girlish shriek of surprise as he came face to face with a second captain. The officer stepped back in shock.

"What do you want?" snarled Noran, masking his fear with anger.

"General Ullsaard wishes to see you," the captain said. "When you're ready."

"I'm ready now," said Noran, walking out of the tent. "Where is the general?"

"Follow me. He's at the bath house."

Noran followed after the captain, confused by this piece of news. Surely Ullsaard would want to deal with this matter in private? His confusion grew as he stepped inside the low building and found it empty. Pushing through the curtains into the main bath room, he found Ullsaard by himself, lounging in one of the main tubs. Through the clouds of steam, Noran saw Ullsaard raise a hand.

"Get your kit off and join me!" Ullsaard called out.

405

Noran hurriedly stripped off and splashed into the pool on the opposite side to Ullsaard, foregoing the customary preliminaries.

"Here I am," Noran said with a weak smile. "You look… You look happy!"

"What's to be sad about?" asked Ullsaard, running fingers through his wet hair. "I've just heard that Nemtun has lost his nerve and retreated behind the Wall. Nalanor's ripe for the picking. With the Greenwater and Narun in our possession, Okhar and Maasra won't be able to put up a fight for long. We're about to win the war."

"Oh," said Noran. "That is good news."

Ullsaard swam across the bath with splashing strokes, and settled next to Noran, elbows resting on the wooden side panels.

"What's the matter with you?" said the general. "You look like a man who paid for a whore and got in bed with a goat."

At first Noran took that as a veiled reference to his exploits with Meliu, but slowly realisation dawned as he looked at the general's concerned face. He didn't know! For reasons beyond Noran's understanding, Luia and Meliu had kept Noran's treachery secret.

"Um, nothing in particular," Noran replied. A little voice inside whined at Noran, telling him that it didn't matter that Luia hadn't given him up: now was the time to come clean. He told the inner voice to shut up as a wave of relief bubbled up inside him, flowing through his body like the warmth of the water. "Just a bit tired, I suppose."

Ullsaard nodded and rubbed his face in his hands.

"How was Magilnada?" Noran asked, trying to sound nonchalant. "It must have been good to see Allenya."

"Magilnada was good," replied Ullsaard. "I would have been back sooner, but I took Allenya and the other two up into the mountains to show them that old rebel camp."

"What about Urikh and Jutaar? Are they well?"

"You sound like some old mother," laughed Ullsaard. "Really, you're in an odd mood."

Ullsaard splashed Noran in the face and lunged at him, pushing his head under the water. Noran panicked, thinking that Ullsaard's innocence had been an act. He was going to drown! He thrashed at Ullsaard's thick arms, but there was no give. Bubbles streaming from his mouth, Noran kicked his legs and grabbed Ullsaard's wrists, trying to push to the surface and prise open that iron grip.

Ullsaard dragged Noran back up and let go, swimming away with a laugh.

"This isn't funny!" snapped Noran between gasps. "Just do it, all right?"

Ullsaard didn't seem to understand and paddled to the centre of the pool.

"You know, it was less than a year ago, I was in your baths and you told me to avoid getting into politics. I can't say this was what I had in mind then, but it hasn't turned out so bad."

Noran said nothing. He had been worried about letting slip Prince Kalmud's illness to Nemtun. It seemed such a stupid thing to worry about in hindsight. Less than a year ago, Noran had a loving wife and a child on the way. Now he had neither, and it was Ullsaard's politics that had killed them. Ullsaard must have seen something in Noran's expression. He swam closer and put a hand on Noran's shoulder.

"I'm sorry," said the general. "I didn't mea–"

"No, no, you didn't," Noran said, a wave of sadness sweeping through his thoughts. He grabbed Ullsaard's arm. "It really isn't your fault. And I'm sorry too."

"What are you sorry for?" said Ullsaard. "Apart from Allenya, you're the only other person I've been able to trust through this whole thing. Anglhan always has his own plans; Luia is possessed at the moment with the thought of becoming a queen; Urikh no doubt realises if I win he'll be heir to the Crown. You? You've asked nothing from me. No favours you want done, no whims to indulge. You could have been governor of Magilnada, but you didn't want it. You have nothing to be sorry for. Of everyone, I owe you the most, and if there's anything I can do for you, just tell me."

It was so tempting to Noran to make his confession there and then. After such a promise, there was no way that Ullsaard could refuse if Noran admitted what had happed with Meliu and asked simply for forgiveness.

But Noran could not bring himself to do it. Looking at the face of his friend, seeing the loyalty and gratitude in those eyes, Noran knew that he could not break that trust. After what Ullsaard had just said, Noran could no more confess his break of faith than breathe the water around him. Forgiveness was not an option, because he didn't deserve it.

His punishment would be to endure the guilt, and that was far harsher now than it had been moments before.

TEMPLE

The prayers channelling the power of the eulanui were swallowed by the dust-filled air. Outside the temple, the winds had grown to a gale, lashing the ziggurat with an unending barrage of sand while the dark skies above flickered with multicoloured lightning. Foreboding seeped from every stone and tile; the displeasure of the eulanui as palpable as the storm.

Lakhyri stared at the apparition of Udaan's features in the carved, distorted face of the acolyte on the slab. The high priest had been assailed by a number of long-forgotten emotions recently: fear, irritation, concern. Now he felt anger as the head of the Brotherhood reported events in the world beyond the temple.

"The king's grip is weakening," snarled Lakhyri. "In one season you have lost an empire that took two hundred years to build. I hold you responsible for this failure."

The bloody parody of Udaan's face contorted into a grimace.

"When the governors no longer listen to us, the Brotherhood can do little to shape events. We have tried our best to firm the hearts of the people against these traitors, but Ullsaard has been sly. He starves them and then feeds them, fills their heads with lies. He promises riches and glory to the legions and the governors are afraid of him."

"They should be afraid of the king!" Lakhyri seized the acolyte's throat in his skeletal fingers, pinning him to the stone table, his face a hair's-breadth away. "You should have dealt with this Ullsaard long before now. Your dithering puts everything at risk. I warned you of the consequences."

The acolyte-Udaan squirmed in Lakhyri's grip, hands flapping uselessly at the slab.

"We have tried to get people close to Ullsaard, but it is difficult, his followers are remarkably loyal. I feel there is some truth that he is one of the Blood."

Lakhyri released his hold and stepped back as if struck.

"That is not possible," said the high priest. His expression creased into a deep scowl. "If a child of the Blood has fallen through your fingers, it is just another example of your failure."

"I cannot see how it is possible." There was an edge of pleading in Udaan's voice. "All of the bastards are accounted for. There are no loose ends."

"Either this usurper is lying, or you have made a mistake. Which is it?"

Udaan's answer was a mute look of helplessness.

"You are clearly incapable of addressing this matter properly," said Lakhyri. "You leave me no choice but to intervene directly."

"I... I thought you could not leave the temple?"

"That may be what you wish to believe, but you are wrong."

Lakhyri leaned over the supine form of the acolyte and placed a hand on each side of the youth's head. The high priest chanted deep and slow, his incantation little more than an exhalation. Closing his eyes, Lakhyri spread his fingers across Udaan's puppet-face. Tissue stirred, turning

410

into sinew and blood and fat and skin, the priest's bony fingertips sinking into the writhing flesh.

The carvings in Lakhyri's skin moved, altering their shapes and orientation, darkening, turning his skin into a web of white and black. The necromantic sigils swirled across Udaan's ravaged features, twisting muscle and nerve into their likeness. Darker and deeper the runes burned into Lakhyri's withered flesh, etching into bone and organ, cutting through every part of him.

With a hoarse cry, Lakhyri slumped, the light in his eyes gone.

ASKH

Summer, 209th Year of Askh

I

The inner chambers of the Grand Precincts of the Brotherhood rang with a drawn-out scream. The wretched sound seemed to come from the rooms of Brother Udaan, and a crowd of concerned brethren converged quickly to investigate.

Upon opening the door, they found the silver-masked head of their order twitching upon the floor, the parchments from his desk scattered around him. Thinking he was having a fit, as sometimes Udaan was known to, one of the Brothers bent over his spasming form and attempted to lift off his mask to help him breathe.

Udaan's gloved hands snapped around the Brother's wrists and pushed them away. With an eerie strength, Udaan placed his feet flat on the tiled floor and pushed himself slowly upward, gracefully rising to his feet. The Brethren shuffled away nervously as Udaan straightened, releasing his grip on the Brother who had tried to help. The head of the Brotherhood flexed his neck and shoulders as if waking stiffened from sleep. He straightened his dishevelled robes and looked at his surroundings with eyes that glittered gold in the depths of his hood.

"Are you all right, Brother?" one of the attending Brethren asked.

"I am well," Udaan replied. His voice was distorted by the mask, but to those who knew their master well, it seemed stretched and thin. "Go back to your duties. I must visit the king."

II

Udaan's body was comfortable. It was old and by no means athletic, but it was not laden with the weight of centuries. Lakhyri walked briskly through the corridors of the Grand Precincts, drawing on the memories of the body's former master to find the shortest route to the palace. He passed the long vaults where shelf upon shelf of the archives stretched into lamplit gloom; the closest records written on vellum and parchments; older testimonies scribed into wax and clay; right the way back through the ages to the darkest recesses where crude symbols were carved into bone.

The archives of the Brotherhood: hidden from all, containing the forgotten reigns of kings who ruled over lands swallowed by the seas; the names of priest-gods who had built shrines of solid gold; the wars of nations whose names had faded even from myth. Back through the centuries, the millennia, to the time when the eulanui had been corporeal and ruled the world, before the waning of their power, when the true Brotherhood had been founded as their immortal servants.

In these dim vaults could be found the ancient mysteries of men and the wisdom of the eulanui, for those who knew where to look. Lakhyri had no need of such reference. He was the embodiment of the Brotherhood, the undying foundation of its purpose. Not for more than two hundred years, as measured by the fleeting lives of normal men, had he stepped foot from outside the Temple.

That he was forced to do so now was a source of deep vexation.

His course took him down flights of stairs lit by flickering oil lamps, whose steps descended beneath the precincts to caves where the ailurs were created and the flaming fuel normal men called lava was concocted. And it was in those deep caverns that the Brotherhood toiled at its other duties, which none save the king and the highest members of the Brotherhood knew.

Striding along a colonnade, Lakhyri came out into the sun. He stopped as the light and warmth hit him. Even through the mask and the robes and the hood, he could feel the summer seeping into him. He looked up with golden eyes and saw a bright blue sky, spotted with wraiths of cloud, and almost directly overhead the gleaming orb of the sun itself.

A doubt entered his thoughts as he walked down the wide flight of steps at the front of the Grand Precincts. Maybe he had waited too long to make his presence felt; not just a matter of days or weeks or years, but perhaps he would have been better intervening a generation ago.

Udaan's memories guided him to a small, unadorned side door in the duskward wing of the palaces. Lakhyri could feel the Brother's presence like a tiny niggling itch at the back of his mind, for Udaan was not gone, merely placed to one side. Spirit and life were one; to remove the spirit entirely was to bring the death of the body. Essence and vitality were entwined throughout the world, from the smallest insect to the mighty eulanui. It was this secret, the knowledge of spirit and life, which the eulanui had bestowed upon Lakhyri and others like him. All life was energy, moving or trapped, active or inert, but always there, never gone.

A rap on the door brought quick attention. Two Brothers opened the small portal and bowed their shaven heads to Lakhyri as he passed into the palace. The corridor within was narrow and straight, leading directly to the throne room of the king. Two hundred paces later, Lakhyri pushed through the curtains at the far end and stepped into the main hall.

The king sat on his throne with Nemtun, Erlaan, Adral of Nalanor and several other self-important officials. Unseen, Lakhyri stopped and listened to their deliberations.

"Ullsaard still does not have Maasra," Adral was saying. "If we perhaps took ship and defended there, we could force him to a negotiation."

"Impossible," said Nemtun. "If he realises we no longer hold the Wall, he will be in Askhor quicker than a sailor jumps in a whore's bed. Whether he has Maasra or not makes no difference."

"I disagree," said Erlaan. "If he has Maasra, he has access to the Nemurians and we do not."

"We cannot defend two places at once," said Adral. "The bastard is still consolidating his hold on Nalanor. If we can get to Maasra first and raise some more legions, we can halt the momentum he has gained."

"What will Kulrua do?" asked Erlaan. "Will he at least try to fight?"

"What do you mean by that?" growled Nemtun, shifting his bulky form to face his grandnephew. "Are you accusing me of something?"

"My grandson is right," snapped Lutaar. "If you had dealt with this problem when you had the chance, we would not be where we are now. I gave you legions and orders, and what did you do? You chased Ullsaard all winter to no effect and allowed him to slip past you into the mountains."

"And you," the king rounded on Adral. "You gave up the crossings of the Greenwater without so much as an arrow loosed or a shield raised. You have fifty warships and yet you let this man walked through Nalanor without hindrance. We have given him these successes without a fight, because the two of you have failed to act."

"I have heard enough," said Lakhyri, striding to the centre of the hall. He turned his masked face to the court of the king. "All of you: leave. I will speak to the king alone."

"Who do you think you are?" said Nemtun, heaving himself to his feet. "You best remember your manners and who you address, Udaan."

Lakhyri did not dignify the outburst with a reply, but simply looked at the king. Lutaar realised something was amiss; his eyes narrowed as he looked at Lakhyri.

"Do as he says, leave us," said the king. He continued to stare with suspicion while the others departed, Nemtun and Adral continuing to voice their grumbling discontent as they did so.

Silence filled the hall as Lakhyri ascended the raised platform on which the throne was placed. He stood directly in front of the king, who watched every move like a hawk. With slow deliberation, Lakhyri raised his left hand to his mask and, reaching inside his hood, unfastened its strap. He pulled the silver mask away, revealing his own rune-etched features.

"I guessed it was you," said Lutaar. "I have been expecting a visit for some time."

"We have much to discuss," said Lakhyri. "Your leniency has been uncharacteristic. Ullsaard and the chaos he threatens must be stopped before winter comes. If he is not destroyed, it will be the end of all that we have strived to create. You cannot fail in your duty to our masters."

Lutaar pursed his lips and his brow wrinkled at the prospect.

"I understand that. I will accept whatever help you can offer. Between us we can deal with this upstart."

"We will, my brother," replied Lakhyri. "We will."

ASKHIRA, MAASRA
Midsummer, 209th Year of Askh

I

The dockyards were a cauldron of ceaseless noise. The thump of wooden mallets was so intense and so prevalent that Jutaar retired to his rooms every night with his head still pounding. The rat-tat-tat of rivet hammers, the buzz of saws, the creak of tensioned rope, the thud of planks and the constant pattering of bare feet intruded into every moment of Jutaar's waking life, and often his dreams.

It had seemed a simple enough job that his father had given him. Build a fleet large enough for fifty thousand men, to sail hotwards along the coast and make landing on the dawnward shores of Askhor, beyond the mountains that separated the homeland of the empire from its surrounding provinces.

And it should have been simple. Jutaar's father had drafted thousands of labourers from the shipyards along the Greenwater, nearly doubling the number of men in the port of Askhira. Carpenters and sailmakers, caulkers and coopers, overseers and ledgermen, all put into action the orders of the general, attended to by a similarly sized army of cooks and traders, wives and whores. To house them, three architects from Nalanor had arrived, with even more men to raise long tenements along the sea front, and to build new docks so that more ships could be laid down. All under the watchful gaze of the Tenth Legion.

Jutaar had only to keep an eye on things, to make sure the monies were paid, the materials supplied and the workers protected. Yet this had proven more difficult than he had been led to believe. Amidst the overcrowded workers' apartments, tempers flared regularly. Small incidents had a habit of sparking large confrontations, and four times Jutaar had sent in companies of the Tenth to suppress potential riots.

It was not just at home that the work force was unhappy; the labourers were constantly fractious with their masters, the captains argued with the harbour masters, and disputes between suppliers often brought the flow of materials to a standstill. Accidents happened every day, most of them minor, but several were more serious and had claimed the lives of nearly two hundred men in total. There were rumours that the endeavour was cursed, but how and by whom nobody would say.

That such superstition had taken root was in itself a symptom of the Brotherhood's absence. Not a single black-robed Brother could be found in all of Maasra, nor in Okhar, or Nalanor or any of the other provinces outside Askhor. It came to light over the course of a few days; in towns and cities across the empire, the Brotherhood disappeared. The precinct pyramids were deserted, their doors locked, their windows barred. This sudden departure had a twofold effect. Most obviously, the machine of state ground to a halt. Without the Brotherhood and their taxes, censuses, marriages, funerals, quotas and archives, people's everyday lives were left without structure, while commerce became sporadic and returned to a small-scale, local trade more common in savage places like Salphoria and Mekha.

It was just not the practical issues that bedevilled Jutaar and the others attempting to run Ullsaard's newly acquired domains. The people of the provinces felt abandoned without the Brotherhood. There was a strange feeling in the towns; a hushed fear around the empty precincts; an unsettled atmosphere in streets where black-robed figures no longer walked.

Jutaar knew that his father and brothers thought him slow and somewhat dim, but he was not without some thoughts. It occurred to him that a Brother might simply take off his robe and be indistinguishable from any other man. It was unlikely that hundreds of Brothers across Maasra were mysteriously spirited away by some strange force; Jutaar firmly believed that the Brotherhood were still around, but had chosen to hide in plain sight.

He had written to his father to warn of the fear that the Brotherhood were agitating against Ullsaard. Jutaar knew enough about the morale of men to understand that it takes little to turn uncertainty into fear, fear into anger. It was Jutaar that had persuaded Allon's legions that they had no chance against Ullsaard, and taken his father's offer of a new allegiance to them. He had seen firsthand the disquiet sown by his father's manoeuvres and half-truths, the lies spread by his men through the ranks of the common soldiers. Now, as far as Jutaar could tell, the Brotherhood were retaliating in kind.

Men already working long shifts to build a warfleet did not need much of a push to start complaining. An act of sabotage, a whispered voice of dissent, could fan the embers of annoyance into something far more dangerous.

Other than asking for advice from his father, Jutaar could not see what else he could do. He kept the Tenth close at hand and walked the docks every day with kind words, resolving disputes, reminding people of the great venture they were embarking upon and the age of prosperity they would all enjoy under the rule of King Ullsaard. Jutaar was lavish with the treasury of Maasra, despite many complaints from the governor, Kulrua, who was by nature a miserly, bureaucratic man. Each ship completed was celebrated with a feast for all and Jutaar continued to build more homes to give the workers more space.

Despite this generosity, he felt that all of the gold in Magilnada, Nalanor and Okhar would not assuage the growing resentment of his newly subject people. Every time the legionnaires broke up a fight, every time a timber cracked and a man was injured, the shipyards bubbled with quiet rebellion. Tools were downed and shifts sent home while tempers eased.

It was even stranger given the placid reputation of Maasrites across the empire. They were known for the most part as peaceful people. A little more than one hundred years ago, the Maasrite tribes had joined Greater Askhor without a fight; famously, their six chieftains cut out their tongues so that they could offer no word of protest and keep their honour. This became the Vow of Service that a proportion of Maasrites still followed. Jutaar had always been uncomfortable with voluntary self-mutilation, but being in Askhira had taught him that the practice was far less common than he had thought. Most of those that took the Vow of Service were servants across the rest of the empire, who had followed their forefathers' act of sacrifice so that they could not dispute the wishes of foreign masters.

Jutaar wondered if the influx of foreigners into Maasra had upset the locals, but there was little evidence. The docile, workmanlike Maasrites had been agitated by far more than the arrival of belligerent, loud Okharans and Nalanorians. Like the other workers, they were fearful of some undisclosed fate and complained of nightmares of the town being swallowed by the sea.

All of this disruption had put Jutaar far behind schedule. Ullsaard was coming to the province to see the delays firsthand and to resolve them quickly.

So it was that Jutaar waited at the gate of Askhira's wall in the summer afternoon heat, feeling downcast that he had failed his father, and fearful of the meeting about to take place. The coming of Ullsaard was heralded by a dust cloud on the horizon, and it was quickly evident that the general had come with a large body of men. As the bells sounded the arrival of High Watch, the marching column of the Thirteenth could be seen in the haze, their golden standards and black shields snaking along the road from the Greenwater.

Jutaar and Rondin had arranged a guard of honour by the Tenth, who lined the road outside and inside the gate, spears raised in salute as General Ullsaard rode into Askhira, while the Thirteenth stopped half a mile outside of the town to make camp. The general had Urikh and Noran with him, both also on ailurs, though Urikh looked far from comfortable on his beast. Jutaar hurried down the steps from the gate tower to greet his father in the square just inside the wall.

Dismounting, Ullsaard clasped his son's hand and clapped him on the shoulder.

"Don't look so worried, son," said the general. "I'm not here to give you a hard time."

"That's good to hear," replied Jutaar with a smile of relief. He turned to his brother. "Urikh. Good to see you."

"Brother," Urikh replied tersely, half-falling from the back of his ailur.

"How are you doing, Jutaar?" asked Noran as he let himself out of the saddle with far more grace, tossing the reins to a waiting legionnaire. "You have been kept busy, I hear."

"Very," said Jutaar.

The group walked down the main street of Askhira, heading towards the docks. The town was quiet, a few women and children around to watch the new arrivals, the bulk of the inhabitants at work. Even from this distance the noise of labour was audible. As they crested a rise, Ullsaard stopped and the others gathered around him.

The harbour was laid out before them, the town sloping gently towards the sea.

Set on an inlet of the Nemurian Strait, Askhira followed the shallow coast around the bay, a thin crescent of red-roofed homes and wooden-beamed warehouses. Warmed by the hotward winds blowing up the Maasran Gulf, Askhira was hot and humid, prone to summer storms that were violent but brief. Even in winter the coast was pleasantly mild and two rearing headlands provided natural shelter for ships. To coldwards the land rose swiftly into the foothills of the Askhinia Mountains, the hotwards range bordering the home of the empire. The hills had once been solid with forests, but centuries of shipbuilding and timber export had cut a large swathe through the trees, visible as a pale scar amongst the dark green, stretching out of sight into the distance.

The sky was clear and Jutaar could see out across the straits, to a dark blotch where sea met sky. That way lay the islands of Nemuria, a chain of active volcanoes that smudged the air with their fumes. When he had first arrived, Jutaar had taken a ship out into the straits to see the islands. By old agreement, no ship approached within a mile of those islands without permission, so Jutaar had tried his best to peer through the smog and gloom to see the lands of the Nemurians. They reared out of the water with high cliffs and steep, ash-wreathed shores. Through breaks in the cloud he had seen huge edifices of black granite standing high above yellow-leafed trees, and thought he glimpsed flashes of red and orange at the tips of the peaks.

The wind, treacherous around Nemuria, had turned foul and forced the ship's captain to tack back lest he break the one-mile limit. Nobody was sure what the penalty would be for breaking the convention, but Jutaar would be the first to admit he did not want to find out the hard way. Little was known of the Nemurians, least of all their numbers, and it was regarded by all to be a good thing that they seemed content to remain on their islands and only came to the mainland to work as mercenaries. Nothing had been seen of them since Nemtun had dismissed his corps of five thousand – even Maasra, their home away from home, was empty of the non-humans. The prevailing wisdom was that the Nemurians were waiting to see who ended up running the empire before they got involved again.

That had been Jutaar's first and last sight of Nemuria, but each time he gazed across the strait, he wondered what else might be seen in that patch of grey.

"You said you had trouble elsewhere?" Jutaar said, tearing his eyes away from the mysterious islands.

"In Parmia and Narun, mostly," replied Noran. Ullsaard was still staring across the sea at the pall of smoke. "A bit of trouble in Geria, but that's to be expected as Nemtun's old capital. Even had a riot in Duuris."

"What did you do to stop it?" Jutaar asked.

"That, my son," said Ullsaard, breaking from his entranced state, "you will see tomorrow."

Wondering what this might mean, Jutaar led his visitors down into Askhira, to the houses he had occupied on the dockside.

II

It was the fourth hour of Gravewatch and Ullsaard was already awake and eating his breakfast. No doubt roused by the commotion of the servants preparing the meal, Jutaar wandered into the small dining room, rubbing the sleep from his eyes, clad in a robe hastily belted.

"You should have warned me it would be an early start," said Jutaar, sitting to his father's left and reaching for a jug of fruit juice. "I would have had the servants wake me properly."

"Early start?" Ullsaard laughed. "You should feel lucky that you're not Anasind. He's been working all night. If

423

you're quick, you can come with me when I join him at Dawnwatch."

"Working all night? Doing what?"

"Come and have a look," said Ullsaard.

He led Jutaar to the wide doors leading out onto a veranda overlooking the harbour. Throwing open the doors, the general stepped outside, his son just behind. The air was cool but not cold, dawn struggling to break through the clouds of Nemuria. Ullsaard waved a hand towards the town below. Bearing lanterns and torches, legionnaires were moving through Askhira from its hotwards tip along the harbour, spreading through the city like runnels of flickering light. There was a greater glow around the three-tiered ziggurat of Askhira's precinct building.

Despite this nocturnal activity, the town was quiet, a sea breeze sighing over the rooftops.

"What are they doing?" asked Jutaar.

"Looking for the Brotherhood, of course," replied Ullsaard. "We did the same in Parmia, Narun, Lepriin, and half a dozen other places. You'd be surprised by the number of them that kept their robes in a chest or under the bed. We've found silver masks on mantels and Brotherhood scrolls in drawers."

"You're searching the whole town?" Jutaar leaned over the rail of the veranda and peered into the streets below. "That's why you brought the Thirteenth?"

"I've got legions spread across all of Greater Askhor keeping a watch for trouble. Donar has the Fifth in Narun, Jutiil's in Parmia, Luamid had the Sixteenth in Geria, plus the two new Magilnadan legions are keeping an eye on things in Ersua and Okhar. Just a precaution."

"What will happen to those Brothers you find?"

Ullsaard joined his son at the rail.

"I'm sending them all to the camp outside Parmia, where they can't do any trouble. The most senior ones tend to put up a bit of a fight and we have to make examples of them. I can't have anyone undermining my claim to the Crown."

"What sort of examples?"

Ullsaard wondered, not for the first time, if Jutaar was really suited to the legions. He laid a hand on his son's shoulder.

"We slit their throats, Jutaar."

"Killing Brothers?" Jutaar was aghast at the suggestion. "Is that really wise?"

"Only a few," Ullsaard replied with a half-shrug. "You'll be surprised the number of them that decide to get out of town when word of that gets around. It saves us the trouble of hunting them down."

"But killing Brothers... If you become king–"

"When I become king," Ullsaard interrupted. "You're worried that I'll lose the Brotherhood? I don't think so. Lutaar and Udaan have them agitated at the moment, but things will return to normal once I have the Crown. The Brotherhood is dedicated to Greater Askhor before any particular king. They may be upset with me for a while, but the empire will continue and they'll see that I am not their enemy."

"And what about the people of the empire? If they learn you've been killing Brothers, what will they think?"

Ullsaard was not sure whether Jutaar was being dimwitted or fearful. Either way, his son's reluctance to accept the facts as they were was wearing the general's patience.

"The people will do what they're fucking told!" he snapped. "That's the other reason the Thirteenth are here. There will be a curfew for the next ten days, enforced by penalty of death. We'll flood the town and docks with legionnaires from the Thirteenth and Tenth and remind these people who is in charge here. Askhira needs reminding that their governor supports me and that means that they do as well."

Ullsaard realised his temper was getting the better of him. Noran had warned that the general could not just order people around as if they were his army. Taking a deep breath, he turned to face Jutaar and leaned casually on the rail, trying to appear calm.

"Look, you've been very good to these people, son," he explained, hoping that some of what he had to say would settle in Jutaar's slow-moving brain. "We've paid them well, brought a huge amount of work and commerce to the harbour, and what have they given in return? They've been muttering and conspiring against you, ignoring your offers and disrespecting your position as my representative. If they refuse to do what they are told when we treat them well, they'll swiftly learn of what else we have to offer."

"I suppose you can't have discipline without the threat of punishment," said Jutaar. "As a captain I'm always quick to enforce the regulations."

"That's right, son," said Ullsaard. "When they see what the alternative is, these people will be grateful to have the kind and understanding Jutaar in charge again. And just like the way a company works, most folks in Askhira will start to take care of the matter themselves. After the next ten days, nobody here will want me coming back, so they'll cast out any Brothers that stay behind, as well as anyone else that wants to upset the wagon."

Realisation crept across Jutaar's face like the dawn spreading across the harbour.

"It's a bit like when Urikh and I were kids," he said. "He was always saying 'I'm telling Father what you did', even when I hadn't done anything wrong."

"Yes," said Ullsaard. "But when I've left and you need to remind people of the consequences of ill discipline, I wouldn't use those exact words."

III

Ullsaard's crackdown on the Brotherhood and the other

malcontents in Askhira rapidly brought work back up to speed. Though Jutaar was still behind on delivering the fleet his father needed, the pace was quickening and there was still a chance that they would be ready to sail with the legions before the winter.

Five days after his father had departed, Jutaar discussed this with Urikh; Ullsaard had left his eldest son in Askhira to help Jutaar ensure progress went smoothly. The two of them were making a tour of the docks, followed by a coterie of scribes with wax tablets and styluses making notes of the work being done.

"This is the sixteenth of the thirty warships we need," Jutaar was saying as they stopped to look at the skeletal timbers of a trireme. Hundreds of men were cladding the ribs with hull planks and putting down decking. "We have four hundred and eleven of the six hundred and fifty transports too."

"It is still taking too long," said Urikh.

Jutaar had always known his brother to be an industrious, ambitious, busy person. Even as a child Urikh had constantly devised ways to take advantage of his younger siblings and their friends, persuading them to lend him money for some scheme or other; money that he almost inevitably failed to repay due to the poor sense or bad luck of someone else. Urikh's apparent appetite for this operation outstripped anything he had shown before. The promise of becoming the heir to the Crown was clearly the greatest incentive Jutaar's brother had ever felt. Since coming to Askhira, he had thrown himself into every aspect of the endeavour, berating any foreman whose team so much as laid one plank or hammered one nail or tarred one seam less than was required each day. Jutaar was pleased that Urikh was around to deal with the more unpleasant practicalities of controlling a work force and Urikh had even admitted, somewhat drunkenly and aggressively the night before, that the two of them made a good team.

"More men won't help," said Jutaar. "There's only so much space to build and so many things that can be done at once."

"That does not solve my problem," said Urikh, squinting in the sunshine. He was obviously suffering from his over-indulgence of wine the night before. "Give me answers, not excuses."

Jutaar thought about the problem as they moved onto the next dock where a flat-bottomed transport was taking shape, waiting only for its mast and cabin to be built.

"Lanterns," he said.

"What's that?" Urikh replied absently, having snatched a tablet from one of his attendants to scribble down some thought of his own.

"If we bring in some of those large camp lanterns the legions use, maybe thirty or so, we could extend the shifts into the night by another watch before it gets too dark to work."

Urikh stared at his brother as if he had suddenly turned a strange colour and spouted Nemurian.

"What?" said Jutaar. "What's wrong with that?"

"Nothing!" Urikh exclaimed with a grin. "It is brilliant! I should have thought of that."

"Well, you didn't, brother," said Jutaar, feeling pleased with himself.

"So, where do we get these lanterns from?"

Jutaar hesitated. He hadn't got that far ahead in his thinking.

"We'll have to send for them," he said.

"That will take too long," said Urikh as they resumed their tour, walking along a stone wharf as the waves lapped over its edge and crept towards their sandaled feet. His smile disappeared and became a frown, but that soon vanished as he came to an answer. "We will get the artisans in the Tenth to make them. I'm sure they have everything they need and it is not like they have much else to do at the moment."

Jutaar thought about this and could find no fault with the plan.

"That would work. An extra watch each day should increase production by another fifth. We would have the fleet ready in time."

Urikh laid a brotherly arm around Jutaar's shoulders and slapped him on the belly.

"With a fleet, we take Askhor," Urikh said. "When we have Askhor, we take Askh. After that, father becomes king. And we will be Princes of the Blood!"

Jutaar nodded and smiled. That certainly sounded good.

IV

Something woke Urikh in the early hours of the morning. He guessed it to be during Gravewatch. He glanced across the bed to see his wife, Neerlima, still asleep. He slipped out from under the blankets and padded barefoot to the archway and into the adjoining room. He peered into the darkness at Luissa in her small bed, nothing more than a splay of dark curls against a white pillow. He watched for a moment but his daughter did not stir, as sound asleep as her mother.

As he turned back to his bed, Urikh realised what seemed amiss. He could smell a hint of smoke in the air, as if one of the servants had improperly put out a cooking fire. Urikh could not understand why he would notice such a thing at this time of the morning. As he was about to slip back under the covers, he saw movement out of the corner of his eye and looked towards the windows. Between the slats of the shutters he saw a flickering.

Filled with sudden foreboding, he dashed across the room and flung open the shutters. He looked towards the harbour and saw smoke rising from flames aboard three ships, slowly drifting towards he docks. He recognised them as ships Jutaar had mounted with legion lamps, now ablaze from stem to stern.

Others had seen them too and bells rang and gongs were struck in warning, but there was nothing that could be done. Urikh heard Neerlima stirring behind him, asking what he was doing, but he was fixed on the scene unfolding in the harbour.

The burning ships crashed into the docks, the sea wind fanning the flames onto the canvas and timbers, the barrels of pitch and oil, and soon the fires were spreading from hotward along the crescent of the bay, growing in strength. That same wind brought smoke gusting over Askhira, stinging Urikh's eyes; but there had been tears in them already as he realised how many ships they would lose. It seemed as if they hadn't found all of the Brotherhood's agents and saboteurs after all. He would have to write to his father.

"Fuck," he muttered, lowering his head into his hands, unable to look any more.

NARUN, NALANOR
Late Summer, 210th Year of Askh

I

The reports from the scouts had been confirmed: Nemtun's army had left the Wall and was advancing on Narun. After a season content to guard against attack, no doubt having celebrated the new year in comfort, the king's brother had decided to take the offensive. Donar gathered his second captains in the headquarters he had made in an old municipal building. Third captains bustled around the room, gathering maps of the area between Narun and the Wall, collating the disparate reports of Nemtun's army and its progress.

"Stand or retreat, that is the simple question," the First Captain of the Fifth told his subordinates, fists on hips. "We have one legion and a few auxiliaries from the docks; Nemtun has four by all accounts, two of them newly raised in Askhor. They lack experience but they'll be well-equipped."

"One legion cannot face four, no matter how fresh they are," said Kluurs, the wrinkled, grey-haired Second Captain of the fifth company. Donar had inherited him from the previous First Captain, and considered Kluurs a dependable if uninspired officer. "Narun has no Wall to defend."

"We can send word to the Twelfth in Parmia and hold the camp," suggested Arsiil. The captain of the second company was a battered man with ugly ears, a broken nose and a scar running from right cheek to chin. Like Kluurs, he had been with the Fifth when it had been under Nemtun's command and knew the king's brother well. Arsiil waved a hand towards the narrow window. "Let Nemtun have the city; he can't do anything with it with us still on his doorstep."

"It'd take four days at least for a runner to reach Jutiil, and six or seven for the Twelfth to reach us, even if they could leave immediately," said Donar. He looked at the maps spread on the table between them. "Nemtun could storm the camp in ten days, no problem. Is there nowhere else we could defend?"

"I have an idea," said Lutaan, captain of the first company and Donar's nephew. He pulled a map to the top of the pile and turned it towards Donar. "Let's not think about defending Narun, let's think about attacking Nemtun."

"Open battle against four to one?" Arsiil laughed scornfully. "General Ullsaard will thank none of us for throwing ourselves onto the enemy's spears for no cause. We need every shield and spear for the attack on Askhor."

"The general will thank us less for giving up the Greenwater without a fight," said Donar. "From Narun, Nemtun can send ships hotwards to Paalun and then retake Geria. The Tenth will be cut off in Maasra and easy to pick off. I don't even know where the general and the Thirteenth are, they could be horribly caught out. We can't allow that to happen. Lutaan, what are you suggesting?"

"Here, at Pallion, the road passes through high hills," said Lutaan, pointing to the defile on the map. "We ambush Nemtun's column there, before withdrawing coldwards and crossing back over the Greenwater at Denerii Ford."

"Nemtun's not an idiot," argued Arsiil. "He'll be treating everywhere outside the Wall as hostile territory. You think we could just sneak up on the man that blazed across Anrair? He'll have a picket out and he'll be doubly wary going through Pallion."

"We'll give him cause to relax," said Donar, liking his nephew's plan more with each passing moment. There was no hope of stopping Nemtun, but at least a short offensive would be something better to take to Ullsaard than a hasty retreat. "We'll make it look like we've burnt the ships, as we would if we were retreating. Nemtun's an arrogant arse, and he knows we can't hold Narun against him. No doubt the king's agents know the legions are spread all over keeping everything under control. Yes, I'm damn sure Nemtun isn't looking for a fight, but he knows if he can take Narun it'll be hard to claim it back before the winter."

"Why don't we just burn the ships and retreat?" asked Nimruun, the captain of the third company. The slight, fair-haired man looked up from a sheaf of scouts' reports. "Geria is safe if Nemtun has no ships to sail downriver. It'll take him a while to get enough vessels together, by which time we can join with the Tenth in Paalun and wait for him."

Donar was about to argue with this course of action, but stopped himself. Was he just looking to keep his pride with the general, or was there actually a military reason for risking an attack on Nemtun?"

Before he could answer, Lutaan spoke.

"Why not send what ships we can down to Paalun before attacking Nemtun?" said the captain. "That way, we give the old fucker a bloody nose, withdraw with the legion intact and stop him getting anything useful out of Narun."

Donar looked at his officers, waiting for further criticisms. None were forthcoming, though Arsiil's brow was furrowed, trying to come up with one.

"Those will be my orders," Donar announced. "We have to move quickly. We need to be at Pallion by midday tomorrow to be sure of getting there before Nemtun. Pass the word to the ships' captains to set sail tonight; tell them that any of them left in the harbour at dawn will have their ship seized and destroyed, that'll get their arses moving. We'll use the camp materials for our fake fires."

"Double sentries on the roads as well," said Nimruun. Donar's look was questioning so the captain continued. "Obviously Nemtun has one or more spies still in the city, otherwise he wouldn't know we're ripe for attacking. All it'll take is one of them to catch a sniff of what we're doing and get to his army and we'll be walking into a trap, not the other way round."

Donar nodded and the second captains saluted before departing. The commander of the Fifth walked up the stairs to the second storey of the building and passed through the upper rooms, where former offices and harbour archives had been turned into storerooms and dormitories. Striding between the bunks in one room, he came to a ladder leading to the roof terrace. Pulling himself up, he walked to the dawnwards edge of the terrace and looked at the mountains jutting into the sky, the natural boundary of Askhor.

"I'll teach you to have a swing at me, you fat swine," Donar said with a content smile.

II

The horns sounded the alarm, ringing back along the column as it marched along the road. Donar grinned to himself at the thought of the consternation that would be going through the minds of the legionnaires below, especially those new recruits who had probably been looking forward to a march into Narun without a battle.

Nemtun had taken the bait, headstrong as always, and had come to the Pallion defile in the late afternoon the day after Donar and his Fifth had left Narun. Nemtun's column was stretched out, the veterans of the Second in the vanguard, the two new legions with their blue shields and freshly forged icons half a mile behind, unable to keep up with the pace of the experienced campaigners. This held back the other blooded legionnaires from the Fourth; the brother legion raised at the same time as Donar's Fifth for the conquest of Nalanor, taken by the Nemtun from Murian before his capitulation to Ullsaard.

Donar was disappointed that he could see no sign of Nemtun with the Second as they hurriedly moved from their ranks of march into a semi-circle of phalanxes facing coldwards towards the advancing companies of the Fifth. Clearly their captain hoped to hold position until reinforced by the following legions. What he didn't know was that Donar had already set in motion a plan to ensure that relief would be some time in coming.

"Let's show these spoilt braggarts what a real legion can do!" Donar shouted to his men as he led them down the long slope towards the road, striding with purpose beside his nephew in the first company.

To his right, black smoke hung in a pall over the Greenwater, where fires still burned fitfully amongst the piers and wharfs of Narun. Everything that wasn't needed had been loaded onto spare boats and rafts made from the logs of the camp wall, and set ablaze in the early hours of morning for maximum visibility, an hour after the last ships had been sent downriver. The conflagration had been something to behold, and Donar had enjoyed some banter with his men as they cheered the pops and explosions.

Looking to his left, along the road towards the Wall, the First Captain could see three hundred hand-picked men led by the legion's engineers and armourers, picking their way through the boulders at the steepest part of the defile. They carried kegs of fuel taken from the lava-throwers that had been set ablaze along with the rest of the camp baggage; the war machines were too heavy to be taken on the Fifth's hasty retreat that would come later in the day.

While the companies of the next legion in the column entered the rock-lined canyon at a fast march, the engineers lighted the tapers on their barrels and threw them down the slopes. Some exploded early, others caught on bushes and trees to detonate harmlessly, but dozens of the kegs rolled down onto the road, spraying hot burning fuel over the advancing legionnaires. Where the lava spilt across the pavement of the road, it spread into burning pools, halting further progress. Those soldiers that tried to pick their way around the blaze by climbing the slope were assailed by a barrage of bellows-arrows and slingshot from the men on the defiles.

There was no time to enjoy the view as Donar raised his sword to signal the charge. Five thousand legionnaires swept down the slope, falling upon the Second with shouts of "Fight for the Fifth!"

Donar could have remained with his second captains, directing the battle, but the temptation to pit himself in person against his foes had proved too much. The battle plan was simple and he would not be needed if things went well and could do little good if things went poorly. Having hacked down savages in Anrair and Mekha, this was his chance to prove himself against another legion, and his blood rushed through his body at the prospect of a proper fight. With the legion's battle cry on his lips, Donar plunged down the slope with his men.

The Second were not content to let fate alone decide their future. Their captain, a wily, political man called Rhantis who Donar had never liked, led five companies on a counter-attack, storming up the hillside to meet the Fifth head-on. Spear crashed against shield as the opposing phalanxes met, the impetus of those charging downhill meeting with the set pikes of those below.

Surrounded by a wall of spearpoints, Donar led the first company directly into the Second's own premier company, heading for their icon bearer. Wooden shafts splintered around him and a bronze pike head glanced from his helm as the two formations smashed together. Pushed onwards by his surging legionnaires, Donar was thrust into the middle of massive melee. He kicked a booted foot against the shield of the enemy legionnaire to his front, smashing it back into the face of the man beside his foe. Another wave of spear thrusts forced Donar into the cover of the shield carried by the man to his right, accompanied by more shivered shafts and broken pike tips.

"By the right!" Lutaan bellowed.

As one, the leftmost men in the phalanx stepped back a pace while those on the right flank heaved forwards, pushed into the enemy by eleven more ranks behind them. Though the movement was slight in the wider scheme of things, this slight change of angle caught the enemy unawares; they stumbled into the space created, allowing Donar's legionnaires to thrust their pikes into the gaps opened. Men of the Second fell, armour pierced, bodies streaming with blood.

These casualties, though relatively few in number, were enough to disrupt the momentum of the enemy phalanx. Donar and those around him in the front rank broke their shield wall and charged, smashing their shoulders into the shields of their foes to force them back a few more steps.

The company closed ranks again, the whole advance taking only a few heartbeats. The momentum continued to shift as the legionnaires of the Second were forced to step back to redress their ranks, but were given no time as Donar's company pushed them further and further down the slope towards the road, using their advantage of the higher ground.

"Beware to the left!" came a cry from behind Donar.

He could see nothing of what was happening, but guessed an opposing phalanx had broken the line and was about to charge. His phalanx stopped to receive this new threat. The men on that side turned their shields outwards, while the back ranks swung their pikes over the heads of those in front and angled them towards the oncoming enemies.

The force of the fresh impact shuddered though the tightly packed men and Donar felt the legionnaire behind him stumble. There were laughs as the man was dragged back to his feet by his companions. The inevitable push came, forcing Donar and the others to step to their right to compensate, as inexorably they were herded along the line of the slope. Ahead, the first company of the Second had rallied somewhat during the diversion and thrust forward with renewed vigour.

"Get at them!" Donar shouted, swinging his sword towards a helmeted head, the blade crashing along the top of a raised shield.

Another deafening crash rang in Donar's ears as the enemy to his left were in turn counter-charged and suddenly his formation was surging into the space vacated by their retreat. This sudden movement turned the enemy in front even further, and Donar could hear the shouts of his men as his legion's third company drove into the enemy from his right.

Step by excruciating step, the first company of the Fifth advanced down the slope, battering and heaving at their counterparts in the Second. The advance gathered pace until the legionnaires in front could no longer contain the pressure. Some lost their balance and tripped down the slope, others turned full around to run away, sensing that this engagement had been lost. With a hoarse shout, Donar urged his men after them, running down the slope, hacking at their backs with his sword.

A horn note, long and deep, cut through the blood pounding in Donar's ears. It was the general order to hold advance. Wondering what his captains were thinking, he ducked back through the lines of men behind, pushing through the ranks until he exited through the back of the phalanx.

The slope and road was littered with bodies from both sides, but it was the formations of men advancing through the right flank of his army that drew his attention. Three of his companies had made it all the way to the road, but had been met by a company from the Second held in reserve, while half a dozen companies from the Second had pushed their way up the hill around them, turning in an arc towards the rear of the line's centre. The first company and those around it were hideously compromised.

"Sound the rally!" Donar shouted, dashing up the slope towards the gaggle of second captains at the crest. "Bring the phalanxes back to the line!"

The captains could not hear him over the din of the battle, and sounded the command for "Halt advance" again. Neither pushing into the enemy to force a retreat nor falling back to mount a fresh attack, the companies of the Fifth were scattered across the hillside, only the centre forming a cohesive line. Screaming with anger, Donar sprinted up the hill, lungs bursting.

"Sound the fucking rally!" he bellowed over and over until he was within earshot of the hornblowers. Three short notes followed swiftly, but as he turned back towards the road, Donar could see it was too late.

Their formation disjointed, the Fifth were being enveloped on their left, where the enemy now had the advantage of the better ground. Those companies on the right could already see what was happening, and were breaking from the line, retreating coldwards towards the Greenwater. For the phalanxes in the centre, there was no escape. Assailed from both sides, their shield walls were quickly broken and a stream of men ran back up the hill as the rear ranks fled from the brutal fighting.

Donar watched in horror as the first company broke ranks and fell back. For a moment the icon of Askhos disappeared and Donar's heart sank, only for the golden icon to emerge from the mass of bodies, held aloft by his nephew.

As legionnaires poured up the slope, Donar was thankful to hear the Second's musicians ringing out the "Halt pursuit" call; Rhantis was more concerned with keeping his legion intact that catching his fleeing enemies.

Blood streaming from a cut across the bridge of his nose, Lutaan fell to his knees just in front of Donar, panting heavily, his shield gouged and split in one hand, the legion icon in the other. Donar helped his nephew to his feet.

"Come on, let's get out of here." The First Captain knew it was a bit pointless, but called out for the horns to sound the general retreat, for appearance's sake if nothing else.

He pulled Lutaan's useless shield from his arm and tossed it away, putting his shoulder under the man's arm to help him along. Between gasps, Lutaan laughed fitfully. He looked at Donar, his hand tightening reassuringly on his shoulder.

"I'm sorry, Uncle, don't listen to me again. This was a shit plan!"

Donar stared in wonder at Lutaan, and at the thousands fleeing up the slope. Despite the defeat that this had turned out to be, he guessed he'd only lost a fifth of his men – so far. More would turn up missing before the legion came together at Denerii, but it was far from being a disaster.

"All things considered," he said to his nephew, "I have to agree with you."

PARMIA

Winter, 210th Year of Askh

I

Using a trick he had learnt from his fellow legionnaires, Gelthius thrust his hands down the front of his kilt and used the heat of his groin to warm his numb fingers. His shield was leant against the parapet of the wooden tower, his spear held in the crook of his arm as he wiggled his fingers to get some feeling back into them. The bell had just rung two hours after Noonwatch, but still Gelthius's breath came in clouds of mist.

"Is it always this cold?" he asked Geddiban, the squat Ersuan standing sentry the regulation five paces to his right.

"Not this time of the year," the legionnaire replied. "Rain, there's always plenty of that, but it ain't usually this cold."

"I overheard the captain saying they even had a night frost down in Maasra," added Jirril to the left. "Imagine that. Ice in Maasra."

"It's queer, sure enough," said Gelthius. "Listen to that wind!"

The ten men in the tower did as Gelthius suggested. There seemed to be voices on the wind, long whispers of words Gelthius could not understand, but he detected malice in their tone.

"Just a trick of the mind," said Jirril.

Gelthius had his own opinions, but knew better than to share them. He had been humiliated before when talking about the spirits, mocked by the others in his company for having such superstitions. It didn't matter to them that their grandfathers had made sacrifices to the same spirits that Gelthius talked about; the Brotherhood had done its work well, convincing them that men alone controlled their fate.

Stamping his feet to distract himself from the strange hisses in his ears, Gelthius looked out across the snow-dusted fields. The early winter did not bode well. It was an omen of the spirits' displeasure, he was sure of it.

The other men always complained about standing watch, but the cold aside, Gelthius quite enjoyed it. He had grown used to monotony in the bowels of the landship, and at least guard duty didn't take the bone-aching toll that was the lot of every cranksman. Standing in a tower or pacing along the camp walls gave Gelthius time to ponder the world, something there had been precious little of since he had been drafted into the Thirteenth.

When he had been a turnsman, he had idled away the long days with thoughts of what he would do when he had paid off his debt. He would picture his wife and children, the village in duskward Salphoria where they lived, helping on the farms in the warm seasons, picking berries and herding swine through the woods during the winter. He could never have imagined how differently things would turn out. On the very day he should have had his freedom, he had been entangled in all this rebel business, and just as he was getting used to that idea the general had turned up.

He'd travelled all over the world since becoming one of the Thirteenth, up to Ersua and Enair and all the way hotwards into Okhar and Maasra. He'd rooted out hiding Brothers in Askhira and patrolled the streets of the harbour town enforcing the curfew. He'd sailed on a bireme on the Greenwater and peed in the gardens of Nemtun's palace in Geria.

For all that he had done, he had not yet seen a battle, not a proper one. He had talked to legionnaires from the Fifth after they met the Thirteenth duskwards of Narun and heard them talk about the blood and sweat, the fear of not knowing what was happening and the cold trickle of dread they had experienced when they realised they had lost the battle.

It had come as quite a shock to Gelthius. Never in his life had he heard of an Askhan legion defeated. He supposed that when legion fought legion, one of them would have to lose. It was all fine when they were cutting down the scattered warbands of the tribes, but when they matched against each other something had to give, and that something was their reputation for invincibility.

"Do you reckon we could beat another legion?" he asked, putting the question out to everyone on the tower roof.

"We're the Thirteenth," said Geddiban. "There's not another legion can match us. You're a lucky fella, Gelthius, to join us."

"Not even the First?" said Gelthius. "I hear they're pretty handy."

There were chuckles around him.

"What's so funny about that?" Gelthius looked at his companions, who regarded him with a mix of tolerant humour and patronising stares of pity. "Tell me!"

"Well, there's a couple of things to remember about the First," explained the watch captain, Huuril. "They're only led by the king himself, and since he's well into his seventies I can't see that happening. And they're all pure-born Askhans, which means they're all short-arses."

"I still don't understand," said Gelthius. "If Ullsaard wants to be king, that means we'll end up in Askh one way or

443

other. And if we're in Askh, the First ain't gonna sit around and just let us wander into the city. And what does it matter if the First are shorter? Their pikes are just as long."

"Maybe you're right on that first one, but size matters in a fight," said Huuril. "They've got spindly little arms and legs, no meat to them at all. One good shove will send them running."

"But the Askhans came up with the idea of the legions… That's what makes them better than everyone else."

"Maybe against your lot, whooping their heads off and running at a spearwall, but against another legion, those Askhans will be on the shitty end of the stick."

Removing his now warmed hands, Gelthius was about to continue his argument when he hesitated, his ears catching a change in the wind. The voices were still there, harsh and cold, but they had grown more strident.

"You must be able to hear that," he said. "That's not just a trick of the mind."

The others were looking around with concern and did not reply. The voices, though no louder, were speaking rapidly, the cadence of their words increasing in tempo. They throbbed in Gelthius's ears, growing in insistence, worming their way into his mind. His heart beat faster, keeping pace with the awful voices as the rhythm continued to speed up. Through the hissing he could hear disturbance in the camp below; shouts of alarm, the sound of running feet, the pause in the hammering at the armouries.

An eerie quiet settled, not a sound made by any of the thousands of men, only the wind and its disturbing voices could be heard within the camp walls.

"That's jus–" began Arsiil, but he choked. Dropping his spear and shield, he clutched his hands to his throat, eyes bulging.

The legionnaire fell to his knees with a crack, gasping. A trickle of blood ran from the corner of his lips, and he looked at his comrades in terror. Geddiban took a step towards him and suddenly fell, convulsing as he vomited blood across the planks of the tower.

"The spirits of plague!" hissed Gelthius, backing away from the afflicted men.

He saw more men falling along the walls and on other towers. He watched one legionnaire stagger backwards, arms flailing, until he toppled over the rampart into the stake-lined ditch outside. Looking down into the camp, Gelthius saw other casualties stumbling between the tents. Some blundered blindly into fires, hoarse screams coming from bloodstained lips. Many were on their hands and knees or crawling on their bellies, leaving crimson trails in the frost-rimed mud.

The voices stopped.

The wind continued to blow, but now screams and groans and agonised shouts were carried on the breeze. Gelthius heard officers bellowing orders, but did not understand the words. His ears still burned and his stomach was a knot of pain. He dabbed a finger to his lips, fearing to see blood, but there was none. Keeping his distance from the bodies of the men on the tower, he made his way to the ladder and hastily climbed down, only to find a contorted corpse at the bottom. Fingers spasmed into claws, legs and arms bent awkwardly, the dead legionnaire stared up at Gelthius with wide eyes, bubbles of red froth still bursting through his gritted teeth.

"You, get away from there!" a second captain called out. "If you're not ill, muster at your drill square."

Gelthius nodded dumbly and staggered through the camp, every turn revealing more dead and dying. He heard something scraping at the canvas inside a nearby tent and broke into a run, dashing for the safety of open ground.

II

"Seven hundred and thirty-eight dead," Anasind announced grimly. "Another seventy or so that won't survive

445

the night, and hundred and six more that will probably live but can barely breathe or walk."

Ullsaard took this news without comment. He rubbed his bristled chin and looked at his First Captain. The prevailing wisdom was illness, but Ullsaard was not so sure. It was not the number infected that shocked him, but the sudden speed of the affliction's onset. And though he had said nothing, like everyone else he had heard those sinister voices in the air. He had been feeding Blackfang and thought it was just the guards outside the corral tent whispering to each other. Then the panic had started.

"How many desertions?" he asked quietly.

"Not too bad," said Anasind. "At last muster, less than two hundred men accounted for, and half a dozen officers. It's not a rout."

"I think they've been poisoned," the general said.

"Poison? How?" replied Anasind. "It's affected men from companies across all three legions here. If it was the food, it wouldn't be so widespread."

"Something in the air, maybe," said Ullsaard. He shook his head angrily. "I don't know how, but it's an attack. Plague doesn't strike in winter. Check all of the food stores, and double the number of men accompanying the caravans. If you find anything suspicious, anything the slightest bit odd, burn it. We can't take any chances."

"Nobody has had access to the food except the men," said Anasind. "And no man in the camp would poison the supplies, because he'd be just as likely to die himself."

"What else would you have me do?" Ullsaard asked, slamming a hand on the arm of his campaign chair. "Stop the men from breathing? While you're at it, send patrols up the rivers, make sure the water isn't being tainted. And check the storage butts too. Something caused this, and we have to stop it happening again."

The gruesome episodes did not stop. Despite every precaution that Ullsaard and his officers could take, there were sporadic outbursts of death and disease. Sometimes the bloody vomiting returned; other times, men were struck blind and deaf, or their bones became brittle so that they snapped with the slightest pressure.

The winter closed in fiercely, colder than anything any man in the legions could remember, even the Enairians. Though the snow came thick and fast for days on end, Ullsaard began to welcome the blizzards; when the snow was thick, he could not hear the voices on the wind, there were no strange episodes and men were unwilling to risk their lives in the wilds by deserting.

The general began to have nightmares. Nothing distinct, nothing he could place when he woke, but every morning he would have a lingering feeling of dread and oppression. He could tell others were affected the same; a surly mood born of fatigue and worry enveloped the camp.

The snowstorm was almost permanent. It became a constant job for the legionnaires to shovel ice and snow into wagons and take it out of the camp. Tents were flattened and the walls needed continual repairs to guard against the weight of the cold deluge.

By Midwinter's day, as close as Ullsaard could reckon it, it had snowed for thirty-eight days without surcease. Sickness, death and desertion since the winter began had robbed him of more than two and a half thousand men. The bodies of a thousand had been buried in the forests a few miles from the camp: the army could not spare the wood to build pyres. Ullsaard had promised that proper ceremonies would be carried out in the spring, but he could feel the will of his legions being sapped day by day.

There was no open rebellion, but the grind of daily life that had once been the machinery of discipline had become a soul-breaking series of never-ending chores without end in sight. Not even in the blasting heat of Mekha had he known the morale of his soldiers to fall so low. There was no enemy to fight, no foe to blame for the misery they endured, and so the grumbling turned against the officers and, with an inevitability Ullsaard had feared, the camp talk began to whisper questions about Ullsaard's endeavour and the wisdom of his bid for the throne.

He discussed the matter with Anasind and the other First Captains, but there was not a lot they could do. Rumour and gossip was part of legion life and couldn't be stopped. The weather was beyond their control. All that could be done to keep the men warm and fed was being done. Ullsaard all but emptied the coin store giving the men advance pay, but it was nothing more than a gesture for there was nothing to spend it on. Parmia was only ten miles away, but in the blizzards it was a journey of several days and no man had neither the time nor the will for such an expedition just to drink wine, eat a fine meal or have sex with a prostitute.

Midwinter's night found Ullsaard walking the ramparts, trying to cheer up his men whilst showing them that he shared their predicament. They were respectful but quiet. He had always enjoyed a good relationship with the common soldiers, having been a legionnaire himself before ascending the ranks, but he sensed a divide. It didn't matter that he could have quit the camp and lived in Parmia in more comfort, but chose not to; it was no argument that he shovelled as much snow as the next man. Deep down, every soldier knew that they were here because of their general, and the old questions came to the fore: what were they getting out of it? Who were they fighting? What were they fighting for?

The questions were unasked; it was legion tradition not to openly defy superiors even in dire circumstances. That made it all the harder for Ullsaard to confront. He asked the men what was on their minds and got the same replies: the cold; the thin stew for dinner; the loss of a friend or officer. Nobody was saying what they were thinking.

Ullsaard returned to his tent feeling exhausted, knowing he had accomplished little if anything on his tour. He dismissed the servants after they had brought hot wine and sat in his campaign chair with both cloak and thick blanket wrapped around him. There he brooded until the early hours of the morning.

IV

Third captain Huuril woke up from a dream of spiralling shadows and golden eyes. Blinking in the darkness of the tent, he stared up, the whispers of the dream lingering in his mind. As he listened to the half-heard voices, the golden eyes came back to him, surrounded by a swirl of dark smoke writhing in strange patterns. The golden eyes hovered in the gloom just in front of him, staring unblinking into his soul.

He could not break his gaze as the eyes came closer, burning into him. He felt them upon his own eyeballs while the twisting black smoke writhed into his ears and nose and mouth. He closed his eyes and the golden orbs were there, inside his eyelids, burrowing into his brain. He could hear nothing except that rapid whispering, a litany of meaningless syllables pouring into his thoughts.

Huuril's eyes snapped open, flecks of gold in their veins. He looked to his right to see the others in the tent rising from their beds. He felt the urge that propelled them and stood. Together they put on their gear and took their weapons from the rack along the side of the tent. They mustered in a line outside, staring numbly ahead.

The meaningless whisper returned and the twenty men stepped together, turning towards the centre of the camp.

V

Noran was instantly awake. It took him a moment to work out what had disturbed him: the quiet tread of feet and jangle of armour. It was out of place, a break in the routine he had become accustomed to in the camp. Quickly slipping on his clothes, skin prickling in the cold, he padded to the door of his tent.

Behind him a servant, woken by his master's movements, asked if he could help. Noran shushed him into silence and peered through the tent flap.

The snow had stopped, but there was an icy tinge to the air, like a frozen mist. There was not a breath of wind, no singing across the ropes, no flap of canvas. Above, there was not a cloud in the sky, and no moon, but starlight shimmered through the strange fog. The stillness was unnerving and Noran instinctively grabbed his sword belt from the table close at hand. Strapping it on, he stepped outside.

A glance to his right showed the two sentries standing in front of Ullsaard's red pavilion. Further along the row of tents, he could see more legionnaires standing guard at the end of the street of wooden planks.

To the left, he saw a group of men approaching through the sparkling light; it was their noise he had heard. Noran shrank back beside his tent as he saw twenty legionnaires marching in step, heading directly towards him, shields and spears at the ready. He could hear nothing else across the camp save for the distant, muffled calls of men on the walls confirming the hour of the watch.

The approaching legionnaires were barely a dozen paces away. Noran looked at their faces and saw slack expressions, like men sleeping. Their eyes were open and by the light of the stars Noran thought he saw a strange glitter to them, with a hint of gold. He stayed immobile as the soldiers marched closer, armour jingling, feet tramping in time. They seemed intent on Ullsaard's pavilion.

Noran was going to shout a warning or a challenge, but stopped.

He was sure that they meant to slay Ullsaard, and he hesitated. Ullsaard's death would solve so many problems. This whole misadventure had been his doing, and with one spear thrust it could be ended. Noran could return to a semblance of normality. He would no longer have to worry about his indiscretion with Meliu.

Ullsaard's death would make life far simpler for Noran.

Crouched in the shadow of his tent, he watched the legionnaires pass, disturbed by their shining eyes. As they came level with him, he heard a faint whispering floating on the edge of hearing. It was not the soldiers, their lips were unmoving.

Guilt at his inactivity gripped Noran, but there was nothing he could do. Twenty men would cut him down in an instant and Ullsaard would still die. He clenched his fists and bit his lip as the men continued past, no more than twenty paces from the door to the general's pavilion. The sentries outside looked curiously at their fellow legionnaires, but they had no more chance of stopping them than Noran.

But the guilt was too much. Noran had betrayed Ullsaard badly enough, he could not salve his conscience with more treachery.

"Hey!" he shouted, stepping out from the shadow with his now-drawn sword in hand. "Stop there!"

The twenty legionnaires halted and turned on the spot to face him, moving in time with each other. Terror gripped Noran as flickering eyes stared at him and twenty spearpoints lowered in his direction. The mesmerised soldiers regarded him for a moment and turned away to continue towards the general's pavilion.

"Ullsaard!" Noran bellowed, running towards the closest legionnaire.

He swung his sword at the man's undefended back,

smashing it against the scale armour, bronze slicing bronze. The legionnaire fell wordlessly, collapsing on his face. The others rounded on Noran in an instant.

"Alarm!" Noran's voice broke into a wordless shriek as a spearpoint caught him in the shoulder.

He batted away another thrust, stumbling backwards. A third spear caught him in the thigh, ripping through the flesh. Noran fell with a cry of pain as the spear was pulled from the wound. He swung his sword blindly, slashing across the legs of the man that had attacked him. The legionnaire toppled to one side without even a grunt, his golden eyes staring at Noran past the bleeding stump of his leg.

More spears closed in on Noran as he shouted again.

VI

Hearing his name being called, Ullsaard snapped out of his fugue. He recognised Noran's voice just outside the pavilion, and heard the familiar sound of a sword blow. The general was on his feet in a heartbeat, throwing off the blanket. Unsheathing his sword, he dashed through the pavilion to the door, where he found his two sentries fighting against other soldiers.

Past the melee, Ullsaard could see Noran lying on the ground, blood bubbling from several wounds. He had no time to spare a further thought for his friend as a legionnaire lunged towards him with a spear.

Ullsaard used the flat of his blade to slap aside the attack and jumped into his attackers, slashing his sword backhanded into a man's face, cutting through nose and cheek. The legionnaire staggered back as blood spilled from the wound, but Ullsaard noticed a blank look in his gold-tinted eyes.

More soldiers had been roused by Noran's cry and they came running along the street with their weapons ready. Ullsaard kicked the feet from under another attacker and brought his knee up into the other's face as he fell, breaking his jaw. The man surged to his feet, spearpoint aimed at Ullsaard's chest. The general stumbled to his right to avoid the thrust and righted himself in time to duck beneath another swinging spear tip. He caught the shaft of the weapon in his free hand and wrenched it from the legionnaire's grasp. Without hesitation, the soldier came on again, swinging his shield against Ullsaard's shoulder.

Rolling with the blow, Ullsaard came to his feet and spun the spear in his left hand so that he was holding it overhand. He jabbed the point into the throat of the next man to come at him, the spear cutting through the side of the legionnaire's neck in a gush of arterial blood. The general waded into his assassins, using his sword to parry thrusting spears, his own finding limbs and guts and faces with each lunging blow.

Even wounded, the traitors tried to fight on, impervious to grievous injuries that would kill a normal man. One by one, they were slain by Ullsaard and those who came to his rescue; one by one, that golden light in their eyes dimmed and disappeared.

When the last of them was dead, Ullsaard tossed aside his spear and ran to Noran's side. Crouching down, he saw his friend's tunic soaked with blood from neck to knee and the ground was red beneath him.

"I'm sorry," Noran said weakly, flapping at Ullsaard with a blood-slicked hand.

"No apologies," growled Ullsaard. "Save your strength."

Ullsaard's eyes quickly took in the injuries: a wound in the leg, three in the gut, one in the chest and two in Noran's left shoulder. It was a marvel that Noran was still conscious. Ullsaard gripped his friend's hand tightly, feeling the blood oozing between his fingers. Noran's eyelids were drooping and his breath hissed through his teeth in shallow gasps.

"Stay with me," said Ullsaard, putting a hand behind Noran's head and lifting him up. "Who else is going to keep Meliu happy while I'm away?"

Noran's eyes flickered wide. His words came in halting gasps.

"You know about that?"

Ullsaard grinned.

"Luia had you stitched up like a legionnaire's sack, but I wouldn't have any of it."

"I... I didn't..."

"Yes, you did, but I forgive you." Ullsaard looked over his shoulder at the legionnaires gathering around. "Fuck off, the lot of you. And fetch the surgeons."

With a grunt, Ullsaard hefted Noran into his arms and straightened.

"Never thought such a streak of piss could weigh so much," he said. Noran hung an arm limply over the general's shoulder.

Ullsaard felt blood trickling down his back. He bowed his head to speak softly into his friend's ear. "I didn't mean to take your wife either, but I did. If you want her, Meliu is yours."

He got no reply as he carried Noran into the pavilion.

VII

Ullsaard looked at the blanket-swathed body of his friend. His skin was drawn and waxy, his eyes closed, his hair matted. His pale flesh had a yellowish pallor and there was no movement at all.

"Will he live?" the general asked.

The man with drooping moustaches, sitting beside Noran, pursed his lips in a way that Ullsaard knew was the surgeon's equivalent of a shrug.

"Injuries like that, it might be better if he doesn't," said the surgeon, Luuarit. "He has lost a lot of blood and there's going to be damage to his organs."

"If he was a legionnaire, we'd have slit his throat already, put him out of his misery," added Anasind from behind the general. Ullsaard rounded on the First Captain, fists balled. "I meant no disrespect!"

"He isn't a legionnaire," Ullsaard growled. He turned his glare onto Luuarit. "You will keep him alive, whatever you have to do."

The surgeon nodded thoughtfully, but there was doubt in his eyes.

"You have a larger problem to worry about, General," said Anasind. "The army is on the verge of collapse. I have them assembled outside the camp waiting for your address. Whatever you say to them, it'd better be good. We've had three hundred desertions since the episode of last night, from companies not returning after forage duty."

Ullsaard stalked out of the pavilion to where a legionnaire was waiting with Blackfang. The ailur seemed as surly as her master, tossing her head in irritation as Ullsaard mounted and rode slowly towards the gate camps.

Outside, the three legions were drawn up in their companies, eyes expectantly following their general as he rode to a spot on a slight rise so all could see him. More than fifteen thousand pairs of eyes looked at Ullsaard, a mixture of hope and desperation, ambivalence and accusation.

The general cleared his throat and cast his gaze across rows upon rows of soldiers.

"You have given me more than I would ever have asked for," he said, pitching his voice to the farthest ranks. "From the sands of Mekha to this treacherous snow, you have followed me; out of respect for my rank; out of loyalty to me; some of you even think my claim is right."

There were scattered chuckles to this poor joke, mainly from the Thirteenth.

"You have done more than I have ever asked for and so I cannot ask for more than you have already given. It is my turn to give. You are my legions, and each of you receives his pay and has his pension, as you have earned. That is not enough reward for such fighting men. You have stayed with me against the wishes of your king. I have lost comrades I loved dearly and so have you. What price could be put on such lives? What reward is worthy of such sacrifice?"

Ullsaard allowed his words to sink in as he considered what he was about to say. In the last year he had thought he had crossed every line he could cross, bartered away every principle he believed in for the greater goal he sought.

He had been wrong.

He had betrayed and killed those he had called allies, even friends. He had bargained away a whole city to Anglhan in return for the support he needed. He had turned on his king, a man he now knew to be his father, and pretty much ordered his half-brother killed. He had raised his spear against his fellow legions and he had spilt the blood of Askhans. All of that he could stomach because they were necessary for the wider endeavour; sacrifices on the road to a greater empire and a stronger Askhor.

None of it counted for anything if he was to fail now; his claim for the Crown would be nothing but a vain venture, an exercise in pride, if he was to falter in his dedication. He had one hand on the Crown; he could feel it in his bones. All he had to do was pry the aging fingertips of his father from it and Ullsaard would be proven right. As king, he would make the dream of Askhos a reality.

He remembered a stone, somewhere in hotwards Nalanor, inscribed with the rune of the Crown. He had made a vow that Greater Askhor would spread from sea to sea, as Askhos had promised. The empire was larger than any man; or any city. For generations Askh had been the empire and the empire had been Askh. Ullsaard saw now that his allegiance to the city and the king that ruled from there had been blind obedience. He had believed in the myths: Askh was the start and end of the empire. No more.

"In the spring we will march on the city of the king," Ullsaard announced. "I want you to march with me. We are all citizens of the empire, and in forging a new empire it is only right that you take your dues. When the city falls to us, we will be the masters of Greater Askhor. To us will come the responsibilities, but also the rewards.

"I have the right to grant my legions the privilege of sacking conquered territories. For years I have been forced to throw you the scraps left behind by others, filling your purses with the dust and sand of Mekha. I offer you something no other man can. In the spring, I shall become king; my legions will get the riches of the capital. The city will be yours, by right of conquest, to take what you have earned through sweat and blood.

"You, the legions of Ullsaard, have my permission to sack Askh."

The reaction was muted at first, the army unable to comprehend what they were being offered. Wiser soldiers made the point clearer: the legions would be allowed to plunder and rape their way through the richest city in the world. Even split amongst the many thousands in the legions, such a prize would make them wealthy beyond anything they could imagine.

As realisation spread, the cheers began. Legion mottos were shouted into the air, but soon all voices turned to chanting Ullsaard's name, over and over, the air split by the thunderous cries. Ullsaard took the ovation impassively. His name ringing in his ears, he turned Blackfang around and rode away from his army.

Ullsaard would have the Crown. The disgust churning his stomach was just another part of the price to pay.

NALANOR
Spring, 210th Year of Askh

I

"I'm surprised such a fat man can run so fast," laughed Anasind.

All that could be seen of Nemtun's army was a cloud of dust spreading towards the distant shadow of the Wall. A few ships and boats burned along the quays of Narun, and there were signs that the retreating prince had attempted to torch the city, but with little success. A smouldering warehouse here and there was testament to the hasty, clumsy arson.

"I didn't expect him to fight," said Ullsaard, standing with Anasind and his other First Captains on the roof terrace of a merchant's house overlooking the docks. He looked at Donar. "He isn't stupid. He has the Wall to hide behind."

The First Captain of the Fifth looked shamefacedly at his feet, feeling the dig at his pride for his unsuccessful attack on Nemtun's army at the start of the year. Ullsaard allowed Donar to stew in his embarrassment for a little while, before clapping him on the shoulder with a smile.

"You'll be able to get even soon enough," said the general. "Nemtun's trapped in Askhor now, he won't be able to run anymore."

"So when do we go for the Wall?" asked Luamid. "I can't see much point in waiting."

"We don't," replied Ullsaard. The half-circle of commanders around the general exchanged confused looks. "I didn't spend a fortune building a fleet in Maasra to needlessly throw my legions at the Wall."

"So we'll be marching to Askhira?" asked Jutiil. "That's a trek and a half."

Ullsaard smiled slyly.

"You have a plan, don't you?" said Anasind.

"Let's go downstairs to discuss it," Ullsaard told them. "I think it's one of my best."

II

Eleven legions on the march, the largest army Jutaar had ever seen: the Thirteenth, the general's own men; the Fifth, Tenth, Twelfth and Sixteenth from the campaigns in Mekha; the First and Second Magilnadan – Ullsaard had been incensed by Anglhan naming his legions after the city where they were raised; the Ninth, Fourteenth, Seventeenth and Eighteenth from across Greater Askhor, taken from the governors under Ullsaard's heel.

In all, nearly seventy thousand men marched from Narun and the people of the city came out to wave them off. They had not enjoyed their brief rulership by Nemtun over the winter and were glad to see Ullsaard back in charge. Another legion, the newly raised Twenty-third, had been left as garrison in the city.

Jutaar had wondered at this. Nemtun had already proven he was capable of sallying forth from the Wall to take Narun, and the fifty-day march to Askhira would give him plenty of time to do so. Ullsaard had emptied the provinces of all but the most skeleton force and if Nemtun realised this, he would be able to run free. Without Ullsaard around to protect them, the governors would quickly flip sides back to the king if Nemtun arrived at

their capitals with his five legions. Once the first one toppled, the rest would follow, just as they had when
confronted by Ullsaard's army.

"Don't worry about it," Jutaar's father had told him.
"Leave the strategy to me."

Jutaar did worry about it, but his concerns were tem-
pered by the trust he had in his father's judgement. It was
that judgement that had placed Jutaar in charge of the
massive supply caravan and tens of thousands of camp followers. Jutaar had thought his experience building the
fleet in Askhira had been daunting, but it had become little
more than practise for the monumental task of keeping
forty thousand civilians in line.

He'd been given half the companies from the Sixteenth
to help chaperone a column that stretched for five miles,
following behind the army. The people were everything
the legions were not: slovenly, intractable, selfish, disorganised and petty. Not a day went by that did not see
Jutaar cajoling a powerful merchant into line; or prevent-
ing families following different legions all but declaring
war on each other over camp space; or settling a dispute
over whose turn it was to travel at the front, closest to the
legions.

"Another forty days of this will drive me mad," Jutaar
confessed to his father on the fifth evening since they had
left Narun.

"I'm sorry, son," said Ullsaard.

It was just the two of them in the main room of Ullsaard's pavilion. The general's servants had brought in a
table and low chairs and the two shared a simple meal together, the first in a long time.

"It's going to get worse for you," said Ullsaard.

"I'll get the hang of it, I'm starting to work out who the
troublemakers are and who I can trust," said Jutaar. He
popped a grape in his mouth and chewed laboriously.
"They'll get into the routine of it too."

"You don't understand," said Ullsaard. "From tomorrow, you'll be on your own."

Jutaar stopped, another grape halfway to his mouth.

"You're right, I don't understand."

Ullsaard looked apologetic as he pushed aside his plate and laid his hands on the table.

"This march is a ruse," said the general. "So is the fleet in Askhira. I've got no intention of trying to land an army on the Askhan coast. There's no more than ten places where I could offload so many soldiers, and you can be sure our enemies have them closely watched. If we failed to get a landing, we'd be driven back into the sea."

"It's not… I don't…" muttered Jutaar.

"It's bait for a trap," Ullsaard continued with a self-satisfied smile. "Of course Narun looks weak, I want it to. Donar may have bollocksed up his attack on Nemtun, but he had the right idea. This time when he comes looking for an easy win, I'll fall on him with ten legions! We'll see how the fat cunt likes that!"

"So who will I be taking to Askhira?"

"The First Magilnadan and the whole of the caravan. You're to make as much noise and mess as possible marching to Maasra; make it look like fifty thousand men came through. I want the king looking towards the sea for as long as possible. When Nemtun comes snuffling out from behind the Wall, we'll smash his army and be into Askhor before anyone realises what's happening. It'll be too late for the legions guarding the coast to come back duskwards and Askh will be ours."

"You're sending me on a diversion?" said Jutaar. "I want to be there when we win. Why can't Urikh do this?"

Ullsaard stood up and gripped his son's arm.

"I'm sorry, but I don't trust anyone else to do this for me. It has to be utterly convincing, and Urikh isn't a legion man. You are. You have the most important job of anyone."

Jutaar understood the truth of his father's words, but it made him no happier.

"I want to fight, Father," he said. "I want to be there when you lead your army. I want to be the first through the Wall with you, and the first into Askh. You're trying to get me out of the way, keep me out of trouble. I don't want to be the prince that led the wives' army!"

"Stand up," said Ullsaard. Jutaar did so. "You will be leading an army, and not just of merchants and children. I'll be making you First Captain. The man Anglhan has in charge of the First Magilnadan is an idiot, some hairy-arsed son of a chieftain Anglhan wanted to keep happy. I'm replacing him with you and giving you some quality officers to help out. You'll be Prince Jutaar, First Captain of the legions."

"First Captain?" Jutaar never thought he would hear those words. He imagined his pavilion at the heart of the camp, every second and third captain doing his bidding. No more tiresome watch rotations. No more drills in the snow and rain. He would be the man in charge.

"Aye, First Captain Jutaar," Ullsaard said, shaking his son's hand. "Congratulations."

MAGILNADA
Spring, 210th Year of Askh

I

It was a solemn crowd that gathered around Noran's bed in the house of Ullsaard's wives. Meliu sat with Noran's limp, clammy hand in her tight grip. Allenya was there too, in a chair by the window, her thoughts and expression distant. Anglhan had come to pay his respects to the friend of his ally, and to perform another duty which he was in two minds about.

"Look who is here," Meliu said in overly sweet tones. "Governor Anglhan."

Anglhan looked at the dull features of Noran. His chest barely moved, his hair lank on the pillow, a thin trace of spit drooling from the corner of white lips, flesh a nauseating yellow. His eyes were closed, for which Anglhan was thankful. The last thing he wanted to look at was a pair of near-dead eyes staring blankly back.

Looking around the room, the governor of Magilnada saw that the comatose man was being given every comfort. Noran lay beneath thick blankets, on embroidered pillows, spring flowers arranged in vases around the room. There was even a blue songbird in a silver cage hanging in the corner, though it was quiet for the moment.

"He seems to be well looked after," said Anglhan.

Meliu smiled up at the governor.

"The physicians see him daily. Ullsaard sent more money to ensure we could afford it. I think the spring air will do him the world of good."

Allenya sighed and moved listlessly.

"And how are you?" asked Anglhan, turning his attention to Ullsaard's oldest wife. "I know it must be a heartache for you to be here, but your husband left you in my protection and if there's anything I can do, let me know."

"Can you spirit Ullsaard here?" she said. Anglhan shook his head sadly. "Not that he would want that. I have never worried so much. He has always been away for long times, on campaigns, fighting battles. I always believed he would come back to me."

"I am sure he will be back," said Meliu, reaching out a hand to her sister. "He always is."

"I am not so sure, not this time," said Allenya. "He sent me a letter with the men that brought Noran. It reads like the words of a man not sure if he will write any more."

"This is his first, last and best chance for victory," said Anglhan. "If he fails, the legions and the governors – the other governors – will lose confidence in him. I've not known Ullsaard long, and know him far less than you, but he doesn't strike me as the gambling sort. If he's ready to go, you can be sure it's because the time is right. The next letter you receive from him will be signed King Ullsaard, you'll see."

Allenya looked unconvinced and she returned to gazing out of the window, fingers picking at a loose thread on her skirt.

Anglhan took a deep breath, wondering if the moment was right for the announcement he had to make. He looked at Allenya and Meliu, both distracted.

"Where's Luia?" he asked. "I have something to say that she should hear as well."

"Making trouble somewhere, probably," said Meliu. "She's being more of bitch than normal, ever since Ullsaard shipped Urikh off to Maasra. I know how she is feeling; it has been so long since I have seen Ullnaar. I know he is safe, but he is growing into a young man and I have not been there to help him."

"It'll be finished soon enough, and your family can be together again," said Anglhan.

His hands fiddled with the letter from Ullsaard, which he had brought as proof of Ullsaard's wishes. With all this talk of families, it didn't seem right to reveal the letter's content. It was something Ullsaard could better deal with in person.

"What is that you have?" asked Meliu. "Is it something to do with what you want to talk to us about?"

Anglhan crumpled the letter into his jerkin pocket.

"It doesn't matter, it'll wait," he said.

He stood there feeling uncomfortable for a short while, but it was too much to bear.

"Thank you for your time, ladies, I hope to see you all at the lord's hall soon," he said, edging towards the door. "With any luck, Noran will be able to come as well."

"That would be nice," said Meliu, standing up. Allenya glanced in Anglhan's direction and nothing more.

"Right, I'll be off."

Anglhan hurried out of the house, feeling like a coward, though he tried to assure himself he was simply being sensitive to circumstance. Ullsaard's letter had included a request that as governor Anglhan legally annul the general's marriage to Meliu, and that of Noran and Anriit. Though it was obvious that Meliu felt something for Noran, Anglhan was not convinced she would be happy to learn that the man about to become king wanted to divorce her.

No, thought Anglhan, I'm not getting involved in that one. He can settle it himself.

II

Furlthia was waiting outside the house. Anglhan's body-guard of legionnaires closed in on the former landship mate as he crossed the street, but Anglhan called them off.

"Sorry about that," Anglhan said as Furlthia fell into step beside him, pitching his voice so that the soldiers could hear him. "Put a uniform on them and they turn into idiots."

"You're the one that gave them uniforms," Furlthia reminded him quietly.

Anglhan replied with a non-committal grunt.

"Anyway, I've got some news for you," Furlthia continued.

"Am I going to like it?" asked Anglhan, heaving himself up the step of a carriage.

Furlthia walked around the other side and pulled himself through the curtains.

"No," he said. "Aegenuis is calling a council of chieftains. He wants the tribes to unite and take back Magilnada."

Anglhan slouched back into the thick cushions and shrugged.

"What he wants and what he gets are different things. Aegenuis could probably count on the tribes that were moved out of the Free Country, they'd want to get their lands back. What does anyone else care?"

"He knows what's going on in Askhor, and the turmoil your friend Ullsaard is causing. He's going to tell the tribes that after Magilnada they're going to move into Anrair."

"That's war with Askh," laughed Anglhan. "Nobody's that stupid, not even the chieftains."

"You haven't been duskwards for years, you haven't got any idea what it's like out there," said Furlthia, leaning towards Anglhan in agitation. "It's getting crowded and all the best timber, ore and grain is coming this way because the Askhans can pay more for it. People are starving, Anglhan, even with plentiful harvests! You don't understand how much hatred there is for the Askhans. Aegenuis has been frightened of poking the beast that's left him alone so far. By taking Magilnada, your general has shown Aegenuis that he can't expect the peace to last much longer. Either the tribes attack now, or suffer later."

Furlthia had been right; Anglhan did not like the sound of this. Not one bit.

"How long?" Anglhan asked, dreading the answer.

Now it was Furlthia's turn to shrug.

"By the end of the summer, surely," he said.

"Ullsaard will be king by the time spring is over," said Anglhan, speaking with confidence, though he was far from certain. "He'll not let Magilnada fall."

"And if Ullsaard fails? What happens then?"

Anglhan didn't answer. I'll be stuck between Lutaar and Aegenuis, he thought. Neither of them wants me here. He put on a brave smile and looked at Furlthia.

"Ullsaard won't fail."

NALANOR
Spring, 210th Year of Askh

I

There was so much shouting; the bellows of the officers, the cries of the men around him, the roars of the enemy. Gelthius never realised battle would be this noisy. He winced as his company crashed into one of Nemtun's phalanxes. As a new hand, he was in the back ranks. All he had to do was shove the man in front and keep his spear from hitting any of his own men. The veterans at the front and along the right side of the phalanx would be doing all the hard work.

It was a far cry from the fights he had been in, stealing cattle from the neighbouring tribes in Salphoria. In those scraps it was every man for himself, and Gelthius fancied himself as quite a handy swordsman in his prime. Age might have slowed him a bit, but on the first charge he had realised why they had spent so many miserable days marching back and forth across the drill squares, raising and lowering their arms, setting their shields and walking in step shoulder to shoulder.

Askhan fighting wasn't about skill, not for the greater part. It was about strength and stamina; grinding down the opposition until they could fight no more. This was the fourth melee he'd been involved in since the battle had begun a little before noon. Sweat soaked his tunic and his kilt chafed against his thighs. Fortunately his hands had been worn hard over years at the cranks, but some of the others around him had wrapped linen bandages around their palms because of tears and blisters. Similarly his back was strong, but his legs ached, despite the lean muscle brought on by miles of marching.

In front of him, Gebriun pulled up suddenly, dropping his spear to clutch at his calf.

"Fucking cramp!" the legionnaire snarled.

"Step up!" bellowed the rank sergeant, Muuril.

Gelthius pushed into Gebriun's place as the legionnaire hobbled towards the back of the phalanx. Passing his spear into his shield hand, he grabbed Gebriun's fallen weapon and passed it back after the retreating legionnaire.

"Lock!"

The order came from the front, probably third captain Lonnir. Gelthius slid his shield across that of the man to his left, while the man to his right did the same to Gelthius. Putting his left foot forward, Gelthius braced himself against the legionnaire in front and felt the pressure of the shield from the man behind along his back. Glancing up from under the brow of his helmet, Gelthius could see enemy pike heads swaying against the cloudy sky.

"Step!"

Gelthius gave a shout and pushed, bringing his right foot up to his left and forcing his left foot another pace. As one, the phalanx heaved the enemy backwards.

"Step!"

Again Gelthius urged himself on, feeling the weight of the rank behind on his shoulders, his right arm tiring from holding his spear above the heads of those in front.

"Step!"

"I'll fuckin' step on 'im when we're back in camp," muttered the man in front.

"Brace to the right!"

And so it carried on, a blur of shouts and aches and surging bodies. Gelthius felt a tap on his right shoulder and he turned to see Loordin, one of the ten-year veterans, who had taught Gelthius how to maintain his kit and stand sentry. His face was covered in blood from a gash just below the rim of his helmet. The legionnaire winked through the crimson mask.

"Welcome to the legions!" the man laughed.

"What's happening?" Gelthius said.

"We're winning," Loordin said with a grin.

"How can you tell?" Gelthius could see nothing of the rest of the battle, engulfed by the press of bodies around him.

"You're still alive, aren't you?" came the reply.

II

From a bluff overlooking the battle, Ullsaard was pleased with what he saw. I'll teach you to patronise me, you old fart, he thought. Nemtun had come running for Narun like a child chasing a ball; straight into Ullsaard's army waiting for him a day's march from the city. Donar and the Fifth had been given a chance to redeem themselves, making a forced march to coldwards before swinging in between Nemtun's army and the Wall, cutting off their retreat. Giving Nemtun no time to turn his legions against Donar, Ullsaard had ordered eight of his remaining legions on a full attack, keeping only one back in case of some disastrous turn of events. The kolubrid riders had pinned the enemy in place with their bellows-bows, their heavy arrows forcing the opposing companies to form into defensive circles, shields raised against the attack while the infantry closed for the kill.

There had been a couple of dubious moments. Nemtun's lava-thowers and spear thowers had been gathered in one place for the march and once set up they had reaped a bloody and burning toll of the Twelfth on the right flank.

Jutiil had pushed his men on into the storm of the war machine fire taking heavy casualties, but had eventually overrun the enemy position.

Nemtun had also feigned a retreat on his right, dragging the Thirteenth and Second Magilnadan ahead of the rest of the army, which allowed Nemtun to turn his centre to attack them. This exposed the legions in the centre of the enemy line, but if Nemtun had broken through he would have turned the whole flank. The Thirteenth had done Ullsaard proud, holding even after the raw men from Magilnada had started to fall back, giving Ullsaard time to move his own central phalanxes to relieve the pressure.

When this gambit had failed, Nemtun had pulled back his attacking regiments and was now resetting his line on a ridge to coldwards. One legion had been left a quarter of a mile ahead of the main army; Ullsaard felt sorry for the poor soldiers in that vanguard, sacrificed to buy time for the other legions to withdraw towards the Wall.

Nemtun's army started to turn away, heading dawnwards away from the battle. Ullsaard could see the covered wagons and ailur-riding officers of Nemtun's staff at the head of the retreating column. The king's brother would be on one of the carts, no doubt shouting at the drivers to whip the abada as fast as they could.

"Fuck that," said Ullsaard, turning to his messengers. "I'm not letting him get away. Send word to Jutiil. Full march to engage the enemy before they reach the road. Tell him to keep Nemtun busy until the rest of us catch up. Everyone else is to concentrate on the rearguard. I want them dead in half an hour. Remind my captains that every man that escapes will be fighting them again at the Wall. That should hurry them up."

As the messengers rode away, Ullsaard swung himself up into Blackfang's saddle. It was time to hammer home the advantage.

Nemtun's army had been broken and scattered. All but the Thirteenth had been let loose on general pursuit, and would chase after their fleeing foes until nightfall. Ullsaard had kept his legion with him, though Anasind had grumbled that the men wouldn't like being denied the spoils of victory.

"Don't worry, I'll give them some extra money," Ullsaard said as he marched the Thirteenth along the road towards the Wall. "And they'll get to see something they'll enjoy."

A quarter of a mile ahead a few hundred legionnaires escorted Nemtun's caravan. It was almost comical; abada plodding along the road, the legionnaires arranged to either side looking over their shoulders at the legion closing on them at a quick march.

The escort finally lost their nerve and bolted for the hills when Ullsaard was two hundred paces behind them. The wagons continued to rumble along the road even as drivers leapt from the boards and followed the legionnaires. Ullsaard urged Blackfang into a loping run and the companies of Thirteenth followed, charging along the road to catch the carts.

This is too easy, thought Ullsaard. He expected to find that Nemtun had sent the wagons away as a lure and was waddling to safety across the hills somewhere.

Catching up with the carts, the legionnaires leapt up onto them and pulled the abada to a stop. Ullsaard rode along the line of wagons and saw a legionnaire leaping down to the road a little way ahead, holding his hand to his side. Blood poured from a cut, no doubt inflicted by Nemtun. Ullsaard felt a moment of happiness he had not experienced except in Allenya's company. The Crown was the grand prize, but repaying the insult Nemtun had heaped upon Ullsaard was a worthy second place.

The general pulled his spear from behind his saddle and dismounted, leading his ailur by the reins until he came level with Nemtun's carriage. He tied Blackfang to the back of the cart and walked to the front, spear over his shoulder. There was nobody to be seen, the curtains at the front of the compartment closed.

"Don't make me poke you until you come out," Ullsaard called.

He waited as the carriage rocked from side to side on its axles. Nemtun appeared through the curtains, a bloodied sword in one hand. The former governor looked at the lines of legionnaires gathering around him and tossed down the weapon.

"Are you surrendering?" Ullsaard asked.

Nemtun nodded with a scowl.

"Even an Enairian cock-eater can win when he's got more men," he snarled.

Nemtun lowered himself to his knees and shuffled to the side of the driving board before swinging his fat legs over the edge and dropping awkwardly to the road. There was no hint of dejection in him as he walked up to Ullsaard, thumbs tucked into his belt.

"You still haven't won, you know?" Nemtun said. "You think my brother will barter for me? He doesn't give two shits for me, and even less for you. Don't fool yourself. You've got this far, but you won't get any farther. Ten legions hold the Wall against you."

"No, they don't," Ullsaard replied. "You're full of shit."

Nemtun met Ullsaard's stare.

"If you do beat my brother, I'll govern Okhar for you."

"No, you won't," Ullsaard said quietly. "I've promised Okhar to my eldest son."

Incomprehension clouded Nemtun's features.

"So what are you going to do with m–"

Ullsaard's spear plunged through Nemtun's white shirt, catching him just below the right side of the ribcage. Red seeped through the cloth as the former governor, a Prince of the Blood, fell to his knees, cheek and chins wobbling.

Ullsaard clubbed him across the face with the butt of his spear, breaking his nose and sending him sprawling to his back. Tossing the weapon aside, he grabbed the dazed man's wrist in both hands and heaved, dragging him a few steps along the side of the wagon.

"You're a fucking disgrace," said Ullsaard, rolling his shoulder as if he had strained something.

Recovering his senses a little, Nemtun flapped a hand at his stomach, blood seeping through his pudgy fingers and dripping onto his bare legs.

"That's it?" Nemtun snapped. "Fuck you, Ullsaard! It'll take more than that to kill me."

Ullsaard said nothing. Nemtun's eyes widened with terror as he heard a growl from just behind him. Blackfang took a step towards the prince, sniffing the air, tongue licking out. Nemtun tried to edge away, sliding himself along the road, but the noise attracted the ailur's attention and her blinded face snapped in his direction.

She pounced, slashing and biting wildly in her blinkered state. Ullsaard watched silently while the legionnaires hooted and cheered the grisly display, laughter greeting Nemtun's girlish screams until he fell silent, flesh shredded to the bone, throat ripped open.

Blackfang settled down to feed, licking at the streams of blood pouring across the stone slabs of the road.

Ullsaard looked away from the ailur's feasting. He gazed down the road towards the grey smudge that was the Wall. He didn't see the miles of stone. He looked upon the city beyond; the towers and walls and streets of Askh; and at their heart, the palaces of the king. His mind's eye arrowed to the heart of the palace, to the audience hall, where an old, bitter man sat with the golden Crown upon his wrinkled head.

"You're next, Lutaar," he growled quietly. "Just a few more days of being king. I hope you're ready."

ASKHOR
Spring, 210th Year of Askh

I

It rained. As if all the clouds above the mountains had come together in one last act to defy Ullsaard, the skies poured down in a torrent that lasted three days. Much to the amazement and amusement of his men, on the evening of the third day of the storm Ullsaard strode out into the central drilling square of the camp, naked save for his spear, helmet and shield. He stood with arms raised aloft, water streaming from his body, dripping from his beard.

"Is that it?" he shouted with glee. "Is that all you have left? Ice and blood and the Wall didn't stop us! You think pissing on me is going to end this?"

Encouraged by their general's odd behaviour, some of the off-duty legionnaires stripped away their armour and joined him, splashing each other and throwing handfuls of mud in defiance of the weather.

A crack of thunder brought them to a standstill. Lightning flashed down, striking the flag pole atop a nearby tent, splintering the wood.

"Come on!" bellowed Ullsaard, staring up into the storm clouds. "You can fucking growl all you like, I'm not going away!"

The deluge continued and the thunder rumbled on. Ullsaard closed his eyes and listened to the rain hammering on helmet and shield, felt the storm clawing at his skin. He had not been so invigorated since he had faced the behemodon single-handed. His flesh tingled with excitement and the Blood coursed through his body, suffusing him with excitement and energy.

He opened his eyes and turned to coldwards, pointing his spear through the haze of rain in the direction of Askh, only half a day's march away.

"I'm coming for you, Lutaar!" he cried. "I'm coming!"

Still abuzz with sensation, Ullsaard laughed and stalked back to his tent.

II

The following dawn brought a cloudless sky. Ullsaard had not slept and at the first bell of Dawnwatch he put on his armour, ate a swift breakfast of dried fruit and bread and left his pavilion to see what was happening. The ground was a mire underfoot despite the plank walkways and he sloshed through the camp to the coldwards wall. He kicked thick mud from his boots and pulled himself up the ladder to the gate tower.

From this vantage point he could see Askh in the morning haze. The Royal Hill stood out in the rosy light against the blues and purples of the mountains. It was a beautiful city, majestic with its white stone and marble.

"General, is that a legion camp?" said the legionnaire behind him, pointing slightly to dawnwards.

Ullsaard could see a makeshift wall less than five miles away, built on a shallow rise. It was undoubtedly a camp, housing four or five legions judging by its size. Ullsaard's mood soured at the sight.

"Who is it?" the legionnaire asked.

"Cosuas," Ullsaard replied.

III

The two armies faced each other across a stretch of farmland filled with the green shoots of cereal. Ullsaard's legions were arranged in two lines of phalanxes along a ridge facing coldwards, the companies interspersed with lava-throwers, squadrons of kolubrid riders and batteries of spear throwers; Cosuas's much smaller force occupied a solitary hill, forming a complete circle about its summit like the Crown they protected. Half a mile separated the two hosts.

At the chime of Noonwatch, Ullsaard mounted Blackfang and rode out towards the enemy, spear slung behind him, sword sheathed. Though the sun was drying the ground, the rutted track he followed was as much stream as road. Cresting a rise on the road, he saw a lone figure breaking from the enemy army, walking slowly down the hill towards him. The man carried a mace in his left hand and a large oval shield in the other.

The two of them met at the gate of a farmyard halfway between the armies. Ullsaard dismounted, tied Blackfang to the fence and waited as Cosuas strode up the road. Ullsaard stood patiently with his hands clasped behind him as the aging general set his shield against a gatepost and slung his mace to the ground beside it.

"I expected to see you here," said Ullsaard. "But I don't know how you made it."

Cosuas gave Ullsaard a lopsided smile and his eyes were bright with excitement.

"Found the end of the Greenwater, lad!" he said. "Can you fucking believe it? Nearly fifteen hundred miles hotwards of here, we reached the sea. Golden sandy beaches, strange trees with nuts the size of your head. Got word of what you were up to, built some ships and sailed all the way up the dawnwards coast, round Nemuria, and landed last winter while you were still stuck in the snow. You've had me running between the Wall and the coast and back again with your tricks."

"Never have a straight fight if you can avoid it," said Ullsaard. "You taught me that."

Cosuas looked Ullsaard up and down.

"Not as big as your nuts, I reckon," Cosuas said. "What the fuck are you doing? You don't want to be king."

"I'm not your son," Ullsaard said. "Just thought you should know that. I'm Lutaar's bastard, one of the Blood."

Cosuas took this news with a nod.

"I never figured for that," he said. "I wasn't sure you were mine, you certainly don't look like me. Thought your mother got knocked up by some other man."

"Why did you save her? Why didn't you hand her over to the Brotherhood like you were meant to?"

Cosuas wiped a hand over his bald head. The breeze was cooling, but the sun was strong and both men were sweating in their armour.

"What can I say?" Cosuas said. "I loved your mother. I didn't know what the Brotherhood would do with her, but I knew none of the poor bitches sent to the Grand Precincts came back. I didn't want that to happen to her."

"And during all those years we campaigned together, you never said a word about it."

Cosuas shrugged.

"It wasn't my place. If your mother wanted her secrets, who was I to stop her? What good would it have done?"

Ullsaard crossed his arms and nodded in agreement.

"That's the past," he said. "We need to talk about the future. Don't fight me."

Cosuas said nothing.

"I know you like to see yourself as the simple general, but you can fucking count!" snapped Ullsaard, stepping towards his mentor. "I've got ten legions; you've got what? Four? Five?"

"Four and a half," Cosuas replied. "In a superior defensive position."

"Bollocks! You could be on a fucking mountain and you couldn't even those odds."

"If you're so sure, why are we talking?"

"Don't let me beat you," said Ullsaard. "What's Lutaar to you, anyway? He's just some cunt whose family killed yours. What do you owe him?"

"My allegiance," growled Cosuas. He waved a hand angrily at Ullsaard. "That's your problem, you traitorous shit. Your word is worthless. What have you done? You think you've solved something? All you've done is reduce the empire to a bauble that men can scrap and claw at each other over."

Cosuas took a few paces away and turned on Ullsaard, spittle flying from his lips.

"Don't you fucking get it, Ullsaard? You've broken everything! What happens the next time a general doesn't like his orders and decides to get even? What happens when a governor thinks he might just raise a legion or two of his own to settle an argument with his neighbour? Askh, the Crown, the Blood, none of it means anything if you take it for yourself."

"I am of the Blood," said Ullsaard. "I have been denied my inheritance."

"That's funny, I thought you were spawned and raised by a court whore in Enair, and succeeded with your own blood and fucking sweat. Doesn't that count for anything?"

Ullsaard would have laughed if it had been anyone else saying these things.

"It's that same blood and sweat that's got me to where I am now. I have *earned* this day, friend. I will become king."

Cosuas turned his back again. Ullsaard called out to him.

"You don't have to join me. Just don't get in my way. There's no need for you to get involved. Let me pass, march your troops back down the Greenwater and spend the rest of your life by the sea. I don't fucking care, do whatever you want to do, just don't make me destroy you. You don't deserve that."

"You want to do something for me?" said Cosuas. He picked up his mace and shield and squared off. "Give me a chance to end this now."

Ullsaard shook his head as the old general beckoned him closer with his shield.

"Why not?" snarled Cosuas. "Afraid?"

"I don't want to kill you," said Ullsaard. "Don't you understand?"

"Why not?" Cosuas said with a shrug. "If I let you do this, what's the point in staying alive? I swore an oath to the king and the empire. That actually means something to me! I can't serve you, and I can't turn the other way and let you destroy Askhor. This is my only choice."

Ullsaard picked up his shield and spear and trudged away.

"Ullsaard!"

The general stopped and looked back. Cosuas was striding down the road after him, mud splashing up his bare legs, caking his sandals. Ullsaard continued to walk away.

"You have to kill me, Ullsaard! It's either now, or your men do it on that hill!"

That stopped him. He looked at Cosuas, saw desperation and hurt in his eyes. Cosuas knew he couldn't stop Ullsaard, but he couldn't bear the shame of failing in his duty. It would be a worse fate for Cosuas to see his army routed and survive with that knowledge.

"All right," said Ullsaard, turning back, hefting his spear into a fighting grip. "I'll make it quick."

"You fucking wish you could!" shouted Cosuas, breaking into a run.

IV

Ullsaard set himself to receive the attack, legs braced apart, shield to the front, spear jutting beside it. Half a dozen paces away, Cosuas slid to a stop and stooped, bringing his foot up to fling mud into Ullsaard's face. Spluttering and partially blinded, Ullsaard reacted on instinct, bringing his shield across his body to block the blow he knew was coming from his right.

Cosuas' mace crashed against the shield, driving it down, its lower edge scraping painfully along Ullsaard's shin. Ullsaard stepped back, trying to wipe the mud from his eyes. He caught a shadow of movement to his left and twisted, ducking to his right as he brought up his shield. Another blow crashed down, numbing Ullsaard's arm.

"By fucking Askhos, you're stronger than you look!" spat Ullsaard, clearing his eyes in time to see the head of Cosuas's mace swinging towards his ankles. He sprang back and the mace splashed into the mud.

Ullsaard acted on instinct. He lunged, right arm stretched out. The spear caught Cosuas in the hip, just below his breastplate. Ullsaard pulled the spear free.

"Shit," he said, stepping close to Cosuas. Blood leaked from the wound as Cosuas tripped and fell to his rump. Red flowed into the puddles of the road. The veteran general tried to push himself up but fell to his right side in a splash of mud.

"Finish it!" Cosuas hissed. "You said you'd make it quick."

Ullsaard threw aside his spear and dragged his sword free. He drew his arm back for the killing blow, looming over Cosuas.

The old man's mace crashed into Ullsaard's body and the general felt ribs crack, breath exploding from his body. Staggering back, he stumbled to one knee as Cosuas pushed himself unsteadily to his feet and limped closer, mace in hand.

"Fucking idiot," said Cosuas. "You think I'd make it that easy?"

Two crashing blows rained down on Ullsaard's upraised shield before he forced himself upright. He raised his sword to block the next, but Cosuas's mace smashed into his hand, shattering fingers. The sword tumbled from Ullsaard's mangled fingers. He looked at Cosuas and saw a sneer curling the old general's lips.

"Have it your way," Ullsaard growled as the two circled each other.

Ullsaard fended off a few tentative strikes from his opponent, his gaze flicking to the stream of red pouring down Cosuas's left leg. For all his grit and stubbornness, the old man was already dying. It was just a matter of time.

Cosuas knew it too and swung his mace at Ullsaard's head. Ullsaard angled his shield to deflect the blow and swung back, smashing the rim into Cosuas's brow. Skin ruptured and bone split from the blow. Cosuas fell backwards, eyes glazed, blood pouring from his nostrils.

Panting, his ribs sending stabs of pain through him, Ullsaard cast aside his shield and snatched his sword from the mud with his left hand. Shaking his head woozily, Cosuas weakly raised his shield, but Ullsaard kicked the other man's arm aside and stepped on his wrist, pinning it to the muddy road.

"You tried," Ullsaard said quietly, driving the point of his sword into Cosuas's throat.

The old man spasmed for a moment, back arching as blood erupted from the wound and foamed from his lips. Then he fell still, eyes staring into the blue skies.

Ullsaard let the sword fall from his fingers and dropped to his knees. He bent over Cosuas and laid a hand on his mentor's chest. He kissed Cosuas on each cheek and rocked back, slumping to one side.

The tears came quickly, washing away the grime in Ullsaard's eyes. His ribs made every breath a torture and he could feel nothing of his right hand. He gazed numbly at his fingers and saw his middle and index finger splayed at awkward angles. Gritting his teeth, he pulled the fingers back into place with sharp cracks and bent his brow to Cosuas's chest, wracked by sobs.

Taking a deep breath, Ullsaard got to his feet, good hand holding his damaged ribs.

"You old bastard," he sighed between painful gasps of air. "Can't leave you here."

He bent down and tugged Cosuas's shield from his arm and pried his mace from his dead grip. Awkwardly, hissing in pain from every movement, Ullsaard hauled Cosuas over his left shoulder. He seemed even smaller now, almost no weight at all.

With slow, painful steps, Ullsaard walked back to his army.

V

Ullsaard growled as he tried to flex his splinted knuckles. Luuarit stepped back to admire his handiwork, stroking his fingers down his moustaches.

"I've set the bones in your hand as best I can," said the surgeon. "Give it a few weeks before you try anything strenuous. There's not a lot I can do about your ribs more than the bandages. If you start pissing or shitting blood, or you feel water in your breath, come to me immediately. There's no telling if there's any damage inside you."

Ullsaard nodded absently and sat back in his campaign throne. It had been brought to the ridge by Anasind, so that the general could watch the coming battle in a little more comfort. Looking to the left and right, Ullsaard saw his legions spreading out around the hill occupied by the opposing army. Heavy bellows-arrows flew between the two forces as kolubrids skirmished for position on the lower parts of the slope. From higher up, spear throwers hurled their shafts down the hill, cutting wounds into the neat formations of the advancing phalanxes.

Cosuas had been right; it was a good defensive position.

Ullsaard's army did not attack from all sides. He had left an opening in his line to duskwards, allowing the enemy room to flee if they chose. Had they been surrounded he had no doubt the proud legionnaires, veterans of the Greenwater campaign, would fight to the death; by offering them a route out, Ullsaard hoped that the bloody toll would be less on both sides.

After bringing Cosuas's body back, Ullsaard had sent messengers to the First Captains now facing him, but to a man they had refused his terms. In a way, Ullsaard was pleased; their general slain, outnumbered and certain to lose, still the legions would not surrender. He knew he expected every man that followed him to act the same and had told his officers to fight this battle with pride and honour.

Not that he wanted a battle, not any more. He glanced at the body of Cosuas laying on a bier to his left. Ullsaard had no qualms about shedding blood if necessary, but enough was enough. After today he hoped no legionnaire would kill another.

As he watched the blocks of bronze and black and red converging on the hill, he wondered how many more lives would be lost today. He felt no regret at his actions thus far, but Cosuas's words troubled him. He thought back to his conversations with Noran – how he missed Noran right at that moment and Allenya too – and wondered if he had unleashed something he could not control.

His mind wandered back to the discussions with Aalun, and the chaotic time of the empire's founding. That time would come again under Ullsaard's rule. The empire would grow larger than ever and generals would be granted the rewards of their success. The hungry, living creature that was Greater Askhor would be filled with new vigour, and Ullsaard would steer it teeth and claws to new heights of power.

Looking at the armies about to clash, thinking of the blood that had been spilt and the dubious acts he had committed and allowed, Ullsaard felt no guilt.

He was doing Askhos's work.

VI

Noran had been right; Askh was far grander than Magilnada. Gelthius had never seen such a place, and it was as far from the mud-and-wood house he'd grown up in as an ailur was from the cats that chased rats around a barn. Peering over the shoulders of the legionnaires in front, he could see the white stone of the palaces and the dark shadow of the Grand Precincts rearing above a sea of tiled roofs. He saw the sun gleaming from golden domes, and minarets jutted from behind the walls like slender fingers, topped with colourful flags. These were places he had not even heard of less than a year ago, and now he was looking at them with his own eyes.

There was excitement in the legion. Today the city would be theirs. Gelthius heard scatters of conversation, as soldiers discussed the merits of what to take.

"No gold," said one. "It's too heavy and the markets will be full of it after we're done. Gold is for fools. Gems and cut stones, that's another matter. Easy to fill a bag with that stuff and it'll never lose its value."

"I reckon I'll get me some tapestries and carpets," said another. "Send them back to the wife in Parmia. She'll be dead proud with covered floors and walls. That'll shut her mother up for a change, the craggy-faced bitch."

"Head for the markets," a third man had advised Gelthius. "You want to make a quick bit of money, get all the grain, flour, fruit, vegetables, meat and milk you can. You'll need some wagons of course, but the first thing people need after something like this is food. All them with pockets of silver and jewels will give you a handful of their spoils for some apples and a leg of pork in a few days, mark my words."

"I'm gonna find me one of those dark-haired Askhan women and fuck her till my cock's raw," came one man's promise, which rather unsettled Gelthius. In his younger days Gelthius had taken his fair share of loot from a raid on another tribe, but had never got on with the rape side of things. He liked to spend a bit of time with a woman, but years on the landship had worn out his lust to the point where the only thing he wanted from his wife, when he eventually got home, would be a kiss on the cheek and a bowl of her wonderful lamb stew.

"Listen up!" barked Captain Anasind. The Thirteenth's commander prowled up and down in front of his men, his stare unforgiving. "The general's got three rules. Break them and you're dead. Rule one: three days. Anyone not back in camp by Midwatch on the third day will be a deserter. Rule two: no burning. We've fought our way all across the empire for this place; let's not have it going up in smoke. Rule three: nobody touches the precincts, palaces or colleges. They belong to the general."

Captain Anasind continued, explaining which parts of the city had been allotted to the Thirteenth. Gelthius shook his head in disbelief. The Askhans even organised their looting! Company by company, Anasind divided the legion's bit of the city. So this is civilisation? he thought. Calmly talking about who could rape who, and who could steal what? It all seemed a little strange to the Salphor. Yet the more Gelthius thought about it, the more it made a horrible kind of sense. Nobody wanted the legions to be fighting each other over the spoils. If everybody got their fair share, there'd be no backstabbing, nobody stealing from each other, setting company against company, legionnaire against legionnaire.

When they were given the order, the Thirteenth moved out in formation. There was no mad dash, no greedy sprint

486

for the open gates. As Ullsaard's favourites, they would be the first into the city, and the officers had made it clear that the eyes of the army would be on them.

Smartly in step, icons held high, spears shouldered, the companies of the Thirteenth entered Askh. The city was quiet; thousands had fled in the night fearing what was to come. The companies split along the streets and after a while Gelthius could hear the splintering of doors being kicked in, angry shouts from those that had remained. He heard a scream from behind and turned to see a middle-aged woman running out of an alley, two legionnaires in pursuit. One tripped her with the butt of his spear and they grabbed an arm each, dragging her back to where she had come from.

At a crossroads, Gelthius's company ran into the fifteenth company and he saw Lepiris amongst the crowd. The two ex-turncranks met at the corner of a tall townhouse.

"Made it this far then?" said Lepiris. Gelthius nodded. "Up for some looting?"

Gelthius shook his head. "I think I'd rather get some sleep, right enough."

Lepiris grinned. "I'm sure we can find some beds somewhere, and maybe something to eat."

Arms on each other's shoulders, the two of them headed after the others.

ASKH
Spring, 210th Year of Askh

I

The sounds of looting echoed from Askh as Ullsaard rode towards the gate on Blackfang. He couldn't bring himself to come to the city earlier; better that he didn't see that first rush of the beast he had unleashed.

Just inside the shadow of the gatehouse he saw two figures sitting side by side, backs against the wall, legs outstretched with shields and spears leaning next to them. Several empty bottles littered the ground around them, along with bones, fruit skins and cores and other detritus of a sizeable meal. One seemed asleep, the other lazily blew smoke from his mouth, a bowl of gently glowing dried leaves held in his hand. Ullsaard caught the pungent whiff of hennek as the man slowly inhaled; a drug from Maasra favoured by the younger generation of Askhan nobility. The legionnaire looked up at Ullsaard, recognised him with widening eyes and attempted unsuccessfully to stand up. He wobbled in an uncertain crouch for a moment before falling back against the wall.

"It's all right," laughed Ullsaard. "No ceremony today."

He recognised the face of the sleeping man.

"Weren't you two part of Aroisius's lot?" said Ullsaard, stopping Blackfang with a tug on the reins. He pulled her head to one side, away from the stupefying smoke of the hennek.

"Well, Anglhan's really," drawled the legionnaire. "I'm Lepiris. My companion is Gelthius. I apologise for his state, as he has, alas, been overcome with weariness. And not a little wine, which he has not drunk before today. I think he mistook it for the strength of ale."

"Enjoy yourselves for the next two days," said Ullsaard. "But don't be late back to camp."

"No, General, right enough," said Gelthius, rearing up from his stupor and banging his fists against his chest in salute. He collapsed backwards, helmet tipping over his eyes.

Ullsaard laughed again and urged Blackfang through the gate. He rode quickly through the city, heading directly up the Royal Way. The last time he had been here, Ullsaard had been fleeing the city, fearful of a mob. The time before he had been parading in triumph with Aalun, the masses of Askh cheering his name. Today, those people cowered behind their doors and shutters, terrified of him.

Give it time, he thought. They'll be cheering your name again when you bring them the wealth of Salphoria.

There were no guards at the palace, and it looked deserted. Taking Blackfang to the stables himself, Ullsaard saw the evidence of a hasty evacuation. Once inside the palace itself, the emptiness was even more pronounced. Statues and tapestries had been taken, and there were empty alcoves where once golden vases and silver busts had stood. He had not seen a legionnaire so he knew the palace had not been looted – not by his men at least, but he suspected the king's servants had taken what they could once the king had fled.

His bandaged ribs ached as he walked along the corridors and halls, and it was with a weary hand that he pushed open the doors of the audience hall.

"I expected you earlier," Lutaar rasped. Ullsaard looked along the hall in surprise.

The king sat in his throne, wearing a golden-threaded robe, a scarlet cloak hanging from his shoulders. And on his head sat the Crown.

"I thought I'd have to hunt you down," said Ullsaard as he walked towards the king.

"I'm not running away from you," said Lutaar. "Besides, what would be the point?"

"And Kalmud? Erlaan?"

"They are not here. They have been taken somewhere safer."

"You know that you don't have to die, don't you?" said Ullsaard, striding up the steps to the throne's dais.

"If you want this," Lutaar took the Crown of the Blood from his head and waved it at Ullsaard, "then you'll have to prise it from my dead fingers."

Ullsaard unsheathed his sword but Lutaar held up his hand, staying the blow.

"Listen to me before you do this deed," the king said. There was no scorn in his voice; instead his words were edged with sadness. "Please do not do this. I do not ask you for myself, but for the empire. As I once implored Aalun to understand, Kalmud must become king; it is Kalmud's destiny to wear the Crown. Rule the empire as you wish, use him as a puppet if you must, but do not make yourself king."

Lutaar stood up and, placing the Crown on the seat of the throne, approached Ullsaard to lay a hand on his sword arm.

"You have won, Ullsaard," he said. "The empire is yours to do with as you wish. You are the most powerful man in all of Greater Askhor. You have defeated your enemies, and your allies respect you. You do not need to become king in name."

Ullsaard pulled his arm away.

"What is it that you are so afraid of, Lutaar?"

"I am afraid for us all," replied the king. "Askhos decreed that the Crown pass from eldest living son to eldest living

490

son; it has done so for two hundred years. There is a chain of the Blood that stretches back to Askhos, and you will break it. The Blood must rule Askh; it is our doom and our privilege."

"I am of the Blood," said Ullsaard.

"I have heard such rumour, but it cannot be possible."

"It is true. You bedded my mother and Cosuas helped her escape before she was handed to the Brotherhood."

Lutaar's eyes widened with surprise for a moment and his expression changed. Ullsaard was not quite sure what he saw, a fleeting glimpse of speculation, perhaps hope.

"How old are you?" the king asked quickly. "Are you older than Kalmud?"

"I am not sure," replied Ullsaard, stepping back, disturbed by the king's sudden interest. "We are of a similar age, but I grew up in a place without the benefit of the Brotherhood's count of the years."

Lutaar dragged the tips of his fingers over his wizened, stubbled cheeks and continued to look at Ullsaard with that strange, calculating gaze. The king walked back to the throne, lifted the Crown to his head and sat down.

"Very well," said Lutaar. "Kill me. Take the Crown. Become king of Askh."

Lutaar craned his head to one side, exposing the artery in the side of his neck. He folded his hands neatly in his lap and waited expectantly, eyes fixed on Ullsaard. The general walked cautiously towards the throne, sword held ready, perturbed by the king's odd behaviour. Ullsaard expected some kind of trap, and his eyes darted left and right as he stood over the frail king.

Lutaar nodded once and closed his eyes.

Blood sprayed as Ullsaard drew the edge of his sword across Lutaar's neck. The gush became a stream and then a slow trickle. Lutaar did not move. Blood pooled in his lap and started to drip onto the marble floor from the hem of the robe.

Ullsaard had killed many men, but he was unnerved by this act. The splash of blood on stone seemed to echo around the hall. He turned away and strode to a high window, throwing open the shutters for a gulp of fresh air. Ullsaard shuddered as he looked over the city, the energy of the last few days draining away from him, leaving him feeling sick and weak. His hand throbbed and his gut ached.

Raising his eyes, he looked duskwards over Askh, where the sun was disappearing behind the city wall. The sky grew red and purple as the sounds of the looting legionnaires was carried up to him from the streets below. Steadying his thoughts, Ullsaard smiled.

He liked the moment. Tonight the sun set on the reign of Lutaar, tomorrow it would rise on the reign of Ullsaard. It was a fitting end to one life and start of another.

II

Ullsaard stood at the window until the moon had risen high above the domes of the palace. Not a single soul had disturbed him as he had admired the city that was his.

He turned, seeing again the body of Lutaar. A small crimson pond surrounded the throne, and the king seemed more slumped than before. Ullsaard's eye was drawn to the gleam of gold upon the king's brow.

There was his prize. All he had to do was reach out and take it.

Ullsaard ignored the slickness underfoot as he bent over the dead king, his good fingers curling around the Crown of the Blood. There would be a proper coronation later, he told himself, but it wouldn't hurt to try it on, just to make sure of the fit.

Looking at his reflection in Lutaar's blood, Ullsaard placed the Crown on his head.

III

Pain lanced through Ullsaard's mind, needles of agony driving into his brain. He fell to the ground and writhed as he felt his mind being shredded and gouged, torn at and pulled apart. His clothes soaked up the blood of Lutaar as he floundered across the floor in a swirl of crimson, a silent scream twisting his face.

Rolling to all fours, Ullsaard dipped his head and vomited as the Crown fell to the floor with a clatter.

The pain stopped and Ullsaard slumped to the tiles, gasping for breath, eyes screwed shut. He lay there for some time, the memory of the pain he had felt almost as much as the pain itself. When his breath came steadily and his heart was no longer hammering against his breastbone, Ullsaard opened his eyes and pushed himself up to his knees.

He looked at his reflection in the blood-spattered gold of the Crown. He could see no wounds upon his head or face, and he looked the same as he had done for the last few years. But something felt like it had changed.

Leaning forward to peer closely at himself, Ullsaard had the strangest feeling that someone else was looking out of his eyes.

"Who are you?" he whispered, looking at his distorted features around the rim of the Crown.

Askhos, replied a voice inside his head.

Acknowledgments

I'd like to thank Marco and Lee of Angry Robot for having faith in my ambitious idea, and Matt Keefe and Guy Haley for their continuing help and support.

About the Author

Gav Thorpe works from Nottingham, England, and has written more than a dozen novels and even more short stories. Growing up in a tedious town just north of London, he originally intended to be an illustrator but after acknowledging an inability to draw or paint he turned his hand to writing.

Gav spent 14 years as a developer for Games Workshop on the worlds of Warhammer and Warhammer 40,000 before going freelance in 2008. It is claimed (albeit solely by our Gav, frankly) that he is merely a puppet of a mechanical hamster called Dennis that intends to take over the world via the global communications network. When not writing, Gav enjoys playing games, cooking, pro-wrestling and smiling wryly. He is currently finishing up the next volume, *The Crown of the Conqueror*.

mechanicalhamster.wordpress.com

A GUIDE TO GREATER ASKHOR, ITS PEOPLES AND ENEMIES

The empire of Greater Askhor has existed for more than two centuries. Over that time, it has relentlessly expanded, bringing a disparate group of peoples under its common banner. Guided by the wisdom laid down in the Book of Askhos, the empire has been brought together not only by military conquest but by advanced trade, technology and organisation. This section looks at some of the factors that make Greater Askhor such a powerful force.

Time

The need for accurate timekeeping was met by Askhos during his formation of the first legions. By use of water clocks and meticulously made watch candles, the offices of state and war can adhere to a routine common across all of the empire.

Askhan time is based upon the rota of duties employed by the legions. The basic element of time is the watches, which run from the start of the day in the following order: Dawnwatch (the official start of the day); Low Watch; Noon Watch; High Watch; Duskwatch; Howling Watch (or simply Howling); Midnight Watch (or Midwatch); Gravewatch.

Each watch is further divided into four equal hours, so the Askhan day is broken into 32 hours in total. The accepted format is to number the hour of the particular watch. For instance, second hour of Gravewatch, or first hour of High Watch. In everyday use this is contracted, so that one might refer to "second Grave" or "first High".

In legion camps and major towns, the start of each watch is signalled by an established pattern of bell rings or horn notes, followed by a number of chimes or blasts equivalent to the hour.

While the Brotherhood has a centralised calendar for taxation systems and organising agriculture, its use is not so widespread as that of the clock and many parts of the empire retain their tribal dating systems. Based upon complex solar and lunar observations, only a few academics understand this calendar outside of the Brotherhood. The only widely accepted date is that of midsummer (where it can be determined) and it is on this day that a new Askhan year starts.

Distance and other measurements

As with the gauging of time, most distances in the empire are derived from legion origins. The Askhan mile is a well established measure based upon the distance a legion can march at a regulated pace. One mile is one tenth of the distance covered in a full watch of marching, so the average marching speed of a legion is two and a half miles per hour.

Other measurements are graded by the Brotherhood, including the "pack" (based on the weight of a legionnaire's wargear), "heft"(the weight of an Askhan spear) and "cast" (seventy paces, the distance a javelin can be reliably thrown). Various commonly agreed crafts, engineering, masonic and trade weights and measures are also used, particularly in the oldest parts of the empire.

Coinage is based on a metric system devised by the Brotherhood. The highest value unit of currency is the

Askharin, a gold-based coin whose weight is also a universal measure. An Askharin is worth one hundred sindins, which are half the size and made of a silver alloy. A sindin is worth ten innats, usually called "tins' due to the metal used in their alloy. There is no formal imperial mint and individual governors and even nobles are free to make their own coinage, subject to appraisal and approval by the Brotherhood. When dealing with imperial contracts, a system of promissory notes are used, and in recent decades these have become a form of paper money when large sums are involved. In many parts of the empire, barter is still the preferred method of trade. Iron is rarer and more valued than gold, but it still in such short supply that by royal decree it cannot be used as coinage.

Politics

The empire is divided into a number of provinces, run on behalf of the king by appointed governors. Each province is a semi-autonomous state, responsible for the raising of taxes and legions, and the payment of imperial contracts and pensions, in addition to providing an agreed stipend to the Crown that is reviewed every ten years. In practice, trade taxes are levied by the Brotherhood and so are consistent across all provinces, while property and personal taxes depend upon the individual circumstances and governors in charge.

The king has absolute rule in law, though he is advised by the High Brother of the Brotherhood, the Council of Governors and various crafts, academic and trade representatives. Alongside this civic administration is a more complex network of influence originating from the ancient noble families, provincial kings and tribal chieftains brought into the fold of Greater Askhor. The majority of non-noble families do not have the wealth for independent investment or trade and are directly employed by the empire or rely upon pensions or contracts originating from the king and governors.

The Blood

The Book of Askhos has a considerable section dedicated to the rights and responsibilities of his descendants. In law, the word of the Blood is sacrosanct and any judgement made by one of the Blood is absolute unless directly over-ruled by the king. By right, all members of the Blood are granted the dual ranks of Prince and General, although in recent generations not all princes have pursued military ambition.

A Prince of the Blood has the right to requisition any resource he requires from a provincial governor. Many Princes of the Blood serve as governors in their later years, although in recent generations the law has been amended so that a prince who does so must relinquish the title of general and may only command legions attached to his position as Governor. Some unruly princes have been forced into Governorship in the past to curb their powers.

The Governors

The Governor is the head of imperial power within each province, second in authority only to a member of the Blood. Appointed by the king, a governor essentially leases his province from the empire through the provision of taxation and supply of soldiers. Within the laws of the empire, he is free to run whatever system of government he wishes within his province. In reality, provinces are run on autocratic principles, with contracted agreements to other bodies such as colleges, merchants' organisations and the nobility.

A governor is required to maintain at least one legion for the defence of the province; the expense of which is deducted from any taxation levied by the king. The king can also compel a governor to raise new legions as required, again at the expense of the Crown. As raising a legion can be a costly and time-consuming business, most governors maintain several in existence in readiness to respond to the king's requests. A governor has nominal command of all legions in his province, unless they are under the authority of one of the Blood or a general named by the king.

The Brotherhood

The High Brother is leader of the Brotherhood and enjoys considerable authority in matters of commerce and law, subject to approval by the king. Individual precincts are empowered to levy taxes, adjudicate disputes, impose judicial sanctions and prosecute criminal law on behalf of the governors and the king.

In addition, the Brotherhood provides personnel for managing the essential tasks of the empire. This ranges from arbitrating trade disputes, managing the maintenance of waterways, roads and other infrastructure, providing supplies and payment to the legions, overseeing the minting of coinage, and several banking duties for the nobility and merchants.

While an individual Brother has little legal authority on his own, as a representative of the Brotherhood he is by extension a direct servant of the king. Any person, even a governor, who defies the wishes of a Brother would need a very good reason to do so, and can expect repercussions if found to be obstructing the running of the empire.

The Legions

It was Askhos who revolutionised the strategy and tactics of war at the founding of the empire. The First King established a professional body of fighting men from the retinues of the Askhan tribal chieftains and organised them into the First Legion. Well-drilled, well-equipped and well-rewarded, these soldiers were more than a match for the tribal warbands they faced and after several crushing victories over the disorganised militia forces of other chieftains in Askhor, their mere existence was enough to subjugate all of the Askhan people to Askhos's rule. Emulating their new king, subservient tribal leaders adopted the legion principles, and with license from Askhos the conquest of Greater Askhor began.

As the empire was established, wary of rebellion, Askhos bought off the legions from their commanders, rewarding the chieftains with the lands they had conquered. The system of governorships was established and the legions were all subsumed into Crown control. All legions swear direct loyalty to the king, and are considered soldiers of the empire rather than any individual prince, governor or general.

In theory, legionnaires are drawn from all across Greater Askhor. In practice, the logistics of raising and recruitment mean that a legion will generally be drawn from the populace of a particular province. Each raising of a legion is given a sequential number; if a legion is destroyed in battle or otherwise disbanded, its number becomes available for the next one created. Certain legions have continued to exist since the time of Askhos through continual replacement of losses, while others had been raised and fallen several times. This means that a legion's number is no sure indication of the length of its current existence, though on principle the First Legion is constantly maintained and so its history is unbroken since it was created by Askhos. Several other legions have earned great distinction in the many campaigns of the empire, either in their current incarnation or in previous raisings.

Each legion bears an icon of Askhos as its army standard. It is on this golden placard that every legionnaire swears his loyalty. It is a matter of pride that no legion icon has ever fallen in battle. Even during the few defeats suffered by a legion, the icon has always been brought back to safety, ready to be raised again at the legion's next founding.

When more than one legion is present, it is termed an army. Command of an army falls to the longest-serving First Captain. This grants the title of First Commander. Above this comes the rank of General. Only the king may appoint the general, and it confers a form of pseudo-Blood status in regards to the law and the command of legions. While a First Commander is subject to the instructions of a governor, a General is not, and can only receive orders from one of the Blood. Generals are usually appointed for a specific campaign of conquest, although its duration is for life unless the rank is later renounced by the king. Like governors, Generals are permitted to raise their own legions at the expense of the Crown, and may even do so at their own expense. By ancient law a General may claim any conquered territories for himself, although to do so he must surrender part of any proceeds from such gains to the Crown. By extension, any lands conquered by a legion must be offered to the soldiers of the legion for lease or purchase, and it is from these rights of conquest that many legionnaires and officers are able to retire after serving their minimum ten years of duty.

At the time of King Lutaar's ascension to the Crown, there were thirty-three legions in existence, though by the end of his reign this had been reduce to twenty. The highest number of legions recorded is forty-eight, during a rapid expansion of the empire that ended about a decade before the start of Lutaar's reign.

Organisation

Askhos's greatest innovation in creating the legions was to approach the formation of the army from a bottom-up approach. Traditionally, tribal chieftains and their nobles each gathered about them a body or retainers who were equipped to fight, supplemented during raids and times of war by armed militia. Therefore the size and quality of troops varied widely depending upon the individual wealth of the nobility and the number of men who were loyal to them.

Askhos established the idea of the company; a set body of men 160-strong that formed the foundation of a legion. The number was chosen in concert with the new concept of the phalanx as a fighting formation. Each company has eight sergeants; in standard phalanx formation they are each responsible for two ranks of troops. There are four Third Captains per company, who are in turn commanded by a single Second Captain. All are numbered within the 160 soldiers and expected to fight in rank.

A minimum of ten companies is required for a force to qualify as a legion, but ideally a new legion will number between twenty and thirty companies, giving a rough manpower of four to five thousand men. Regardless of size, a legion is commanded by its First Captain. A First Captain is supported by a staff of Second and Third Captains, the number dependent on the size of the legion, but typically one Second Captain and two Third Captains for every five companies. The staff officers act as messengers and subordinate battlefield commands, and take on responsibilities for supplies, recruitment, training and the running of the camp.

All legionnaires are required to learn skills necessary for the functioning of the legion. There are no non-combatants in a legion, even engineers, surgeons and armourers must be able to fight. Such men with these prestigious additional duties are usually given the rank of at least Third Captain.

Since the discovery of kolubrids in the grasslands of Maasra, there is an additional cavalry wing to many legions. The size of this varies with the availability of kolubrids, and so is typically larger in legions raised in the hotwards provinces of Nalanor, Okhar and Maasra.

Between two hundred and four hundred kolubrid riders is typical, divided into squadrons fifty-strong.

Legionnaire

Any man of the legions may call himself a legionnaire, and it is an honorific kept until death. A legionnaire is a professional soldier, paid from the legion coffers. All training and equipment is also paid for, as is basic accommodation, food and drink whilst in the legion. Some additional benefits can be bought or hired whilst in camp, though their price effectively limits their availability to officers. Food and shelter are often better than that available to labourers and other menial workers, so there is no shortage of able men willing to fight in the legions.

A legionnaire is expected to lay down his life for the empire; in fact if he survives grievous wounds in battle and is unable to fight he will be slain so that he does not become a burden. In return, he receives a salary that can be paid in coin, salt and other produce, or accumulated as an allotment of land available on his retirement. In addition, should a legionnaire be slain whilst on duty, his immediate family may claim his pay as a war pension, extending to sixty years after his death. Such generosity is balanced by the rigorous training, harsh discipline and long campaigns that are the lot of the imperial legionnaire.

A legionnaire is provided with his weapons, kit and armour by the legion, though replacements for breakages outside of battle must be paid for by him. This gear is divided into march kit and camp kit. A legionnaire's march kit is carried at all times, though when in camp or on hard labours outside camp, a legionnaire is permitted to divest himself of his pack and wargear as long as he is never more than ten paces away. March kit consists of a pair of hard-soled sandals, a stiffened leather kilt, water canteen, woollen undershirt, bronze breastplate, single-bladed bronze knife and sheath, whetstone, leather belt, bronze helmet and a spear. In addition, a legionnaire's camp kit includes a bed roll, replacement sandal soles and belt, five replacement spear tips, a wooden cup and bowl, a bundle of wooden faggots for firemaking, a spare undershirt, helmet crest and a money pouch. Often legionnaires treat their money pouch as march kit.

When campaigning in coldwards climes or expected to fight into the winter, legionnaires must also be provided with a hooded woollen cloak, a tarred waterproof sack, two pairs of knee-length stockings and woollen gloves. Though seen as generous by many, these provisions have allowed legions to fight in exceptionally poor weather when other warriors would be forced to remain in camp or even return to their homes.

A legionnaire is also entitled to two meals per day, at breakfast and at night. When supplies allow, both of these meals must contain some form of meat, a rarity for many folk of lower social standing. Standard march fare is a starchy porridge of ground oats or grain, and Second Captains that wish to engender greater loyalty in their troops will often provide sugar, honey or salt at their own expense. The evening meal must also contain some form of vegetable or fruit. Flat loaves of unleavened bread are used as march rations, which can be supplemented with honey, jam or other fillings at the legionnaire's own expense.

Alcohol is permitted in camp, and each legionnaire has a ration of weak beer every day. Stronger drinks such as wine and mead are often given out as rewards for dutiful service. Legionnaires are permitted to carry additional alcohol in their camp kit, but any drunkenness in camp is punishable by company flogging, while any dereliction of duty is punished by death, so legionnaires are moderate drinkers when on duty.

A legionnaire must serve for at least ten years, at which point he is eligible to leave the military and take his pension. He has the choice of continuing to stay with the legion, signing on for further stints of five years at a time. Officers of Second Captain rank and above may not retire until they have served for fifteen years, and if they choose not to do so at this time, their commitment is for life.

GLOSSARY

People

Aalun – Prince of the Blood, second son of King Lutaar. A patron to Ullsaard, who sponsored his promotion to First Captain and later persuaded King Lutaar to name Ullsaard as a general. It is Aalun's concerns over the health of his older brother, Kalmud, that pitch the empire into a war of succession.

Adral – Governor of Nalanor.

Ahsaam – A revolutionary academic who made fundamental changes to the civil law of the empire, and famous for championing the causes of non-noble families.

Allenya – Eldest of Ullsaard's wives and mother of Jutaar. As matriarch of the family, she is responsible for the running of the household, and tempering the worst excesses of her sisters.

Allon – Governor of Enair. Ullsaard served in Allon's provincial legion before gaining the patronage of Prince Aalun. He later returned for a while as First Captain. Jutaar serves in Allon's legion.

Anasind – First Captain of the Thirteenth Legion.

Anglhan Periusis – A debt guardian of Salphoria and owner of a landship. Ambitious and manipulative, Anglhan is supported by a network of support and favours throughout Salphoria and the Free Country.

Anriit – Eldest of Noran's two wives.

Ariid – Chief servant of Ullsaard's household.

Arnassin – Former king of Salphoria, Aegenuis's great-grandfather.

Aroisius the Free – Former Salphorian chieftain who became a rebel leader after falling foul of Salphoria's strict debt laws.

Askhan – Collective term for both the native people from the tribes of Askhor and those peoples brought into the empire of Greater Askhor.

Askhos – First King of the Askhans, founder of the empire and sire of the Blood. Charismatic and ambitious, Askhos united the tribes of Askhor and subjugated the surrounding peoples to create the fledgling Greater Askhor. Before his death, Askhos laid down his teachings and beliefs in the Book of Askhos, a tome of law, military organisation and customs revered by many people throughout the empire and rigidly adhered to by the Brotherhood.

Asuhas – Governor of Ersua.

Barias – Hillmen chieftain in the pay of Aroisius the Free.

Beruun – visionary architect and engineer commissioned by Askhos to build Askh and the Askhor Wall. He fled the empire and built the city of Magilnada to rival the Askhan capital, in what was then the wild lands of Salphoria. He was eventually captured by agents of Askhos and executed as a traitor by the Brotherhood.

Brotherhood, The – A widespread administrative sect responsible for many of the functions of the empire, including criminal law, taxation, trade, infrastructural organisation and the suppression of pre-empire superstitious beliefs. Proselytisers of the Book of Askhos.

Caelentha – One of the peoples living in Salphoria.

Cannin – One of the peoples living in Salphoria.

Cosuas – A general of the empire of long years and staunch ally of King Lutaar. Son of King Tunaard II and last survivor of the dynasty that ruled Ersua prior to Askhan conquest.

Deaghra – One of the peoples living in Salphoria.

Debt Guardian – In Salphorian law, a man who pays another's debts gains ownership of that man until he has paid off what he owes. Such debts are stamped into tin lozenges and are often used as coinage. Most debtors end up as farm serfs, miners or galley slaves, while some are used by merchants to pull hand carts in their caravans, or act as turncranks of the landships.

Demeetris – A pre-imperial tribe of Askhor living in the foothills of the mountains. They refused the rule of Askhos and every man, woman and child was slain by the First Legion and their villages razed.

Donar – First Captain of the Fifth Legion.

Enairians – Native peoples of Enair. Considered dour, headstrong, sometimes rebellious. Enairians are typically of larger build than the other peoples of Greater Askhor and are valued as soldiers in the legions.

Erlaan – Prince of the Blood, son of Prince Kalmud, grandson of King Lutaar. A youth still in his late teenage years, Erlaan is second in line to inherit the Crown of the Blood.

Ersuans – The peoples native to Ersua. In recent generations, Ersuan tribes have interbred with Nalanorians, Anrairians and hillmen from the Altes Hills and so are considered something of a swarthy, mongrel people in other parts of the empire.

Freyna – Loremother of Ullsaard's home village, Stykhaag.

Furlthia Miadnas – First mate of Anglhan's landship, Furlthia fears Askhan expansion into Salphoria and though he remains loyal to his master for as long as he can stomach it, he eventually cannot abide the Askhan domination of his homelands and leaves to foment opposition to Ullsaard and Anglhan.

Gelthius – A former fisherman, farmer and bandit of the Linghan people in Salphoria, Gelthius has served as a debtor on Anglhan's landship, joined Salphorian rebels, been involved in the fall of Magilnada to the Askhans, was drafted into the Thirteenth Legion and fought in the overthrow of King Lutaar. He longs for a return to a quiet life.

Gerlhan – Salphorian chieftain, ruler of Magilnada.

Griglhan – Salphorian brigand and rebel chieftain.

Hadril – One of the peoples living in Salphoria.

Hannaghian – One of the peoples living in Salphoria.

Heriot – A master of law and philosophy who oversaw the transition of the rights of conquests and control of the legions from King Askhos's warlords to the Crown.

Hillmen – Catch-all term for various tribes found in the Ersuan Highlands and, more numerously, the Altes Hills. The hillmen come from a mix of Ersuan and Salphorian stock and are known for their fierce territorialism and banditry.

Huuril – Third Captain in the Thirteenth Legion.

Huurit – A lightweight champion wrestler of Maarmes, purchased by Ullsaard for Luia.

Jutaar – Son of Allenya, second eldest of Ullsaard. A diligent if dull captain in the legions, eager to follow in his father's military footsteps.

Jutiil – First Captain of the Twelfth Legion.

Kalmud – Prince of the Blood, eldest son of King Lutaar, father of Erlaan. Infected by a devastating lung disease whilst campaigning along the Greenwater River, Kalmud's disability precipitates a crisis of succession in the empire.

Karuu – A young captain of the Thirteenth Legion, personal messenger to Ullsaard.

Kulrua – Governor of Maasra.

Leerunin – Treasurer to Ullsaard's household.

Lenorin – Chancellor of Magilnada, aide to Anglhan, with anti-Askhan sympathies.

Lepiris – Salphorian, former debtor on Anghlhan's landship, recruited into the Fifteenth Company of the Thirteenth Legion.

Linghar – One of the peoples living in Salphoria.

Luamid – First Captain of the Sixteenth Legion.

Lubrianati – Hillmen chieftain, one of Aroisius's lieutenants.

Luia – Second eldest of Ullsaard's wives and mother of Urikh. Wayward, headstrong and adulterous, Luia tests the patience of her husband constantly and owes her continued prosperity, perhaps even her life, to the intervention and protection of her older sister.

Luisaa – An infant, daughter of Urikh, grand-daughter of Ullsaard.

Luriun – One of Askhos's warlords, later governor of Nalanor. Rumoured to have killed his brother and raped his widow due to his own wife being barren.

Luuarit – Second Captain and surgeon in the Thirteenth Legion.

Maasrites – Natives of Maasra, of normally tanned skin due to the sunny climate of their homeland. Many undertake the Oath of Service and have their tongues removed so that they may not speak out of turn to their masters. This has led to the rise of a secret sign language unknown to other peoples.

Meaghran – Salphorian chieftain, ruler of Carlangh.

Medorian – Son of King Aegenuis.

Mekhani – Savage desert-dwelling tribes of Near- and Deep-Mekha, with distinctive dark red skin. Dispersed hunter- gatherers that utilise stone weapons and tools. Led by shamanic tribal chieftains.

Meliu – Youngest wife of Ullsaard and mother to Ullnaar. In her early thirties, Meliu is utterly devoted to her husband, son and eldest sister.

Murian – Governor of Anrair.

Muuril – Sergeant in the Thirteenth Legion, Gelthius's leader.

Muuris – One of Askhos's warlords, later governor of Okhar. The most successful general of Askhos's reign (after the king).

Nalanorians – The peoples native to Nalanor. As the oldest members of the empire outside of Askhor, Nalanorians are generally staunch supporters of the empire, and seen as traditionally conservative in outlook and politics. The presence of the Greenwater's headwaters means that most Nalanorians are accomplished fishermen and sailors, valued across the empire, and they are also respected for the productivity of their farms.

Neerita – Youngest wife of Noran, sister to Anriit, from the Aluuns noble family.

Nemtun – Prince of the Blood, younger and estranged brother of King Lutaar and governor of Okhar. Nemtun brought Anrair into the empire by means of an exceptionally bloody campaign that lasted two years. Married to Lerissa.

Nemurians – Non-human species that live on a chain of volcanic isles lying off the coast of Maasra. Standing more than twice as tall as a man, and of broad girth, Nemurians are heavily muscled, covered with thick scales and possessing a prehensile tail. Extremely secretive, the only Nemurians known to the people of Greater Askhor are those who hire out their much sought after services as mercenaries. Nemurians are also well known for the skill in metalworking and the quantity of iron in their weapons and armour; an element still rare in the empire.

Nidan – Second Captain of the Fifteenth Legion.

Noran Astaan – A noble of Askhor, sole heir of the Astaan family and royal herald in service to Prince Aalun. A long time friend and ally of Ullsaard. Noran's wealth and estates give him considerable influence in the court of Askh. Married to Neerita and Anriit.

Nurtut – A heavyweight champion wrestler of Maarmes.

Nuurin – Fourth King of Greater Askhor, Lutaar's great-great grandfather.

Okharans – The native peoples of Okhar. Most populous peoples of the empire, Okharans are seen as listless and lazy by the natives of other provinces, and the bountiful wealth of their province encourages a culture with little love for physical labour and a deserved reputation of indolence within the Okharan nobility.

Orsinnin – One of the peoples living in Salphoria.

Pak'ka – Nemurian mercenary captain in the employ of Anglhan.

Poets – A much-maligned profession in Askhor, regarded as worse than prostitutes and criminals. Why this persecution exists is not known for sure, but it is believed to date back to Askhos's personal execution of a poet whose bad verse annoyed the First king.

Pretaa – Mother of Ullsaard, former courtesan in Askh and lover of Cosuas.

Rainaan – Headman of Thedraan.

Reifan – Salphorian rebel, one of Aroisius's lieutenants.

Rondin – First Captain of the Tenth Legion.

Thyrisa – Headwoman of Thedraan.

Udaan – The High Brother, head of the Brotherhood and chief advisor to King Lutaar.

Ullnaar – Son of Meliu, youngest of Ullsaard. Clever and cultured, Ullnaar is studying civic law at the colleges in Askh, under the tutelage of Meemis.

Ullsaard – General of the Askhan Empire. Native of Enair. Ally of Prince Aalun. Bastard son of King Lutaar. Married to Allenya, Luia and Meliu. Father to Urikh, Jutaar and Ullnaar. Pretender to the Crown of the Blood.

Urias – Rebel Salphorian, lieutenant of Aroisius.

Urikh – Son of Luia, eldest of Ullsaard. As heir of the family, Urikh has spent considerable time expanding his personal assets and influence across the empire.

Vestil – One of the peoples living in Salphoria.

Places

Altes Hills – Low mountain range stretching coldwards from the Magilnadan Gap to the coast of Enair. This range forms the duskwards boundary of coldwards Ersua and all of Anrair. Sometimes referred to simply as the Altes.

Apili – Ullsaard's estate in coldwards Okhar.

Askh – Founding city of the empire, capital of Askhor, birthplace of Askhos. The largest and most advanced city of the empire, boasting the Grand Precinct of the Brotherhood, the Royal Palaces, the Maarmes arena and circuit and many other wonders of the world.

Askhan Gap – The widest, and only easily navigable, pass in the Askhor mountains. Protected by the Askhan Wall and dominated by the harbour at Narun.

Askhira – Large port city on the coast of Maasra, with a harbour on the Nemurian Strait.

Askhor – The homeland of the Askhan empire, situated in the dawnwards region of the empire, bordered by the Askhor mountains and the dawnwards coast.

Askhor Wall – A defensive edifice stretching the entire width of the Askhor Gap, built in the earliest years of the empire to defend against attack from the neighbouring tribes. The Askhor Wall has never been attacked.

Atanir – A small harbour town on the Greenwater, used as staging point between Okhar and Mekha.

Caprion – A small town in Ersua with a growing reputation for the quality of its copper and bronze smelteries.

Carantathi – Current capital of Salphoria and seat of King Aegenuis's court. Lying far to duskwards of the Greater Askhor border, its precise location is unknown to the empire.

Carlangh – Walled fort and town on the border of Salphoria and the Free Country.

Enair – Most coldward province of the empire, brought into the empire during the reign of King Lutaar's predecessor. A land of strong winds, frequent rain, large marshlands and heavy forest. Enair has no major cities and relies on timber trade and sea fishing for its low income. Birthplace of Ullsaard.

Ersua – Most recent province of the empire, situated dawnwards of Nalanor and separated from Salphoria by the Free Country. Consisting mostly of the foothills of the Altes Hills, Ersua is now Greater Askhor's main source of ore for bronze.

Ersuan Highlands – A range of mountains that separates Ersua from Nalanor, curving several hundred miles to duskwards between Ersua and Anrair.

Geria – Harbour town on the Greenwater, capital of Nalanor, whose quays are owned by the Astaan noble family.

Grand Precincts of the Brotherhood – An imposing black stone ziggurat situated on the Royal Hill in Askh, predating the founding of the city. The centre of the Brotherhood's organisation, it is here that ailurs are bred, the fuel known as lava is created and the great library of the empire – the Archive of Ages – is found, and adjoining the precinct are the highest law courts of Greater Askhor. No one other than a brother of the king has ever set foot within.

Greenwater River – More than seventeen hundred miles long, this is the greatest river of the empire and main route of trade and expansion.

Karnassu – A town in coldwards Nalanor. The site of a massive fortified bridge across the Greenwater, protected by four huge towers.

Khar – A meeting place of the Mekhani tribes, razed by Ullsaard at the outset of his campaign in Mekha.

Khybrair – Town situated in the dawnward forests of Enair.

Labroghia – Salphorian region situated on the duskward slopes of the Lidea mountains, infamous for its mines run by debtor labour.

Landesi – Village in Salphoria, populated by a tribe of the Linghan peoples. Birthplace of Gelthius.

Ladmun River – River that runs along the border of Anrair and Enair from the Altes Hills.

Lehmia – Settlement in coldwards Ersua, which rebelled against Askhan rule and was destroyed by Ullsaard prior to his Mekha campaign.

Lehmin – Town in Maasra, where the great aqueduct taking mountain water to the farmlands to hotwards begins.

Lidean Mountains – Range of mountains separating Ersua and Near-Mekha from Salphoria, marking the coldwards edge of the Magilnada Gap and extending more than a thousand miles coldwards to the sea.

Maarmes – Area of Askh, dominated by the sporting circuits and arena of the same name, where ailur chariots are raced and wrestling tournaments take place. Maarmes is also home to the bloodfields of Askh, where nobles can resolve disputes in mortal combat. All duels on the bloodfields are to the death. Commonly, such duels are over marital disputes; if a marriage proposal is opposed, a noble that kills the head of a noble family undertakes to marry the daughters of that family.

Maasra – Province of the empire situated hotwards of Askhor, with a temperate climate and long coastline. The chiefs of the Maasrite tribes acceded to the empire without battle, though they initiated the Oath of Service by cutting out their tongues so that they could raise no opposition to the conquest. Its people are known across the empire for their placid disposition and its wine is considered the best in the empire. Nemuria lies just off the coast of Maasra.

Magilnada – A city founded by Baruun at the coldwards extent of the Altes Hills, in opposition to the rise of Askh. Magilnada has changed hands through many Salphorian chieftains since its founding, until its status as a free and protected city was guaranteed by agreement between King Aegenuis and King Lutaar. Though fallen into much disrepair, Magilnada remains a formidable fortification on the border between Greater Askhor and Salphoria, and the presence of its garrison protects the vital trade routes between the two.

Mekha – An arid land hotwards of Nalanor and Ersua, divided into the semi-scrub of Near-Mekha and the deserts of Deep (or Far) Mekha. Home to the Mekhani tribes.

Menesun – Ullsaard's estate in hotwards Ersua, granted by right of conquest.

Mount Litheis – One of the highest peaks of the Altes Hills, overlooks Thunder Pass.

Naakus River – A river in Near-Mekha, considered the border between Greater Askhor and Mekha. Site of Ullsaard's camp during his Mekha campaign and proposed location of a new Askhan settlement in the region.

Nalanor – Province of the empire lying to duskwards of the Askhor Gap and first to be conquered by King Askhos. Consisting of rich farmlands, Nalanor was once the centre of trade of the empire, but as Greater Askhor has grown, the province faces stern competition from Salphorian importers and growing farmlands in Okhar. Despite this, Nalanor is considered the gateway of the empire, as it is linked by the Greenwater to other parts of Greater Askhor and sits next to the only secure route into Askhor. Its capital is situated at Parmia.

Narun – Largest harbour on the Greenwater, situated on the border of Nalanor and Askhor. Known as the Harbour of a Thousand Fires due to its many light towers that allow safe navigation even at night. Many decades of construction have made Narun a huge artificial lake-town boasting dozens of docks and quays. Almost all trade along the Greenwater passes through Narun at some point on its journey and most of the empire's ship-building is centred in Narun. The jewels in the crown of Narun are the stone built docks at the King's Wharf.

Nemuria – A chain of smoke-shrouded islands situated to dawnwards of the Maasra coast. Home to the inhuman Nemurians, little is known of this realm other than its volcanic nature and richness of iron. Nemuria is protected by arrangement with the empire so that no ship may approach within a mile of its shores.

Nemurian Strait – A narrow stretch of water separating the shores of Maasra from the isles of Nemuria.

Okhar – Province of the empire flanking the Greenwater River coldwards of Askhor and bordered to dawnwards by Maasra, duskwards by Ersua and hotwards by Mekha; of rich farmlands, vineyards, forested uplands and numerous harbour towns. After Askhor, the richest province of the empire, due in large part to its much-prized marble and linen. Governed by Prince Nemtun from the capital at Geria.

Oorandia – Former capital of Nalanor, now mostly deserted but still home to the second largest precinct of the Brotherhood.

Osteris – Town in Maasra, situated in the parched farmlands in the hotwards region of the province, where the great aqueduct terminates to provide irrigation.

Royal Way – The broad thoroughfare running from the main gate of Askh up to the palaces on the Royal Hill.

Salphoria – Lands situated to duskwards of Greater Askhor, separated from Ersua by the Free Country, of unknown size and population. Populated by disparate peoples and tribes, nominally ruled over by King Aegenuis from the capital at Carantathi.

Sea of the Sun – The body of water lying to dawnwards of Askhor and Maasra.

Straits of Lebrieth – Stretch of sea to dawnwards of Askhor.

Stykhaag – Ullsaard's home village in Enair.

Talladmun – Town in hotwards Anrair on the banks of the Ladmun River, garrisoned by the Second Legion.

Thedraan – Ersuan town situated a few miles from the Altes Hills.

Thunder Pass – Mountain valley in the Altes Hills, former debt mine and lair of Aroisius's Salphorian rebels.

Creatures

Abada – Large herbivorous creature with prominent nose horn, used as a beast of burden throughout Greater Askhor.

Ailur – Large species of cat bred by the Brotherhood as beasts of war and status symbols for Askhan nobility. Possessed of savage temper, only female ailurs are ridden to war, and do so hooded by armoured bronze masks. Known to attack in a berserk frenzy when unmasked.

Behemodon – Large reptilian creature native to the deserts of Mekha. Employed as beasts of burden and war mounts by the Mekhani tribes.

Blackfang – The ailur owned by Ullsaard.

Destiny – The ailur owned by Prince Aalun.

Kolubrid – Large, snakelike beast native to Maasra, employed by Askhans as mounts for messengers and skirmishing cavalry.

Render – The ailur owned by Prince Erlaan.

Thunderbolt – The ailur owned by Noran.

**ANGRY
ROBOT**

Teenage serial killers
Zombie detectives
The grim reaper in love
**Howling axes Vampire
hordes** Dead men's clones
The Black Hand
Death by cellphone
Gangster shamen
Steampunk swordfights
Sex-crazed bloodsuckers
Murderous gods
Riots **Quests** Discovery
Death

Prepare to welcome
your new
Robot overlords.

angryrobotbooks.com